The Rhise of Light

Book One of the Darkness Overcome Series
By Max B. Sternberg

Dedicated to Crystal, Cameron, and Aiden. I love you more than mere words can say.

E-book ISBN: 978-1-7369989-0-8
Paperback ISBN: 978-1-7369989-1-5

This is a work of fiction. Names, characters, businesses, events, and incidents are the products of the author's imagination– with the exception of Adonai and Biblical quotes. Any resemblance to actual persons (living, dead, or undead) and events is purely coincidental.

Front Cover Design by Robert Sternberg

FIRST EDITION

You can find more about the Rhise of Light series and the author at:

www.maxbsternberg.com
https://www.facebook.com/maxbsternberg
https://mewe.com/i/maxbsternberg

Map of the Kingdom

Table of Contents

Act One: The Broken

Whenever the LORD raised up judges for them, the LORD was with the judge, and they saved them from the hand of their enemies all the days of the judge. For the LORD was moved to pity by their groaning because of those who afflicted and oppressed them.
- Judges 2:18 ESV

Prologue: The Ship

Leon Rhise had always felt a sense of freedom when he was flying– even if it was on a warship.

As he stepped up onto the top deck of the *Dawnfire*, he inhaled deeply and smelled the varnished wood of the decking. It mixed with the scent of the clean wind that whipped through his long hair. Up amongst the clouds, there were no armies or war, no undead or politics of the kingdom– just the sun, sky, and the airship gliding through it all.

During his formative years, Leon had only flown on airships a few times. There had been occasional business trips with his family on merchant's vessels and the rare outings with his family over the nearby countryside. All of the happiest moments in his life seemed to occur while in the air. So it was only natural for Leon to gravitate towards the Naval Academy when he left home.

The bustle of the crew on deck also comforted Leon. Everyone had a job to do. He performed his duties remarkably well, and after four long years spent working his way up the ranks, he knew without a doubt that he had earned his position as First Mate. The peace of knowing that hard work, duty, and dedication paid off was likely shared by the other crew members as well. Leon knew those who manned the flagship, *Dawnfire*, were the best of the best from the Xaelon Armada. Sure they played the occasional jovial prank, or participated in harmless ribbing, but every man and woman on board knew their duty to protect the kingdom– and the crown prince. Or, as Leon knew him: Captain Gelan.

Prince Gelan was kind, fair, and commanded respect. When work was to be done, the captain pitched in alongside his crew. If there was a shortage of rations, he sacrificed his plate along with the rest of his men. When battles were fought with the undead menace, he fought shoulder to shoulder with those under his command. His respect was well earned. He was a living symbol– a symbol far better than Xaelon's flag of Last Bastion's tower. Prince Gelan was an exemplary leader and would soon be a great king.

"Master Rhise," Gelan called, after seeing Leon emerge from belowdecks. Leon reflexively put his goggles on to protect his eyes from the wind, and made his way to the wheel at the aft of the ship. Prince Gelan was gently guiding the vessel back from the battlefront for repairs. Their last battle in the Dead Wars had taken an unfortunate toll on the *Dawnfire*. While the ship was still operational they were low on ammunition and had even less by the way of supplies. Luckily, they were making good time, even with the needed repairs slowing them down. After they had reviewed the navigational maps that morning they were confident that the *Dawnfire* should be at the Agaprya shipyards later in the day.

"Yes, Captain Gelan?" Leon replied, stepping next to the wheel.

"I'd like to have your counsel on a matter. Take the helm."

"Of course, Sir." Leon stepped in and took the wheel as Prince Gelan had instructed. The navigational wheel looked like that of a traditional naval vessel– except for its ability to move up, down, forward, and backward. The control gem that was located in the center of the wheel directed the large, precious, and rare Levigems that kept the ship afloat.

"Alright, Master Leon, tell me if you feel anything... concerning."

Leon understood that this was a moment of instruction, just like the many that had come before. He felt the weight of the Prince's growing dependence on him. The Prince's upcoming marriage, which was to be immediately followed by his coronation as King, would force him to step away from the frontlines. Leon was confident that after the Prince's wedding to Princess Schalae, his name would be on the shortlist for taking over his command. After all, the Prince had taught him directly.

First, however, Leon needed to get through this learning exercise. He thought about the northeasterly direction the flagship was flying. To stay in the air it relied on two large, elongated Levigems which skewered either side of the ship. They were carefully cut to be ten-sided, and eight feet in overall length. They stuck out from the hull of the ship, and ran part-way along the outstretched length of the wings. If anything went wrong with them, the *Dawnfire* would be rubble on the surface below. There didn't seem to be any issue with maintaining altitude.

Leon's thoughts shifted to the crew of the *Dawnfire* next. Normally crewed by thirty people, their number was down due to the last battle they had fought. The undead had rushed at, and routed, their failed offensive attack. Many of the *Dawnfire's* crew members perished in the battle or had succumbed to their wounds shortly thereafter. Though the ship was low on crew, the various races still seemed to be well represented onboard. There were humans and elves, gnomes and dwarves, as well as orcs and even a goblin. All members recognized that mutual survival was more important than their past racial grievances. While the

4

Dawnfire was indeed shorthanded, it would still fly as long as someone manned the helm. After another moment of thought, Leon concluded it could not be the crew that Prince Gelan was looking for him to provide comment on.

Thoughts of the ship itself filled his mind. It flew through the sky at a brisk pace, and there seemed to be no listing, or drifting, of the vessel. Beyond the repairs needed to the railing, and replacing the boards taken from the captain's cabin to patch the hull, Leon could think of no other issue. He then concentrated on the feel of the wheel in his hand, and noticed a faint tremor as it shuddered slightly.

Wait, tremors?

"There's a vibration to the wheel sir. What's causing that?" Concern laced his voice.

Gelan sighed and put a friendly hand on Leon's shoulder, "I had hoped it imagined. It may be a few things, but all of them are bad. Prepare to land the ship immediately. We need not risk falling out of the sky."

"Yes sir! All hands, prepare for descent!" Leon shouted. He took one of the leather straps that were attached to the safety harness every crew member was required to wear, and clipped the end of it to one of the many iron rings strategically placed around the ship. The order echoed through the ranks as the other sailors all copied Leon— ensuring they were secured to the airship at their designated positions. Prince Gelan also clipped his strap while Leon gently pushed forward and slightly to the right on the wheel. Leon leaned forward with the movement of the wheel and felt as the airship gave a slight shudder. *That's not normal.*

The *Dawnfire* glided down into a lazy corkscrew maneuver, spiraling among the low hanging clouds. All was blanketed in white as moisture began to cover the ship.

"Scouts look alive for landing areas when clear!" Roared Gelan.

"Aye, sir!" Echoed the unseen replies from the bow of the ship. They were still covered by the cloud, preventing all visibility.

After a few minutes, the *Dawnfire* emerged from the white, cloudy, landscape it had been immersed in. The early morning sun now shone directly onto the vessel as it passed over grassy fields. The pale green and brown elven scouts signaled with one another, and agreed on an acceptable landing area near the Southern Forest that bordered the Lost Lands. Leon course-corrected and they spiraled further downward, still quite high in the sky.

"The vibration's getting slightly worse, Captain." Leon commented.

Gelan leaned into Leon so that his voice would not carry, "Let's stay the course and land. Hopefully it's just a loose portion of the wheel, and nothing more."

The landing area drew ever closer as the lazy corkscrew motion of the vessel continued on. The wind whistled at the crew and was the only noise that kept them company. All else remained quiet and calm, until the distant roar of a massive beast broke the silence. It was an unmistakable bellow of challenge.

One of the elven scouts at the front of the ship did a double-take as her hand shot up, "Dragon! Dragon off to starboard, two miles off! Climbing to the ship's elevation!"

Everyone who could, watched the deadly reptile continue to approach. Drawn to the prize of the red Levigems, and what they could add to their hidden treasure horde, dragons were a known issue to airships on the front. However, it was rare to see them in the kingdom itself– and inconceivable to have a dragon so close to the capital!

Prince Gelan did not waste a moment, "Man your posts! Dragon attacking! Starboard cannons at the ready! We need to get to the ground!"

Then to Leon, "I'll take the helm."

The shocked stillness of the crew was broken, as the bustle of activity immediately resumed on the ship. Crewmembers unlatched the straps that had been hooked to the deck so that they could be about their work with practiced speed and efficiency. Almost all of the crew that had been above deck disappeared below to help the shorthanded cannon crew. Those who remained above armed themselves with crossbows that were stored in a centrally located crate.

Leon relinquished control of the wheel back to Gelan. Standing now at the captain's side, he unslung a large tower shield from his back to protect the Prince while he also supervised the crew. Captain Gelan looked at the oncoming lizard and turned the wheel– an effort to buy the crew as much time as possible.

The bustle of activity from below produced five large cannons that protruded from the gun ports on the side of the vessel. The activity above deck resulted in the bow chaser being turned to face the dragon as well. The nervous tension among the crew was almost visible. Everyone battled the fear that tried to invade their minds as the dragon continued to close the distance between them.

Within minutes, Goro, the orcish cannon master appeared at the entrance to belowdecks and looked to Captain Gelan. "Cannons ready sir, but permission to approach."

"Proceed."

The cannon master stepped next to Leon and Gelan and lowered his already deep voice, "Sirs, we were already low on resources. We only have enough for two barrages."

Prince Gelan took a deep breath, "Thank you good sir. Leon, your thoughts?"

The same scout who initially spotted the dragon shouted to anyone who would hear, "One mile!"

Calculating thoughts raced through Leon's mind. "We'll never outrun it, but we could send a volley towards it and then continue to land. Take the fight to the ground. At least then we stand a chance. If it breathes at us in the air–"

"I agree." Captain Gelan nodded and looked past Leon to the ever-growing threat. The ground was still a half-mile off. Their ability to make it to the surface, before the dragon overtook them, seemed more and more doubtful as the seconds ticked by.

When landing safely was no longer an option Gelan nodded to Leon, "I'll turn hard to line up our volley. Have courage Master Rhise. We'll see this through and bring home quite the story when all is done."

Leon scoffed, "How do you do it, sir?"

"Do what?" Prince Gelan asked.

"Stay so… fearless in the thick of it sir."

Prince Gelan of Xaelon gripped the wheel tighter as he glanced at the incoming dragon, then back to Leon.

"Master Rhise, when we land safely at the shipyards, I'll tell you the secret."

The dragon loomed closer– now a mere quarter-mile off, its wings beat at the air in a frenzy.

"Ready for a hard turn and barrage!" Gelan shouted.

Close enough to accurately gauge, Leon surmised the size of the enormous beast was half the overall length of the ship. Its scaly green hide was unmarred by war or previous battle. Leon wondered again how a dragon this large could live in the kingdom unnoticed.

Coiled muscles tensed throughout the ship, waiting for word from the captain. Fire too early, and the creature would dodge and react. Fire too late, and even if hit, the dragon's forward momentum would carry its massive bulk crashing into them. Suddenly the ship jerked and pivoted, lining the cannons up with the beast. Leon's chest tightened and his pulse throbbed.

"FIRE AS YOU BEAR!" Prince Gelan screamed.

Six cannonballs exploded from the ship. Every one of them arched and converged on the green menace. The dragon roared its own challenge, and attempted to dive out of the way.

The smaller bow chaser cannon fired too early. The volley went wide and to the left. One of the round shots went over its head when it dipped. Three cannonballs hit its wings close to center mass, punching through bone and sinew. The last ball seemed to hit its stomach, as the dragon made a guttural sound and dropped below the ship. Shouts of relief and triumph echoed through the crew as the cannon master called for reloading.

"Find that beast! Scouts!" Gelan shouted. He pushed forward on the wheel, causing the ship to start gliding forward and towards the ground again. A shudder and ripping sound reverberated through the ship as the bow suddenly angled sharply downward. Gelan fought the wheel for control and shouted again, "It's on the front of the ship! DISLODGE IT NOW!" Sure enough, a green scaly head that was the size of a horse rose above the deck on the bow. It instantly saw and cut off the screams of a petrified sailor. It had only taken one rapid snap of its enormous maw.

Everyone above deck struggled to regain their footing on the slanting surface. Archers continued to fire the occasional crossbow bolt towards the dragon, but the bolts did nothing to stop it. A foreclaw clasped the front deck railing, as the dragon reared back. Cries of alarm and terror rang out– the crew knew what inevitably came next.

Fire and death. Ship and crew caught alight, as the fate of the *Dawnfire* was sealed. The beast's flaming breath billowed out across the deck, its reach ending just before the aft stairs. Prince Gelan braced himself and continued to fight with the wheel in an attempt to affect their fall.

Leon held his tower shield in hand and dangled from his securing strap next to Gelan. The Prince and Leon looked at each other in despair. In that moment of anguish, they knew with certainty that at a quarter-mile above the ground they were doomed. Either the dragon, its fire, or the crash landing would kill them all.

Chapter 1: The Homecoming

One month later…

Talking his way past the guards at the gate, and trudging up the path to his family estate, Leon saw evidence of quite a large gathering at Rhise manor. It would be highly unlikely that it was to honor his return home after almost five years in the service. After all, Leon had not written to his family that he was coming home.

Why should I, when I didn't hear from anyone at all the whole blasted time I was gone?

Passing parked carriages with the crests of different court families decorating them, Leon quickly realized this was quite the affair his family was hosting. Practically all the landowners around the Lord Gardens were present. Leon saw a smattering of famous merchant and caravan owner crests on display as well. The only notable family crest Leon did not see was the royal family, for which he was quite thankful.

All the same, company at the house would be inconvenient, to say the least. The dirt and gravel path up the hill to his father's house was well maintained, which was a stark contrast with the dirt and grime that covered Leon from his journey home. His untamed, grizzled, patchy beard and unkempt long hair were as dirt ridden and filthy as his clothing. The only clean-looking items in Leon's possession were his sheathed naval issued sword, and studded naval coat that had been kept in his backpack.

Looking quite the vagabond, Leon scoffed internally at the prospect of seeing lords and ladies carouse with him or his family. Leon hadn't cared for court politics before he enlisted in the airship navy, and he cared even less for them now. Almost none of those pruning peacocks had ever served to defend the kingdom. Yet they held their dances, and their parties, and dined at their fancy banquets. Meanwhile soldiers lived on rations and danced with death daily.

Reaching the end of the path at the top of the hill, Leon noticed a brand-new fountain standing before the manor house. Multiple tiered, it seemed to have an endless supply of clear water spouting from the top of the spherical blob-like statue. The water divided into several streams that crisscrossed at multiple odd angles, then landed on and around other different sized blobs, before finally converging at the bottom in a shallow circular pool. After staring at it for a few seconds, Leon finally realized what it was meant to be: a representation of the large floating Levigem mine that the Rhise family fortune was tied to.

The Rhise family name was long tied with the history of the Xaelon kingdom. Leon's ancestors had served in both the noble court and in many battles throughout history, as the Dead Wars fluctuated. Leon's grandfather, Liam, was the first who tied their family to the ore and mining business. As airships were a relatively new creation during his lifetime, Levigem mining was a new enterprise to be explored and capitalized on. Becoming the first family to provide a steady stream of Levigems to the kingdom, the Rhise standing and influence in court soared to new levels. Their Levigems were crucial to the development of the airship invention: which held the hordes of the undead at bay.

Leon's father Lucien had taken the family business a step further: after a falling out one day with the (up-until-then friendly) dwarven mining guild, Lucien Rhise added iron ore mining to the Rhise family business. He then sacked all his dwarven employees, and privatized his mining and security for the Rhise mines. Refugee ogres, orcs, and goblins, as well as various other friendly races, signed up to be mercenaries guarding the iron mines and the precious floating landmasses that housed Levigems. His name was a curse to dwarves, but praised by many of the other races. Lucien Rhise was seen as a benevolent man for almost all. Providing jobs and homes for those fleeing the Lost Lands: and from the undead hordes that ravaged them.

Lucien Rhise also found rich undiscovered iron ore veins to the south-east of Xaelon, snatching them up almost overnight due to their proximity to the Levigems. One closed-door meeting with the recently-widowed King Garinth later, and the Rhise family became practically the only source of Levigems and of all the iron in the kingdom. In just a few short months, the Rhise family was perhaps the second most powerful family in the kingdom: save for the Xaelon royals themselves.

And so it had been for twenty years. For almost Leon's entire life; his father poured himself into his business first and family second. *One of the reasons I left in the first place.* Leon thought.

He strode up to the fountain and looked at it more closely. A few horses, unhitched from their carriages, drank freely from it. Various footmen and pages tasked with supervising them cast furtive glances Leon's way: quickly meeting his eyes before looking away.

Looking past the fountain to the manor itself, the two-story brick "home" appeared every bit as ostentatious as the fountain. Oversized dark wooden doors, framed windows, large balconies, eastern and western wings, servant quarters, and spiral staircases. The best that money could buy for the war profiteering, but friendly to almost all races: Lucien Rhise. After fighting on the front Leon thought that the Dead Wars needed more than just floating gems and job security for thousands from his father. There should be more than just lines drawn in the sand, and cliffs like Bulwark Fortress. Xaelon needed to rally and push back the hordes that had advanced over the decades.

The Dead Wars. An unending conflict that had plagued the world for an immeasurable amount of time. Whenever anyone died – anyone – within minutes they returned as undead. If that dead person was very lucky, someone was close enough to dispatch the newly undead before it wreaked havoc with unnatural strength, speed, and savagery. However, the undead could occasionally retain some of their power or memory and become something else. Something worse than mindless killing machines.

When enough undead gathered together, causing significant destruction and death, the Dead Wars could renew: as this one had. Unfortunately, the latest war turned quite apocalyptic as, after almost two centuries of fighting, the last living kingdom appeared to be Xaelon.

"So why not just throw a flipping party while we're at it?" Leon thought aloud, scowling at the manor house.

"Um, excuse me, sir?" said a voice, stirring Leon out of his ruminations. Leon looked and saw a tanned, older, grey-haired, man; and two young, thin, teenagers huddled with each other. Looking slightly past them, he saw a gaggle of

14

drivers and servants all watching him. He surmised these three were either elected, or had perhaps chosen, to come over to see who this dirty, rough-looking, vagabond was.

"Can I help you, sir?" The driver asked, with a mildly confused look on his face.

"Good afternoon gentlemen. I'm returning home from naval service. My name is Leon Rhise."

"Master Rhise! Yes, that is you, isn't it?" The driver squinted at him. Leon thought he looked vaguely familiar. Probably from some gala or function long ago.

"What fortunate timing sir!" One of the young boys exclaimed. The carriage driver cast a quick dark look at the boy for speaking out of turn.

The older man tried to brush it off by continuing, "Yes, good Master Rhise, you seem to have the fortune of coming before the end of the party. I am Reginald, the driver for Countess Serina. Boys, do be good chaps and let Lord Rhise know his son's home."

The boys turned to race inside when Leon held a hand up to stop them, "Ah, why ruin the surprise gentlemen? I'll be inside shortly. Besides, I must clean up, eh?"

Crestfallen youthful faces turned and trudged back towards Leon. He smiled at them, but must have looked slightly feral, as the teens shifted uncomfortably.

Deflecting, Leon asked, "But why is the countess, and for that matter, so many others, here?"

Confused, Reginald remarked, "Tis a party for your sister sir. She's engaged to be married."

Married? Liara?

Liara was not just his sister, but Leon's closest friend. They had been almost inseparable as youths. Not only had they lived and played at the manor while growing up, they also had shared a classroom at home– along with their older brother Laric. Always together, they snuck into their father's study to find stories to read, told each other secrets never to be shared with anyone else, and stole food from the kitchens when they thought the cooks were not looking.

The indecision that plagued Leon when he had initially wanted to leave the house was primarily due to concern for Liara and his mother, in his absence. Swearing to keep in contact with them, he wrote to his mother and sister throughout his five years of service. Those letters had become less frequent as time went on, since he had never received a single one in return. The pang of heartache he felt at not knowing that she was being courted, and being unable to celebrate with her, blossomed. Along with questions that asked what else had he missed.

Blast it, now I guess I do have to clean up in there, he thought. "That's– That's wonderful! I guess I'll just pop in and say hello after getting cleaned up." Leon smiled as non-threateningly as he could, excusing himself from the trio. He fished a few copper crows out of his pocket and passed the coins to Reginald. "Please share these amongst yourselves, and thank you for the information." He nodded to them, and headed to the front doors of the manor house. The trio had to wait until he was out of sight before turning and speaking with the other servants, who all quickly approached wanting to ask who he was and what was going on.

The heavy oaken manor doors were attended by two more servants, who opened them to admit Leon into the grand foyer. Upon entering, he was met by a familiar checkered marble floor that spanned outward toward a grand staircase. The staircase had been designed to curve elegantly up either side of the large foyer to the second floor. An elaborate crystalline chandelier, arcanely enchanted to glow, was centered above it all. The walls of the foyer were ornately decorated with an assortment of

16

paintings, ancient weapons, and gifts from kings and other nobility at court. The east and west wings of the manor house had their doors closed. This left the only available avenue of travel on the ground floor, the one between the staircases: towards the ballroom, dining room, and kitchens. Two of the family's large ogre bodyguards were standing on either side of the foyer at the base of the stairs, ensuring no guests attempted to deviate from the areas they were permitted to access.

Nothing's changed.

Leon hoisted his pack onto his shoulder and approached the left stairwell: towards the bedrooms. There he could sneak into his room, get cleaned and dressed, and then find his sister.

The bulbous, bulky, ogre bodyguard that stood at the bottom of the stairwell tried to look as imposing as possible as he stepped in Leon's way, and sized him up. He was two heads taller than Leon with arms as thick as Leon's torso. He held one of his beefy arms out in Leon's direction, promptly stopping him.

"Yer going the wrong way." He grumbled.

"I beg your pardon, friend?" Leon chuckled in response.

"No servants upstairs, go to the kitchens where ye be working." He said, pointing behind Leon towards the kitchens.

Leon looked the guard up and down with a slight grin, while he hooked a thumb inside his undershirt and pulled a necklace out. A small Levigem pendant on a silver chain emerged to rest on top of Leon's worn and stained travel clothes. Exclusively given to the Rhise family, it was a status symbol that was easily recognizable.

There was a sharp intake of breath, as Leon had caught the guard completely by surprise. After taking but a moment to think, the guard's entire demeanor changed. "Um, begging yer pardon yer Lordship. I wasn't uh, was not aware of you returnin' today for the party." Suddenly, the big ogre couldn't bear to meet Leon's eyes.

Leon didn't want to dally in the main hall in his disheveled state, so tried to hurry the conversation along.

"Perfectly alright friend," Leon clapped the guard on the arm with enough force to suggest that he move aside– which he did. "Just freshening up before making the surprise appearance." With that Leon started up the grand staircase as he called back, "Let's be quiet about it though. Shall we, eh, gents? Wouldn't want to ruin anything."

"No, sir." Boomed the ogre behind him, as he resumed his post.

Leon hurried on his way toward the family rooms, thankfully not encountering anyone else. He passed many portraits of Rhise family members, dating back generations– all depicting the classic resting frown that Leon had grown up seeing on his father. Reaching his door he opened it carefully, and with no creak from the wood or hinge, moved stealthily inside.

It was just as he had left it. No layer of dust was present, signifying that the maid service still entered and cleaned regularly. His bed, cantered against the far wall, had nothing but a straw mattress. Plopping his backpack on top of it, Leon turned and saw his math book on top of a small wooden desk: which still stood against the wall adjacent to his bed. A gnomish-made, toy miniature airship sat atop a bookshelf in the far corner. Along with many of his other learning materials. *Everything looks so much smaller.* Leon thought.

Entering the bathroom he shared with his older brother Laric, Leon knew instinctively that the door on the other side (which led into his brother's bedroom) would be locked. Years of him sneaking in would have built a habit after all. Not as though he would be in there now anyways. Knowing Laric, he would be entertaining and dining with the guests at the party: trying to seem as important as humanly possible.

Turning to the mirror that spanned the bathroom wall, Leon had to agree with the guard that stopped him. He certainly didn't look like a Rhise. In recent weeks he'd become disheveled and his cheeks had sunken in from malnourishment. Unruly hair, so dark that it was almost black, and a patchy beard, which seemed to jut out in odd places, had all combined to cover his face. Once he had taken a hot bath, the beard would be the first thing to go.

After soaking for a short bit, then hurrying through what he could, he got out of the tub to finish getting ready. He heard the fourth-afternoon bell chime as he finished putting on the only nice pants he had that still fit: his studded leather naval armor. Knowing the party was in swing, but also eager to surprise his mother and sister, Leon rushed to the mirror with his razor to shave in a hurry.

"Master Leon?" Asked a familiar voice.

"Gaaaah!" He exclaimed, as he recoiled with the razor that had almost been pressed on his skin. Turning, he saw the one man who had always managed to sneak up on him in his youth.

A tall, thin man in his mid-fifties with dark, shoulder-length hair that was streaked with grey and pulled into a small ponytail stood outside the bathroom. He was immaculately dressed in a black formal coat, and gentleman's outfit. The deep red rose poking out of his coat pocket contrasted his almost unhealthy-looking pale skin.

"Master Leon, you look… well." He said, without emotion.

"Seneschal Silas. It's good to see you." Leon replied politely. Silas paused as his left eye twitched ever so

19

slightly. *That's right, abbreviations. Leon thought.* "It IS good to see you." Leon corrected himself.

The Seneschal stepped aside as Leon made his way into the bedroom to finish preparing for the party. Without missing a beat Silas stepped next to Leon and helped him into the shirt and studded naval coat that were laid out on the bed.

"Your return was– unexpected sir." Silas droned, almost disapprovingly.

"But hopefully not unwelcome, and quite opportune, I hear." Leon countered.

"Yes, your sister, most of the family, and guests, are downstairs in the ballroom."

"Most of the family?" Leon asked.

Silas brushed off the shoulders of the dress coat– aiming for perfection. "Well, yes of course. Your mother is resting in the bedroom."

"Is she ill?" Leon backed up from Silas, concern etched on his face.

Silas looked genuinely confused, a foreign emotion on his usually neutral face.

"Master Leon, you did receive the missives sent to you?"

Leon's protective nature towards his mother flared, as it had in his youth, and the jovialness of the occasion shattered like a mirror. "I received no letters while I was in the service. An act of reciprocity I was going to inquire about. What happened to Lady Rhise?"

Seneschal Silas's confused look gave way to resignation. "I am sorry to be the one to inform you Master Leon. In short, she had a seizure and fell down the stairwell in the great hall three years ago. She is alive and aware, but Lady Erika Rhise can neither walk nor talk since."

Leon felt guilt wash over him like a wave. *How could I not have known? How could I have not been there for her?* "I must see her, Silas."

Silas nodded expressionlessly, "I understand sir. She just went down for a rest. I can look into her alertness while you reconnect with your sister, and then retrieve you from the celebration if you would like."

How much have I missed?

Why did I even leave?

Could I have saved her?

Dark thoughts blanketed the guilt that threatened to overwhelm him. He breathed deeply, and reviewed the facts in his head. After spending a few moments trying to look at the situation with logic, instead of emotion, Leon decided he would have plenty of time to attend to his mother. He was already dressed and ready for the party, plus Silas had offered to fetch him if she was awake. *This is the best I can hope for, at least for now*. Leon finally thought to himself.

"Very well then. Thank you, Silas. Perhaps I should see to the rest of the family for now." Ready and dressed, Leon gestured for the door. The Seneschal gave a short bow and opened it for Leon. "Would it be ok if I left my travel pack here?" Leon asked.

Glancing at the pack for a moment, the master of the servants replied, "Of course, Master Leon."

They exited and headed back towards the grand hall. Leon had hoped that he could surprise his family with his sudden appearance– as if the last five years had not happened at all. He had not, however, counted on the Seneschal. Although he knew that he should have. The man seemed to know whenever anything was out of place in the house– it was his penultimate responsibility, after all. Wondering how much else had changed, Leon thought perhaps he would be out of place now.

"How does the rest of the family fare?" Leon asked, trying to shake himself out of his thoughts.

"Your elder brother Laric is doing well. He is learning to take over much of the family operations."

Leon sighed, hoping whatever fences he could mend with his brother would be easier now that they were both older and wiser.

Well, at least I hope Laric is wiser.

They reached the stairwell that had treacherously taken the mobility of his mother. Leon reflexively grasped one of the rails on his way down. "Yes, and how's Liara? Besides being engaged?"

Silas paused behind Leon on the stairwell. As panic over his sister was about to set in, he remembered, and chastised himself.

"Sorry Seneschal, how IS Liara?"

Silas resumed his descent down, and nodded at the beefy guard Leon encountered when he came in. The ogre guard at the bottom of the stairwell quickly shuffled aside and averted his eyes. Leon and Silas both turned left and continued towards the ballroom doors.

"She is also well, Master Leon. As you shall soon see." Silas reached for one of the handles on the door but paused before he opened it. For a moment he looked as if he was contemplating saying something more. The moment passed, and Silas decided to simply open the doors that led into the ballroom instead.

They entered an elegant, spacious, ballroom that had an identical copy of the crystalline chandelier from the foyer perfectly centered above a large dance floor. Surrounding it, murals covered the gently arching ceiling. Floating mountains and mounds of dirt on one side slowly transitioned on their journey across the expansive space, finally transforming into a depiction of the uncovered

Levigem cores that were at the center of the floating globs of earth.

The walls boasted more paintings, and held additional trophies of war or tribute– just as the foyer had. To one side of the ballroom were massive windows filtering in the afternoon sun, while on the other were lines of tables overflowing with meats, cheeses, exotic fruits, and vegetables. Leon nodded his thanks to Seneschal Silas for escorting him to the ballroom then turned to see quite a few pairs of inscrutable eyes resting upon him.

From the far corner of the room a string quartet filled the air with the notes of a waltz, while many nobles danced in concentric circles across the large dance floor. Lords and ladies, barons and baronesses, and young suitors all spun elegantly across the highly polished surface. They all fenced with their movements and fashion choices, when they weren't busy fencing with their words.

The older generations of partygoers were discussing good times from long ago, while younger nobles stood about gossiping in whispered voices. He saw the elderly Countess Serina engaged in an animated conversation with a couple of fawning men, each scrabbling at one another to garner her favor– and the subsequent access to her well-guarded riches. Her estate adjoined the Rhise's and she had been a warm smile and a welcome neighbor while Leon was growing up. Her patience with Leon, and his siblings, far outweighed the patience of their father. Leon would have to be sure to talk to her later.

All of the guests seemed to be having a wonderful time, which irritated Leon slightly. He remembered days of half-rations and only eating one meal a day. All while he fought for civilization's mere existence. Yet here was an overabundance of food and drink. The many actions, battles, and rescue missions that Leon took part of stood in stark contrast to the dancing and wooing of those rich enough to avoid service in the military.

"Brother?" Asked a hesitant voice from his left. He turned, stunned to see his older sister Liara. Her surprised expression mirrored his own. She had grown only slightly taller in her early twenties, but was still as youthful in spirit as ever. She wore a dark green ball gown and long silk gloves. Her chestnut brown hair was tied up in such a way that only wispy locks were allowed to escape in artfully arranged ringlets. A small, red, cut gem sat embedded in a short necklace that rested on the lace top of her gown. Liara's matching brown eyes narrowed at Silas for a moment before she rushed over to Leon and grasped his hands, with eyes aglow. "I didn't know you were coming! I'm so pleasantly surprised!"

The seneschal's eye twitched a few times as he turned to them and stated, "I will leave you both and look after your mother." He then turned and made an abrupt exit.

"Did you do that on purpose? You know it drives him batty." Leon asked, leaning slightly toward her.

"Would I do that?" Liara batted her eyes innocently.

Exhaling theatrically, Leon grasped her thinly gloved hands, "If you are the same older sister I know, then yes… yes you would."

Her impish smile cracked a little as she withdrew her hands, "Well if you would write once and a while, you would know if I was the same."

The light from the joy of coming home seemed to flicker internally for Leon. "Wait, what?"

Her exuberance returned for a moment as she grabbed his hand, and almost dragged him to one of the food tables. Neat piles of different cubed cheeses awaited them. She grabbed a small gold-embossed plate and piled food onto it before handing the plate to Leon. Dumbfounded and stammering he could only utter, "You– You never– Never got my letters? Any of them?"

"Not a one. Did you get mine?" Liara asked, while biting into a cube of cheese from his plate.

"No, Silas broke the news about our mother to me when I got here. I had no idea! Otherwise, I would have asked for leave." Came his exasperated reply.

To Leon's eyes, she seemed hurt– and understandably so. Where did the communication breakdown happen? The hurt in Liara's eyes gave way to resignation, as she looked at getting a plate for herself. Before apparently deciding against it.

"Well, you're here, and safe. That's something at least!" She said, as she popped a cheese cube in her mouth. She ate directly from the tray this time, breaking all social niceties.

"So, um, congratulations on being engaged?" Leon said.

Her face betrayed a flash of something that Leon could not place. She popped a few more pieces of cheese in her mouth before responding. "Thank you," she replied quietly.

"Sooooo..." Leon prompted.

She averted her eyes from him.

"Who is the lucky fellow that managed to avoid my approval?" Leon grinned, looking around the room.

A long pause ensued, then Liara's stony facade cracked even more. She mumbled her response as she ate another piece of cheese.

"I didn't quite catch that. Who did you say?"

"Baron Halomir."

Stunned and confused– he was certain he had heard her incorrectly.

"I, uh, I was unaware that the old windbag had a son our age. Congratulations..." He replied half-heartedly.

Silence.

"He does have a son, right?"

The general murmur and hubbub surrounding them became overwhelming as he waited for a response.

"Liara?" Concern caused him to press her.

She huffed, glancing about nervously, and anxiously popping yet another cheese cube from her hand into her mouth. After chewing for a moment she responded, "Leon, Baron Haldis Halomir does not have any sons."

Leon looked over her shoulder and saw the Baron laughing among several other older gentlemen. Halomir's lumber empire was well known, and his influence extended across much of the kingdom. He was highly esteemed in the courts, wealthier than most of the noble families, and knew business much like Leon knew battlefields. His slovenly appearance and rancid odor were also well known, but never talked about. These unappealing qualities became even more so when one took into account that he was more than twice Liara's age! Leon simply couldn't fathom any reason why Liara would be engaged to him. Unless…

His brain felt as if it would explode. Between receiving no letters, hearing the tragic news about his mother, and now this. Something inside of him snapped. Things had gone terribly, horribly, wrong as of late– and Leon wanted answers. Now!

"Now, before you say anything–" she started.

Leon ground his teeth together, his suspicions confirmed as soon as she started speaking. "Where is father?" He briskly cut her off.

Apprehension erased any previous appetite Liara had. "Leon–"

"Where is he, Liara?"

"Leon, you need to control your temper. Ok?" She pleaded.

"I'm fine." He took a steadying breath, "I'm. Just. Fine. Now, where is he?"

She sighed, and led him toward a more unoccupied corner of the ballroom. Looking around again, to make sure no one was too close, she turned her back to the party and hurriedly asked, "Are you sure you didn't get any of my letters?"

"No! Why are you marrying Halomir? He's twice your age and almost as old as father! What is going on here?"

"Listen, Leon, I didn't want–"

"Liara!" A stern voice broke in from behind her. Leon looked past her shoulder to see a man with a mane of shoulder-length, dark hair. He had gained more than a few long white hairs since the last time Leon saw him. His face was also creased with more frown and worry lines than Leon remembered. He was taller than most at the party, and his elaborately embroidered black formal suit was accented by the red Levigem pendant he wore.

He approached the pair and placed a commanding hand on Liara's shoulder. Leaning towards her he quietly ordered, "Please do not monopolize time with your dearly returned brother. Why not meet us in the study? We will be along shortly to talk and reconnect properly."

Due to years of formal training on how to pick up signals from distant airships; examining surrounding terrain and threats; plus regularly practiced observational skill drills, Leon was able to see his father give his sister's shoulder a nigh unnoticeable squeeze as her face processed a myriad of emotions. It finally settled on apologetic– giving a small brief smile to Leon, then dutifully turning in a curtsy to Lucien.

"Yes, father." She said meekly, as she excused herself. The various guests at the party cast quick glances towards her as she left, before promptly returning to the celebration.

Lucien turned his gaze to Leon after Liara left the ballroom. "Welcome home, Leon." His voice was formal and his face another unreadable mask.

"Father, I don't understand. Why is she betrothed to the Baron of all people?" Leon asked with indignation.

"Keep your voice down Leon." Lucien hissed. He sighed and pinched the bridge of his nose, "Of course, you do not understand. You have been gallivanting around the continent on your adventures instead of being here where you belong."

Here we go. Leon thought. He closed his eyes and started counting. It was a trick he had developed to avoid feeling his blood boil quickly. This was why he left. He and his father could never communicate properly with one another. They were like flint and steel: when forced together, sparks would fly. Tempers would rise and voices would escalate– Leon regretted those evenings the most.

"I was not gallivanting. I joined the military, father! I served our kingdom. The last kingdom!" Leon exclaimed.

"You ran away from your responsibilities to your family." Lucien countered. "Now, your sister has accepted her responsibilities, so you need to–"

"She's accepted what responsibilities?" Leon interrupted, "She's betrothed!"

Lucien Rhise briefly gave in to his temper. With narrowed eyes and a sharp edge in his voice, he spat, "Just... Stop!" He closed his eyes and proceeded to take a deep breath himself. Opening them once again, he beckoned Leon to join him. "Come with me. I will explain everything."

With that, Lucien turned, gave a thin-lipped smile, and shook a few hands before leaving the ballroom. Leon knew he would need to follow if he wanted any answers. He started to walk out, but something caused him to pause. He looked back across the ballroom. All of the dancers still turned circles around the floor, and the food was slowly being devoured from the rows of tables.

Not a fighting man or woman among them. Leon thought.

Leon was about to turn back and exit the ballroom when he caught the eye of the eldest Rhise sibling. Laric was staring straight at Leon from across the ballroom. For half a minute they stood staring each other down. It was as if nobody else was in the room. All of their former animosity returned. The rivalry immediately recurred without words. Indeed Leon realized he was wrong. There was at least one fighter in the room: Laric. He stood, contesting with Leon from across the room. Gauging who was the new alpha between them. Leon had grown in his five-year absence. He was now made of lean muscle born from hard work, and determination that had been forged in the heat of battle.

Laric looked like a younger version of their father. One without the worry lines to mar his face. Being the firstborn, the obvious favorite, and the inheritor of the business empire his father magnified, he had matured through trials of his own. Their stare down ended abruptly when Laric scoffed at Leon then turned away dismissively. Feeling as though he had won, the elder brother went back to chatting up the group of nobles that were gathered across the room. Most of whom were the young daughters of lords and ladies, vying for his attention.

Well, I guess some things haven't changed.

Chapter 2: The Argument

Leon followed his father back into the grand hall, where he was impatiently waiting on him. Wordlessly, they climbed the curving staircase to the second floor. Leon knew better than to try and talk to his father while they were walking. It would only anger him further. Lucien would say his piece on his terms– where he wanted and when he wanted. At the top of the stairs they turned away from the bedrooms. Instead they headed toward the family study, where Liara waited.

Opening the dark wooden door to his study, Lucien stepped briskly inside and deposited himself into the oversized leather chair that sat behind his desk. Stacks of papers that contained status reports on mining and shipping were neatly organized in front of him. A large, and highly detailed, map of the Xaelon Kingdom hung from the wall to his left. It displayed every known geographic feature– everything from the highest mountains to the smallest streams, the largest cities to the most minuscule villages. The map was then made complete with all of the kingdom's trade routes. Nothing was ever hidden from Lucien– that was in large part, due to this map. Bookshelves overflowing with various works by highly esteemed authors, volumes of business publications, and record ledgers from the Rhise family operations lined the wood-paneled wall to his right. Large windows primarily encased the wall behind him, providing Lucien panoramic views of the Rhise property.

Cherished memories played through Leon's mind– memories of being young and sneaking into this study with Liara trying to peruse the bookshelves. Their father hardly had any interesting books, but that hadn't taken away from the excitement of discovery and stealth. Those excursions were always ruined by the Seneschal– who invariably, inevitably, always found them.

The golden late afternoon sun shined through the high windows of the chamber. It illuminated Liara who sat quietly in a chair facing the front of the desk. She averted her eyes from her father as he walked in. When she saw Leon enter she tried to communicate with him, without speaking a word. The message her eyes sent to him was very different from what Laric's had been. Panic. Confusion, anger and frustration all roiled inside of Leon. Emotions that were only made worse by the look on Liara's face.

Leon refused to play his father's game. Closing the door behind himself, he stood leaning against the bookshelf on the wall. The room was silent for several minutes as Lucien shuffled through the papers at his desk. Here was yet another wordless battle. Leon realized his father would not speak first, and that Liara would never break the silence either. She was, by her very nature, outgoing and outspoken. Except when it came to their father. Lucien's private temper, and the tortuous repercussions he inflicted upon them in their youth, had molded them from an early age.

Leon's patience finally met its end, "Well?"

Lucien's eyes flicked up, then back down to his desk and papers, "Have a seat, Leon."

"I'll stand." Leon countered.

The room fell silent again as Lucien withdrew a sheet of parchment from his desk and began writing. After a couple of minutes Leon sat in the chair next to Liara. He would allow his father to enjoy winning his little power play.

"You wish to know why your sister is engaged to Baron Halomir?" Lucien asked, without looking up.

"Yes."

Lucien looked up at Liara. She smiled as genuinely as she could at her father. He then looked to Leon, "He is a good match for your sister. It will elevate the Baron's standing, and it will help both of our families to prosper together." Lucien's eyes dropped back to the page he was writing on.

An arranged marriage? Being the third born son of a powerful family, Leon had known that it happened sometimes while he was growing up. However, with the public persona that his father tried to put on, the Baron would have been far down on the list of choices for his sister. Leon looked at his sister– she had never been able to hide a secret from him throughout their entire lives. She gave him the same smile that she had given her father. It was a smile without her dimples, without her eyes. It was a facade. She wasn't happy. Why would she be?

Leon tried to make sense of it all. "How long has he been courting you Liara?"

Her eyes flicked to her father as she replied, "Well, not long but–"

"Do you love him?" Leon interrupted.

32

The silence told him more than an answer would.

"I will be honest; love is not something that factored into the decision." Lucien stated. "In time perhaps it will come, but the union is to be in a month. That gives them ample opportunity to become acquainted."

"Wait– Acquainted? They don't even know each other?" Leon demanded.

Lucien's voice rose slightly, "It is not your concern! And watch your words Leon, you are not a lowborn!"

Liara's grip on her armrests tightened slightly. She calmly turned to Leon and said, "It is okay, brother. I have accepted it."

Lucien gestured towards Liara, "See, there is nothing for you to worry about."

Continuing on he said, "Now. Your return, albeit unexpected… came at the perfect time." He rolled up the parchment he had written, and launched a pointed question. "I take it you are no longer beholden to the navy?"

"No. I finished my five years honorably," Leon replied quickly.

Lucien smirked. He took a ribbon and wax seal to the rolled parchment. "In any case, I need another foreman for our Levigem mines. We are increasing production even more to meet the king's needs. I have written you a letter of introduction. You can leave tomorrow morning and be there within a week." At this Leon's father offered him the rolled parchment.

A job offer, and an excuse to leave tomorrow? *Here I am, no more than two hours at home. Not even unpacked, and I am all but shuffled out the door again?* Leon raged internally. His father's almost callous disregard shocked him. The door behind them opened, and Seneschal Silas slunk in and looked to Lucien, "The Baron is asking for Lady Liara. I believe toasts and gifts are soon."

Lucien issued another tight-lipped smile and looked expectantly at Liara. She stood, as did Leon, and hugged him briefly, "It will be okay Leon. Look for me down there, and we can catch up tonight." She then turned and exited the study. As she walked past Silas she said, "Let's go Silas. They're waiting for us, aren't they?"

Silas closed his eyes, and his teeth clenched as he moved to close the door.

"A few moments more, Seneschal," Lucien said, stopping Silas. He reentered the room and stood at the door, hands clasped behind him.

"Well?" Lucien asked.

Still irritated that he had been reprimanded for his manner of speech, but his sister faced no such condemnation, Leon couldn't help but be adversarial. "Well, what?"

"Will you take the job?" Lucien shook the rolled parchment in front of him testily.

"Why? Why can I not stay and support my sister during her engagement? And what about mother? I have not even seen her yet!"

Lucien sighed and closed his eyes. When he opened them, they were as hard as the iron that he sold to the kingdom. "Your mother, I assure you, is well taken care of. As your sister will be in a month, by her new husband. Let us be honest with each other Leon. We are both stubborn, both headstrong. As much as we have tried, we have never really gotten along well together, have we?"

Surprise washed through Leon at his father's unexpected honesty. "That is… something I can agree with you on."

Lucien continued, "Then you will also understand the need for distance. Neither your sister's engagement, nor your mother's health, needs to be marred by our squabbling. Right?"

For the first time that he could remember Leon heard his father talking to him, and not at him. It was bittersweet. Unfortunately, Leon knew what he was doing. Reasoning, negotiating, just like one of his business deals.

Lucien pressed the issue further, "I can look past your abrupt exit five years ago. Even you running from your responsibilities to your family. However, now you are here, and you can help the family business just like your brother and sister. Be grateful that you–"

"Wait, what?" Leon interjected.

"Do not interrupt!" Lucien admonished, "As I was saying, be grateful that you have this opportunity. One does not typically have much of a career after such a spectacular failure in the navy." He glared across the desk at Leon.

So, he knew.

The *Dawnfire* crash, and what happened afterward, was still prominent in Leon's nightmares. Leon's shame and guilt was like an itch that he couldn't quite reach to scratch– it just wouldn't go away. To top it all off, his father knew. Lucien nodded imperceptibly as he watched Leon's face, confirming his suspicions. For a moment there was silence as Lucien dropped the letter onto his desk, rubbing his temples.

"How do you think the whole kingdom does not know? I kept it quiet. I kept our family reputation intact. You ran away, Leon. I kept that quiet too. Your rash actions in leaving this house took you to the navy. Where for five years, I monitored your progress from afar."

Leon couldn't move, awestruck that his father had opened up to him in this manner. Lucien sat back down in his chair, looking like the years apart aged him all at once. He gestured for Leon to sit. It was a respectful gesture, and respect had come rarely from his father in his youth. Leon sat back in the chair as Lucien continued.

"You carry the Rhise name, and that means something. We have always served this kingdom with pride. I had to come to accept that your way of service would be different than mine, different than your brothers. So, at the urgings of your mother, before her seizure, I started to help you along where I could. Having a high ranking family member in the navy could be beneficial, and you seemed to have a promising career."

Cold dread gripped Leon's heart, and his pulse quickened at what he knew was coming. *It was all my fault.*

"After one five-year enlistment, surviving in battles where your superiors did not, you were second in command on the FLAGSHIP of the Xaelon Armada. After his wedding to Princess Schalae, when Gelan would then take over the kingdom, I had every quiet assurance that you would take command of your own vessel. Possibly one day even the flagship itself."

It's all my fault they're dead.

My fault.

His father's iron stare returned. He splayed his hands on top of the desk and pushed himself up to take advantage of his intimidating height.

"You had ONE job. Keep the Prince alive. You failed. King Garinth is as distraught as when the queen passed all those years ago. Of course, that was before your time. You were the second in command. The ONLY survivor. Therefore YOU were held responsible. I had to buy practically ALL the heralds in the kingdom to keep our name away from the public."

"I did what I could, what I was asked–" Leon started.

Lucien's voice rose again, "Do NOT give me excuses Leon!"

"Would you rather I had died?" Leon fired back.

Leon felt as though Lucien replied a little too slowly when he finally said, "No– No of course not." Lord Lucien gathered his thoughts and started again, before Leon could interrupt. "What I am offering you is a second chance. A chance to still make a difference on this end of the war. To make something of yourself. Apply your talents towards an endeavor where they could still make an impact. Will you take it, Leon?" Lucien picked up and offered the letter again.

Indecision crashed through Leon like a wave. A second chance? Offered by the very man that he detested? Leon knew he was responsible for his failure in the navy. According to his father though, only a handful of people must know about his role in the *Dawnfire* disaster. His past failure could be kept hidden. Nobody else would ever have to know the truth.

He did want another chance at life, but as a Levigem mine foreman? Part of the danger associated with uncovering a Levigem was clearing away the dirt and debris that surrounded it. There was the always present danger of sliding to your death with the earth you had cleared. Or of getting crushed from falling debris. His father was offering him an extremely dangerous job, but it would get him out from under his oppressive rule. Lucien was right that it would probably be best if they were not under the same roof. Almost everything his father said made sense.

Almost…

"You said Laric and Liara are helping the family business?" Leon started.

"Yes. Of course, Leon."

"Laric is your firstborn. Your successor. Your apprentice." He continued.

Lucien brushed away the trivial statement with a waved hand, "You would not report to him directly Leon. If that is a concern–"

Leon interrupted, continuing his train of thought, "How does Liara marrying Halomir help the family business?"

Lucien paused slightly, "She is... doing her part."

Hesitation. Evasiveness. He was trying to find the right words.

"By doing what? As soon as she marries Halomir she goes with him to his estate, right? What part of the family business does that help exactly?"

Silence. Lucien slowly walked around his desk and stood in front of the kingdom map that hung on the wall. "The Baron is a good match for her and can solidify an alliance, of sorts."

"An alliance?" Leon stopped, and thought. He rose from his chair and turned his attention to the map his father now studied. Memories of everything he knew about the Baron and his business tried to resurface in his mind. Halomir dealt with lumber. Not iron or Levigems. Though all of those had one thing in common:

"Airships." He stated.

Lucien turned with the first genuine smile that Leon he has seen since his return home. It seemed almost unnatural. "See Leon, there is hope for you yet in the family business." He became more excited as he continued, "We would not only supply practically everything needed to build the airships, but we could do it all ourselves! The kingdom could buy the finished product! We would control the entire process! That is why you should be thankful to have this chance to work at the Levigem mines. Thankful that the Rhise name is not tarnished. Prove to me that you can be a part of this family again Leon!"

"So... my sister... is just some common good to trade for allegiance? A business deal? A bargaining chip?" Leon ground out.

Lucien's smile fell into a sneer.

Leon lashed out even further, "Are your children nothing more than pawns in your game of fortune? Are you even conscious of the fact that maybe she wants something different? That she deserves someone better?"

Lucien's voice became cold, "You do not understand. You are young and foolish."

"I am a fool!" Leon railed. Rage boiled to the surface, "To think that five years away from you was long enough! A fool to think you might change!"

"LEON!" Lucien roared, drawing closer.

He couldn't stop. The frustration and anger at his father was back and in full force. Leon yelled with all the strength his voice could muster, "Instead you are STILL the same SELFISH, CONNIVING, CONTROLLING MAN WHO DOESN'T CARE ABOUT ANYTHING OR ANYONE BUT YOUR OWN POINTLESS INTERESTS!"

Lucien stepped close to Leon, stopping only a few meager inches from his face. Still several inches taller than him, Lucien looked down on him with cold fury. His fists tightened and clenched as he opened his mouth to speak, "Choose your next words very carefully, boy."

Leon's anger overflowed. He couldn't take the machinations of his father any longer. He hated the undead that he had dispatched in the war less than his father in this moment. Voice oozing with contempt, Leon said, "I apologize father, but five years is a long time. With that said, I can't quite remember... Was it usually me who got beaten at this point during one of your temper tantrums, or mother? Or was it both? Tell me, is that why she is the way she is now?"

The room was silent as the two men stared at each other. Indignation boiled inside of Leon, and he regretted that things had come to this point. He regretted that his return home had devolved to such a sad state, so quickly. His father had been a sore spot in his life, for so long, that the words had tumbled from him without hesitation. Lucien had inflicted too much emotional damage throughout his childhood. Leon had felt so unwanted due to so many things his father had done. The scars that had been left ran to his very core.

Much like his beloved son Laric had done earlier, Lord Lucien Rhise scoffed. He turned and strode back around his desk. Lucien picked up the rolled parchment that he had offered Leon and, staring directly into his eyes, tore it in two.

"Silas." One calm word was all that was needed.

Leon registered that the Seneschal still had not left the room to follow Liara. It was too late to react– a black-gloved hand suddenly closed around the back of his neck. Momentum carried Leon's body as he was lifted off the ground. Immediately flashing with immense pain, his head slammed, and slid slightly, on the top of Lucien's wooden desk. Grimacing while glancing up sideways, he saw Silas' impassive and emotionless face looking down at him. He held Leon in place with a strong hand and the simple leverage of his body angle. Leon struggled to release himself from the Seneschal's grip. He couldn't break free from the pressure that pinned him or from the immense pain in his head that urged him to be still.

"I see where I went wrong with you boy. It is unfortunate that it has come to this. Maybe if I had broken your stubbornness and independence earlier, things could have been different. Now I see nothing but disappointment and defiance. A stallion, with so much time invested, that cannot be broken."

"I hate you." Leon croaked.

Lucien sighed, "I know. I tried with you, Leon. Whether you choose to believe it or not. I did try to help you. Now I see you are beyond redemption." Lucien strode around them and went back to staring at the map– which was now out of Leon's limited field of view. There was a long pause before Lucien said, "I want you to leave. Now. You chose to run away once, you will do so again. Only this time, you will not return."

Leon couldn't tell if the tears in his eyes were from the pain in his head or the one in his heart. It was unfathomable for him to never see his mother or sister again. He could live without his father and brother. Their verbal, physical, and emotional abuse had caused enough damage for one lifetime. But to never see his beloved sister and mother again? That would hurt more than if he compiled all of the beatings he had ever suffered as a child.

"Silas, release him."

"Yes, sir." The emotionless butler, and master of the servants, let go. The pressure on Leon's head was immediately relieved. He rubbed his neck as he stood and stepped away from the Seneschal. His head throbbed, but he did not want to give Silas, or Lucien, the satisfaction of seeing his pain. Silas looked at him impassively while he pulled the black gloves he wore up slightly. He seemed to have no remorse over having hurt someone.

Lucien opened the door of the study and gestured to Leon, "Now, get out of my house."

Leon stepped warily around Silas, sure to keep his distance. Silas slid behind Leon as he slowly walked past his father, staying a few paces back.

"I want to say goodbye to Mother and Liara."

41

"What part of 'leave now' did you not understand?" Lucien snapped.

"The person it came from." Leon shot back.

Leon walked into the main hall where the only people present were the two ogre guards– still stationed at the base of the grand staircase. Every other guest seemed to be behind the closed doors of the ballroom. Leon heard the faint sounds of music, and the muffled sound of laughter coming from inside.

The Seneschal shut the door to the study before he followed in step with Leon. Lucien walked past him, to the center of the upstairs hall, and leaned on the banister. Leon winced as he realized his father had effectively blocked him from being able to access the bedrooms and his mother. Leon tried to walk down the stairs slowly, giving himself time to think. He may yet see his sister. If he could just get past the guards at the bottom of the stairwell.

How badly would I disrupt the engagement party?

Enough to punish Liara?

Would Liara suffer for my misdeeds against him?

Leon didn't know if he could risk his sister or mother getting hurt because of him. As he descended the stairs a higher-pitched, though still masculine, voice called from below, "What is going on here?"

Laric Rhise sauntered up holding a glass of bubbling liquid, and took in the sight of Leon being escorted by the Seneschal. Leon knew he hadn't expected this sight when he had walked into the foyer from the ballroom. The eldest of the children, he and Leon had been at odds almost as much as Leon and their father had been while growing up. A fair number of Leon's thrashings were due to Laric's sniveling, and his going to Lord Lucien about personal slights– both real and imagined.

42

"Leon was just leaving. He does not seem inclined to share, or fit into, our family vision." Came their father's cold reply. He stood at the banister visibly gripping the dark wood tighter.

"Oh, and I thought the party today was just for Liara!" Laric exclaimed. He smiled at Leon, "I did not realize that it was for me too!"

"Five years, and that's the best you've got?" Leon's voice was laced with acid. Silas, behind Leon on the stairwell, groaned faintly.

Laric's smile broadened, "I do not know Leon, still a self-righteous runaway?"

"Oh, I don't know Laric, still think father's boots are your favorite food?" Leon retorted. He thoroughly enjoyed hearing Silas' frustration behind him.

"ENOUGH!" Shouted Lucien. "Ever the last word, Leon. Guards, throw him off my grounds!"

Seeing the ogre in front of him, and knowing the fast Seneschal was behind him, Leon's reflexes kicked in. He grabbed the railing and jumped over the stairwell to the floor of the foyer below. In his descent he knocked an oil painting and an old spear with a rusted spearhead from the wall. They crashed down with a loud clatter. Upon landing, Leon saw the ogre guard rushing towards him from the bottom of the stairwell. Quickly assessing the situation, he realized would never get to his belongings, or his sword, in time to do any good.

Leon grabbed the spear that was clanging end-to-end next to him, and felt a static shock. He tried not to flinch, and figured the room must be too dry for the old artifact. He brought it up with one hand and held it, tip pointed out, towards the guard. The ogre stopped advancing. He had his hands up, and looked at Leon in confusion. A Rhise, who he was supposed to obey, but also apprehend. Leon almost felt bad for the simple ogre guard. With a quick glance at the stairs he had just jumped from, he saw that his acrobatics had indeed paid off. Silas stood there, gripping the banister, looking... furious.

Most emotion I've ever seen from him.

Nobody advanced towards him. In fact, nobody moved except for him. He slowly walked towards the door. With the spear still pointed at the closest ogre, Leon glanced at everyone in the foyer and said, "I'll walk out of here on my own two feet. Thank you very much."

Lord Rhise spoke in a deadly low voice. That voice was more ominous than if he had screamed at Leon in rage.

"Get. Out. Before I have MY men draw weapons as you have. Do not consider yourself a Rhise any longer."

Leon scoffed as he gazed first at his father and then Laric's faces for what he sincerely hoped was the last time. He single-handedly opened one of the dark oak doors and felt it swing wide. A servant from outside half-stumbled and yelped. Their ear had been pressed to it in an attempt to hear what all the commotion was about.

Leon couldn't help himself as he made his exit. The final word was ripe for the taking, just one last time. "Well, I wouldn't want to dishonor the name of Leon with it, would I?"

Chapter 3: The Departure

Everything has changed. Leon thought, as the door shut with finality behind him.

Without a word he staggered past the speechless door attendants, down the front steps of the manor, and straight to the ostentatious fountain. His mouth was as dry as the hardtack he had been forced to eat on the airship, and his stomach was churning. He dipped a hand into the clear water and slurped a little of it– in the most undignified manner. The churning that had resided in the pit of his stomach suddenly exploded, and Leon retched into the expensively crafted fountain.

"Are you alright sir?"

Leon wiped his mouth and looked up to see one of the boys he had spoken to before entering the manor. The young boy was eyeing both Leon and the old spear he still gripped tightly. He had forgotten it was even in his hand. The spear felt comfortable. The wooden shaft was light, and its overall height equaled his own. The blade was wide and angular– yet at the same time, almost flat, and oddly thin.

He had thought its edges were serrated, but upon closer inspection he saw it was merely coated in rust. In its prime, the blade would have been good for both stabbing and slashing at foes.

Well, at least it appears to be sturdy. He couldn't keep the bitterness from his thoughts.

"I'm fine. Just had some, uh, bad food." Leon lied. He tried not to think about the taste of bile in his mouth.

"Sorry to hear that sir. Can I get you anything?" The boy asked.

Leon thought quickly. He had no future plans to speak of, and would need a job immediately. He couldn't serve in the military again, nor could he live as a vagabond. Leon didn't even know if his father... 'former' father... was truly finished with him. Would he try to send one of his henchmen to finish him off? Today had certainly taught him that Lord Lucian's anger was more pervasive than he had thought. If word of him being disowned by his father spread quickly, offerings of help like this could become fewer and farther between.

Hope and despair warred inside of him as he asked the boy, "Could you please help me prepare a horse, backpack, and supplies for a week's journey?"

The boy brightened at the prospect, "Certainly sir! Should I have everything at the stables for you?"

"Yes, thank you." After another moment of thought he added, "Two silver sparrows for you if you can do it in fifteen minutes."

The boy's eyes lit up at the sudden opportunity, "Yes, SIR!" He quickly ran off and left Leon alone with his dark thoughts.

Leon never would have imagined this as the end result of his coming home. Not even in his wildest dreams. Any hope of reconciliation was now gone. Due to the decision he had made to run away five years ago he had learned duty, honor, and how to be a better man than he thought his father was. So why was it that as soon as he came home he had been unable to control his temper? Why couldn't he stop himself from lashing out, even for just one night? He just couldn't keep his mouth shut. At the time he had thought his actions were justified. Those that were in defense of his sister, at least. But at what cost had they come?

He looked around and noticed several of the carriage drivers, and servants, whispering and glancing in his direction. They all clearly wondered what it was that he was doing. Their curiosity would soon be satisfied. The door attendants looked to simply be waiting for his gaze to shift away, so they could run and spread the news that had been overheard.

Leon finally stood, walked around the fountain, and began trudging down the short hill to the stables. On a whim, he looked back at the manor and tried to imprint its image into his mind one final time. It took a moment to capture the expansive building that he had called "home" for most of his life. Just as he was about done he gazed towards the left wing, where the family's bedrooms were. There, at a second-story window, he thought he saw movement. With the curtain partially open, Leon could swear he saw a gaunt, light-haired, older woman. Looking through the window directly at him.

Mother!

She was too far away, and obscured, for Leon to see her face clearly. Somehow, deep down, he knew it was her. He wished he could say his goodbyes to her in person. If only he could hug her and tell her that it would be okay. That he would be okay.

Will I be okay? He shook off the dark internal question and refocused on the woman in the window.

Leon raised his hand, kissed it, and held it out to her. She didn't appear to move or budge even an inch. Maybe he had imagined the movement after all. He wanted to believe that she had seen him though. He wanted to let that belief carry him forward as far as it could. Thinking his goodbyes to this cursed family, Leon turned back to the path that ultimately would carry him away from them. The lingering taste of bile in his throat once again made itself known as he finally began to make his way down the hill toward the stables. It seemed to pair well with the feeling of desolation that had taken root. A sense of despair that seemed to win in a battle against any other emotion.

Halfway down the path the boy ran up from behind, and handed Leon a sack. "Water skins and travel food, sir! I even got some leftovers from the party for you!"

Smiling as best he could, Leon took the sack. He wordlessly handed the boy two small silver coins in exchange. The boy quickly put the coins in his pocket and ran ahead, calling back, "Thank you, sir. I'll get the horse saddled up for you now, sir!"

He called me 'sir'. That means he doesn't know, or perhaps doesn't care. Either way, it was a welcome feeling. The boy ran off and disappeared into the stables a short distance ahead. The sun was fading fast, and Leon knew he wouldn't make it to any nearby town until very late– or early. He would have to hope that there would be a small inn, or perhaps a tavern, open still.

Eating some of the rich food the boy had given him, Leon walked the last few steps to the wide door of the stables. A dim light was cast inside, courtesy of a candle that flickered by the door. Upon entering the stables he saw that half of the stalls were empty. He walked down the row, until he arrived at the stall where he observed the boy carrying out his job with speed. He worked furiously to secure a bridle, then to strap a saddle and travel bags on a chestnut mare– guided only by torchlight. Leon remained silent, letting the boy earn the pay that he had already been given. After just a few minutes, as the boy began to lead the horse outside, Leon turned and saw a silhouette standing at the door.

"Moving on up in the world, aren't we? From vagabond to horse thief?" A smug voice asked.

"Laric, get out of my way." Leon growled.

"Ah, that is Lord Rhise to you now. You are, after all, a commoner. Which means that is not your spear, and that is not your horse."

Refusing to address his brother as 'My Lord', Leon sighed, and spoke through gritted teeth. "Laric, have a heart. It's getting dark, and you want me gone– I can put more distance between us with a horse."

Laric was silent. *He must be thinking about it.*

"I'll even send the horse back once I get to the nearest town." Leon bartered.

"If you take that horse," Laric drawled, "I will sack that boy behind you for helping you steal Rhise property."

What a jerk. Just like 'his' father. "Fine! He didn't know that Lord Rhise disowned me. Keep your blasted horse."

Leon started moving back towards the door, but Laric's silhouette did not budge.

"And the spear?" Laric asked, "Hand it over."

The spear? Leon had forgotten that it was in his hand again! *How odd.* "You know, before I left this just sat on the wall, in the same place, for years."

Lord Laric didn't miss a beat, "Do not forget Leon. I will thrash that boy, and then I will sack him!"

Leon deposited the sack of food that had been given to him on the ground and stepped closer to his brother, unafraid. He grasped the spear in both hands. "He wasn't

49

there when I took the spear, and you know it. On top of that, you have my backpack still in the house. That has everything I own, including my travel gear and my sword. Since I can't get it and you don't have it, then I assume you're keeping it. Which makes you a pack of thieves. So, I'm taking this spear Laric. You want it? Try to take it from me."

Leon enjoyed that his older brother broke the stare down quickly– now that they weren't separated by a room full of people. "Really, Leon. How petty of you," Laric scoffed. "Fine. I hope that rusty twig snaps in half on the road. Enjoy your new life, peasant!" Laric stormed off into the night. He headed back up the road, presumably to tattle to Lord Lucien. Leon had to leave, and quickly, before anything more nefarious could happen.

The boy piped up behind Leon, "Thank you, sir. You didn't have to do that."

Leon turned to address him, "I did, and you don't have to call me sir anymore. Just Leon is fine."

The reality of the situation crashed through him again, as he realized that everything he owned was on his back or in his hand. He was no longer a Rhise. Leon shook himself out of his thoughts to focus on the present. He needed to get out of here. That meant he had to walk to a town. Then he would have to find a job. Maybe mercenary work? He could never debase himself to become a brigand– it didn't matter how desperate his situation became.

The young boy, Leon guessed about eleven or so, led the horse back to its paddock and began to untack it. Leon knew every second was both precious and dangerous on the road after dark. Especially now that he had to travel on foot, which would cause a journey anywhere to be much lengthier than if he travelled by horse. None of these factors stopped him from stepping over and helping the boy as he situated the horse back in its stall.

"And what is your name young man?" Leon asked.

"Telon, sir."

"Well Telon," Leon continued, "Do you have family in any towns close by? I am suddenly without a home or a roof to sleep under."

"No, sir. Just my mom and me. She works in the kitchens here." Telon said sadly.

Leon sighed. *Guess there is no one that he knows who I could stay with while I figure things out.*

"Well, I thank you both for the provisions, and encourage you two to leave here as soon as you can." Leon concluded.

"Oh, yes sir." Telon nodded.

Leon winced, "You really don't have to call me sir, Telon."

There was a small pause, "Yes, I do, sir."

"I'm not a noble anymore." Despair tapped on Leon's heart. A small reminder that it was, in fact, still there.

"You are nobler to me than that bully that just left, sir."

Leon chuckled grimly as the boy locked the paddock, his job now done. Leon checked his coin purse. Luckily it still held a small amount of money from his... 'severance'. He pulled another silver sparrow out and handed it to Telon.

"I am serious. Get your mother and get out when you can. Lord Lame-o will throw a fit that he didn't get his way. I don't want either of you IN his way." He warned, using an old name for his brother.

"Yes, sir." Telon chuckled.

Leon turned to leave.

"Sir?"

"Yes?"

Telon assessed the situation and asked, "Would you, like me to… try to get a message to the Lady Rhise? Or Lady Liara?"

Leon's grim smile turned genuine. He wished he had more coins to spare for this boy. He looked down at the wise child and said, "Tell them that I will be alright. That they need not worry about me." After a moment he added, "And if you can, tell them that I am sorry."

"Yes, sir. Where– Where will you go?"

Leon thought for a moment. "Of the towns close to here, Everbright makes sense for now. After that, maybe Agaprya. Who knows? Wherever the road takes me." Leon held out his hand, and Telon reached out and shook it as an equal. "Good luck to you Telon."

"And you, sir." Came Telon's solemn reply.

And with that, Leon left the stables, and the world he thought he could rejoin, behind.

✦✦✦✦✦

After what must have been several hours of walking along the dirt road, Leon was grateful for the almost full moon that dimly lit his path. It also provided faint light to the brush that ran along either side. The interspersed trees that lined this road were small to medium in size, but none were large enough for him to climb in and rest for the night.

Recalling his survival training Leon knew random, stray undead – and other dangers – could come across a sleeping person on the ground. However, they could not reach a person who was up a decent sized tree very well. Emotional exhaustion had long since begun bleeding over into his physical exhaustion and Leon knew he was rapidly running out of energy. He desperately needed to find something that could work for the night.

A slow, continuous, yet ever-increasing noise arose from behind which caused him to turn his head and look. He saw a row of several lantern-lit carriages, coming from the Rhise estate. *Perfect! Some of the partygoers must have to use this road to return to their homes!* Leon turned to walk backward and stuck his thumb out. Hopefully, one of those carriages would stop and let him hitch a ride. Even if it was only as far as Everbright.

Four carriages, at an easy night's pace, lumbered along. None of them stopped. Leon sank further and further into the pit of despair with each one that passed. As the last one trundled by his hope for an easier evening faded. Then the sound of someone shouting unintelligible words caught his attention. He looked and saw a dark shape as it was dropped from the last carriage, just a short distance ahead.

Leon scrambled forward in the moonlight darkness, carefully watching and trying to not step on anything. Eventually, he came across a bundle the size of a loaf of bread. In the dim light, Leon felt and saw what he thought was cloth, a coin pouch that jingled (slightly larger than his own), and something else that was tiny and wrapped in parchment. A note had been pinned to it all, but the lettering indicating who it was from was indecipherable in the dim light of the late hour. Leon silently thanked whomever this mystery benefactor was as opposed to shouting out after them– there was no need to attract unwanted nighttime attention. He would just have to read the note in the morning.

His desperation to find a place to sleep rose to a pitch. He couldn't camp or sleep on the ground, to do such a thing while alone would be suicide. The mere idea caused dark memories (of a not-too-distant past) to resurface. Leon spotted the dark shape of a relatively tall tree, with only a few low hanging branches in his peripheral vision. He approached it and, with much relief, found it to be satisfactory for getting a few hours of sleep. He started to climb up, getting as high off the ground as he possibly could. Leon found a sturdy branch, higher than arms reach of a normal person's height, and carefully nestled the pack Telon gave him on a nearby bough. Resting his back against the trunk, he exhaled a long breath. At least here, in the tree, he should be relatively safe from night prowlers.

Why be safe though? A stray thought popped into his head.

His chest tightened and anxiety crept into his mind. The realization that he had nothing in the world left suddenly flooded through him again. Nothing but the clothes he wore, the travel food Telon had pilfered for him, the newly acquired mystery bundle from the carriage, and the old spear he used as a walking stick on the road. He was cut off, abandoned, and alone. A far cry away from a powerful noble's son, or even a warrior in the navy. Dark thoughts, darker than the night he was sleeping under, seeped into his head.

You couldn't control your temper for one night when you got home, could you?

Your sister and mother are now defenseless.

You let them down.

You let everyone down.

You should just end it all on the tip of that spear you're holding.

It's all your fault that they died.

It's all YOUR fault HE died.

IT'S ALL YOUR FAULT.

Exhausted, and emotionally overwhelmed, he cradled the old spear against himself. Tears began to flow down his cheeks, as they had on many a night recently. Only now, there were entirely new reasons for Leon to cry himself to sleep.

Chapter 4: The Vision

Leon's nightmares returned as he slept. He had dreams of his brother fist fighting with him when he was only ten years old. Five years his junior, Leon held his own as best he could. Finally he went running to Lord Lucien with a broken nose– compliments of Laric. His father's cold disapproval, for not defending himself better, was present even then. It was as if, somehow, the trouncing he received from his father was supposed to motivate him to try harder the next time he fought with his brother.

Leon then dreamt of the time he spent at the training grounds in the Naval Academy, and his very first encounter with the undead. A long-dead skeleton, with a dull red glow coming from its eye sockets, was trapped behind the bars of a small cell. Bone and sinew reached through the openings towards the students. The creature grasped and clawed while its bony jaw clacked viciously, desperate to end more life. It was an example to the students of the enemy they faced. One that was meant to show them that death was something to fear, but undeath was something far worse, and to always be keenly aware of it. A lesson that everybody dies. Then everyone un-lives.

The nightmare shifted to his service in the war and his countless actions against hordes of undead. Lifeless eyes glowing a sinister, dull, deep, red; and burning villages, devoid of all life, plagued Leon's unconsciousness. The latest advancement in this cycle of the Dead Wars was to bombard groups of skeletons and shamblers with airship cannons. It was an advancement that strove to finally give the living an advantage over the un-dead.

While humans and non-humans alike worked tirelessly to create a fleet of airships to protect the kingdom, new and still dangerous threats emerged to face them. There were the intelligent, sinisterly-aware, undead to deal with; savage creatures who were chimeric in nature; giants, and even others still. Airships had their drawbacks, due to the attention they garnered from dragons (and others) who sought the coveted Levigems. A new danger to be faced was ever present, and the war machine kept churning. Even with the technology and advancement of airships people still died. It seemed there would eventually be no one left alive to fight.

Heaviness of heart filled Leon in his dream, as he revisited some of the worst moments of his life. It all just seemed so strange. The dream was less like a dream, and more like one long agonizing flashback. It was rare for him to be this cognizant while dreaming. He wanted to wake up! He didn't want to relive the horrors of his conscious past, yet again, in his sleep.

"You have had a hard life, Leon." A disembodied, deep, voice resounded around him. The nightmarish image displaying the lifeless body of Prince Gelan faded away into nothingness. What remained was a pale grey expanse. The sky was grey, the ground was grey, everywhere around him was a blank landscape– as far as his eye could see.

Leon looked down and could see his body, his hands, his feet, but he could not see where the voice came from. Behind Leon, high in the monochrome sky, there was a distant pinprick of what appeared to be a multicolored light. He examined the vast empty expanse and couldn't find anything or anyone. There was just the pinprick of light in the distance.

"Where are you?" Leon asked into the void.

"I am here." Replied the voice.

"Um, okay. Then, who are you?"

"I am Rohiel, an angel of Adonai. And you, Leon, have been called."

"Angel?" This nightmare had just become even weirder. He held no opinion on religion or deities whatsoever. The Rhise family did not have any idols or household gods, as far as Leon knew. Of course, he had been gone for the past five years. One thing Leon clung to with absolute certainty was that he wanted no part of any deity that Lucien followed.

Even when he was in the military, Leon's strength was what carried him through the day. While others made little charms, or had strange idols near their sleeping quarters, Leon viewed it all as odd. Why would you worship something that you had made? Or as he had called it, 'a glorified statue'. What power could those trinkets possibly hold? He had gone through his entire life without any sort of relationship with any sort of deity– why should he encounter one now?

"And where has that gotten you, Leon?"

An image of himself appeared. It showed him unconscious, sleeping in the tree he had climbed that very evening. A pale light emanated from the moon above, and seemed to highlight the spear with the rusty head that lay across his lap as he slept. It looked like he was still cradling it. *What was that old spear doing in the manor in the first place?*

"It was there for you."

"The spear?" Leon questioned, as he continued to stare at himself sleeping.

Somehow, in this dream that wasn't a dream, even his thoughts were an open book to this Rohiel voice. Even while knowing this, Leon could not stop the questions from racing through his head. The most prevalent question easily rose to the forefront of his mind.

"You said 'called'? By this Adonai? Who's this Adonai anyway?" Leon asked. If Rohiel could read his thoughts, there would be nothing lost by speaking his questions aloud.

The pinprick of pale, glowing, multicolored light in the distance flashed. A wave of white light and a surge of warmth exploded from it. It washed over Leon and dissolved the image of himself sleeping. A sense of calmness, peace, and contentment stirred at the very core of his being. Looking back, the light in the distance was still there– unchanged and glowing.

"He is the creator of all, the God of the universe. He knows all, sees all, and is the light of the world. Whoever follows Adonai will never walk in darkness but will have the light of life in them."

The cold reality that Leon truly might not be dreaming washed over his consciousness. He was truly out of his depth if this was real, and some otherworldly being was talking to him. Gods and angels were not beings that he was familiar with in the least.

"Adonai is love. Perfect love. The love of a creator for its creation. He has created you, Leon, for a purpose. His purpose."

Confusion began to overtake him. "How could I bear his spear if I've never heard of him before?"

59

"Adonai has been waiting patiently for a new Judge, and there were but few choices in the manor."

Judge? The term sounded familiar, but Leon couldn't quite figure out why. It was like a hazy memory, one that sat just out of reach.

"Judges. Heroes of old. Chosen against the schemes of the Fallen."

A different image now appeared in front of Leon. Like sand shifting into place, it resolved into a picture from the past. It showed young Leon and Liara, reading a book together in their father's study. The study had scarce reading material for youngsters, but they were undeterred. After searching, while Lord Lucien was away on one of his business trips (and while dodging the Seneschal), they managed to find a few books that had piqued their interest.

One book had described the adventures of several heroes. They were portrayed as always slaying monsters, rescuing damsels in distress, and saving far off lands from evildoers and secret plots. Those heroes always fascinated Leon. They invariably had to not only always save the day, but often had to solve moral quandaries too.

They were warriors, they were leaders, and they usually lived happily ever after. Then there were the other stories– ones that depicted some of the supposed heroes meeting quite gruesome fates. The heroes who persevered, who saved the day, were apparently called Judges. They were the leaders of their time, from centuries past. One would rise and help usher in an era of peace, then they would lay down the mantle until the next Judge was needed.

Maybe I am dreaming. Maybe this is me going mad. All of my recent trauma has caught up to me, and is robbing me of my sanity. It didn't seem all that farfetched. Alternatively, he was without a job. Perhaps this was his deluded dream of grandeur– a career made entirely of being a hero.

"Yes, Leon. It is time for another Judge to walk the world again."

Right. He can hear my thoughts. Ok, I'll play along. "Why me?"

"You have been called by his name, whom he created for his glory, whom he formed and made."

"Called to do what exactly?" He wondered if he would wake up crazy and frothing at the mouth.

The pinprick of light pulsed again, sending another wave that washed over him. It felt like a breath of fresh air.

"The time has come. The people have forgotten Adonai. They cry out for a savior but do not know who can save them from themselves. You will remind them of Adonai, of light, hope, and truth. You will help them understand that only Adonai can save them."

"Save them from what, the undead?" Leon joked.

The voice of Rohiel was noticeably silent as the frozen image of young Leon and Liara disappeared. For a moment, there was just the grey horizon and the multicolored spot in the distance. Then image after image of atrocities, both large and small, surrounded Leon. It seemed not to be just his memories anymore. As Leon looked through the eyes of strangers, he witnessed the depravity of the living world.

Leon saw rich lordlings (like his father) line their pockets, while children starved to death in the streets. He saw murders over trivial trinkets, and lecherous adultery. The old and infirm were begging by the roadside, struggling merely to survive the day, while merchants blatantly ignored them. Forests were purposely set on fire, over minor disputes with elves.

He had never dreamt of himself throwing up before, but some of the things that Leon saw made him want to do just that while clawing his eyes out. Ritual sacrifices in acts of worship to beings who wanted nothing but the perversion of their followers. Children being slaughtered by drunken fathers and mothers. Hypocrites who did in private exactly what they told others not to do while in public.

Mass graves and genocide. Theft. Pillaging. Slavery. Violations of both body and mind. All creatures were guilty– from Giants to Gnomes, and all shapes and sizes in between. Hundreds of images. Thousands. It was enough to truly drive one mad. For Leon, it didn't seem to be a joking matter anymore. Indeed he no longer believed that this was a random, depression-induced dream.

Leon saw the images of the world's great atrocities played out right alongside his own wrongdoings. The indignation at being accused by a God that he had never heard of quickly gave way to self-examination. This self-examination was punctuated by more flashes of his life playing before him.

Lie after conscious lie that had escaped his lips. Those said to benefit himself, or for really no reason at all. The moments when Leon crept into Laric's room to steal his toys. His jealousy towards another officer in the navy, for being promoted before he was– when he thought he deserved it more. Outbursts of anger, and a temper that spiraled out of control. Even the murderous rage he occasionally felt towards those that had wronged him. More and more infractions from his life replayed before him in the grey expanse.

Leon was quite ashamed of some. Such as when he felt a small victory after getting a promotion– one that was due to the death of a commanding officer. Or the vanity and pride he felt after he received the attention of young ladies at parties and balls. That specific guilt was made worse by the knowledge of how he and his brother had compared them based on their assets and level of attractiveness– as if those young women had been nothing more than objects to be played with. Since then of course, that mindset had changed. The women he had served with quickly taught Leon that they worked just as hard as the men, and more than deserved his respect.

Of these offenses against this God, this Adonai, there was no rebuttal and no defense. Yes, Leon had done wrongs in his life, but then again hadn't everybody?

"Yes, Leon. All have fallen short. There is no one unmarred, not one. And thus, presents the problem. You can be a solution. You can help Adonai save them."

The incredulity of such a statement left Leon awestruck. The images around him dissolved as if in a whirlwind. "Save them? Save… people?"

"Yes."

Leon tried to understand. "From their… bad actions?"

"From the repercussions of their actions after death."

The incredulity gave way to dread. *After death you become an undead, right?* He did not want to ask, but he needed to know.

"What repercussions exactly?" Leon asked.

"Your soul is separated from Adonai for all eternity. The marred, stained, soul cannot co-exist with the pure love of Adonai. It is set apart. The evidence of that separation is something you are quite familiar with."

Leon felt as though the grey expanse tilted sharply, his sense of balance eluded him, and he fell to the ground. When he stumbled to his feet again, guilt and panic gripped his heart. Once more his past haunted him. However, instead of a mere image, his entire surroundings had changed into a nightmare– the wreckage of the *Dawnfire*.

It was as if Leon was there again. While the trauma, and willing-himself-to-forget, had created a haze over his memory, this dreamscape made every blade of grass and shard of wood appear real enough to touch. It seemed the

63

dragon that attacked the airship had died upon impact. The bowsprit at the front of the *Dawnfire* was embedded into its skull, not letting it rise again. Black blood and toxic fluids dripped from the beast's open toothy maw.

The airship itself had the bow and stern cracked in half– like a giant, wooden, broken, egg. The middle of the ship had splintered and exploded outward from the impact. Debris littered the grassy field and the nearby treeline of the Southern Forest. Most of the wreckage was on fire and a vile stench filled the air.

Bodies of the crew lay strewn about– motionless. Some bodies were pinned underneath the wreck, while some bodies lay thrown a good distance away. This had been caused by the few remaining munitions on board exploding upon impact. All was still, except for the crackling of the fire. A fire that was composed of the woodpile that had once been known as the mighty flagship of the kingdom.

Leon never could remember exactly how he and the Prince had survived the fall. He had blacked out upon landing. His best guess was that both he and the Prince had jumped away from the impact at the exact moment the powder room exploded. The blast would have propelled them from the crash site. As Leon watched himself hobble close to the wreckage, holding up Prince Gelan, he saw that the splinter of wood impaling Gelan's right arm was smaller than what he remembered.

"How long… were we… unconscious?" Gelan gasped, holding his bleeding limb tenderly.

"I don't know, but we don't have much time." Leon saw himself say in a hollow voice.

"No, we don't. Look." Gelan pointed with his arm that wasn't mangled.

For the second time in his life Leon watched as his comrades in arms, his brothers and sisters in war, stirred jerkily. The bodies of the dead began to rise from the crash. They clawed their way up, and were moaning listlessly. Leon saw Midshipman Dawes with his neck broken. He watched as Dawes twisted his head at an unnatural angle towards past-Leon and the Prince. The dull, red, lights glowing from his eyes signaled that any sense of life or humanity was gone. All that remained was the urge to kill and spread undeath.

"Leon, I don't know if we can fight them all off." Prince Gelan said in a low voice.

"We must try." Past-Leon said, as he drew his sword from the scabbard strapped to his leg. He set Prince Gelan down on the ground gently. Then he turned to put the friends who had served with him to rest.

A burnt husk of a crewmember, which Leon could not identify, ran towards him with its arms outstretched and moans escaping its mouth. Past-Leon swung his heavy short sword and chopped the crewmember down. To make sure it did not rise again, the past version of himself reversed his grip on the sword and stabbed through its head. The light that came from his once-crewmember's eyes winked out. Moments later, the orcish cannon master, Goro, stumbled out of a hole in the wreckage. He appeared relatively whole.

Leon fell to his knees watching the past. Watching the hope fade from his past self's eyes, hope that another person had survived, was too much. When Goro turned past-Leon saw the gaping chest wound. Goro's glowing red eyes had met his own, and narrowed. A gurgling shout escaped between the tusks that protruded from Goro's mouth. He charged at past-Leon with a speed unhindered by wound or fatigue. The sword stroke and sidestep that past-Leon managed only served to anger his undead friend. In true undead form, the Orc had caught the blade in a now split hand. Goro then used his other hand to grab Leon's shoulder and push him to the ground.

About to lunge down and rip out Leon's throat, the blade of a longsword suddenly pierced the dead orc's neck–severing both bone and tendon. Prince Gelan gasped due to the effort it took to save Leon. He held his injured arm against his chest as he strained to cut through the large orc, and then pull it off of Leon. The glow from Goro's eyes faded, and Leon rolled out from under him in order to get back up and protect the injured prince. Gelan tried unsuccessfully to get up, and instead collapsed next to the permanently dead orc.

Midshipman Dawes stumbled around the side of the wreckage. He had been a small man, made smaller now by his head sitting at a ninety degree angle. In life he had served alongside Leon since the Academy. They had always shared a fierce but friendly rivalry. Now, the man Leon had known for so long was gone. Past-Leon had to raise his sword against him, and end his undeath also.

"PLEASE MAKE IT STOP!" Cried out Leon from the dream. He had already been taken to his knees, but tears also ran freely down his face now. Just as he saw the neck of the Midshipman fully severed, and his undead comrade drop to the ground, the dark vision of his past disappeared. Once again he was left in the dream world's blank expanse. Guilt and shame pounded Leon, as he tried to process his experience all over again. "I had to kill them. My friends, my crew. I had to, because they– they turned."

"You are already forgiven for it all Leon. If you would accept it."

Leon heard the angel, but the words of Rohiel were like stones that bounced off the window to his remorse.

Leon wailed, "He told me that I made a mistake, that it was my fault! That I was to blame!"

66

"The events of the past cannot be changed. They are written into the very fabric of the universe. But so has your salvation been, and the salvation of all. You would only need to accept Adonai's forgiveness."

Forgiveness?

"Then, and only then, would you have any chance of ending the cycle and stopping the plague once and for all. At bringing faith in Adonai back to the world."

THAT caught Leon's attention. "Wait, stopping undeath?"

"Do you think it normal that bodies of the recently departed rise? That the egg that your spirit matures in transforms into a monster, instead of a marvel?"

"So… following Adonai… would prevent you from turning?" Leon struggled to comprehend a fact that opposed everything he had ever known.

"You are learning."

Stop the dead from rising? Stop the Dead Wars itself? The world seemed to be on the brink of annihilation. Xaelon was the very last living kingdom. This was all because people had forgotten about God? Could it be that everything this Rohiel said was true? Could the Dead Wars end? Was forgiveness from this Adonai really all that it took to make people stop rising again?

The guilt he carried since the crash, had become an all too familiar boulder weighing him down. It made the very air he breathed heavy enough to crush him. He felt he just had to accept the weight that came with the knowledge that he alone had survived and returned. The maneuvers to engage the dragon had been his idea. He was to blame for the death of the crew. He was to blame for the death of the Prince himself.

Leon now realized that the rage he displayed was not just due to his father and his upbringing. He was also full of anger at himself. Maybe that was why he had asked his father… 'former' father… if he wished he had died in the crash. A part of Leon wished that he had indeed died alongside his crew. If he had, he would have been saved from this inescapable pain.

"And what purpose would that have served Leon? If you had died, Adonai would wait for the opportunity to choose another. Every moment of your life has brought you here to this choice. Rather than face oblivion, you can choose Adonai to carry this burden for you. His forgiveness and mercy will follow you all the days of your life."

A yearning and eagerness blossomed within Leon, one that he had not known was there. A desire for acceptance, for conquering the turmoil within himself, for peace. For almost five long years, Leon fought in the navy and felt as if no difference had been made. The dead still rose. The war machine still churned.

And yet this voice, this Rohiel, this angel of Adonai, said that the war could be ended? That the recently deceased rising as undead was somehow not normal? For all of Leon's life that had been the status quo. It was a fact of life, a part of the culture of the world. You died, you came back. Until someone dispatched you again. Preventative measures were sometimes taken, when the opportunity was available, but this was the way life was supposed to be– right?

"It doesn't have to be this way."

Thoughts churned around his head faster and faster. *If there's a chance of me relieving myself of this pain, and at the same time maybe – just maybe – ending the Dead Wars and the suffering of others, shouldn't I take it? Could I, in fact, be a Judge after all?*

An unfamiliar spike of hope penetrated Leon. It permeated as deeply as he thought was physically possible within this dreamscape. What had begun as a nightmare, was in fact an otherworldly encounter. The pinprick of light in the distance flashed and pulsed again. A wave of peace and light flowed over him. It left him both convicted and convinced.

Why not? Why not give this Adonai a try?
At this point, what do I have to lose?

Leon took a shaky breath. Which, upon reflection, felt odd in a dream... vision... whatever this truly was. Then he asked, "What– what must I do?"

"Ask Adonai for forgiveness for your transgressions, ask him to come into your life, and help you. Thank him for saving you. Then go Leon, and transgress no more."

As Rohiel's words echoed around him, Leon spoke the words aloud that seemed so normal, but a peace unknown to him stirred. As the thoughts came to him, Leon saw the light in the distance pulse yet again. A tidal wave of that light washed over him again, and Leon felt a part of it remain within him this time. It left a warmth that could not be described– and the sense of a weight that seemed to be lifted off his shoulders.

"Forgive, as you have been forgiven. Love others as you are loved. Adonai is with you, Leon. Always."

Emotion overwhelmed him. He did not want the dream, or the peace, to end.

"We will speak again, as I will teach you more about Adonai."

"Thank you Rohiel."

The expanse faded, as Leon awoke from his slumber. Pale light of the early morning hours was beginning to shine behind the opposite tree line. His spear had remained securely in his lap through the night, and the tears he had cried were still wet on his face. A new day had dawned.

Chapter 5: The Village

Leon rubbed a sleeve across his face, drying the evidence that remained from his strange dream. A fresh vigor filled him this morning, one he hadn't felt in quite some time. After scrambling down from the tree Leon pulled out the bundle that the carriage had dropped for him the night before. He opened the note that had come with it and quickly read what looked to be a hastily scrawled message.

Dearest brother,

I must be quick as I'm not sure how long I can be away unnoticed. My hope that we would be reunited for the next few months is shattered, and my heart is broken.

Father is in a rage. Anything that reminds him of you will be gone by the morning. I beg of you– DO NOT return! I can't assure you of your safety here.

I don't even know if this will reach you. As our history suggests, our correspondence doesn't seem to be successfully delivered. Know that in a month I'll no longer be here, as I will be Baroness Halomir. Hopefully, I may be able to reach you then, but I doubt it. Sometimes it feels as though I am trading one gilded cage for another.

I'm glad to have seen you one last time Leon. Just as you instructed the boy Telon to say– please also don't worry about me. We all have our parts to play. Yours is whatever you make of it. I would gladly give up every title and possession I own to have that freedom. Sadly, all I can give you is enclosed with this note.

Be safe, Leon. I truly hope that Countess Serena's footmen are trustworthy enough to get this to you.

Liara

Silently thanking his sister, those who helped her, and even Adonai, tears that had so recently been dried, fought to run freely again. Leon delved into the food sack Telon had given him for breakfast, and scrounged through the burlap sack his sister had sent. His heart overflowed with the love he had for her. Inside, there was a hefty amount of salted beef, a bar of soap carefully wrapped in parchment, forty golden eagle coins, and a small blanket. Leon packed everything away, reorganizing both sacks, then started on the road toward Everbright once again. He knew if he was very lucky, he would arrive slightly after sunset.

As far as Leon could tell he was making good progress on his trek to the small town. He ate from his rations as he walked and only stopped to rest a few times. Visions from the night before and memories of his life up until this moment played through his head as he walked. Leon had no idea how he was going to stop the undead hordes, or share the news of Adonai. Beyond the small amount Rohiel had told him, he hadn't the clue about this God. Leon was grateful that Rohiel said they would speak again. There were just so many questions bubbling up inside of him that still needed answering.

Those questions, thoughts about Adonai, Rohiel, his life, his mother, and Liara all spun through his head like a whirlwind. They kept him constant company on his journey towards the village. Having taken so few rests during the day, Leon traversed the road in incredibly good time. It was nearing sunset when the tree-lined road curved slightly, then straightened in a line towards Everbright. His journey to the village was almost over.

To Leon's best recollection Everbright was a small farming village, and had all of the very basic amenities expected in a rural community. It was another few days' journey on foot from Everbright to the trading routes that crisscrossed the Xaelon kingdom. Leon hoped he could rent passage on a small mail carrier– if they had one visiting. A mail carrier being permanently attached to a village of this size would be a rarity. Passage had been unavailable when he initially journeyed home to the manor. Though if he were fully honest with himself, he hadn't really wanted to fly in an airship at the time anyways.

As he crested a small hill in the road and exited the edge of the forest, Leon's eyes wandered over Everbright and the farmland beyond. It was currently the beginning of springtime. Farmers still spent their daytime hours seeding and tilling the almost bare fields. Their widespread barns and outbuildings encircled the central village of small one-story houses. Occasionally a taller building could be seen, standing out from among the mass– an inn here, a town hall there. All were of stone or woodwork construction, and were topped with thatched roofs. Candle and torchlight had begun to pepper through Everbright at this hour, making it appear as if the star-filled heavens had reached down in their splendor to invade the earth. It painted a beautiful picture, contrasting with the last vestiges of sunlight that slowly dipped under the horizon. Leon took in the peacefulness and quiet of the village as the last hues of orange and yellow quickly faded from the sky.

He was two-thirds of the way down the dirt road, crossing through the farmland, when the peace and quiet came to an end. It was rudely disrupted by a loud horn blast from somewhere inside the village. Leon tensed as he listened. Three short blasts in a row. A universal sound throughout Xaelon– an undead horde was approaching.

Adrenaline began to race through him and he took off towards the village at a sprint. As he ran, he looked around in the dim twilight for any sign of the attack. Even from a distance, he saw the village start to come alive. The light from handheld lamps and torches appeared against the dim evening sky. As indicated by their movement, people had begun to rush around. He guessed they were preparing to either hide, or defend Everbright.

Leon noticed there was a basic palisade around the village, but that it had no gate which could be shut. That would make it a challenge to beat back large numbers of undead. Why wouldn't a town have a proper wall in the first place? It was a standard practice for villages and cities near the Lost Lands! *But this village isn't near the Lost Lands.*

So, why would a village so far in the Kingdom have undead attacking it?

As he continued to run towards the village, his makeshift backpack bounced behind him. Leon ran through his mental wartime checklist, to prepare himself for what was coming. All he had for battle was his studded armor and the rusty spear in his hands. With minimal experience in using the weapon, he struggled to remember the rudiments of it. In the navy he had excelled more with the sword and focused his training solely on that. He now wished he had better balanced that with other weapons as well. *Oh well, it will have to do.*

Leon thought he saw the horde to his left. They were still a good ways out from the village, but moving quickly. The distinct red glow that marked them as undead came from their eyes. There were enough of those dancing red lights for Leon to know that this wasn't just a random shambler or two approaching the village. Furthermore, it looked as if they came with a cart that held a cage of some sort– and it was led by a team of four skeletal horses! All of Leon's mental preparations suddenly collapsed like a house of cards. *What is going on here? Since when do the undead take prisoners?*

Leon finally passed through the closest entrance of the village. His feet were pounding from having walked all day, but he did not slow down. He careened sharply to the left on the cobblestone street and continued to run down the road– directly towards the undead's closest possible point of assault. As he ran he saw some village children inside their homes. They poked their heads up to their windows, hoping to see something exciting. One pair of children were abruptly yanked away from the window they had been looking through. Thankfully they had not been grabbed by undead, but by their much more fearsome mother. Leon continued to clearly hear her scold them long after he had passed by their home.

A few of the village's men and women were congregated at the street intersection ahead. They were armed with torches, swords, knives, farming tools, and pitchforks. Before Leon could reach them to help, they all ran off towards another street. He was about to jog after them but quickly decided to keep bearing left. Instead, he would try and see about flanking the horde. It was at that moment he heard the sound of distant screams, paired with the clash of metal. The horde had reached the village, and the fighting had begun.

Leon entered another intersection near the edge of the village. A few of the small one-story houses to his right had their front doors broken in. A wretch walked out of one, and looked directly at him. It was like the many others that he had encountered before: undead, yet not mindless like shamblers. Their thin smaller stature was humanoid. Grey, mottled, and rotting skin stretched tautly over their skeletal frames. This particular one seemed to be clothed solely in rags. Their hands were elongated and their fingers made to be sharp as daggers. One scratch from them left a toxin that would cause someone to become sluggish and unfocused.

The wretch hissed at Leon. Behind it a second one shoved a teenage man and woman outside. Two shamblers then exited. The first wretch pointed to Leon, before following the second and their prisoners.

Abducting people from houses instead of killing them on the spot? Seriously, what is going on here?

The shamblers that Leon had encountered during the Dead Wars looked similar to these two as well. Rotting flesh hung in strips, along with whatever clothing (or other debris) remained attached to their hollow frames. A majority of these two walking corpses were bone and sinew. Bleached white skulls stared at Leon with a glowing, dark-red, energy emanating from the eyes. Without the encumbrance of emotions, like fear or hesitation, they launched their attack with unnatural speed and reflexes.

One shambler held a sword that it swung high at Leon. The other had no weapon, and dove for Leon's legs in an effort to knock him over. Leon dodged the lunging corpse while simultaneously swinging to parry the shambler with the sword. He knocked the sword aside and swiftly jabbed the spearhead into the shoulder of the shambler's sword arm. What happened next was unexpected to say the least.

The rusty spear emitted a small flash of pale light from the impact. When Leon withdrew the spear, the shambler's shoulder (and the surrounding area) were pure white. It seemed to be dissolving in the small breeze that blew through the town. The red eyes of the undead continued to follow Leon. It registered no pain as the arm with the sword detached and fell to the ground.

Okay. This is getting more and more confusing. Leon thought, as he tossed his makeshift backpack behind him. If he was going to be victorious against these undead he would need as much freedom of motion as possible.

He quickly glanced at the spearhead, which was still as old and rusted as ever. There was no change to it, or light that he could see anymore. The now one-armed shambler lumbered forward. Leon reacted and whacked its armless side with the wooden shaft of the spear while sidestepping–shifting his position again. His eyes returned to the agile, weaponless, corpse that had lunged at him. It now stood next to the one-armed shambler. They began to rush at him together. Leon shuffled the other way, and swung the shaft of the spear against their legs in an effort to trip them. The corpses stumbled and fell, just as Leon wanted. He followed up by slashing the two-armed shambler across the back of its neck. The spearhead flashed again, and a line of white appeared where the spear had made contact.

The dissolving rapidly began again. The neck of the corpse separated from the rest of the body. The progression stopped then, as the head of the shambler rolled to rest a few feet away. The jaw was half dissolved and the dark-red eye sockets, looking towards Leon, winked out. He knew it would not get back up again.

Alright, so the spearhead makes them dissolve, but not the shaft. Leon observed.

The other shambler had no issue regaining its balance after being tripped. Mindlessly, it pivoted and charged again. It was too close, already inside the spear's defensive range– the one-armed shambler tackled Leon to the ground. Leon's back flashed in pain as he landed, but luckily he was not winded. He had been brought to the ground many a time before, and knew how to take a hit.

The corpse was scratching and scrabbling at Leon in an almost rabid frenzy. He winced through the pain and grasped the mushy neck of the shambler in his right hand. Lifting it slightly, he shifted and rolled, so that it was pinned to the ground beneath him. Gripping his weapon close to the blade, he held the corpse down, and penetrated its skull with the tip of the spear. The pale light flashed again, and its eyes winked out. The corpse's head turned into a white mound, its body falling limp.

Up close, Leon could see that the head had not dissolved as he had thought, per se, but had *turned into* a white sand-like material. Leon looked even closer and when this close to it, he could smell a familiar scent. One that he often enjoyed on airships, high among the clouds, while flying along the coast: salt.

He wondered at the many mysteries that seemed to be in front of him. A scream suddenly pierced through his thoughts. The new sound of terror seemed to come from a few streets over. He jumped up and retrieved his discarded backpack, then ran toward where he thought the next attackers were.

He jogged down the street, which followed the interior edge of the village, headed in the direction the scream had come from. As Leon ran, he collided with a wall of smoke from a burning building nearby. The red glow, and thick smoky haze, made it difficult to breathe and see. He pushed forward anyways, and could tell that he had reached the other entrance to the village. This was where the main force of undead had attacked. Coughing, and forcing himself even deeper into the smoke, the sound of fighting began to surround him. Leon rushed into the fray, and saw a shambler with a pickaxe reach for a young villager armed only with a pitchfork. Using his forward momentum he swung the spear. He grasped it near the end of the shaft and was able to neatly trip the corpse with its spearhead. A small glowing flash indicated to Leon, even in the smoke, that he had indeed cut the creature. When it fell face down onto the road Leon promptly skewered it. The awestruck young man he had just saved stared at him in amazement.

Stepping further into the haze, Leon saw more figures moving around in the choking smoke. Obscuring friend from foe, he tried to gauge the enemy by their movements. It was nearly impossible to see what the figures actually looked like. His attention caught on the jerky movements and thin outline of a wretch directing a few shamblers. The wretch's back faced him which enabled Leon to run up, and with a thrust of the rusty spear, skewer it through the chest. An internal glow formed around the wound, growing continuously brighter until the wretch exploded in a shower of salt.

After a few more minutes spent helping others out of perilous situations, no more moving undead were to be found. The assault was over mere minutes after it had begun. Leon knew, however, that there were more out there. He saw no sign of the undead carriage, or its cage, from earlier. All that remained in the village now were the cries of the traumatized, and the pumping adrenaline of battle.

✦✦✦✦✦

"I thank you for your assistance, kind sir." Wheezed the town elder named Fanem. He was a white-haired, wisp of a man, with deep wrinkles and tanned skin. He shook Leon's hand with surprising strength. One that had come from a lifetime of farming and hard labor.

"Rhoxmas knows that you came at just the right time." Fanem continued, while Leon stared at one of the undead's remains.

For the past few minutes, with a lit torch in hand, Leon found himself standing over a decapitated shambler. He wanted to be able to understand why this attack had happened. This was one of the "fresher" corpses that had assaulted Everbright. He still could not figure out why the undead were taking prisoners. What need did they have for those, like the two teenagers, the two wretches had escorted away? Everything seemed off, even this corpse in front of him.

None of the events that had occurred since the crash made sense to him. Leon felt as if he had been given puzzle pieces, without a picture of what they fit together to make. He realized that the elder was still talking to him, and tore himself away from examining the corpse.

"I'm sorry, who?" Leon asked.

Elder Fanem nodded vigorously, as if expecting confusion, "Rhoxmas! The God of the harvest. He sows and reaps us at his will." A small, sad, shake of his head was all it took to refocus the elder's mind back on Leon in front of him. "But you, strong warrior– You have in turn reaped the undead! Ha, that'll show 'em!"

A god of harvest? Why not just have a god for every little detail of your life? Leon thought. *Then again, I only knew about the God of the universe last night. If Adonai is God of the universe why would there need to be any others?*

"Yes, well um, you're welcome and I am glad I was here to help," Leon replied, slightly distracted. Still puzzling over the undead. *What was it that was wrong with this body? Besides the obvious...*

Fanem peered past Leon to the headless corpse on the ground, "What are you looking at it for?" The elder asked.

Leon seized upon this opportunity to try and get some answers, "How often do they kidnap people? I've never seen that before."

Fanem's head continued to bob, in what Leon now thought was an uncontrollable tic. "They took people? Do– Do undead do that? I– I thought you slew them all."

True, Leon counted that he had dispatched seven shamblers and one wretch by the end of the assault. However, there had been many more red eyes than that in the horde, and at least one more wretch that wasn't accounted for. Leon refused to believe that he imagined it.

"Didn't you see the carriage? The skeletal horses?" Leon questioned.

Elder Fanem stared at the corpse with Leon, mumbling, "I saw nothing."

Leon processed the infallibility of the elder's statement. Leon knew what he saw. *Didn't someone see the horde coming and alert the town in the first place? Wouldn't someone have noticed people missing?* The resolve to do something, anything, grew in Leon as he recalled the charge given to him in his vision the prior evening.

"Good sir Fanem, I tell you plainly, as you can see from my coat I am from Xaelon naval service. Although recently... retired. I know that there were more undead in this attack, but I do not know where they went. I would be honored to attempt to find the remainder of the undead horde plaguing you."

80

Elder Fanem's eyes widened at the unexpected act of chivalry from the stranger who had helped save his village. "Um, thank you, young man, but you really don't need to trouble yourself furth–"

"Wait a second, Master Fanem, I think I am onto something…" Leon interrupted, as he examined the body a section at a time.

He looked back to the corpse on the ground, needing to figure this out. It was a dead body that had rough, ragged, dirty clothes hanging off its torso. The shambler's hands were the dirtiest. Its nails were cracked and broken, with dirt stuck underneath. The feet were shoeless and bone protruded in some areas, from the flesh having been worn off. The skin on the headless neck was grey and necrotic, but Leon had finally spotted what he thought was unusual. Two desiccated holes in the base of the neck.

"Oh, no." Leon groaned.

"What?" Fanem asked.

Leon pulled himself to his feet and ran over to the other unmoving, undead bodies. Bringing his torch close, he checked them for the same marks– hoping he was wrong. The stink of the long dead corpses, at this close a proximity, almost made Leon gag. After he found another with the same two holes in its neck, Leon realized this village faced more than just simple undead hordes and horses.

"Elder Fanem?" Leon asked, as he turned to the village leader.

"Yes, young man?" Fanem replied, looking worried.

"You have an Alukah problem." He said, as he pointed out the teeth marks along the neck of the corpse.

Elder Fanem covered his nose with his sweat-stained shirt, and leaned closer to inspect for himself. After a few moments the elder stepped back from examining the corpse, and spoke to Leon in a slightly different tone than before, "An Alukah? What is that?"

Leon silently reminded himself that not everyone could afford an education, or had served on the front lines.

"An Alukah is another undead fiend. One more dangerous than wretches or shamblers." He explained, nudging the body with his foot, "They drink the blood of live victims, hence the need for the capture of your villagers. I can assure you that the Alukah is commanding the undead plaguing your village. They are extremely cunning, fast, and some on the front even use some type of hypnosis to command you to do things you wouldn't normally do."

Leon watched the white-haired farmer wring his hands together in worry. Looking back into Leon's eyes, Elder Fanem seemed almost nervous.

"How can we defend ourselves from something like that?" Asked the exasperated elder.

"We hunt it. It must have a lair nearby. It hates sunlight, so it hides in there during the day and sends its horde out during the night. My guess is to collect its victims."

Elder Fanem's head began to bob vigorously, "You said they kidnapped villagers!"

"Exactly. How many villagers are missing since the attack?" Leon asked.

"I... I don't know." Fanem replied.

"Well, has anyone gone missing before? Alukahs are notorious for picking people off– trying to be unnoticed."

Fanem ran a hand over his balding scalp, looking stressed. "Possibly– Yes, maybe a few over the years. We always thought that it was just people moving away."

The inaction on the part of both the villagers, in having not built better defenses; and the military, in having not purged the decent-sized horde before now, was still confusing to Leon. Something still did not add up for him. He didn't like not knowing all of the facts. However, if there was an undead problem here, and if people were indeed missing, Leon felt he needed to find them and end it.

"Then there is no time to waste. We must hasten after the horde and find their hideout before it's too late. Are there any in the village who would go with me?" Leon asked.

Fanem's head kept nodding, and Leon hoped that was a sign of agreement– not simply the elder's tic.

Elder Fanem spoke a few hushed words to a couple of farmhands, after which word seemed to spread quickly. Before long, it appeared as though the whole town had gathered around the large well in the center of Everbright. There were a couple hundred people of all ages and races. The Elder, and some of the other older people in the village, joined Leon on the wooden landing that led up to the well. Torches and candles dotted the crowd, as the people strained to see during the evening meeting.

Fanem raised his hands, and the murmurings of the crowd quieted when he began to speak in a wheezing bellow, "Unfortunately, we have suffered a reaping. We must all understand that this is the will of Rhoxmas. Though this is a dark moment for Everbright, it seems that this time we have a glimmer of hope." Fanem then gestured to Leon, as his eyes scanned across the crowd.

Leon shifted slightly under the weight of the villagers' stares. Their eyes all fell upon him, and the murmurings that had begun again suddenly quieted. Even their silence sounded resigned and mournful to his ears.

"We were able to defeat the undead thanks to the timely assistance of this heroic individual." Fanem gestured again, and Leon knew it was time to get to the point. After all, time was an important factor in this endeavor. He stepped close, smiling briefly at Fanem, before turning to address the crowd.

Leon started, "There are also villagers missing, presumed taken by the wretches that attacked. Did anyone see anything like a cage, being drawn by undead horses?"

More blasted murmurings washed through the crowd. After a few seconds, a high pitched, feminine, voice piped in from the crowd. "That thar carriage cage was full of o' people! I thought I saw them newlyweds, the Cales, in there I did!" The people around her tried to quietly shush her.

Leon's pulse quickened as he tried to think of how much time had passed since the battle ended. No more than an hour, maybe? Any pursuit would be against four horses drawing a carriage, so speed would be essential. Suddenly, every moment was precious.

"Then we must try to rescue them. Presumably, they retreated to where they came from. Did anyone see where they went?" Leon asked.

The silence from the crowd was almost deafening.

"I mean to find their trail and to follow them immediately. Let any able-bodied person come with me, and I swear I will do everything I can to help rescue your people."

The crowd began to stir uncomfortably while Leon stared out at them. They were a bruised and beaten people– a people who were tired from a long day's work and defending themselves from an attack on their town. Leon hopped off the platform, then strode into and through the crowd. The common people, which he reminded himself he now was a part of, parted for him like gates opening. All too quickly, it seemed he reached the other side of them. After a few more steps Leon turned to look back. He saw that there was, in fact, nobody following him. A few husbands were pulled gently back by their wives, as well as an exuberant child or two.

Crestfallen, Leon had to mentally remind himself that they were not trained and conditioned soldiers. He couldn't fault families for not wanting to be divided, but living in a place where this happened made no sense! Why not build a gate? When people went missing, why not ask for help from the military? Why would people simply up and move for no reason or warning– except to possibly escape this madness? Questions abounded as he stared at the unmoving people of the town. Some looked uneasy, others looked guilty. All were unwilling to follow him into danger and death. Even so, Leon couldn't bring himself to admonish them for it.

So Leon silently turned around, his back to the crowd, determined to find the way the undead had come and gone.

If I must do this alone, I will.

Chapter 6: The Outcasts

Leon figured the burning building would be a good place to start investigating where the horde had come from. It was the point of attack closest to where they had entered the town, so he thought he may be able to pick up their trail from there. He jogged down the street, and headed back towards that entrance of the village. As he approached it, he began to hear angry yelling and screaming. Oddly enough, it came from the direction of the smoldering building which was still covered in a smoky haze.

Through the haze Leon saw a smallish figure shaking his fists, jumping up and down, and ranting and raving at the building itself. He was a dwarven male, dressed in an apron, over what appeared to be polished chainmail that had been cut off at the shoulders. Leather pants hung below a tool belt, which was slung full of tools that jingled and clanked as he shook with anger. His black braided and dreadlocked hair was covered in ash and soot. Leo thought that it shook with more fervor than his fists did.

Burning with curiosity, he walked around the dwarf until it saw him. Leon quickly realized he may have gotten more than he bargained for, as the dwarf stepped uncomfortably close to him and waved a well-used mallet in his face.

"They burned down me house! Me shop! Everythin' I have! I'll kill 'em! AGAIN!" he yelled.

The dwarf, standing at full height, was almost up to Leon's shoulder. Though he didn't need height to seem intimidating. He looked menacing enough with his corded, rippling, oversized shoulder and arm muscles— which exploded out from the spotted leather apron he wore. The angry dwarf looked Leon up and down and, in a rage, asked, "Who the rust are ya? Ya ain't from this here hick village."

Leon held up both open hands to the dwarf, to show him he meant no harm, "I was passing through Everbright when the undead attacked. I helped to fight them off, and am now trying to pursue them, to hopefully rescue the prisoners they've taken."

The dwarf looked Leon up and down, evaluating him for a few seconds. Grunting, he sheathed the mallet in a loop at his side, and growled. The dwarf's gaze turned wary, "Ya daft lad? Undead don't take no prisoners!"

"A carriage, pulled by skeletal horses, ran off with villagers locked in a cage. Some of the bodies of the undead that attacked had Alukah marks on their necks. They will take the people they kidnapped to the Alukah, and feed them to it."

The dwarf threw up his hands in anger, "Well that's jus' great. Been here not even two years, an' lost everythin' settlin' in tha wrong, dumb, hick town."

Leon ignored the slight against the villagers, and instead saw in front of him a prospect. The dwarf was fit enough, angry enough, and could certainly be of help. "Well, if you want revenge for them burning down your home, I could use the help in going after them."

The dwarf seemed to only half-listen. Instead, he turned to gather a satchel. It appeared to be filled with the few belongings he had been able to scrounge from his now ruined home. Dropping a few things from his belt onto the ground, the dwarf hoisted the satchel over his shoulders, then pointed the small mallet at Leon again. "An' don't ya go slowin' me down now, boyo. We are leavin' right this instant!" And after a pause added, "As soon as we know where they went!"

Patience. Leon thought. "I have a modest amount of skill at tracking, and they would surely leave a trail with the carriage."

The dwarf grumbled, and muttered something Leon could only half make out about relying on strangers. In a huff, the dwarf extended a rough, calloused hand, "Duamé."

Leon shook his hand and tried not to cringe. Duamé seemed to be making a valid attempt to crush Leon's hand in his grip, "Leon."

"Well mista meat shield, lead tha rustin' way already!"

Meat shield? Leon had to think for a moment before he realized what the dwarf meant. He tried not to massage his hand as he glanced down the cobblestone street and jogged to the edge of the village– just past the remains of Duamé's still smoldering home. As they continued out of the wide palisade opening of the village, the road abruptly turned to dirt and fields lined either side. Crops barely poked out of the ground, and in the dim torchlight Leon carried it was hard to see any sign of a trail. He knew that he had seen them in this general area when they approached the village, but where had they gone when they left it?

They continued to follow the road by torchlight, in silence. Leon's thoughts strayed to the fact that should they stay on this route for a few days, it would take them to his father's mining camps. The carriage could have easily come from that direction, with some sort of hideout for the Alukah nearby. Giving way to that line of thought, Leon started to jog ahead. Then, the dwarf he had just met suddenly shouted from behind.

"Wot kinda tracker do ya think ya are exactly?" Duamé blustered.

Trying to concentrate, Leon asked. "What do you mean?"

"Ya walked right past their trail boyo!" Duamé explained, pointing to an area behind Leon.

Leon turned back, and brought the torch closer. While one side of the road looked relatively unchanged, the other side of the road had the barest evidence of two rut lines that branched off into the fields of barely-growing wheat.

"Guess me seein' better in tha dark beats yer 'trackin' any day o' tha week." Duamé commented. They both started to jog towards the treeline, now following the carriage's trail. Leon noticed the trees were wide enough at one spot to allow for a small path through the woods.

No wonder the carriage seemed to come out of nowhere! He thought.

Leon paused, and looking over his shoulder, wondered if Duamé knew about it. He called back to the dwarf, "Hey Duamé, where does this path through the woods lead?"

Indignant, the dwarf countered, "Certain death an' dismemberment? How should I know where tha path goes?"

"Don't you live in this village? It looks like a well-worn or used path."

"Again, I only lived here fer two years, lad. These hick farmers never mentioned anythin' bout no… Oi, WATCH IT!"

Leon, hearing the tone of the dwarf, wasted no time. Without looking away from Duamé, he dove to the side, dropping the torch and spear to the ground. The buzz of an arrow whizzed past where his head had been only a second before.

Leon looked up and saw a wretch, with its eyes glowing red, snarl at them from the treeline. The creature stood right where the path entered the trees. It held a bow and was drawing an arrow from a quiver on its leg, hissing all the while. Two shamblers lumbered forward from behind it. They had crude woodcutting axes and old leather armor that hung loosely off of them. They rushed forward towards Leon and Duamé, mindlessly wanting to add to their necrotic numbers.

As Leon picked up the spear he had dropped when he rolled, he saw a small hammer whirl end-over-end past him. It flew straight at one of the shamblers and hit it in the shoulder. The strike connected with such force that it caused the shambler to spin as it hit the ground. Duamé shouted in exhilaration as he hefted a large, two-handed hammer from over his back and charged at the downed shambler– determined to finish the job.

Leon saw the danger of leaving the wretch standing, and allowing it to use them both as pincushions for its arrows. So, choosing to deal with it first, he rushed at it. After having seen the basic tactic work earlier, Leon grabbed the spear from one end and swung it with both hands at the other shambler's legs– tripping it while he ran past.

When Leon was only about ten feet away the wretch drew the bowstring back, preparing to fire. Knowing he only had seconds, and that he couldn't roll or dodge out of the way without potentially dropping the spear, Leon gambled. With the first thought that came of how he could strike before the wretch, he hurled the spear directly at it. He then immediately dove into a roll towards his adversary. It was a desperate attempt to avoid the arrow that he was certain had been launched straight towards him. A flash of light caught on the edge of his vision.

As Leon came out of the roll he saw that the wretch was staring at the spear protruding from its left side. The surrounding flesh that was rapidly turning to salt and spreading across its body. While it still stood, it was unmoving. The red glowing eyes winked out, changing to a pale colorless white.

As Leon removed his spear it caused the top of the wretch corpse to bend. Then it proceeded to fall over and off of the bottom half of the body. Salt grains had divided the body in half, and formed a small pile on top of the remains.

Leon turned to deal with the shambler that he had tripped. He saw it several strides away, lit by the torch on the ground, atop Duamé. One of its hands pinned the dwarf to the ground by his neck, while the other hand held a woodcutter's axe– raised high, and ready to strike.

Leon ran as fast as he could in an effort to save Duamé. It seemed hopeless, he would never get there in time to save the dwarf. Then, suddenly, the shambler was launched off of Duamé with a puff of smoke– straight towards Leon's feet.

No, not smoke.

Fire.

The shambler landed with its face in the ground, its head aflame. Still and unmoving, it posed no immediate threat. Duamé sat up exclaiming, "Wot tha heck happened?" Turning, Duamé and Leon saw a figure purposefully striding towards them.

She was dressed in a long brown robe, and had a wild bush of dark red hair. Clearly untamed, it went about in every which way. She was fairly young, and had no wrinkles marking her features. Her face, however, was smeared with dirt– almost as if she didn't care about her appearance at all. Her green eyes were fierce, but also seemed to have a hollowness to them. The most prominent feature about her, though, was the torch-like flame coming off of her outstretched hand. She closed her palm, and the fire extinguished.

Duamé did a double-take as he hoisted himself off the ground, "Oi! Miala, wot are ya doin' here? An' how'd ya know ta burn faces off?"

The woman, named Miala, glanced towards Leon as she answered Duamé in a soft voice that belied her wild appearance, "I have always known, Duamé. And I followed you both to help. Once you were clear of the villagers, that is."

Leon approached her and inclined his head, "Thank you for the assistance Miss Miala. My name is Leon."

"No family name?" She asked curiously.

"Not anymore."

She paused a beat before she replied, "Miala. No last name either."

"Well, mancer Miala I thank y–" Leon started.

Miala quickly cut him off, "Pyromancer."

Duamé was dusting himself off as he piped, "Thank ya lass! No wonder tha village steers clear o' ya! Tha rumors about ya bein' a witch–"

"Only apply when I am in a bad mood Duamé. Otherwise, I am a simple mancer trying to live out her life." Changing the topic, she turned to Leon and said, "We should keep moving if we have any hope of catching them."

"Agreed." Leon chimed, "Are you well prepared, miss? You do not look as if you packed much by way of provisions." Leon couldn't help but notice that she had not seemed to pack for the journey at all. She was just in a simple brown robe. Even Duamé had his satchel.

"I will be fine Mister Leon. Now let us go to save those people." She strode purposefully past them, and had followed the trail almost into the forest when she came across the bisected wretch in the salt pile. Raising a brow, she asked, "How did you do that?"

Leon held up the rusty spear. Duamé looked on as well, cackled, and pointed at the spear, "Wot is that? A spear saltshaker? A spearshaker? A pointy saltlick?"

Feeling as though now wasn't quite the right time to tell the people he had just met about Adonai, and dreams about angels, Leon took the jests and smirked. "Magic." Then he walked ahead to take the lead.

Miala explained as they went that while she lived outside of the village, she had seen the undead assault. Unfortunately by the time she arrived it had been too late to help.

"And to top it all off," Miala whispered in frustration, "Kelleren is missing."

"Kelleren?" Leon asked.

"My dog."

"Oi, that mangy mutt? Good riddance!" Duamé sniped.

Sighing, Miala whispered quietly, "You're just saying that because Kelleren stole your sweetroll that one time."

"Right! Wot kinda dog eats sweetrolls?" Duamé raged.

They continued down the forested path for what seemed like several hours. Duamé began to grumble about wanting to rest for a bit; Miala and Leon finally acquiesced for a few minutes when they came upon some conveniently cut tree stumps. Duamé took off a boot and kneaded his aching foot while they sat. Miala, however, never relaxed or stopped scanning the surrounding trees. She always seemed to be on high alert for any possible dangers, even while they rested.

Leon thought about the situation they were in, and how much his life had changed in a mere day's time. He knew there was a reason that things from the village didn't make sense to him– it was time to open up to these two a bit. Perhaps his new traveling companions could provide some insight.

After a few more minutes of thought, hung up on the behavior of the village elder, and how no one from the town meeting came along to help, he decided to ask, "So, Miala, have you seen raids at Everbright before?"

"The last one was supposed to be around five years ago." Came her quiet response.

"You weren't there?"

"No." She was still looking around the forest, and very distracted from what he was asking her.

Perhaps she is looking for more than lurking threats, maybe she is also hoping to find her dog out there. Leon thought to himself.

Seeing that was a dead-end conversation, Leon tried a different tactic, "Either of you fight the undead before today?"

Flat stares were his only reply. Leon made one last-ditch attempt at solving any of his mysteries: he decided to fill Miala in on what he had found in Everbright. "I saw two undead in the village with bite marks in their necks. I think that an Alukah is behind the attack somehow."

Miala sighed as she got up, dusted her robe off, and walked off ahead. "Don't let it talk to you. It could hypnotize you to attack me, and I really would rather not kill anyone who is still alive."

Leon tried to remember the last time that he had this much difficulty conversing with people. Well, people other than his 'former' father, that is. The surly dwarf and standoffish Pyromancer may prove to be helpful traveling companions, however when it came to conversation– things might be difficult, to say the least. Duamé didn't help any. He chuckled while putting his boot back on.

"Boyo, do YOU got a way wit' tha ladies." He croaked. Then he walked ahead cackling some more.

Leon decided to quit while he was behind. Following the path deeper into the woods, they were grateful to not suffer any more skirmishes. Even so, Leon knew that every step they took, even at a good pace, they would be far outdistanced by a horse-drawn cart. *A skeletal-horse drawn cart for that matter. They would never tire.*

After tripping one too many times on the tree roots that ran along and across the path, Miala had enough.

"We need to stop. I could use some rest." she said, her frustration clearly evident.

"I could as well actually. Before arriving at the village, I had been walking all day." Leon added.

"Well, I could go on, but seein' as how ya all can't see in tha dark, an I need ya– Fer protection. Ya know– meat shields." Duamé commented.

Miala looked about and sighed, "I didn't find Kelleren. I know he went this way, but he always comes back."

"I am sure we will find him." Leon reassured her.

"Spare me your empty platitudes." She snapped. After a moment Miala took a deep breath, "Sorry, that was unnecessary. I miss him terribly and should not take it out on you."

She is just stressed. Leon thought. "It's ok, but if we are stopping for the night we should get in a tree branch–" he started.

"…above arm's reach, to avoid a possible random undead." Miala finished. It was almost verbatim what Leon was going to say. Her eyes widened slightly, and then she turned away quickly, looking for a tree to inhabit for the night.

Duamé grunted before he too looked for a promising spot up a tree.

Soon they found a tall elm, adjacent to the path, just a little ways ahead. Duamé climbed up first, putting to rest the question of if the boughs would hold their weight. Leon offered Miala the next spot up– to which she snapped, "Look away, please!"

Without waiting for Leon's baffled response, and while he looked the other direction, she deftly scaled the tree. After she got settled, as Leon climbed to the branch that was closest to the ground, he heard Miala ask softly, "Do you think the captives will be alive when you… when we get to them?"

Leon had been trying hard not to think about what they might find– but since it had been brought up, "I hope so. I have to believe they will be. We can take a short rest. Sunrise will be in just a few hours. Besides, we are no good to anyone if we are too exhausted to actually free them."

Miala seemed to think about his answer as she settled into her branch. "Hope is not something I'm used to having."

Me either. Not lately. Leon thought. Pessimistic thoughts didn't seem to be the correct way to go about this situation. Nor the right attitude to respond with either. He tried to think of something that would be inspiring to the mancer. The best Leon could sputter were the words Prince Gelan had once said. Words that had always stuck with him. "Well, um, let's hope for the best, and prepare for the worst."

Miala scoffed and laid against the tree trunk, apparently putting an end to the conversation. Leon decided to try and rest as well, yet again cradling the spear against himself. He wondered if he would dream as he had in the tree from the night before, and he mentally reviewed all of the events from the day. While Miala was silent, Duamé's snoring punctuated the questions that floated through Leon's head.

Seriously. Why does Everbright have no solid protection against even a basic undead attack?

Are the captured villagers even alive anymore?

Did Miala have survival training in the military as well?

As his thoughts continued, somewhere between wondering about both his sister and his mother's well-being, Leon finally drifted off to sleep.

Chapter 7: The Lesson

Leon immediately felt the difference in his dream. The battles he waged with the spear the prior day replayed in his mind as watched himself from the outside. From this perspective it looked as if he spent more time fumbling with the spear than fighting. The shamblers he had dispatched were lightly armed with pickaxes and woodcutting axes, which was a far cry from a fully armed and armored undead. Overall, Leon counted himself fairly lucky after yesterday's encounters.

"You must learn."

A musical, feminine, voice echoed through the flashbacks and they all froze– as if time had stopped. Leon stood transfixed, staring at his frozen memories. Then they began to dissolve away like salt in the wind, revealing the grey expanse from his previous dream. He couldn't see anyone or anything, just the same pinprick of light in the distance.

Leon called out, "Rohiel?"

"I am not him."

The voice came from behind Leon. He turned and saw a figure step forward out of nothingness, as if there were an unseen doorway that she had walked through. In a moment she was simply– there. She was outfitted in heavily detailed, form-fitting, plate armor. Armor that was polished to a bright sheen. Muscular, and as tall as Leon, the armor she wore gleamed a pale blue and had gold trim along the edges. Her armor was intricate– beautiful in and of itself. He had never seen anything like it. When Leon looked up at her face he saw it was covered by a sleek rounded helm, with a low hanging nose guard. What looked to be long hair of pure sunlight, grew from the helm and fell down behind her. Where a face would normally be shadowed, due to being covered by the helm, it was instead obscured by radiant light. The light shone through the helms openings, but still allowed for definition around her unusual eyes. Eyes with irises that matched the brilliance of her shining hair.

"I am Lochemetel."

Her voice echoed around Leon as she started walking slowly around him, keeping several feet away. She held out one of her hands and a long golden spear coalesced in it. She pointed it at Leon, which caused him to look down at his own hand. The spear he had fallen asleep cradling once again, suddenly appeared.

"Lochemetel?" Leon asked. As he looked back at her.

"It means 'Warrior of God'."

Then she lunged at him. It seemed as if she was fully intent on skewering him with her spear. He blocked her attack instinctively, and then had to continue blocking attack after attack as she whirled and wailed at him. She was fast– faster than any enemy Leon had ever faced before. It only took a few seconds for her to maneuver inside Leon's defenses. Then Lochemetel struck him. The flat of her blade connected solidly with the back of his head. Stumbling forward while rubbing the area she hit, Leon suddenly realized that she was training him: it was a training through combat.

A little over two months had already passed since Leon last engaged in combat drills on the *Dawnfire*. It had been one of his favorite activities on the ship. However, that included using a weapon he was much better versed in. He now fought an angelic being, not crewmates, and used a spear he was inexperienced with. This would prove to be much more of a challenge. He turned to Lochemetel, who held her spear ready. Leon readied himself before nodding for the bout to continue. She immediately attacked, while Leon defended himself again– repeatedly.

For what seemed like hours Leon defended and attacked, parried and riposted. All the while he watched and analyzed her movements. He picked up different techniques to use with the weapon as he became more and more familiar with it. It seemed to him that Lochemetel would repeat a few sequences of attacks and blocks, until she was sure that he knew them, before she would move on to new ones.

When she (all too often) knocked Leon to the ground, and delivered what would be a killing stroke, she would display her unbelievable control and halt her golden spear mere inches from slicing him open. While Leon could never best her, the smile that played on his face throughout the entire engagement was genuine. This sparring session was one of the more enjoyable exercises he had experienced in quite some time.

Strangely, Leon did not feel tired. For that matter, he didn't even break a sweat. The dream version of him felt as though he could keep fighting for hours more. However, Lochemetel had other plans. She held up a hand, signaling to stop, after his latest defeat.

"Enough. You must learn more."

"Then let's keep going!" Leon was more than ready to continue their training.

"Not from me."

He sighed and lowered his weapon, then showed her respect with a nod of his head.

"Thank you, this was... fun." He said. She began to fade– becoming more and more blurry until she disappeared completely into the grey, formless, expanse. Left alone once again, Leon looked to the pinprick of light glowing in the distance. As he did, it pulsed and washed him with its warm light that made him feel weightless.

After a moment Rohiel's voice resounded all around him, filling the expanse.

"You learn quickly, Leon."

"Lochemetel is a good teacher. She would certainly best all of the warriors I have ever known." He replied.

"Well she has been fighting for thousands of years..."

Leon's feeling of comfort after being bathed in the wave of light gave way to awe, as he tried to process the idea that he could learn from such a being. What would it be like to live for thousands of years? To fight for thousands of years? With such mastery of her weapon, he thought surely no one would be able to stand against Lochemetel in battle.

"Fighting what exactly?" He asked.

"The Fallen, and their armies."

Leon had heard Rohiel mention 'The Fallen' before. While it sounded ominous, if they fell once, how could they honestly be that big of a threat?

"You must see before you can learn."

Leon wondered what Rohiel meant, until his eyes started to tingle and itch. Then an ache began in the back of his head. As he tried to fight through the strange feeling coming over him, Leon looked at the light in the distance. It seemed to have changed too. It appeared to have become more saturated with red and violet colors than before.

"Observe."

The grey expanse shifted and Leon's sense of balance was thrown off– similarly to the way he felt when an airship took a sharp turn. Much like when Rohiel showed Leon the wreckage of the *Dawnfire*, Leon felt the unending grey world change around him. Just like a new recruit on their very first airship flight, he stumbled. He had to regain his balance and right himself as his surroundings transformed. Then Leon watched as the grey expanse was replaced by another familiar sight: Rhise manor in the daytime.

The manor, however, looked different– the colors were innumerable. Brights were brighter and darks were darker. Everything was more vivid. He had never seen the manor like this before. Of course, that could also be because Leon was seeing it from an odd angle. He was several hundred feet in the air! As he looked down he realized nothing was supporting him and panic momentarily gripped him; then he realized that he wasn't falling. He seemed to be standing on nothingness. His body was just floating weightlessly in the air.

Leon looked up and saw that the sun was hidden behind thin, rolling clouds. The sky grew progressively darker as he looked across the horizon– towards the Lost Lands. The rest of the world appeared to be consumed by that darkness. It evoked a sense of oppression and foreboding which matched the magnitude of the dark, voided, lands. Spotting movement in the manor courtyard below, Leon turned away from the darkness, and watched as more than a few servants went about their day. They went back and forth, inside and outside of the large house, completely unaware of his presence.

"This was earlier today. They cannot see us."

Us? Leon thought, as he felt a hand on his shoulder.

He looked and saw another armored figure floating next to him in the air. The plate armor on this angel was bulky. It looked almost oversized and exaggerated, yet was still beautifully crafted. It shone with the same blue brilliance that Lochemetel's had. The golden edges of this bulkier suit seemed to have tiny symbols written across them, spread apart at various locations.

Unlike Leon's recent sparring partner, this figure had no helm. However, his head shone so brightly that the light itself obscured all of his features. The luminescence of the angel's face was like staring into the sun. Leon couldn't look for long without feeling pain in his eyes from its intensity. He did see the edges of long, flowing, bright white, hair, which settled around his armored shoulders.

"Rohiel?" Leon asked in amazement.

"Indeed. Observe."

The figure pointed, and Leon looked. He saw that the servants below seemed to have others following them. In fact there were many things flitting and moving about like little gusts of wind. There were small, winged, leathery, creatures– who tried to fly right by the servant's heads. Every so often, one of those creatures would land on a servant's shoulder and whisper into their ear. Somehow they remained completely unnoticed and unseen. They would then fly off for a bit before coming back to that person; sometimes they stopped to also visit someone else. Before Leon could even ask about them, the angel answered his question.

"The Mazzikin."

Other creatures were around as well. Some of them looked like miniature humans, while others looked almost like falcons, or birds with human heads. Leon had rarely seen hostile chimeras during his naval service; they were usually dispatched from afar, via cannons or arrows. These creatures, however, didn't seem as nefarious as the chimeras he had encountered. In fact, there was a quality to them that felt as though they just exuded goodness. Rohiel pointed to a group of them huddled around a maid, as she brought air dried clothes into the manor.

"The Malakhim."

They guarded the people, and chased the little leathery creatures around. Occasionally the two types of creatures became entangled in a little clash. During one such incident, Leon observed a Mazzikin being bound in chains. Then he was dropped like a stone into the earth, disappearing through the ground without having even disturbed it. Leon even saw that the creatures would suddenly stop fighting each other, as if on some unspoken cue. They would then repeat the entire cycle: flitting about, whispering in people's ears, skirmishing, then ceasefire.

Leon suddenly caught sight of rapid movement from the corner of his eye. Several shadowy clouds soared through the air, heading towards the manor from the direction of the Lost Lands. These were being chased through the sky by an angel armored similarly to Rohiel and Lochemetel. This angel, however, held a flaming sword at its side. A sword that clearly spelled doom for the black clouds trying so desperately to evade it. Just as the armored angel was about to overtake them, the cloud beings scattered apart– racing in all different directions. Watching as the clouds scattered, Leon saw the treetops sway. It appeared as if their sudden movements caused an actual breeze to blow through the leaves that clung to the branches. The angel and its fiery sword kept chasing after one unlucky cloud, well off into the distance.

"Observe." Rohiel directed again.

He pointed to one small servant on the ground. Upon Rohiel's command, they seemed to shift closer to that person– and as they did recognition dawned on Leon. It was the boy, Telon, who had helped Leon leave the manor. Why did he seem to have a worried look about him? Leon watched as he stepped up to the fountain in front of Rhise manor and filled a pail from it. His muscles strained lifting the pail, but he hefted it and headed towards the stables. Leon and Rohiel glided over, following him down the hill, then through the stable door.

As Telon entered the stables, he grabbed a brush, and brought the pail to one of the horses. Leon knew this horse, it belonged to Laric. A brute of a black stallion, its disposition matched the surly, brutish nature of its owner. The horse shifted as Telon nervously opened the stall door and entered. He then proceeded to carefully close the door behind himself. Clearly uncomfortable around the horse, Telon shuffled along the edge of the stall. He pressed his body tightly against the wall, and made sure to keep a tight grip on both the pail and the brush in his hands. The horse, in turn, started to slowly clop towards Telon.

Leon watched as the horse used its bulk to pin Telon to the wall. The several-hundred pound animal's flanks assaulted Telon– spilling the pail, and knocking him to the ground. Telon hurriedly scrambled back up in a huff. He dusted himself off and screamed angrily at the horse, "You did that on purpose! Jerk!"

As if summoned from afar, a leathery winged creature flew through the stable door, and zipped over to Telon. It landed on his shoulder, and whispered into his ear. Telon had no idea the creature was there, and stood still as he began to shake with rage towards the horse. The horse had already started on its way back from the other side of the stall, in an attempt to body-check him again. Telon quickly

105

climbed over the stall's wall, before the horse could hurt him.

He had picked the brush back up in the stall, and he now cocked his arm back to throw it at the horse. Then Telon's hand paused, and quivered, until he finally lowered his arm altogether. Closing his eyes, he took a few deep breaths. The brush dropped to the floor and he opened his eyes again. He looked at the horse, clearly still irritated with it.

"Look, I don't like you," he said, as he turned and grabbed a carrot from a nearby barrel. "And I know you don't like me." He picked the brush up again and held the carrot out to the horse, brandishing it as if it were a weapon. The horse eyed him warily.

"I have to brush your coat, so unless you want this to take all day, you might as well stand still so we can get this over with." Telon reasoned.

The horse nickered softly as it slowly approached Telon and the carrot. Soon, the horse took a bite out of the vegetable while Telon started brushing the side of its head.

"See, not so bad, huh?" Telon commented, smiling at his small victory.

"*Observe.*"

The small, leathery, creature howled in frustration as it flapped its wings and zipped around in a temper fit. It flew up and started to head out the door when, from just outside the stable door, a golden spear suddenly appeared. It pierced the creature with unnatural speed. Leon saw his recent sparring partner, Lochemetel, suited in her battle armor, as she stepped into the strike. She made sure the creature disappeared in a puff of smoke. Just as he had seen before, the smoke dropped to the ground and seeped down into the earth. The warrior lingered in the doorway for a few moments, scanning the stable for other adversaries. Once she was satisfied that there were no others, she turned and exited– leaving the completely unaware Telon to his task.

A bestial roar came from outside as Leon and Rohiel were moving to the doorway of the stables. Outside, they saw Lochemetel defending herself against a giant sized version of the creature she had just killed. This one seemed to almost be made of shadows, as if the light actually bent away from it. Several heads taller than her, its dark claws swiped at her again and again in fury. Lochemetel dipped, whirled, and dodged around the creature. She used her spear with the same familiarity as a limb that was attached to her body. It would knock a claw away, then she would turn her wrist and stab, before she again parried the next blow.

Leon wanted to start forward and assist her, but felt as though he were rooted in place.

Sensing his eagerness to help, Rohiel patiently explained again, *"This was earlier today."*

The creature rushed forward at her, as she stood holding her spear. Its shaft had been lifted high and its blade pointed low. This move seemed to be exactly what she had been waiting for; the creature suddenly roared out again, in anger and then pain. The spearhead had sliced upward, cutting across its kneecap, as Lochemetel pivoted out of its way. The monster's claw caught hold of her shoulder armor, eliciting a shriek of tearing metal combined with a familiar flash of light. Leon, mesmerized by the battle, saw the hiss of the monster's claws as they dissolved away due to their contact with her armor. Concern for the warrior angel raged through him when he saw the three dark jagged holes the monster had rent in her armor.

Lochemetel started running to the side of the shadowy creature; it tried to turn and keep her positioned in front of it. She seemed to make note of the fact that the creature had been slowed down due to the cut across its knee. When an opening presented itself, she took it. Lochemetel dove to the side and thrust her weapon through one of its dark wings. It penetrated through the appendage as if it wasn't even there. A bright flash occurred and instantly dissolved a hole in the wing, which allowed the spear to continue deep into the chest of the creature. Its bellow of pain turned into a strained gurgle. The creature then began to shake violently before finally exploding into minuscule particles that dropped and disappeared into the earth.

Lochemetel scanned the surrounding area for signs of any other threats, as a rainbow-like light began to radiate from the claw wounds in her shoulder armor. After the light faded her pauldron was unblemished– as if it was brand new. She whirled the golden spear in her hand for a few seconds and it simply disappeared while mid-spin, over her wrist. After that, the warrior ran off. She headed towards the manor, and out of their sight. Rohiel spoke as she left.

"She defeated the Nephilim, so it could not plague the world further."

Leon turned to Rohiel and asked, "Why can't people see all of this happening?"

"You have eyes to see but do not see, and ears to hear but do not hear, for you are also rebellious people."

A secret war was occurring that nobody could see. One that was all around them. Leon would never have believed it if he hadn't seen it. After that thought passed through his mind, Rohiel laughed.

"Of course not. Only a fool thinks they know everything based on what they see and hear. There is only one who knows how creation truly works."

For once, Leon thought he knew the answer. "Adonai?"

"Indeed. He is the father of all, but as you well know, some children's relationship with their fathers are complicated."

The angel's words resounded around them, and seemed to vibrate the very air. Rohiel extended a gauntleted hand and grasped Leon's shoulder. Their surroundings dissolved back into the grey expanse. Rohiel remained with him as the light in the distance pulsed and sent a wave to wash over them both.

"Those beings then, the Mazzikin and the Nephilim, they are children of Adonai too?" Leon tried to reason.

When Rohiel responded his voice sounded sorrowful— mournful even. The light around his face dimmed slightly; just enough that Leon could almost distinguish his features.

"They rebelled against our father. Our creator. They were my friends. My family."

Leon was reminded of the drama between his family members. Yet, no comparison could be made. His entire lifespan was just a blink of an eye to these beings. The angels he'd met and observed had been fighting this war amongst themselves for thousands of years. How much pain and sorrow must they have gone through fighting with each other? How much drama and loss must they have endured?

"I'm sorry, Rohiel." Leon replied.

The light around Rohiel grew bright again and a warmth exuded from him once more.

"Thank you. Hold on to that compassion, Leon. You will need it for the days to come. For your battles ahead."

Leon was slightly overwhelmed. He had already decided to take on becoming a Judge, a hero— fighting in a whole new way, in a war that spanned centuries against the undead. How could he try to take a side in another war, one that he couldn't even see? He would be a pawn. Worse than a pawn. Could he even last for one second against a shadowy monster? Those Nephilim? When he couldn't even endure against Lochemetel?

"Leon, you are still learning." Rohiel's voice echoed around him, *"Our struggle is not against flesh and blood, but against the rulers, against the authorities, against the powers of this dark world, and against the spiritual forces of evil in the heavenly realms."*

Leon tried again to fathom the gravity of it all. His life felt so very insignificant up until this point. How much of a difference he could actually make in this other war? A war he couldn't even see when he was awake.

"You are more significant than you know. You are but a spark, but that can become a flame. A flame, which can then in turn become a spreading fire. That fire can burn bright, and purge the darkness from this world with the light of Adonai."

The responsibility weighed heavily upon him as he tried to understand the cryptic answers of the angel.

"How do I do that? How can I bring the 'light of Adonai'?"

"Talk to Adonai. As a friend. As a father. Even if you cannot hear him, he is there with you. Even in the darkest depths, Adonai will light your way."

As Leon resolved to do what he could the light in the distance pulsed again. The same warm peace he felt before settled over him once again. It took the place of the weight that he had felt just moments ago. Leon knew, deep down, that the vision would be over soon and he would awaken. He wondered what impact his upcoming battle against the Alukah would have on the unseen war he had just witnessed. Before Rohiel could answer, Leon awoke to the darkness of early morning– and the faces of Duamé and Miala staring at him with concern.

Chapter 8: The Mine

"Do ya always talk ta yerself in yer sleep like that?" Duamé grumbled from the next tree branch over.

"Well I would have to be awake to know if I talk in my sleep, wouldn't I?" Leon replied, as he rubbed the sleep from his eyes. It seemed his vision had returned to normal at least.

"Sarcastic meat shield, aren't ya?" Duamé fired back, as he swung down to the forest floor.

"You were talking about a war between things with weird names, and someone called Adonai. It was really odd." Miala said, from her tree branch.

"My apologies if I woke you." Leon replied, "What time is it?"

"We slept for about three hours." Miala volunteered. How she knew that, Leon could only guess. Though the light of the sun seemed to be almost poking through the tree line.

"Bout dawn, I think." Duamé hollered as he stretched.

"Hey! Be quiet! There may be undead about!" Leon hissed at the loud dwarf.

Miala and Leon both dismounted from the tree; Miala waving away Leon's offered help.

Once they arrived back at the trail they took a moment to regain their bearings, then resumed their journey along the overgrown forest path. The trio ate trail rations as they walked, causing the trek to be made in near silence. After finishing their breakfast, Miala stepped closer to Leon. Her eyes were alert as she made every effort to pay attention to the trail while also scanning for unseen enemies. Finally welcoming some social interaction, Leon tried to think of what she would want to talk about. Perhaps the Alukah? Or maybe her magic. Before he could speculate further, she whispered, "So, who is he?"

"Who?"

"Adonai. You said his name a few times in your sleep."

Leon's mind raced, as he thought about Rohiel. About the instructions he had given regarding spreading the word of who Adonai was. Feeling the pressure to say something, he tried to start simple, "Adonai is… God."

Miala's face seemed disappointed somehow, "Oh. The god of what?"

"Um… life. The Universe. Everything. All of creation."

"Hm. I haven't heard of him before." she mumbled.

"Apparently he has been… forgotten?" Leon tried to explain. He didn't want to misrepresent something so important as the God of the universe, "I only really learned about him recently myself. He has something to do with this." Leon held up the spear that he was walking with.

Miala looked like she was about to say something when Duamé piped in, "Well, that's a crock!"

Leon turned to the dwarf, thought better of asking him to keep his voice down, and instead just asked, "Why?"

Duamé scoffed, as he shook his head, "Everythin' in this world stinks. Almost tha whole world is dead– or undead–

an' here we are trudgin' towards almost certain death. Fer wot? Ta get revenge, find a rustin' dog, or ta save people we don't even know– from their certain death!" He scoffed again as he looked Leon up and down, "Ain't no God o' anything, an' even if there were, he doesn't care bout nuthin' down here."

Sympathy for the dwarf filled Leon. Less than three days ago, he might even have agreed with Duamé. Leon had certainly seen enough horror in his life to question such things. But he also knew his dreams were too vivid, too real, to be just dreams. The magic that came from the spear when he struck the undead was evidence that there was something to this path he was on. It was something that neither Duamé nor Miala had seen or experienced for themselves yet.

Deciding against using Rohiel's words about fools thinking they know everything based on only what they could see and hear, he thought back to another memory. *What was it that Prince Gelan used to say when surveying the landscape?* "It has been my experience, good friend Duamé, that the absence of knowledge about something doesn't mean it's not there."

Duamé grunted and spat, "Ya ain't my friend. Right now ya ain't nothing but a meat shield fer me ta hide behind."

Miala held up her hand and crouched down. She looked back at the two of them mouthing, "Shut up!"

Leon and Duamé both buttoned up and, following her example, also crouched down. Leon watched Miala furrow her uneven brows in concentration, and then smirk when she saw bushes rustle ahead. A decent sized, short-haired, tan dog leapt out of the brush at the side of the trail and tackled Miala. She rolled on the forest floor with it and laughed. Miala was happily rubbing its belly while the dog's tongue lazily lolled about.

"Oh great, watch yer food meat shield." Duamé advised, as he rolled his eyes.

Leon scanned his field of vision for any undead that might be chasing the dog. "I take it that this is Kelleren?"

"Yeees." Miala smiled, as she got up and dusted herself off. She reached into a pocket of her robe and pulled out a treat, which quickly disappeared into Kelleren's mouth. She scratched behind his ear a little more before she turned to Leon and Duamé, fidgeting and looking nervous.

"I, um, I didn't know that I would find him this quickly." Miala began.

"Well that's good, right?" Leon asked.

"Yes, but now I need to…" She started to say, but then trailed off. Her soft voice fell quiet, as she looked at her dog. Leon thought for a moment and tried to read between the lines to figure out what Miala was not saying– just as much as what she was saying. It had been a useful ability while he served in the military; one he had picked up from working with female counterparts.

On a hunch, Leon asked, "So, you're leaving Duamé and me to do this alone?"

When Miala cringed, Duamé huffed and hissed, "Wot? I'm down tha other meat shield? Jus' great!"

"Why would you abandon those people?" Leon chided.

Miala snapped back at Leon, "I haven't done anything to them! But what have they ever done for me? Call me a witch? Cast dark glares my way, and spit in my direction every time I thought to give them another chance and go into the village myself? How about daring each other to throw rocks at my cabin? Need I go on?"

There was a long awkward silence where no one said anything. Interestingly, Leon noticed that rather than looking angry, or guilty for leaving them, Miala kept turning towards her dog and staring at him for a few minutes at a time. The dog looked at Duamé and sat on its hind legs. After it had stared at Duamé for a few seconds, the surly dwarf looked right back at the dog and snapped, "Wot?"

Kelleren let out a small woof, turned, and padded over to Leon. Leon watched patiently and let the dog rear up on its hind legs and put its forepaws on his chest. The dog stared at Leon a moment, and while Leon contemplated the strange behavior of the animal, it made another small woof then padded back to Miala. She reached out to it, and held the dog's chin as it intently looked into her eyes. She sighed and pressed the heel of her hand to her head as she rolled her eyes, "Fine."

"Fine?" Leon asked.

"FINE! I will go with you on one condition," Miala explained.

"What would that be?"

She sighed again as she walked over and poked a finger right into Leon's studded armor, "If we all get through this alive, I can't stay here in Everbright. I'll leave, and YOU will escort me somewhere that I can be left alone again."

"Why would you need to leave?" Leon still didn't understand.

Miala stared at Leon, then shook her head and grunted in frustration. She stomped off, with Kelleren close behind her. Leon looked bemusedly at Duamé, who fired back as he walked off after her, "Don't look at me boyo, I don't understand ya humans an' yer matin' rituals."

They walked mostly in silence, with Leon taking the lead and Duamé close behind. Miala walked at the rear, with Kelleren bounding around them all. He romped across seemingly random areas of the path, and sniffed at the ground. The forest grew more and more dense, until only the path could be comfortably walked. It was when they reached that area of the path that Kelleren rushed forward and stopped in front of Leon– he froze and uttered a low growl. The dog looked straight ahead towards a small hill in the path. A hill just high enough to obscure what lay beyond it. Miala whispered for everyone to stop, "He knows there are undead ahead."

"How tha bloodstone do ya know that?" Duamé whispered back.

"I just do. We are, however, coming up on where the carriage stopped. It must be just ahead." she responded.

"Now jus' wait a–" Duamé started.

"Shhh, let me think!" Miala hissed. She looked at her dog and they locked eyes for a moment. Kelleren silently ran off ahead and came back a few minutes later. They stared at each other again, then Miala turned to the rest of them, "Okay, there is an old mine opening up ahead. A wretch is just inside the opening as a lookout. The carriage is parked outside the opening of the mine, but I guess the skeletal horses are inside."

"An' ya got all that from a starin' contest with yer dog?" Duamé scoffed.

Miala rolled her eyes at Duamé before she replied, "Let's just say Kelleren and I have a connection, and leave it at that."

Leon made a connection in his mind, one that was based on a few of his memories which paired well with her behavior. For now he would keep his suspicions quiet. Instead, he thought over the scouting report she had given and turned to Miala, "How far can you throw your magic? Could you take out the wretch without it seeing you?"

Miala shook her head, "Not likely. To get close enough I'll need a distraction."

Kelleren woofed quietly and ran ahead, putting distance between them. Miala turned towards her dog and hissed as loud as she dared, "No! You can't!"

Kelleren woofed quietly again, then he turned and silently bounded down the trail towards their destination. Miala pursed her lips in irritation. "Come on! Hurry!" She snapped, as she went after her dog. Leon and Duamé obediently followed. A short distance ahead the trail inclined again, sharply this time, before disappearing into the large hill directly before them. The mine entrance had wide cut beams that appeared to frame the tunnel, which led down into the rock and earth. The dense tree line was broken on one side of the mine entrance, with roughly cut tree stumps peppering a small clearing. That was where the carriage and its accompanying cage sat.

Miala abruptly turned and hissed, "Hide!"

They scrambled to the trail edge and squeezed behind the largest trees they could find. Now hidden as best as they could be, Miala closed her eyes and concentrated. Seconds later Kelleren raced back down the trail– chased closely by a thin, slobbering wretch. It carried a bow and quiver just as the other wretch had, and stopped to nock an arrow, right outside of where they were hiding.

When Kelleren ran past and looked back at its pursuer, Miala stepped onto the path and grabbed the wretch. She held it by its head and by its arm that held the bow. Her hands glowed bright as they burst into intense flame. The dry, stretched, skin ignited as if it were parchment. Its body twitched and convulsed, as her hands burned hot enough to turn the wretch's head and arm to nothing but char and ash. The body collapsed on the ground, twitching again slightly, before going still.

"Wow. Nice work." Leon commented, as he stepped out of his hiding spot. He looked at the wretch's smoldering

117

neck, appreciation for a job well done clearly marking his face.

"Quite tha 'heated' exchange." Duamé quipped.

Leon snorted with a stifled laugh as Miala's hands continued to burn; making sure whatever detritus that remained from the wretch was gone. Once it had all been burnt off, her hands turned back into normal skin again. She smirked at Duamé, then turned to her dog, and glared at him. Kelleren whined a little as he padded towards her with his tail between his legs. He leaned against her leg, allowing her to scratch behind his ear again.

"And good job to you too, Kelleren." Leon said as he squatted down to talk to the dog.

Kelleren looked at Leon with a doggy grin, while Miala spat out in annoyance, "He put himself in danger. Again."

Leon scratched under the dog's chin which caused Kelleren's back leg to start thumping on the forest floor, "He's a great scout, and he wanted to be a distraction to get the wretch close enough. He's a smart companion."

Miala froze as if paralyzed. "Wait. You– You, know?"

"I assumed," Leon explained, "I served with a few mancers, some had companions. The last one I knew had a platypus. A water mancer."

"Aquamancer." Miala corrected.

"Wot's a companion?" Duamé asked.

Miala recited her explanation as if speaking from a textbook. "Some call them animal familiars. I can hear his thoughts and he can hear mine. Earning a companion happens sometimes when you are a mancer. You can't pick just any animal though, you have to find each other."

Duamé looked at Kelleren, "So he's a smart dog?"

"He is smarter than most people." Miala said, as she walked away again, Kelleren close by her side.

After thinking about what she said Duamé piped, "Oi, was that supposed ta be an insult?"

Keeping more concerns to himself, Leon was (yet again) somewhat confused. Miala was a strong enough mancer to have a companion, and she was a Pyromancer to boot. Their powers were of great use in the Dead Wars; which would mean that she must have served in the military as well.

What was she doing in Everbright being a hermitess instead? Leon questioned to himself. He added it to the ever-growing pile of mysteries that had surrounded his life lately. He hurriedly moved to rejoin the others.

They walked into the entrance of the mine and were hit with the smell of dust and decay. Miala made a fist as they shifted into the shadows and her hand began to glow a dull torchlight red. She advanced slowly, with Duamé in front of her, able to see into the darkness without issue. However, as Leon stepped into the shadow of the mine, something unexpected happened.

The spearhead flashed a pale light that illuminated both Miala and Duamé. Rather than fading back into a normal spear, the rusty spearhead stayed lit in the dark entrance– better than any torch or flaming fist would.

Miala extinguished her hand with an arched eyebrow and Duamé snarked, "Works fer me. Maybe they'll see ya first an' leave me alone. Good thinkin' meat shield!"

"It's never done this before!" Leon whispered.

"Well maybe ya shook all tha salt out of it then." Duamé quipped. Miala covered her mouth to keep herself quiet, as her shoulders shook with suppressed laughter.

The mine looked to be very old. Cobwebs had formed all along the cracks and crevices of the entrance. Layers of dust that had accumulated were disturbed in the middle of the entrance– marked with recent footprints. As they moved a short distance into the mine they encountered no resistance.

All that held them back was their own cautious pace. They eventually reached a junction, and were faced with a choice to go right or left. A noise came from the left, and the trio unanimously decided it warranted exploring. What they discovered was a long, thin, room that had been converted into a makeshift paddock.

Four skeletal horses were housed in tight stalls, with nothing but dark magic holding their bleached bones together. Instead of snorting or whinnying as the group approached, the broken teeth that lined their skulls clacked together frantically. Duamé unslung the huge hammer from across his back, "Guard tha entrance. These are mine."

Leon agreed that it was a good idea to handle the horses and turned to make sure the noises didn't attract anyone. Miala stared at the furthest horse, trapped in a stall so narrow it couldn't even turn. Instead, it moved its skull up and down in an effort to avoid the fate it knew was coming. The smith's muscles rippled as he brought the two-handed maul from behind his back and crashed it into the horse's head– right between its glowing red eyes. The eyes winked out as the skull shattered, sending pieces scattering everywhere. The rest of the skeleton lost the magical spark that held it together and collapsed into a clattering heap on the floor.

Miala joined Leon as a lookout and Duamé repeated the process with the remaining horses. They stood in silence for a moment before Leon just couldn't help himself, "Miala?"

"Yes?"

"Did you serve in the military as well?" He tried to pose the question as innocently as possible.

She whirled on Leon with an unexpected ferocity. Inches from his face, voice low but cold, she spat, "Do yourself a favor. Don't try to figure ME out. DON"T become interested in ME. DON'T EVEN THINK about anything other than keeping each other alive until you help me disappear to somewhere else, far away. GOT IT?"

Taken aback, Leon couldn't think of anything to say or do. Taking his silence as assent, Miala nodded and distanced herself once again. Duamé gave a short yell as he crushed the last horse's head. Sauntering up to Leon and Miala, the maul slung over his shoulder, the dwarf huffed, "That was satisfyin'. Ready ta keep goin'?"

After coaxing Kelleren to leave the piles of horse bones alone (much to his chagrin), they went back to the intersection, and in the only other possible direction. The tunnel quickly started sloping downward at a curve, and Duamé commented they were spiraling down into what would probably be the main chamber.

"Now, I ain't no minin' dwarf, but that's how these places usually look." He said.

Sure enough, the path opened into a large circular chamber littered with piles of broken tables, chairs, and barrels. The cobwebs that once covered most of the walls had been cleared away; only the ones out of reach, draping across the high ceiling, still remained. The air was musty, and permeated with dust particles that swirled all around them. Debris had been moved apart to make a path of sorts. The makeshift path led through the enormous chamber to an opening in the wall on the opposite side. As they continued to look around the cavernous room they saw that there was a second wall opening. It was located to their right, also quite a distance away from where they stood at the tunnel exit. This second opening was even larger than the one the path led to across the cavern.

"Look here," Miala whispered, as she pointed to one of the old wooden pillars that stood against the wall. They gathered around to look at it, and jaggedly carved into the pillar was the same name, over and over again.

121

"Isn't that…" Leon started to ask.

Miala and Duamé exchanged a look, as they whispered their response simultaneously.

"The god of the harvest."

"Tha god o' tha harvest."

The name Rhoxmas was scrawled over every spare space of the wooden support beam. Perplexed, they crept further into the room. A few moments passed before Miala whispered, "It's carved into that pillar too."

"It's on some o' tha broken tables." Duamé piped gravely.

Kelleren whined at the other side of the room and padded back to Miala. "Kelleren said that way leads to a cave-in," Miala whispered.

Leon stepped back from inspecting more pillars. They all had the harvest god's name scrawled in multiple places. The new mystery of this mine eluded him. There still seemed to be no sign of the captured villagers– other than the carriage that sat outside.

"The villagers must be deeper in the mine." He noted.

Duamé grunted before he replied, "If they're still alive at this point ya mean?"

Leon ignored the negativity and shone the spearhead near the ground. He saw among the heavy dust and debris exactly what he had hoped for: a clear path of footprints, and rock with no layers of dust. Signs of recent use that pointed down another corridor.

"Here." He said. The others came over to look. "They lead down that way." Leon pointed to the remaining tunnel shaft with the spear.

They crept down the main tunnel, moving slowly as more and more Rhoxmas graffiti lined the support pillars. The pillars soon stopped and gave way to a different type of construction. The walls of mined rock shifted abruptly to crafted blocks. As large as Duamé, they intersected at irregular angles, and seemed to fit perfectly against each other. There was no mortar between them and the walls flared, angling slightly outward at the bottom, which created a trapezoidal shape in the hallway. The ceiling and floor transitioned to the stone blocks as well, and their footsteps began to echo. They slowed their pace, making a conscious effort to step as lightly as possible. The musty air took on the stench of decay again, one Leon was all too familiar with.

As they continued down the corridor they began to hear faint noises that echoed in the distance. Hunching down to creep even further, Duamé silently held out his hand, signaling the others to stop. He then turned and whispered as quietly as Leon had ever heard him speak, "Ya lot can't see in tha dark, an' yer liable ta get us all killed getting too close with tha thing on." Duamé pointed at the spearhead shining as bright as a torch, "Ya cannot turn it off can ya?"

Leon hadn't the faintest clue how to turn it off. He shook the spear slightly, tapped the flat of the blade with his finger, and even closed his eyes and thought a command towards it as hard as he could. The light resolutely remained shining, despite his hardest efforts. Duamé arched a brow at Leon as he motioned for everyone to wait there.

The dwarf silently shuffled forward, into the darkness, and out of the light of the spear. Time crawled by as Miala and Leon exchanged glances, trying to hear every sound from up ahead, and anxiously awaited Duamé's return. Miala turned sharply, breaking from the watch she and Leon kept, to look at Kelleren– who had been staring at her. After a few moments, she rolled her eyes and dug a strip of jerky from the pocket of her robe. Just as quickly as it had appeared Kelleren snatched it from her hand, causing it to disappear once again.

Duamé reappeared, and as he crept towards them he motioned for them to head back to the main chamber. After retreating through the hundred foot long section of tunnel, they gathered together amongst the broken woodpiles. "What did you find?" Miala asked.

"Ferget tha villagers. We need ta keep walkin' right on outta here." Duamé said, as he kept moving straight towards the exit.

"What? Why? What did you see?" Miala questioned.

Agitated and grumbling, Duamé stopped. He grabbed a few scraps of wood and made a small diagram on the floor, "Tha hallway turns left inta a room as big as this here chamber. Now this here wall," he said, as he pointed to the wall to the left of the entrance, "Got all tha bumpkins chained up against it. Tha other wall over there's got some sorta underground water pool."

Leon watched as Duamé outlined the room in dust and pebbles, "Are the villagers all alive?"

"Looks it. They won't be fer long. Tha real problem is in tha middle an' back o' tha room."

"How many undead?" Leon asked.

"I counted twelve o' those bug buffets right here," He pointed in the middle of the room. Duamé moved his finger to the back of the room, "An' there, sittin' on a throne, is tha pointy-toothed Alukah ya went on an' on about."

A long, heavy, silence oppressed the room.

"Thirteen against three," Leon stated.

Kelleren gave a small whine.

"Thirteen against four." Leon corrected.

"Are ya mad ya daft fool? We can't win this. It's suicide. Besides," Duamé jerked a thumb at Kelleren, "He counts as a half at best."

Kelleren whined again and licked Duamé's thumb, which he promptly rubbed on his leather pants. Miala sighed and squinted at the rough outline on the floor.

Leon contended, "We did not come all this way only to be defeated by fear."

"What are the undead armed with? Did you see?" Miala asked.

Duamé looked up from the floor to stare contemptuously at Miala, "Pickaxes. Superior numbers. An' no rustin' idiots on their side."

Leon let the insult pass. "The villagers chained to the wall, could the chains be broken?"

"So sorry 'meat shield'. I fergot ta look, as I was busy checkin' tha size o' the Alukah's feet. Can we go already?"

Miala caught on to Leon's thought process, "The villagers? That's your plan? You mean to even the odds?"

"Well, if we could somehow get them free–" Leon started.

She interrupted him, "You don't know their condition. They may not have eaten this whole time they've been gone. Their strength may be sapped. If they are indeed still alive at all."

She has a point. Leon thought, as he tried to formulate a new strategy.

"At least tha witch has good sense." Duamé grumbled.

"Don't call me that!" Miala snapped.

"Wot? Sensible?"

Silence again. Kelleren sat on his haunches and gazed at his mancer while she looked at him curiously, "What?"

"What is it?" Leon asked.

Miala's brows furrowed in thought, "I may be able to take care of a majority of the horde."

"Tha DOG had an idea?" Duamé asked– a little too loudly.

"Shhhhh!" echoed Miala and Leon.

They waited in silence to see if the noise had attracted any undead. After a few minutes passed without incident, they resumed their planning.

"How?" Leon asked quietly.

"Boom." She said, as she put a red, glowing finger in the middle of the outline of the room.

Leon winced, "Could you do it without hurting the villagers?"

"Could ya do it as we walk outta here an' seal tha blasted mine shut?" Duamé countered.

"I could aim it away from the villagers, though it would depend on how close all of the undead are standing to them. However, I cannot say for certain I'll be of any use afterward. My powers may be drained." She continued.

Leon sighed. The longer they bickered, the bigger the chance they would be discovered– or the villagers could be hurt. If Miala could take down most, if not all, of the horde of shamblers then that would just leave the Alukah to confront. "Do we have a better option?"

"Not really." Miala replied softly.

Leon turned to Duamé and asked, "If Miala takes down the horde, I'll take the Alukah. Can you take any stragglers and free any villagers who may be able to help?"

"Yer takin' this 'meat shield' thing ta heart now I see." Duamé said flatly.

"Can you do it Duamé?" Leon repeated.

"Tch. Fine."

Leon turned to Kelleren last, "If Miala is drained, can you protect her?"

The dog got up and wagged his tail.

Leon looked at his recent companions and nodded at them each in turn. With a calming breath to regulate the adrenaline that coursed through him, Leon turned and started to walk towards the undead once again.

"Yup, we're going with the dog's idea."

Act Two: The Rumors

It is the glory of God to conceal things, but the glory of kings is to search things out.
-Proverbs 25:2 ESV

Chapter 9: The Judge

Leon checked the spearhead again. In a fit of inspiration he had ripped a linen strip of his undershirt sleeve off and wrapped it around the glowing blade. The light was muted, but had not been completely smothered. Afterward, they stealthily headed back down the corridor, quietly approaching the corner that turned into the chamber Duamé had scouted.

Leon hoped the spear was dim enough to not be noticed as they crept closer. He hoped that Miala had the power to eradicate the undead horde. Hoped that Duamé was as good in a fight as he was with his bickering. Mostly though, he hoped that they could prevail against overwhelmingly poor odds. If ever Adonai, God of the universe, the one who had created everything, needed to lend a helping hand, this would be it. Remembering the words Rohiel had told him, Leon berated himself inwardly for not talking to Adonai more before now.

Adonai, if you could, we could really use your help. If you don't mind.

Pressing tightly to the corner of the wall Leon looked behind him and saw Duamé with his huge hammer in hand, eyes wide, and breathing fast. Behind the dwarf, Miala and Kelleren also stood ready to play their parts. With a nod from everyone else, Miala began to concentrate. She brought up both of her hands, and her fingertips started to glow a dull red– rivaling the eyes of the undead.

"Have you also come to be harvested for the great Rhoxmas?"

The voice that spoke was a hoarse, guttural rasp, and echoed all around them. Leon, Miala, and Duamé exchanged panicked looks as Miala whispered to them, "I can't stop it now!" Her fingertips had brightened significantly and her nails looked almost molten.

Thoughts raced through Leon as he processed hearing the voice of what he knew was the Alukah. He had known that certain undead could talk, could even evoke magic like a mancer, but hearing it first-hand was a chilling experience. That feeling mixed with the confusion that abounded in him already. Rhoxmas? Why were the undead worshipping a harvest god?

"It is good that you have destroyed my insolent wretches. They tainted my offerings with their poison. They deserved their fates for delaying the harvest."

They were alive? Leon silently thanked Adonai that the villagers had not been harvested yet! Apparently, the Alukah didn't want to feed on them due to the wretch toxin that kept them docile. *Wait, what did it just say?*

"You will replace my wretches, and then when the poison fades, I will feast on my offerings."

MY offerings? The pieces began to fall into place. The Alukah was Rhoxmas! It thought itself a god? Leon remembered the words Elder Fanem had spoken about the harvest god reaping. Which meant Elder Fanem knew? The blood pumping through him quickened as Leon's anger started to surface. It was a righteous anger, one that

130

continued to build against the monster that plagued Everbright. This Alukah had been a blight on the people of that town– for who knew how long!

Then there was the fact that this creature considered itself a god! Leon kept circling back to that idea, it was unfathomable to him! Since having been in the presence of angels, and the power of Adonai himself, the thought of the Alukah trying to compare itself was... beyond wrong. What type of god had to survive by feeding off of others? Leon could think of no words to describe how nauseating it was to think about. He remembered the sense of peace he felt when the wave of light would repeatedly wash over him during his visions. He thought about what a stark contrast that was to the fear these villagers must have felt coming to this mine to be harvested. *This was no god!*

"Um, guys, I really can't stop this! What do I do?" Miala cried, as lines of pure fire crisscrossed over her bright red fingers like some child's string game.

"I am Rhoxmas, and you will bend to my will. Now come forth. Let me see my new wretches."

Duamé, Miala, and Kelleren started moving around the corner as if in a trance– directly towards the opening of the chamber. The Alukah's voice seemed to command them to do its bidding unconsciously. It beckoned them closer, so that it might add to its followers. Watching from around the corner, unaffected by the voice of the Alukah, Leon saw that even in her trance Miala's hands held a small ball of fire. The ball swirled and grew ever larger, being fed by the tendrils and strings of fire that poured from her fingers.

A rage unlike any he had ever felt before started to burn hot within Leon. Their plan of surprise attack was ruined, Miala's spell was ready to go off at any moment, and certain death seemed inevitable. Leon suddenly didn't care if he survived.

He just wanted to turn this Rhoxmas into an Alukah sized pile of salt.

Stepping around the corner and next to his companions, Leon ripped the linen sleeve from the spearhead. It shone from the entrance of the crafted stone room, and its light dimly covered the chamber. Directly in front of Leon a few decent sized steps led down to the floor of the chamber. Roughly thirty feet beyond the steps several shamblers (at various stages of decomposition) huddled together around a small, horned, stone altar. All of them wore assorted bits of clothing and scraps of armor. They were also equipped with various mining and lumber tools to use as makeshift weapons.

The captured Everbright villagers were indeed chained along the wall to the left. They were collapsed on the ground, silent, and clearly still drugged from the wretch poison. Without Leon and his compatriots they would have awoken to nothing but darkness and terror. Their last memories would have been of the red glowing eyes that belonged to the creatures that brought impending death.

The spear's light also allowed Leon to faintly see the Alukah at the far side of the chamber. At least eight feet tall, he was bald and appeared to be completely hairless. Rhoxmas wore a simple loincloth which highlighted his lean muscular figure. He stood in front of a crumbling stone throne with a shocked expression spread across his face.

Leon slammed the butt of the spear on the floor and yelled words that came to him unbidden. Without a thought he shouted in a clarion call, "FALSE GOD! ADONAI CALLS FOR YOUR JUDGEMENT!"

The dim light that fell on Rhoxmas displayed a snarl of pure hatred. However, it seemed to Leon that the Alukah's glowing red eyes had grown wide– hopefully in fear. *"Kill the Judge! Kill him! Servants! Now!"*

Leon's compatriots were jerked out of their trances as the spear's light fell across them. The shamblers that the Alukah had just screamed his command at turned and started to advance on Leon. Miala, seeming to come out of her daze, looked down at her hands– and the ball of fire that almost touched her palms. She suddenly exclaimed, "Oh, crap! Cover your ears!"

With reflexes born of self-preservation, the strings of fire that had formed from her fingers launched the ball as she pulled her hands apart. Much like a stone from a sling, it landed next to the horned altar near the middle of the shamblers.

The explosion was deafening and the horde was blown apart across the room. Bodies and flaming debris scattered and landed everywhere. The shockwave even blew Miala back down the entrance passageway towards Kelleren, who immediately bounded over to guard her. Leon and Duamé had taken her last second advice and braced themselves against the walls, making sure to cover their ears, just before the blast. After checking on Miala's safety, Leon looked back and could see that Rhoxmas had been knocked over by two flame engulfed shamblers. The villagers cringed and cried out as debris rained on them. Apparently her blast had awakened them from their trances and whatever other residual effect the wretch toxin had.

One second Leon saw that the burning top half of a shambler was clawing its way up the stairs. The next it sailed away, towards the underground pool, as Duamé solidly connected his hammer with its undead head in an upward swing. Yelling, he jumped down to the center of the chamber, towards the ruined altar, and looked for more moving foes.

Ears still ringing, Leon recovered as quickly as possible and sprang down the short stairwell towards the prisoners.

Checking to make sure there were no moving undead near them, he pivoted, and then bounded over to the small dais. Knowing that every moment was precious, he headed directly towards the stone throne where he had seen Rhoxmas bowled over.

Rhoxmas clambered to his feet with unnatural speed, hoarsely screaming in a rage. As Leon moved closer he saw how overly defined the vain Alukah's muscles were. The false god immediately bared its large fangs and claws at him. Leon decided not to dally either, and after taking a few steps he leapt towards the Alukah with his spear outstretched. Rhoxmas easily dodged out of the spear's path and punched Leon before he had a chance to land. The impact forcefully knocked him down the dais.

Leon's chest ached from the blow but he tucked into a roll from the momentum nonetheless. Springing back up he found Rhoxmas almost upon him already– spittle flying from his open maw. Leon had just been able to catch sight of Duamé, watching for a split second, as the dwarf knocked a flaming shambler down near the pool– before the incredibly fast Alukah crashed into him. Rhoxmas grabbed him by the shoulders, and forcefully bent him backward over the broken altar.

The Alukah reared back, ready to sink its fangs into him. Leon twisted his hand bringing the shining spearhead between them, in an attempt to cut the faster and stronger creature. Rhoxmas' hairless face recoiled from the spear's light. It grasped Leon's arm and twisted, forcing the spear and the light away from its body. Leon's teeth gritted together, as he clenched his jaw shut to keep himself from crying out due to the pain the Alukah was inflicting on him.

Leon's childhood had seen plenty of wrestling matches with his taller, heavier, and older brother Laric. Through both experience and necessity, he had quickly learned how to fight up close and dirty. Seeing an opening when Rhoxmas moved to bite him again, Leon punched the Alukah in the neck with his free hand. The muscles of the Alukah spasmed just enough for Leon to scrabble for, and grasp, the monster's ear. The dead flesh of the Alukah was strong, not weak and squishy like the flesh that composed the bodies of its underlings. Leon yanked on its ear as hard as he could, causing the creature to yelp as the action pulled it off balance.

This false god could feel pain. It could be outwitted. Seeing its reaction from the spear earlier, Leon knew one more thing– it could feel fear too. He stabbed forward with the spear, causing Rhoxmas to cringe away again while still clutching its ear. He seethed as he rasped, *"I will CONSUME YOU!"*

Leon slashed upward with the spear, again reminded of how Laric had taunted him as a kid. When Laric was angry he made foolish mistakes. He imagined this Alukah as his older brother raging at him, and needled the monster. "I'm pretty sure I'm bad for your health!" Leon charged forward again, this time making sure to remain on the ground.

While Leon was determined to stay on the offensive, he also wanted to keep himself and the spear between the Alukah and the chained villagers. The spearhead bathed the room in light, which allowed Leon to see all the shamblers that Miala's fiery blast had taken out. Stepping amongst and through their remains, he thrust purposefully off-center from Rhoxmas to block any path towards the helpless prisoners. Rhoxmas sidestepped and dodged away from the spear, headed back towards his throne. Through the light that shone across the pale Alukah's face, Leon saw ever increasing fear in its eyes.

For however long this Alukah and its decent sized horde had been here, its food source had been Everbright. There had been none who ever possessed the ability to challenge it. Its entrancing voice and its cunning had been used to establish a secure reign. Leon now knew that the light from the spear seemed to cancel the effects of the Alukah's voice. Someone had finally come who could stand up to Rhoxmas. It had called Leon a Judge. It knew that Judges slayed monsters, and it knew that its turn had come.

Rhoxmas ducked and dodged every swing that Leon took. The speed of the Alukah removed any advantage Leon thought may have had due to the reach of a longer weapon. Leon thought of the many times he had been bested by Lochemetel in his dream. Often it was because she stepped inside his guard, just like Rhoxmas initially had. Ironically, she moved fluidly and fast, much like the Alukah. He already knew that the Alukah was deadly if it stepped too close, but unconventional tactics had surprised and bested this monster before.

Armed with that knowledge, Leon kept swinging his spear and waited for the right moment to strike. As he continued slashing at the Alukah, showing how dependent he was on the spear, he watched for the tell-tale sign that Rhoxmas had fallen for his bait. Crouching down under a diagonal slash, the Alukah finally dove forward. Its claws were extended, ready to tear Leon apart after tackling him.

He had moved just like Leon wanted him to.

Taking one hand off the spear, Leon punched as hard as he could. He heard the bone shattering crunch of Rhoxmas' nose as its face slammed into Leon's fist; colliding with a force that equaled the Alukah's unnatural speed. Its head snapped back as its black blood sprayed, and the false god screamed while covering its face with its claws. To Leon the high pitched screech of the bloody Alukah was reminiscent of pigs squealing. He took the opportunity that had presented itself and slashed the exposed chest of the

136

undead monster. The already glowing spearhead flashed brighter as a thin, white, line of salt bisected the muscular front of the Alukah's dead flesh.

The Alukah cried out again as it scrambled away from Leon. Pushing himself up off the floor, the wide red-eyed Alukah seemed to turn almost feral. Its eyes darted around, above the bloodied black mess of a face, looking for a way to escape. Leon harried Rhoxmas backward, stabbing and swinging the spear in an effort to cage the Alukah in. It staggered and dodged away from Leon's strikes, getting ever closer to the far corner of the room, near the underground pool.

When Rhoxmas' back hit the wall, a hoarse snarl escaped its lips. Then it lunged forward, out of pure desperation, with its claws outstretched. Leon brought the butt end of the spear up to knock the Alukah back again. On reflex it seemed, the outstretched claws of Rhoxmas grabbed hold of the wooden shaft of the weapon.

Any residual ringing that remained in Leon's ears, both from the explosion and the squealing of the Alukah, dissipated. It was replaced by what he could only describe as a long continuous bell sound. It sounded to him almost like the tuning fork against a lute, but it resonated from the spear instead. Loud, but not uncomfortably so, it filled the chamber as Leon watched the Alukah convulse uncontrollably while grasping the spear.

The clawed hands that held the spear started to smoke and sizzle, as if in a hot flame. Its pale skin turned black then flaked and fell apart, and the once fast and deadly claws of the Alukah turned to ash and crumbled to dust. It stood twitching slightly, red eyes staring at the charred stumps that had once been its hands.

With a battle cry, Leon brought the spear back and impaled Rhoxmas in the stomach. Light pulsed from the wound, and with immense effort Leon brought the blade upward, granulating the false god's body as it went. When the blade reached the Alukah's head there was a bright flash as its body collapsed. All that remained was the sound of an Alukah-sized pile of salt, as it softly fell to the chamber floor.

For a moment all was quiet. Taking a deep breath, Leon turned from the salted corner, only to come face to face with another shambler. Singed but otherwise unscathed, it was already bringing its rusty pickaxe down towards his head.

Inches from his face, the pickaxe trajectory suddenly reversed course. The shambler fell backward, its feet having been swept out from under it. Leon saw Duamé sweep the two-handed hammer up from under the shambler. Then, with a mid-swing adjustment, he brought the hammer back down onto the undead's head with a grunt.

Huffing, Duamé checked that the shambler's eyes winked out before hoisting his hammer across his shoulder. "Ya alright lad?" He asked.

Leon, heart racing from his fight and the near-death experiences, nodded. "Thank you Duamé."

The dwarf looked at Leon warily, "No problem. Ones that were left all ignored me, an' only went after ya."

They both walked over to the prisoners, who were still chained to the wall, shaking and squinting at the light that came from the spear. Miala apparently had recovered at some point during the fight, because Leon saw her by the villagers, pulling dried meat from somewhere inside her robe.

A *pack maybe?* Leon wondered. He watched as she carefully fed the chained villagers then gave them water from a skin that she had also produced from some hidden compartment. As the light fully fell across everyone Miala, Duamé, and Leon exchanged surprised glances. They had destroyed the Alukah, laid waste to the undead, and not only were they all still alive, but the captured villagers were as well. It seemed almost miraculous.

Duamé put away his maul and pulled out a smaller hammer along with some other metal tools. Then he proceeded to walk over to the farthest people in the chamber. "Alright, let's getcha all fr–" he paused, and in a low, even, tone called, "Oi. Meat shield. Over here."

Leon walked over and the light of the spear revealed the furthest two prisoners– twin boys, no older than their eighth year. They huddled close, touching their moccasins together as their chained hands couldn't reach each other. They flinched away from both the dwarf and Leon, traumatized by their harrowing experience.

Leon's teeth clenched, and took a steadying breath before he said as gently as possible, "Don't worry, everything is going to be okay."

Duamé hunched down to the boys and also spoke in hushed tones, "Don't ya worry now wee lads, I'll have ye outta there in a jiffy an' then we'll getcha home alright?"

Leon had to step back, moving out of Miala's way as she rushed over to feed the young boys, and give them some water to quench their thirst. Having just seen such a nice gesture from what he viewed as a normally surly dwarf, he realized more questions and peculiarities existed than he was entirely comfortable with. Thoughts raced through his head as he connected the different threads of questions, answers, and assumptions over the mystery of Rhoxmas. *Was the village even safe if the Elder had known about the Alukah in the first place?*

For that matter, did Miala or Duamé know about the village elder's relationship with the Alukah? They had certainly acted surprised when they saw the writing on the pillars. Leon surmised they must not have been aware. *They couldn't put up an act like that for a whole day, could they?*

Clangs echoed as Duamé used a hammer and chisel to break the chains from the wall, and free the villagers. Besides the twin boys, there were the newlywed teenagers, a middle-aged woman, and two farmhands. Other than bumps and bruises, and the cuts from wretch claws, they seemed to be physically healthy. The twins huddled close to the older woman, and they all seemed to be quite shaken by the experience.

After a few minutes they all walked through the tunnel and into the chamber with the broken furniture. Duamé took on more of a leadership role, directing the teenagers and the farmhands to pick up specific scraps of wood. After a sigh of resignation, Miala helped fashion them into makeshift torches. When her hand glowed hot and erupted into flame, the villagers flinched and edged away from her. It was as if they feared her. Leon didn't understand. *Shouldn't they be grateful? Appreciative?* Instead, they eyed Leon and Miala warily, whispering amongst themselves words of, "The Judge," or, "The Witch," whenever either of them passed by.

Miala walked up to Leon, who had kept himself apart from the others, while Duamé talked to the villagers. "They all know him. I, however, am the weird hermitess who just revealed that she actually does have powers, and you're the stranger who showed up out of nowhere to save them."

Scoffing at the villager's behavior, Leon turned away from them to give them a break from his staring. "Did you know about people being 'harvested'?" Leon asked pointedly.

Miala looked over her shoulder to the twin boys, "Of course not! I came to Everbright shortly after Duamé. After...," she paused, "After I left the last place I lived."

Leon sighed, "Look, I will respect your boundaries and your past. I have my own. But you were hesitant before about saving them, so I had to ask."

She nodded, "I understand your suspicion, but I do not advertise that I actually have powers. I would rather just stay to myself. Now I have proven that I am the 'witch' they say I am. I will have to leave Everbright." Miala again looked over at the villagers, "But I know now it was the right decision to come here."

"You're not a witch Miala. You ARE a good person." Leon praised.

Miala was silent for a moment before looking up into Leon's eyes– glaring, "I told you– don't get interested. And no. No, I am not."

Before Leon could inquire further, Kelleren woofed from the darkness and bounded up to Miala. He had come from the throne room, tail wagging. She looked at him and arched a brow, "Really?" She turned to Leon, "Kelleren has found something."

"Duamé, we will be back." Leon called.

"Yeah, ok." Duamé mumbled. As Leon left the chamber, he could hear some of the villagers talking to Duamé about them. He couldn't make out what they were saying, but made a conscious effort to shrug it off. *Let them say what they want.* Leon and Miala followed Kelleren back, and they eventually ended up at the wall behind the empty stone throne.

The dog was staring intently at the stone block wall. "He says the air smells different here, and that it moves around the wall?" Miala said with confusion.

Leon moved closer and he reached out to run his hand over the rough surface. He looked at the irregular, huge blocks that made up the slightly slanted wall, and saw one about chest high that was much smaller than the rest.

Shrugging, Leon pressed on it, and the grinding of stone on stone began to rumble around them. They tensed as Kelleren's hackles raised, but soon saw it came from one of the large blocks in the wall that slowly slid into the floor– right next to the stone Leon had pressed. When the stone finished its descent it appeared to just make up another small piece of the chamber floor. However, it revealed there was a decent-sized alcove that had been well hidden behind the wall. An alcove that was about the same size as Leon's large closet at Rhise manor. Leon held out his spear, lending its light to the room so he and Miala could see inside.

All Leon could do was stare, speechless.

Miala peeked in and gasped.

Kelleren sat back on his haunches and panted happily.

"Oi! I gotta tell ya guys something that might be a wee bit–" Duamé walked up from behind them and stopped at the opening to the alcove, right next to Miala. "Flint an' Feldspar!" he exclaimed.

The alcove was filled with an enormous pile of treasure.

Chapter 10: The Treasure

The only sounds that could be heard were Kelleren's quiet panting and Duamé's foot tapping. Everyone stared at the sizable pile of coins that just lay there. Golden eagles, silver sparrows, and copper crows all covered a small chest. It managed to barely peek out from underneath portions of the pile.

Duamé pinched the bridge of his nose and closed his eyes. He was still tapping his foot and had begun mumbling to himself. After patiently waiting for a few minutes, Miala couldn't take it anymore.

"Duamé, what are you doing?" She asked.

"I'm thinkin'! Okay, so here's tha thing. I say we take it. Finders' keepers. It's ours, we split it three ways. Reward fer a job well done."

Kelleren whined softly, and Miala smirked. "He wants a share too, he found it after all."

"Oh come ON, he's a DOG! Wot's he gonna spend it on? TREATS?" Duamé argued.

"She does have a point." Leon conceded, smiling. His smile quickly faded as the dwarf whirled on Leon, pointing an angry finger into his face.

"Speakin' o' points, wot's tha point o' ya holdin' out on us?"

Leon was baffled by what Duamé meant, until he continued, "Ya didn't tell us that ya were a Judge, meat shield! That there Alukah called ya a Judge! I heard it!"

Miala piped in at that point, "That's right! He did, didn't he? Why didn't you tell us?"

If Leon needed confirmation that the dreams he experienced were more than just dreams, this had been it. Rhoxmas had indeed called him a Judge and the shamblers had only come after him. They had followed the Alukah's orders and ignored Duamé, to their own detriment. It was strange to Leon that he still felt the same as he had before. He had thought that once he earned the title some sort of superhuman strength would overtake him. The heroes he read about as a child were larger than life– yet he still felt like himself.

"I was told that I could be a Judge, but this was the first time I was called one." He reasoned.

Casting him a sidelong glance, Duamé still looked quite suspicious. "So, yer a new Judge. Can't remember tha last time there ever was one. Didn't think there were any anymore."

"It's a recent development."

"Well, as a new Judge, I can see why ya would make a simple error in judgement as ta think ya can give a rustin' dog a share o' treasure!" Duamé responded.

Kelleren whined again, as he laid on the floor and covered his eyes with a paw. After a moment Miala doubled over with laughter. Duamé looked between her and Kelleren then exclaimed, "Wot? Wot did he say?"

Still chuckling, and with a voice full of mirth, Miala managed to sputter out, "It... it wouldn't... translate well."

"Try." Duamé said, squinting at her skeptically.

Kelleren got up and wagged his tail. After a moment Miala haltingly translated, "If... if only closed minds... had closed mouths."

It was Leon's turn to laugh. Duamé exclaimed, "Oi!" Before he smiled and chased Kelleren around the stone throne a few times. It seemed that everyone was in a light-hearted mood for once. *And why wouldn't they be? No matter how it's divided, that's a lot of treasure!*

Running back to Miala, Kelleren looked at Duamé and then back to her, still wagging his tail. She held up a hand and said, "Kelleren will give up his share if you use his name from now on. No 'dog' or 'mangy mutt'. Just Kelleren."

The dwarf's outraged face fell to confusion, then disbelief, and finally looking at the dog with suspicion he said, "Deal."

Kelleren, without missing a beat, sat on his haunches and held up a forepaw to Duamé. Miala held her hand in front of her mouth and snickered.

"Ya still laughin' at me?" Duamé muttered, as he shook the dog's outstretched paw.

"I am SO not." She replied, hand still held over her mouth.

Duamé sighed as he put his hands on his hips, "Alright. Well as I was sayin' then, um, good job then, uh, Kelleren. Fer, uh, findin' tha, uh, trove."

Leon couldn't help himself, "Wow. That looked incredibly painful for you."

Miala suppressed another laugh and turned away, her shoulders shaking.

"Right, well ah, look, we got a new problem." Duamé said. "Tha villagers are uh, askin' me ta take 'em back."

Leon shrugged, "Okay well, we will leave in a second here Duamé, once we collect all of that." He gestured to the treasure to accentuate his point.

"They want me ta take 'em back alone, genius." Duamé snapped.

Miala whirled around, shocked. "Are you serious? After we saved their lives? They still don't trust us?"

Leon couldn't believe it either, "Why?"

Duamé shrugged, turning to Miala, "They were kinda freaked out I guess. I mean they always thought ya were a witch an' ya jus' proved it ta 'em. An' you," he said, enunciating the words, as he whirled on Leon, "YOU, they are right petrified of."

Leon's confusion deepened, "Again, why?"

"Ya killed their god boyo- One they all were scared of. Tha only god they have ever known, an' ya up an' turned 'em inta dust."

"Salt." Leon muttered.

"WOTEVER! Tha point being," Duamé gestured at Leon, "tha only reaction they know ta a god is fear. Ya killed it, so guess who they're afraid o' now?"

Comprehension dawned on Leon. Of course, they would be afraid. They had been conditioned to always fear. The entire village of Everbright had been molded by fear. Fear had turned them all into sheep ready for the slaughter. Then Leon had come along, killed the shepherd, and burned down the slaughterhouse. That thought reminded Leon about another possible shepherd.

"I think Elder Fanem knew about the Alukah. His behavior before I left seemed off. When you pair that with the village's worship of the 'harvest god', and then finding Rhoxmas' name all over the wooden pillars, too many things just add up." He speculated, looking at Miala and Duamé.

"I never liked tha geezer." Duamé commented.

Miala's temper flared, "He was one of the ones who championed the village's hatred of me."

"Well, if we are going to confront him, we should do it together. Not when you're there alone with the villagers, Duamé." Leon reasoned.

"Ya don't have ta worry about me beatin' up tha old geezer by meself. We can do it together!" Duamé agreed.

"That's not what I meant!"

"Ya sure?" Duamé asked, "Could be yer thing. You'll be just like tha Judges of old– only judgin' tha old!"

After the laughter died down, Miala began to look slightly confused. "But wait, you just said they don't want us to return to the village with them."

"Ya can head back separately. Not like they'll stop ya." The dwarf stated.

Leon thought that was a rather obvious solution. "Alright, well I guess Miala, Kelleren, and I can head back by ourselves. If you're okay with that Miala."

Miala threw up her hands, "Fine."

"Well, I'm not okay with it!" Duamé commented. When nobody said anything he continued, "How do I know ya lot won't run off with me share?"

Leon laughed again thinking the dwarf had made another joke– until he saw that the serious expression on Duamé's face didn't change. He was scrambling to come up with a way for Duamé to trust him, when Kelleren woofed and padded over to sit by the dwarf.

Miala pressed the heel of her hand on her forehead and explained, "He says he will go with you to make sure that Leon and I come back to get him." She cocked her head at the dog while she stared at him, their mental conversation kept private. Kelleren simply wagged his tail and Miala threw up her hands, "Ugh, fine! We can get back before dark anyway. It's not even noon."

"How do you know that?" Leon asked.

Miala wiggled her fingers at him, "Ooo, magic."

Leon smiled, and turning to Duamé asked, "Does that work for you?"

Duamé pulled a small hammer out and pointed it at Leon threateningly. "Ya better not short me share, meat shield." Kelleren woofed and padded off, which left Duamé no choice but to turn and holler, "I'm comin', I'm comin'!" before following him back to the villagers.

Miala watched her companion leave until he could no longer be seen by the light. With a sigh she turned to Leon, "Well then, let's see what we've got."

Leon, still smiling, nodded, "Why don't we?"

As they searched the alcove they separated all of the coins by their type. Once they finished separating everything, they decided to count the copper and silver coins first. There proved to be a generous amount of both types. When they got to the gold coins they counted much more than the other two types!

"Isn't it odd that a simple farming village had such a trove next to it?" Leon asked.

Miala thought about it before she responded, "You mean, that it's odd for the villagers who were brought here to have come with these 'offerings'? They never could have had this much money on them?"

"Yeah, exactly."

"I don't know, it does seem unlikely." she admitted.

They continued to count and divide the piles; all the while Leon was lost to the questions that swirled in his head. He had some serious inquiries to make of Elder Fanem when he got back. *How long must this have been going on if the villagers thought this creature was a god?*

After they finished dividing the piles, Leon scooped his share into his bag. He hefted it and wondered how he might be able to adjust it to accommodate the added weight, as he would have to carry Duamé's share as well. He looked over, intending to offer help to Miala, but was astonished to see both her and Duamé's piles had disappeared! Miala was instead eyeing the small chest with interest.

"W– What? Where did… where did they go?" Leon spluttered.

"Don't worry about it, I have them." She replied.

"Where? You look–" Leon stammered.

Miala flashed him an apathetic look, waiting expectantly. Knowing he was treading dangerous waters, Leon thought fast. "Um, no different."

"Nice save." She went back to inspect the trunk.

"Aren't your and Duamé's shares heavy?"

"No. Why, did you want me to carry yours?"

Leon wracked his brain as to how she could be carrying everything. *There are no noticeable bulges from her brown robe, where does she put it all?* He thought.

Finally, Miala shrugged and picked up the chest. Turning it this way and that, she studied it and tried to open it, but it was locked.

"Did you want to look for the key?" Leon asked.

"No need." Miala responded, as she turned the chest around and set it down to face her. She held up her pinky finger and it turned a bright whitish color; then she held it against the lock and tilted the chest forward. The lock itself seemed to heat up and after a minute her pinky sank into it. She withdrew her finger, and the now molten lock poured out onto the ground. Once it finished, she carefully tipped the chest back to its original position. Then she glanced at Leon, "You ready?"

"That was amazing!" He exclaimed.

Miala opened the chest and cast a smirk his way.

A smirk that was suddenly obscured by the puff of white powder which plumed up from the opening.

Leon had wasted no time, as soon as he heard the audible click– just as the powder escaped– he tackled Miala. They rolled away from the trapped chest and the powder that filled the air. He had dropped the spear while diving at her and the instant it left his hand the light winked out, plunging them both into darkness. Holding his breath, Leon did everything he could to protect both of them. The momentum of their roll ended, with Leon on top of her.

Without any audible sounds of breath coming from her, Leon could only hope that she had held her breath and was not injured. His answer came when she suddenly screamed, "DON'T TOUCH ME!"

Miala's hand appeared, glowing a dull red in the pitch black, and slapped Leon across the face with enough force that the walls echoed its sound as he fell off her. His cheek stung, but was also burning hot. Reeling from the strong blow, and the heat coming from his cheek, Leon staggered over and felt around in the darkness for the spear. As he grabbed it the light from the spearhead returned and revealed the powder settling to the floor around the chest. Confused, hurt, and also somewhat concerned, Leon turned towards Miala to see if she was okay.

The light of the spear revealed Miala curled into a ball on the cold mine floor, her back facing towards him. Her shoulders were shaking, and she appeared to be sobbing quietly to herself. Faintly, she tried to speak in between sobs. "I'm sorry… I'm so… s– sorry… I'm sorry."

What happened to her to make her react this way? Leon asked himself, not daring to speak to her yet.

Reaching out to console her, Leon stopped himself, and refrained from putting his hand on her shoulder. Not knowing how to deal with the situation, or the right thing to say, he just tried to comfort her with words. "I AM okay Miala, are... are you?"

"Just... just give me a minute ok?" she croaked, unmoving and sniffling.

Leon shook his head, unable to comprehend this, and just stood there. He faced away from her, giving Miala her space, but still offering her his light. For a while she just laid there– curled in a ball, not saying a word. He eventually heard the sounds of her shuffling around, indicating that she had gotten up and was brushing herself off.

"I am... really sorry. Are you hurt?" she asked softly.

"I'm fine. Are you? Did the powder–"

"No. You got me away in time." Miala paused briefly, "Thank you for saving me."

She walked more into the light, and seeing Leon's face winced slightly. "Hopefully that will fade by the time we get back to Duamé, or we will never hear the end of it."

"How bad is it?" He asked, as his cheek still burned slightly.

"I'm really sorry." She said again.

"It's okay. I am not going to ask you to explain, but if you need to talk...," Leon left the invitation hanging.

With a heavy sigh, she dismissed his offer with a wave of her hand. "We should hurry up if we want to make it back in time."

Understanding her deflection, Leon nodded, and they went back into the alcove. Using the back end of the spear Leon pushed the chest out of the powder that surrounded it. After the chest had been removed from the powder he stood behind it, checked that Miala was a good distance away, and flipped the lid up. Seeing that the trap mechanism embedded in the lid of the chest was expended, they both came close, and peered inside.

What lay within was a short, straight, stick and a nondescript bag that took up the rest of the space. Reaching in, Leon picked up the pouch and loosened it. He carefully peered inside and saw a multitude of both cut and uncut gems– in varying sizes and qualities. Rhoxmas appeared to be quite the material collector, even though he could never show his face anywhere to spend it.

When Leon looked back up, he saw Miala reach in and pick up the stick. The air must have been dry because just before she grasped it, a static shock leaped up to her fingers from the object. She looked at the short stick with a sense of wonderment in her eyes. Trying to remember what it was called, as he had seen a few like it in the field, Leon asked, "That's… a wand, right?"

Miala turned it this way and that, staring at it as though it were more valuable than all of the coins and jewels they had just pocketed. She nodded at him and held it in both hands with reverence. "It's a wand alright. I've never had one before. I never earned one before."

Leon saw her fascination and realized this was a great opportunity to pull her thoughts further from the traumatic event earlier. "What does it do?"

She closed her eyes and spoke as if reciting from memory, "It is a focus point, a channel for inner power. It will help me better control what I have, and allow me to do more."

Leon smiled, "Lucky find for you."

"If there was a wand here, does that mean that Rhoxmas killed a mancer?" She asked.

"Either that or he was one when alive." Leon speculated.

"Hey, what's that?" Miala peered into the chest.

Bringing the light back over the chest, the shadows disappeared to reveal that under the bag of jewels had laid an old, intricate ring. It looked to have three distinct bands painstakingly woven together to make one singular band. It was clearly ancient, as part of it was so rusted that it crumbled slightly when he held it.

Leon couldn't see any identifying marks on it. "Do you know what this is?"

"Not a clue." Miala replied, leaning over to examine it more closely. "It looks old, see the rust on one of the bands?"

"Could be magical."

Miala backed away slightly, "It could also be cursed, I mean we did just barely escape whatever that powder was."

"Good point." Leon shrugged and pocketed the ring, thinking he would examine it later. "We can always have it appraised later, along with the jewels."

"Jewels?" Miala asked, instantly interested. Leon showed her the bag and she opened it under the spear's light. "Ooh! Yes, we definitely need to get these appraised and divide them later." She closed the bag and put it under a flap of her robe. When her hand came back it was empty, but just as before she looked no different. Leon was yet again flabbergasted. *Maybe it's a mancer thing?*

"We should get going then." Miala commented, looking around. "I really don't like it in here and it looks like we've picked it clean."

Tired of trying to puzzle through how she carried it all, Leon nodded. "Agreed."

They made their way back from the throne room and were not surprised to see that the other two members of their party had already departed with the villagers. As they retraced their steps, spiraling back up the sloped tunnel of the old mine, few words were spoken. Miala trailed slightly behind Leon, obviously still a bit shaken by everything that had occurred. As she walked, crossing one of her arms in front of her body to hold the other, and clearly avoiding

153

making eye contact, Leon thought she cast the picture-perfect image of human insecurity. Whatever her past was, it clearly haunted her. He hoped for her sake that she could overcome it.

As they neared the opening of the mine the sunlight began to peek inside the entranceway. Miala and Leon stood in silence as they waited for their eyes to adjust to the newfound brightness, allowing them to proceed. Once they stepped out into the daylight the spearhead winked out, but it did not return to normal.

"Leon, look!" Miala pointed.

What was once a rusted spearhead– all but corroded away– was now a perfectly unblemished blade. It was an elongated, rhombus shaped, blade that had a razor sharp edge all the way around. A very unique spearhead indeed, one that Leon had never seen the likes of before. It did not quite look like iron or steel. The metal had an oddly familiar, yet very distinct, pale blue tint to it. In the very center of the blade etched with precision (as if it was part of the spearhead itself) was a symbol unfamiliar to Leon:

"What does it mean?" Miala questioned, awestruck.

Leon stared at it, just as stunned. "I– I have no idea."

Chapter 11: The Rescued

"Okay, so let's try this again. Who is this Adonai?" Miala asked.

Leon and Miala were on the trail, making their way back towards Everbright, and soaking in the afternoon sun. The initial shock of the spear having changed in appearance soon gave way to full blown curiosity. Not even five minutes had passed since they left the mine before Miala's interest overpowered her self-control, and her questions began.

Leon found he didn't mind though, as he also felt the need to review what he had been told for himself. So, over the next several hours he talked about his dreams– of Adonai. How everyone in the world fell short of God's perfection. However, in Adonai's mercy, if you believed in Him and asked forgiveness, then He gave it and you would not rise again as undead.

"You do realize how crazy that sounds, right?" Miala criticized.

"Crazier than a spear that goes from rusted to new in the span of one morning?" Leon countered, holding up the strange artifact.

"How does that happen? Where did you even get that thing?"

"It was hanging on the wall in my family home."

Which immediately made Leon stop and wonder. *Why was this spear hanging on the wall in the first place?* If this was the spear of Adonai, or something, what was it doing in Rhise manor of all places? There must be more appropriate places for it to be housed than with his corrupted family.

Miala's thoughts seemed to be drawn to his family as well. "So, your family are all followers of Adonai?"

Leon laughed so hard he started coughing. He wiped the tears that had formed from his eyes, and Miala answered her own question with a sarcastic, "So, that's a no."

Trying to catch his breath, while still coughing a bit, Leon explained, "Sorry, sorry, it's just that my family isn't exactly what you would call the 'religious' type." *I can't even call them my family anymore, can I?* He reminded himself.

"Besides, if you want to delve into my past... I mean, can I even ask you about yours?"

Miala scoffed, "What? You mean a question for a question? And answer for an answer?"

"Does that idea interest you?"

She smirked, "Don't flatter yourself. You're not that intriguing." Leon laughed again as they continued walking on their way.

A short while later a low repeated rumble started to reverberate through Leon's legs. He looked at Miala and her expression told him she had felt the vibrations in the ground too. The sensation continued to grow in intensity until the realization of what it was dawned on him. Wide eyed and heart racing, he whispered, "Giant."

Miala started to shake, her hands visibly trembling, as panic gripped her and she hissed, "We're going to die Leon!"

Run, fight, or hide. Run, fight, or hide. Leon mentally debated their options before quickly stating, "We need to hide. Come on!"

They rushed over to a few large oak trees which stood off to the side of the forest path. One tree looked to have fallen over long ago– the dirt and clay covering its root system creating a natural wall. Not knowing where the origins of the shaking were coming from, Leon could only hope they had chosen their hiding place well. They crouched low, and pressed into the roots as closely as they possibly could. Miala closed her eyes, her entire body quaking in fear, hardly daring to breathe for fear of making a sound. Leon couldn't fault her because he was terrified as well; however, that didn't stop him as he quietly whispered encouraging words to her, "Hey, Miala. Look at me– we're going to be okay. Just keep looking at me."

She opened her emerald green eyes wide as the rumbling grew closer. Every time there was a vibration the leaves and tree branches shook in synchronization. Hugging the roots even tighter, Leon and Miala felt the low rumble get louder and louder, the shaking becoming more violent with every single step. Then the creaking and cracking of wood signaled the approach of something unnaturally large nearby– it was just on the other side of the fallen tree.

Standing at least twenty-five feet tall, a shape loped through the forest a short distance behind Miala. It had long, straight, bright-red hair that surrounded an elongated, misshapen skull, filled with gritted and sharply pointed teeth. The giant clearly moved without fear or pause– this creature knew it was the true apex predator of the area. A very detailed and intricate bronze plate armor covered its

157

body, one that was covered in etched symbols reminiscent of spiderwebs. An assortment of bags, bleached skulls, and a huge broadsword hung from its belt, rattling and clanking as it jogged across Leon's view.

Please don't come this way! Don't notice us! He said to himself, noticing that Miala was still looking unswervingly into his eyes. She knew that when he wasn't looking at her, he was looking at it. The Pyromancer was shaking her head almost imperceptibly, and Leon could see her mouthing the word, 'No' repeatedly.

His chest felt physically constricted due to worry. He knew that if the giant noticed their presence, their lives would be forfeit. The sword that hung from the giant's belt was at least as tall as Leon, and could easily cleave them in two. Of all the creatures and races in this fallen, undead plagued, world, the giants alone remained unperturbed.

Savage. Highly intelligent. Highly skilled. They feared nothing– and for good reason. Entire villages could easily be depopulated from just a few giants. To them, everything was either food, free labor, or entertainment. Leon's first dream, about the transgressions of the world, involved quite a few actions of the giants. Some of them were so unspeakable that he almost physically recoiled in disgust of the memory, a possibly fatal mistake while he was hiding.

Fortunately, the huge monster kept its pace. The quaking of each of its steps grew less pronounced as it continued on in its westerly direction. When the rumbling finally stopped, Miala and Leon pried themselves away from the roots of the fallen tree. Leon tried to ignore the muscles that quivered through his legs, which he could no longer blame on the giant's vibrations. He now had to admit that they were shaking completely due to the fear that coursed through him.

"I have never been that close to a giant." Miala said, hugging herself tighter than she had during the ordeal in the mine.

"In the airship navy we tried to bombard them from the air, keeping a safe distance away." Leon responded. "Of course, the giants would just throw the cannonballs right back. That's why every ship also carried a few canister shots as well."

"Tell me more about the navy. Please, I– I need to get my mind off of how we keep just barely escaping death today." Miala pled.

More than happy to acquiesce, for the same reasons, Leon began to tell her more about the airship navy. He filled the time as they walked by talking about the warships and transports that made up the Xaelon Armada. Even the smaller, unarmed mail carriers were revolutionary to mail delivery– which played a key role in faster response times for the military.

"A lot of the ships in the service are those that were repurposed from when we used to travel on ships by sea. That all ended of course. It makes no sense to put them in the water now, they would just–"

Miala held up her hands in surrender, "Thank you Leon. That's um, that's enough for now. I feel better."

Leon understood, immediately regretting his lengthy monologue on airship life. Some people found airship life quite interesting. He guessed though, gauging by the glazed look in Miala's eyes, that she wasn't one of them.

After they had walked for several more hours, but before sunset had quite hit, Leon beheld the village of Everbright for the second time in as many days. The whole town looked alive this time, with everyone gathered in the center of the village where the well was. Miala stopped short as

Leon started to make his way down to the town. "I… I can't." She stammered.

Leon's brows furrowed in concern. "It'll be okay. You saved them, they all have to see and respect that. Plus, Kelleren is probably still with Duamé."

She sighed, and after a few more minutes of inner turmoil, followed him. Miala managed to stay physically close to him, yet somehow be miles away emotionally. As they neared the village they began to hear random shouts, cheers, and laughter.

It was when they got to the ruined rubble of Duamé's home at the edge of the village that Kelleren excitedly bound up to Miala. She met him with a warm smile, and happily ruffled his fur. Leon saw that both Duamé and Elder Fanem were sitting on a broken wall of the home. Duamé held, and gently stroked, a small object– before he glanced up, noticed Leon, and put it in his satchel which sat behind him. The village elder stood shakily, leaning on a cane to support himself. A myriad of emotions played across his face as he watched them approach. Then with a heavy sigh, he stepped forward to greet them.

"You've returned," Fanem stated.

"I have questions." Leon couldn't help but issue his retorted statement as a challenge.

"I imagine you do. But first, I would like to tell you about our village. Please, hear me out." The elder's weight rested heavily on the cane and his head bobbed slightly already. Miala eyed the elder distrustfully as she sat down on the wall near Duamé. Leon stood, arms crossed, waiting for whatever excuses the elder decided to provide.

Fanem closed his eyes and breathed deeply, before he opened them once again and recited his tale, "Long ago, when I was a young lad, there was a mine not too far from here. The city of Agaprya used it for prison labor. As I

160

understood the tale, an accident one day caused a cave-in to occur– which revealed an ancient chamber that had been buried underground. Many of the miners perished and the mine was quickly abandoned and forgotten."

As the words tumbled from him his back seemed to straighten. It was as if unburdening himself verbally removed a physical weight from him. "Afterward, villagers began to disappear, one at a time, and it was discovered that an Alukah was somewhere nearby. The village elder back then went to Agaprya for help. Naturally, a squad of soldiers came to investigate– but they failed. The Alukah told them all to go home and forget him. Don't you see? The power of his voice could not be denied."

"Afterward, Rhoxmas showed up in our town and demanded punishment. He told us we would have to choose an offering for him, from amongst ourselves, every five years. He said we would be punished again if we called for help. He was toying with us– playing! It was all a game to him, and we were his pieces! And then he took his sacrifice. An elder volunteered that year."

Tears appeared in Fanem's eyes, and his voice wavered. "I can still remember his laughter as they left. For a while, we lived in resigned fear that every five years one of us would have to go. Each time, we chose the sick and the dying. We knew where they went, but were not willing to do anything to stop it. The knowledge that any further infractions against him would bring more misery held us hostage. Until finally, one year we decided to take a risk. I was not much older than you when the villagers all decided to pool their money, and hired mercenaries and even a witch, to slay the Alukah."

Kelleren's head, resting on Miala's lap, turned toward the elder. His ears went back and the dog growled. "Steady

161

boy." Duamé said, as he held a hand on the dog. Miala, to her credit, didn't react at all.

Fanem looked at the dog impassively before he continued. "But they too failed– never returning. We figured they died. When three of our own went missing during the next 'harvest', we knew that we had lost our right to choose those who were 'reaped'."

The elder's head, which normally bobbed due to age, remained still and Fanem lifted his eyes to look straight into Leon's. "When I became elder, I thought I could solve the problem. I swallowed my pride and asked a traveler, who mentioned he was going to the king's court, to carry my letter to the king. It begged for assistance, explaining our situation with the creature. Either he went and the king did not care, or was accosted and never made it there himself. Rhoxmas then began to send his horde of undead to claim us each harvest. That was five years ago."

"I honestly never thought you would return. I never thought that you would overcome the hypnotic voice of the Alukah. I just knew that one way or another, our village was doomed. We were afraid to try and move the village, afraid to build more defenses, afraid to do anything other than defend our very lives. If we did more, we feared that next harvest Rhoxmas would decide to just end his game and kill us all."

Leon's indignation at the elder deflated as the defeated man stared at him. The cries of delight and celebration had continued in the background, all while the elder shared his village's tragic history. Fanem saw that the story he shared had elicited no response from anyone, and a resigned look appeared on his face. He walked up to Leon, stopping an arm's length away, and spoke with the first indication of defiance laced in his voice, "I thank you, truly, for vanquishing the Alukah. Those you rescued, they remember

162

what happened. All of it. They have recounted what you all did, numerous times. We don't know your name, but we know what you are. What he called you. I remember the stories of old. I know you are a Judge."

"I know I am responsible for this attack– just like the last one. I am ready for your judgement. However, I would ask you one question. What would you have done differently if you were me?" With that, the elder got down on his old knees in front of Leon, bowed his head, and awaited death– if that was the sentence he wished to pronounce.

Looking around, he saw that everyone's eyes were focused on him. Miala's piercing green eyes, Duamé's with his brows arched high, and Kelleren's with his head tilted to the side. All were waiting to see what Leon would do.

What would I do? Leon asked himself. *What would I have done differently?*

The military's focus has always been to defend the front lines. They tried to make the kingdom unassailable. Build and defend the cliffs at Bulwark. Destroy the hordes that threatened to invade. Recover dwindling resources, in order to defend the front all over again. Yet somehow, even so close to the capital city Agaprya, this small little farming village was overlooked.

The simmering rage Leon felt towards Everbright and it's leaders, letting those here be sacrificed for years – decades even – gave way to sympathy. With the village's lack of available resources, and with the rest of the world falling apart too, what was one small village to the world? What was one, or for that matter several lives, compared to the lives of many? Yet if the military did try to help here before, and the hypnotic voice of Rhoxmas had defeated them so thoroughly, what else could be done to survive? Still struggling to understand, trying to grasp the complexity of the situation, Leon pushed. "There were children, elder. Children being taken!"

The elder beat his cane on the ground in frustration. "You think I didn't know that? What could we have done other than keeping the children inside during the harvesting? Hide them to make sure they were safe? Cover their ears so they couldn't hear the Alukah's voice? We did everything we could!" The elder looked back up; there were tears streaming down his face. "How old are you?" he fumed.

Taken aback by the abrupt, seemingly unrelated, question, Leon replied almost by reflex, "Twenty years."

Elder Fanem scoffed and lowered his eyes again. "You just wait. You're still a boy. You think the world exists in black and white. Right and wrong. Wait till you are my age and have to live with the hard choices you were forced to make. You'll realize there are a lot more choices than just right or wrong. A lot more colors in the world than just black and white."

Leon's heart broke for the old man who had just unburdened his very being. This man had been stuck in a situation where no positive outcome seemed achievable. Fanem truly felt he had done the best he could.

What do I do here?

What would Adonai want me to do?

What did Rohiel tell me during the dream?

"I don't know what I would have done," Leon said honestly. "What has passed has passed. I cannot change it. The… the events of the past cannot be changed. They are written into the very fabric of the universe. What I do know is that while the world may have many more choices than just right or wrong, what matters is that you never stray from making decisions based out of love. If you love right, you can't be wrong."

164

As he looked at Elder Fanem, he felt he understood the miserable man that knelt before him. One who had endured a life full of fear. This man lived in an almost impossible situation and he could not fault him for it. Leon reached down and unhooked the pouch that carried the golden eagle coins from his sister. Taking the pouch, he grabbed the elder and pulled him to his feet, then he placed it into his hands.

Fanem, overcome with emotion, spluttered, "I– I don't understand."

Leon clasped Elder Fanem's shoulder and instructed, "Buy weapons and build a better wall to defend yourselves. If Bulwark Fortress falls then gather your people and make your way to Last Bastion."

"You, you aren't going to kill me?" The elder asked in a small voice.

Words tumbled from Leon's lips, ones that just made sense, given his recent visions. "No, you are forgiven. Just as I am."

✦✦✦✦✦

Leon had no clue what he was doing, but for some reason he felt the need to address the villagers. Since choosing to forgive Elder Fanem and let him live, he felt an internal tugging almost– a feeling that his work here was somehow not yet done. As Leon walked away from the speechless and smiling Elder Fanem, towards the village center, his recent battle compatriots rushed to join him.

Duamé hustled up to Leon and grasped his sleeve. He then turned to confront him, "Oi, meat shield, what tha hematite was that?"

"What do you mean?" Leon asked.

"You gave him money. And then you… you forgave him." Miala blurted.

165

"That was to defend the town from further attacks."

Duamé raged at Leon, "Wot kinda Judge are ya exactly? That's comin' outta yer share, not mine!"

"Relax. That was out of my share."

"Great! Now that that's cleared up– where's me share?" Duamé asked, as if he hadn't been ready to explode just a moment before.

"I have it." Miala replied.

Duamé looked at Miala and then back at Leon incredulously, "Ya let a woman carry two shares? Wot kinda MAN are ya exactly?"

"She took it before I could! I– I was going to–"

But the dwarf peered closer at Leon. "Is that a handprint on yer face too?" Duamé snickered, "Ha, gave ya two a moment alone an' ya blew it!"

Miala's face went red, and Leon scrambled to think of an easier way out of this conversation. "Uh, hey, what is that Kelleren has?" He asked desperately.

Kelleren kept pace with them, and had something prominently sticking from his mouth.

"While goin' back, I got a few o' those bones from tha skeletal horses fer 'im." Duamé explained.

"That was nice of you." Miala complemented.

"Completely self-servin'. This way, maybe he won't take me food anymore."

Miala cocked her head for a moment and laughed, "Or he could still take your food, and now has a few nice bones too."

Duamé stopped Leon with a hand. "Listen, lad I… I'm sorry that I suggested that we shoulda turned tha other way. If I had known that children were in tha next room–"

"It's okay Duamé, everything worked out." Leon consoled him.

The dwarf continued, "I ain't heartless or gutless, we dwarves are just prudent, that's all. If a kid's in danger though–"

"Speaking of danger, we are just glad you made it back," Miala said. "We had to hide from a migrant giant on our way back."

"Whoa, wot? Yer pullin' me leg!"

Miala and Leon explained how the giant passed them, moving westward. The only things out that way were the southern forest, Bulwark Fortress, and the Lost Lands. Why it was going in that direction Leon couldn't fathom.

Duamé shook his head at the news. "They're right savage they are. Dwarves tryin' ta settle Masterwork Halls almost lost half their number in gettin' rid o' tha giants that were living there."

They reached the village center, where it seemed an impromptu party had begun to take place outside. A few people with rough instruments played discordant music together– though it was off key and not quite on beat, it didn't stop several people from dancing and singing. Laughter abounded, kids were chasing each other while playing, and pure merriment was coming from all around.

"Never seen tha town this happy 'fore." Duamé commented.

A few people noticed them walking, and like a wildfire, whispers began to spread. The merriment gave way to wonder and stares. A few of which were curious, though some were full of shame. However, just like when Leon moved through the crowd to see who would follow him to the Alukah's lair, the villagers opened a path that led directly to the well again.

Leon heard the whispers of, "The Judge." and, "Witch." He stepped up to the well, as the crowd gathered around once again. Miala and Duamé stood behind him, with

Kelleren in tow. The whispers quieted, and Leon saw the twin boys they rescued shuffle together to the front of the crowd. Crouching, Leon smiled at them and said, "I am glad to see you two are ok, but where are your parents?"

They looked at each other before one piped up and said, "They was harvested when we was littler."

Leon's heart lurched as if he felt somehow responsible for their plight. Almost as though he had left people in the mine unsaved. "Who then... takes care of you both?"

"The people in the village all help." The other twin replied, as he sheepishly fiddled with his rope belt.

Leon's head bowed as he processed the news. These boys probably did not even remember their parents. The reasons why, and elder Fanem's story, didn't matter anymore; this tragedy should never have happened in the first place. Something needed to change. Here was the clearest example that could be made about the effect of the undead on a peaceful village. If Rohiel was right, and belief in Adonai could stop the turn after death, then Adonai needed to be known again!

Leon knew now why he felt he needed to talk to the people of Everbright.

And so he spoke to them. He didn't know a lot about the creator of the universe, only what Rohiel had told him thus far– so, Leon told them everything he knew. How love was stronger than fear, and that they didn't have to fear anymore.

It was during this moment, whether through divine timing, or Adonai's assistance himself, that the sun set behind the horizon. As the last glimmer of sunlight faded from the sky the spearhead began to glow. Its pristine blade, with no rust to be found, brightened into a radiant light, just as it had in the mine. The village people gasped and gazed at it in amazement. Leon heard Duamé mutter behind him, "Are ya flintin', kiddin' me?"

When Leon finished speaking he looked out to gauge the faces of the now silent crowd. Some stood watching him, mesmerized by his words, and waiting for him to share more. Others looked confused, and turned to their neighbors mouthing words like, "He's crazy!" While some had even left the gathering. Those headed back to their homes while shaking their heads, or looking back at Leon angrily– fearful of the next things he might say. He thought to himself that there were too many unreceptive people. Still, he tried to be happy about those who remained: a few of the villagers, all those that they had rescued, and even Elder Fanem– who had joined the crowd after Leon started.

Leon felt the moment for him to speak was over, and turned to look at his fellow village saviors. Miala's eyes held tears which she quickly wiped away, and Kelleren happily wagged his tail, his doggy expression unreadable as he gazed back at Leon.

Duamé, however, looked... angry. Furious even! Poking Leon repeatedly, he seethed, "Listen ta me boyo! I don't want any part o' yer 'God o' love' an' all that nonsense. Ya got that?"

Crestfallen, Leon thought he would have at least gotten a better reaction from those he had relied on and entrusted with his life. Leon nodded begrudgingly to Duamé, and stepped down from the platform. He walked away, finally feeling as though his task in Everbright was done.

Kelleren padded up next to him and slipped his head next to Leon's hand. Leon smiled and scratched the dog behind the ears.

"He liked what you had to say." Miala said, catching up to Leon. She seemed more composed and spoke in her usual soft tones. Then she asked, "What will you do now?"

169

Leon thought for a moment, "I made a promise to you, to take you wherever you needed to go to start over. I intend to keep it."

That seemed to be the answer she wanted to hear. Duamé piped in, "Oi! I still want me share!"

"I'm exhausted Duamé, can we do it tomorrow? I need to sleep and pack up the important things in my home."

"That's fine missy, but I ain't leaving ya till I get it."

Miala poked Duamé in the chest, just like he had done to Leon. "You can sleep outside the cabin then."

"Fine by me." Duamé stated.

"Fine." Miala countered.

"Fine!" Duamé shouted.

"I could just find an inn–" Leon interjected.

Duamé interrupted with a short laugh, "I doubt he'd let ya stay after that speech. Never seen ol' Norm hobble away so fast."

Leon cringed inwardly. "Guess I'm sleeping outside too." Looking to Miala, "If that's ok."

She nodded and they started the trek towards her home.

From the exterior the cabin seemed small, just as Miala said it was. Kelleren bounded towards it, looking back at the group excitedly. He clearly intended to lead them to the home, which was located at the edge of one of the farming fields, near where the horde had left the forest. It was a quaint cabin that looked to be solidly constructed, and had no outside features to even hint that someone lived there. They trudged up to the cabin feeling the ache of every mile they had walked that day, and every undead they had slain. Just anticipating sleep that evening seemed to make Leon feel even more tired than he already was. Looking over at his companions, he didn't seem to be the only one battling exhaustion.

Miala said her goodnights and stumbled into her cabin with Kelleren. Duamé crouched down and leaned against the house, and Leon did the same in another spot. Eyelids heavy with sleep, Leon shifted positions trying desperately to get comfortable. While trying to adjust his body, Duamé cracked an eye open and asked, "That thing gonna be on all night?"

Leon looked at the spear glowing brightly in his hand, and instinctively felt that letting it go, allowing the darkness of night to surround them, would be wrong. "Maybe."

"Afraid of tha dark are ye?"

Leon, hardly able to keep his eyes open, and so tired he couldn't even think straight, mumbled, "Not as much anymore." Before he promptly fell asleep.

Chapter 12: The Attributes

Surprised and slightly disappointed, Leon awoke to the pale light of early morning– just as the spearhead's glow winked out. He'd had no dreams or visions last night. *Was that a message from Rohiel? Was something wrong? Did I do something I wasn't supposed to?*

Leon looked around and saw that Duamé was already awake, and munching on his breakfast. When Duamé noticed he had woken up, he gestured to the house with a strip of bacon and grumbled, "Somethin's goin' on in there."

Leon immediately tuned in to the sounds of Miala's muffled voice, followed by a few loud crashes, and then shuffling around that came from inside. While he couldn't make out most of her words, shouts of, "I don't want to!" and, "You can't make me!" penetrated the thick walls of the cabin. These exclamations were punctuated by occasional barks and a few howls as the 'conversation' continued between the Pyromancer and the companion.

"Thank you. Know what they are arguing about?" Leon asked, gratefully taking the strip of bacon the dwarf had offered him.

"Ya got me, lad. I'm not goin' in there. A woman gets like that, best ta just stay outta sight."

They munched on their breakfast in companionable silence, and continued to listen to the occasional noises that broke through the walls. Duamé eventually got fed up waiting for Miala, and pointed to the rubble of his building on the other end of the field. "I'm goin' over there, an' gettin' what I can from me shop. I can see ye all from there. So if ya leave, I will find ya. An' this," he continued, pointing at the two-handed hammer on his back, "will taste a lot worse than bacon." Without waiting for a response, he stomped off towards his former home.

Amused by the dwarf's antics, Leon smiled at the threat, and waited until he was about halfway across the field before shouting after him, "Hey Duamé!" The dwarf turned around to look back at him.

"Thanks for the BACON!"

It only took another moment for the door of Miala's house to open, and then Kelleren shot out from it like a cannonball from an airship. Leon burst into laughter as the dog started to frantically jump around the dwarf. He sniffed all around him, in an effort to find whatever scrap of meat was left to scrounge. Duamé growled in frustration and shouted at the dog, "No, NO! Kelleren! Go get yer own! NO! Yer own! Aaaugh!"

Finally, Kelleren saw that he wouldn't win against the dwarf and raced back to the house, scratching at the door. After the dog had scratched for a minute, Leon heard Miala's laughter from inside joining his own. Then the door cracked open, and she held out a small pouch with a note attached. The dog took the pouch (which jingled a little) in

173

his jaws, and loped past the dwarf down to the village. Duamé shot Leon a dark look before he turned around and once more walked towards his ruined home.

Leon continued to sit outside of Miala's home, and was speculating on how beautiful the sunrise had been, when Kelleren finally returned with a different pouch in his mouth. Grease dripped through the soaked bottom, and Leon chuckled as the understanding of how Miala had remained a successful hermitess for all this time dawned on him. The dog scratched at the door and promptly entered when it opened slightly.

Curious about how much longer Miala was going to be, Leon mustered the courage to knock. "Is everything okay?"

"Yes! Just a few more minutes!" She snapped.

A 'few minutes' turned out to be what Duamé needed, because he returned with an organized pack, stuffed full with more tools. "Wot? Is she still not ready? Typical o' women lad. One day ya will learn they run on their own schedule. Especially dwarven women."

"I take it you know from experience?" Leon asked, thinking back to his own sister, and her similar behavior.

"Married fer a time."

"Oh. For a time?"

Duamé's face darkened, as he seemed to recall something unpleasant. "It ended." He spoke in a tone that Leon knew indicated he was on dangerous ground.

"Sorry to hear that."

"So 'Judge'," Duamé mocked, making sure to say Leon's title as sarcastically as possible, "how big was each share?"

At that moment Miala's door opened, and she stepped out with Kelleren in tow. Her dark red hair, which just yesterday had been unkempt, wild, and uncared for, was now straightened and lightly curled down one side outside her freshly cleaned robe. Her face had been washed as well, and her eyes pierced Leon and Duamé as she enunciated, "Not. A. Word."

Leon, speechless by her transformation, could only nod his head. Meanwhile, Duamé said nothing, but raised an eyebrow and smirked. Miala then pointed an accusatory finger at Kelleren, who sat sporting a pleased doggy grin. "This was all HIS idea. So, again, not a word!"

"Can ye give me tha rustin' share already lass?" Duamé demanded.

Satisfied that her metamorphosis was not going to be commented on, Miala strode over to the dwarf. She reached a hand into her robe and visibly strained to withdraw, before shakily handing over, three different sized burlap bags. As far as Leon could tell, the bags hadn't been there a few seconds ago. She deposited each of them into Duamé's hands and recited with precision, "Four hundred and thirty-two gold, one hundred and seventy four silver, one hundred, and seventy-one copper."

"We also have a bag of mixed gems, both cut and rough, which still have to be divided." Leon chimed in.

After checking them, Duamé put the coin bags into his pack. "Lemme see."

Duamé poked through the bag of gems and grimaced. "We're gonna hafta get these appraised an' exchanged. Too many different gems. Should double tha money though! Anythin' else we got?"

Miala pulled her find out from her robe. "I got a wand– that is NOT for FETCH!" She exclaimed over her shoulder to Kelleren.

Lastly, Leon pulled out and tossed Duamé the braided ring they found. He figured that the dwarven smith might know what it was. "There was also this. We think it might be magical, but have no idea what it does or if it's dangerous. Got any ideas?"

Duamé caught it in his leather work gloves, frowned, and held it up to the morning light. With a muttered, "Wot tha…," he looked at it from all angles and handed it back to Leon. "Too right ya are. Could very well be magical, might even be dwarven or elven made. Beyond me skill though, an' that's sayin' somethin'."

"What are the metals woven into it?" Leon asked.

As a parent would with a child, Duamé patiently started to explain, "Well, ya had iron there, which looked like it was rustin' a bit, then ya had elvenwood on there, which makes me think it's magical– ya know, like yer spear, an' her wand."

"Elvenwood?"

"Yeah, it channels inner energy." Miala also helped to explain.

"I didn't know this was elvenwood." Leon replied, as he thoughtfully gazed at his spear with a new perspective.

"Ya didn't ask boyo." Duamé stepped over and clapped Leon hard on the back. "If'n ya ever need ta know how tha world works, ya shouldn't be afraid ta ask those who are older an' wiser."

"Gee, thanks for the advice."

"Free o' charge. Next one'll cost ya." Duamé bantered.

Miala held up a hand to interject, "So here's a question, where are we going?"

They all looked at each other, and Leon thought only one place nearby would possibly enable them to spend their shares of the treasure. Miala and Duamé had apparently come to the same conclusion, because all at once they said, "Agaprya."

Having made the decision of where they would go, Duamé and Kelleren promptly headed into the town and bought the food they would need to make the three day journey to Xaelon's capital city. In about an hour's time

they were on the western road that led out of Everbright–
towards the last great city left in the kingdom. This road
would carry the trio and Kelleren across the grassy plains
and rolling hills, before it would follow alongside the Sigrit
River, and up to the southern entrance of the great walled
city.

After a while, Duamé, who seemed to be in a spirited
mood, rubbed his hands together and started up a
conversation. "So, in tha interest o' passin' time, what are ye
all goin' ta do with yer money?"

Leon started to think more about his share of the
treasure, and wondered the same thing. As he thought
seriously about his options, Miala piped in, "I suppose I
could use it to buy a new house, or perhaps some land in the
middle of nowhere. Kelleren has proven lately that he is
trustworthy enough to bring back most of the food I send
him to get for both of us."

Miala had changed. Besides the obvious difference in
her striking physical appearance, she seemed to be slightly
more vocal today than yesterday– especially when it came
to bickering with Kelleren. The dog didn't appear to mind
though; Kelleren just seemed to be excited for the journey,
as the rest of them were. For that matter, after he thought
about it, everyone seemed to be in a lighter mood. *Maybe
this is how they all normally behave– when they're not
rushing off to save people.*

"Oi, meat shield! Wot about ya?" Duamé asked.

*Then again, we bantered while heading towards 'certain
death and dismemberment' too.* He reminded himself. "Um,
maybe I'll get new armor? I'm not exactly in the navy
anymore, so it's a little awkward wearing this."

"Ya do know yer talkin' ta a smith right?"

"You want to make my armor?" Leon asked
suspiciously.

177

"If ya want somethin' better than anythin' any human can make, yeah I can do that fer ya."

Genuinely surprised at the offer, Leon was impressed by the dwarf's generosity.

"Thank you, Duamé. I'd be honored."

"Course I'd have ta charge ya. Materials, an' labor, ya know…"

"And there it is." Leon understood.

"Might give ye a discount. New 'Judge' an' all." he continued.

"Gee, thanks again."

"Don't want ya dyin'– when yer jus' startin' out."

"Okay, Duamé."

"Might give Judges a bad name an' all."

"Would you STOP that?" Leon exclaimed.

Miala doubled over in laughter while Duamé chuckled at his own humor. All of the jesting made Leon think. *What were past Judges like? Did they also carry the spear? Was his family somehow related to the ancient Judges, and that's how the spear got on the wall?* Leon almost laughed out loud at his internal joke. *How far had the apple fallen from the tree if his father and brother were the descendants of Judges?*

"What about you Duamé?" Leon asked.

"Well, mista meat shield, after much deliberatin' an' plannin', I have an idea, but I got a question fer miss Miala first, an' that may help me with a better answer."

"I notice you're not calling me a witch anymore," Miala commented.

"Well, ya don't look tha part now, do ya?" Duamé replied.

"Hey, I said not a word!" She cried, pretending to be hurt.

Duamé, mimicking what she had done earlier, enunciated very clearly, "I know– That's. Why. I. Said. Several words."

They all broke into laughter again at the dwarf's antics. Leon was reminded of the jesting he and his crew of the *Dawnfire* had engaged in. It had kept everyone sane while doing a very insane job.

"What did you want to know?" Miala asked, after everyone had stopped.

"Alright, so when yer hands go all burnin', does it hurt ya?"

"Um, no heat doesn't really bother me. It sort of, tingles I guess." She answered, her eyes narrowing.

"Okay, okay, next question. How hot can ya go? Like a campfire, or a forge? Ya ever heat metal right enough?" Duamé seemed almost hopeful of her answer.

"Well, I've melted my fair share of locks. It's how I opened that chest."

"YES! Okay, last question: how long can ye do it?"

Miala looked at Kelleren for a moment, then back at Duamé, "Longer, the more I practice. It's like using your muscles or swinging your hammer to make something. Most mancers just get better with increased time and use."

Leon watched as Duamé went from walking at a nice leisurely pace to jumping up and down while shouting in celebration. "Would ya mind doin' a short experiment tonight at camp?"

Some of Duamé's excitement must have rubbed off, because Miala readily agreed with a smile.

The rest of the day flew by, and before they knew it Leon's spearlight had come on once again. It at least confirmed for him that it would be a regularly occurring event. They decided to stop along the side of the road and rest at an old campsite they spotted tucked in a thin copse of

179

trees. Leon and Duamé agreed to each take a watch through the night, since they would all have to sleep on the ground. A small stream cut through the trees and appeared to run parallel to the road ahead. After they settled in, Duamé dug through his pack until he found a strange pan-like implement that had a handle and deep grooves. He set it on the ground in front of them, and Kelleren began to sniff at it with curiosity. He also took out his sack of copper coins, and launched into an explanation using the same informative voice he had employed earlier.

"Right. So this here is called an ingot mold. Normally ores get mined an' go through a smelter, which gets rid o' tha impurities. Then tha heated metal goes into tha mold ta make ingots, which can be smithed inta wotever. I want ta see if ya can melt these inta that." Duamé gestured from the sacks of coins to the mold.

Miala cocked her head, curious about the whole affair. "Why? Don't you want the coins?"

"Ingots are easier ta carry, an' fer a smith they are more valuable."

Leon tried to contribute to the endeavor as well, "Don't you need water to cool the metal?"

"Hmm. Oil's usually better, less crackin'. But, good point! Go get some from that there stream." Duamé fished a tray from his pack to put the water in and handed it to Leon.

Leon headed off to complete his task, and when he returned set the pan back in front of Duamé. The dwarf then held the ingot mold underneath as Miala grasped a handful of tinkling coins from the bag. She held her hand over the mold and squeezed. Her hand glowed, changing from red to off white, altering the very temperature of the air around them. Soon hot melted copper dripped and ran from her hand into the pan– halfway filling one of the molds.

Everyone's eyes went wide with the realization that Duamé's proposed process was working!

As her hand returned to normal Miala's face lit with a genuine smile, then she took Duamé's bag and poured more coins into her palm. She continued to repeat the process, until she soon had all of the molds filled. Duamé, steady and silent, took the mold tray and deposited it into the pan of water. It hissed steam, causing a small cloud to envelop the makeshift camp. Once the steam cleared, Duamé removed the tray from the pan. He then turned it upside down, and with a good-sized hammer, hit the back of it–knocking three copper ingots out onto the ground.

Without saying a word Duamé bent down and picked up one of the copper ingots, wearing the biggest grin Leon had ever seen grace his face. Leon, awed by the experience, couldn't help but smile as well. Miala leaned forward and picked up another ingot herself. Looking up at Duamé she asked, "Want to do it again?"

Late that night, all of Duamé's copper and silver coins had been turned into ingots. The experience had tired Miala though, even causing her to develop a small spontaneous nosebleed. Kelleren whined at her, and that was the point at which they had to stop. She assured them that as time went on, and she kept practicing, her strength and endurance would increase.

"Fire usually destroys. It's not often I get a chance to make something." Miala grinned.

As they prepared to get some sleep, Duamé volunteered to take the first watch. His overflowing ideas were causing him to almost ramble, a complete contradiction to his earlier silent behavior. "We could be a 'travelin' smithy'! We might be able ta even recycle used metals easier. Just hafta get more tools, oh an' oil too. An' can have a almost unlimited supply, an' better quality than those human smiths! That means demand too!"

As Duamé muttered excitedly to himself, Leon began to wonder if he would dream again. Then he drifted off to sleep.

The grey expanse that greeted him told Leon he had indeed dreamt again– but something about the expanse was different this time. As he looked around, his eyes fixed on the light in the distance. He may have been imagining it, but that far off pinprick which emanated the faint glow, seemed slightly larger. It flashed as Leon lifted his head and a wave of light washed over him. The warmth and peace that it provided returned, and for a moment Leon felt that he would be content to stay there for the rest of his life. Perhaps he could simply enjoy the warmth and the feeling of weightlessness forever.

"You are on the path, but you must be careful Leon."

Rohiel's voice sounded from behind Leon. As he turned, he saw an enormous pile of gold and jewels set before him. Easily as tall as himself, it was just a few short steps away. Leon could reach for it and fill his pockets with more wealth than he had ever known. More wealth than his father had, more even than King Garinth probably had.

The light behind Leon pulsed again, and he felt as it passed through him. This time it continued onward and dissolved the pile of treasure. The particles of gold seemed to be blown away in the wind. Leon turned back towards the light and heard Rohiel's voice around him again.

"You cannot love both God and money. For where your treasure is, there your heart will be also."

Leon felt the truth of those words reverberate deep inside of him. With the words Rohiel spoke, ideas were conveyed that equated to more than the mere words themselves. Money was a distraction. A worldly creation and concept.

The value of money was due to its rarity and perceived value. While having money was not inherently bad, when gaining more of it became an obsession a person could be overtaken. That obsession to always increase your wealth would distract, consume, and direct the thoughts and actions of those whose focus should instead be on God's desires for them.

"Blessed is the one who finds wisdom, and the one who gets understanding."

There was a disturbance in the grey expanse as Rohiel stepped out of nothingness in front of Leon. The angel still had a radiant face and wore his scrolled and detailed bulky armor. He did not stand still, but instead paced around Leon in circles. With a sudden flash of insight, Leon realized the angel's metal armor looked like it was the same blue metal the spearhead was composed of.

Rohiel continued his circles around Leon, as the angel's words repeated and burned themselves into Leon's consciousness.

"Love. Joy. Peace. Patience. Kindness. Goodness. Faithfulness. Gentleness. Self-Control."

Leon lost count of how many times the angel revolved around him. He could not say how many times those same words repetitively echoed through him. When Leon was confident he knew all of the words by heart, Rohiel stopped in front of him. With a sudden burst of speed the angel grasped him by the shoulders and leaned close, stopping his too-bright face only a hair's breadth away. While the rest of his face was still featureless, Rohiel's eyes sharpened and clarified until Leon saw eyes that seemed to belong to an ancient man. The very center of his eyes glowed instead of having an iris or pupil. A sense of urgency exuded from the angel.

***"You must learn. Of Adonai. Of Judges. Of yourself.
You must–"***

"Oi! Yer turn, ya mumblin' meat shield." Duamé shook
Leon's shoulders as he quietly woke him from his slumber.

Disappointed, Leon realized Duamé must have cut off
the dream. Leon's vision was blurry as he tried to rub the
sleep from his eyes, and stood to take over the watch. He
was careful not to make too much noise and awaken Miala,
who slumbered nearby, or Kelleren, whose head rested on
her stomach. He took Duamé's place for watch, as the dwarf
went over and propped his back against the same tree that
Leon had slept against just a moment ago. Within minutes,
Duamé was sound asleep and snoring lightly.

Leon looked out into the night and held the spear close–
allowing its light to radiate like a solitary bubble designed
to keep the darkness at bay. Rohiel's words and voice
seemed to resound in his head still, helping to keep him
awake. He thought of the chanted words: Love. Joy. Peace.
Patience. Kindness. Goodness. Faithfulness. Gentleness.
Self-Control.

If Adonai was love, then the other words the angel
chanted should go hand in hand with love. Self-analyzing,
Leon knew that he loved his mother and sister, but couldn't
think of anything or anyone else that he could say he
'loved'. Joy was a feeling he missed. He had known joy
when flying in airships and amongst friends. He hoped the
banter and company of his new companions could perhaps
develop into a camaraderie. The last time he felt he had a
true friend was…

Leon shook his head in an effort to prevent himself from
falling into a dark memory, and brought himself back to the
words Rohiel spoke. Peace was something that he felt only
in the grey expanse of his dreams– when the pinprick in the
distance washed its light on him. Xaelon was anything but

peaceful. Most were scrabbling to survive, and fought a losing war against the tides of undead. Those who didn't fight had either given up, were too young to fight, or were wealthy enough to avoid it.

He thought again about the absurd parties and power plays of the kingdom's courtiers, while the world all around them died. Leon felt his anger at their callous disregard for what was occurring start to simmer again. However, before his anger built too far, he felt a sense of insight into it. Maybe the peace Rohiel was talking about wasn't the worldly peace he thought of, but a peace within himself. These words were all traits of a person after all. With that realization, he had to admit that he still held a great amount of turmoil locked within himself.

Leon moved on to the next trait and chuckled to himself. He would be the first to admit that patience was not in his nature at all. Kindness and goodness he thought were possibly his strengths, but didn't want to seem boastful of himself. Which again made Leon chuckle– at the pure absurdity of the thought.

Faithfulness? Leon spent at least an hour on his night watch wondering what exactly faith was. Gentleness was not something that was encouraged when fighting the undead, so he wasn't sure how to work on that trait either.

Dawn was not far off and Leon dreaded going over the last attribute the angel mentioned: self-control. Leon knew his lack of self-control was why he hadn't been able to manage one successful conversation with his father. It was why he repeatedly blamed himself for the *Dawnfire* wreckage, and the excessive guilt he carried over having to kill the undead shells of his friends. This would be the hardest attribute about himself to face. This would be harder than patience, and that said a lot.

The light of dawn poked over the grassy hills. As it did Leon's spearhead winked out, and returned to its naturally blue metallic sheen, with its strange etched symbol.

He roused the others, and after a quick breakfast they broke camp and continued their journey towards Agaprya. Duamé and Miala talked in more detail about the idea of a traveling dwarven smithy. When Duamé was explaining the different processes and the metals and alloys that he would work with, Leon piped in, "Duamé, don't you need something like an anvil to smith? Isn't that heavy? How would you carry that around everywhere?"

The dwarf thought for a moment before he cast a sly look at Miala.

"I can't carry anything that big or heavy Duamé!" she preempted, raising both hands.

"Why couldn't you use a cart?" Leon asked.

"I was hopin' ta avoid that," Duamé muttered. After a few moments, he shouted, "Dolomite! It was such a good idea!"

Curiosity overwhelmed Leon, "What do you keep saying?"

"Wot ya talking about, meat shield?"

Leon tried to give examples of the things he had heard. "Dolomite, feldspar…"

Duamé cackled, "Those are minerals an' stones in tha ground lad. Every dwarf from tha Commerce, Military, an' Craftin' Guilds know their minerals like their alphabet."

Leon suddenly saw an opportunity. He held out the spear, with its odd blue metal, and asked, "Which one is this?"

Duamé shuffled away a few steps. "I ain't touchin' that thing! It'll turn me ta salt, or char me hands off!"

Smiling, Leon pressured the dwarf. "I don't think it will Duamé."

"Well, I'm not takin' any chances. Ya keep yer saltshakin' nightlight ta yerself!"

Chapter 13: The Grieving

As the lively group continued to walk they came upon a fork in the road– one branch splitting to the west and the other continuing to the north. The western path led to an old stone bridge that crossed the Sigrit River and led into the Southern Forest, then to Bulwark Fortress, and finally the Lost Lands. The northern branch ran alongside the river, and headed towards Agaprya. Leon, Miala, and Duamé stayed on the northern branch and began to encounter more travelers as they drew ever closer to the capital. They passed a family of gnomes here and a merchant carriage there. Similarly to the group, many appeared to be carrying everything they owned on their backs.

More than a few of these travelers had fled the Lost Lands due to the undead hordes that ravaged them. Those that survived had the foresight to escape early or were lucky enough to be evacuated by airships. Many of these survivors journeyed to Agaprya, looking to start a new life for as long as they could live it.

Duamé currently chatted up an orcish father. He was a stout man named Lorog, who carried not only his backpack, but his very young orc daughter as well. There had been a time when open hatred had existed between the dwarven and orcish races. However, both races had set aside old grievances due to the threat of mutual extinction. A threat which came from a force that killed indiscriminately whenever either race warred against the other.

"The ancestral clans that remain there are all stubborn fools." Lorog stated as his young daughter pulled on his chin hair. Wincing, he removed her hand and hoisted her onto his shoulders. "They think bravery is staying put and fighting for their homes– while leaving to find a new home and staying alive to fight another day is stupid. Well, we don't need them! We've got all the clan we need right here." He said, gesturing to his daughter, wife, and son– a small newborn who was slung across his mother's back. His wife smiled warmly, her tusks protruding past her lips. She didn't seem to speak very much, content to let her husband talk as she walked peacefully beside him.

"Wot o' tha dwarven halls out there? Had ya heard anythin' about em before ya left?" Duamé questioned.

Lorog shrugged and then winced again as his daughter, who was fixated on his beard, tugged at it again. "Nothing. Mean no disrespect, but dwarves are just as stubborn as orcs. Some still stay trying to hold out, but others say they'll move to halls here in Xaelon. We lived near Shatterhasp, and nearly all the dwarves there stayed put. They refused the last airship evacuation."

"Nooooo…" Duamé drawled, disbelief written on his face.

"Not one got on. So when we saw there was room we took it at the first opportunity. Dropped us off near the southern forest before the ship had to go back out, pointed us towards Agaprya, and here we are." Lorog finished.

Leon listened to Duamé and Lorog's conversation and privately wondered how much longer the races could evacuate and act defensively against the undead onslaught. Every long-term offensive excursion into the Lost Lands thus far had failed. While the Bulwark could continue to build its walls higher and higher, similarly to those that surrounded Agaprya, Xaelon only had so many resources available for refugees. Once those were exhausted they would be forced to reclaim some of the Lost Lands.

Leon thought about his time in the service, the evacuations he had executed, and the undead he had blown up with the airship cannons. Miala and Kelleren, who walked along in silence, sidled up to Leon while he was lost in thought. "There should be a waypost up ahead, right?" she asked.

"Yeah, we should reach it before nightfall. Then it is another day's walk until Agaprya."

Sure enough, the waypost appeared after just a few more hours of walking. It looked as though it had been repeatedly and hastily added on to time and time again. Two long slapdash buildings stretched on either side of the road. Tents and stalls could be seen off the road, dotting the landscape. They had popped up, surrounding the more permanent buildings, and were filled with people looking to hock their wares or to avoid the waystation's exorbitant lodging prices.

Leon heard a person on horseback yelling faintly in the distance, and noticing the small crowd that surrounded the individual, pointed it out to everyone. "I believe that's a herald."

"Perfect! It has been some time since we have had news of Xaelon!" Lorog exclaimed.

They drew closer and saw the herald dressed in the standard puffery travel clothes denoting their office. Paid to speak the truth and spread anything of interest throughout the kingdom, mail carrier airships transported them all across the land. While growing up Leon had thought that having a loud voice was the only critical component to be a herald. However, he had learned that their ability to spin a captivating tale was also quite useful. The Naval Academy held a longstanding belief that fear-mongering was all the Xaelon Herald Guild was good for. Battles and skirmishes in the Dead Wars were routinely embellished when retold; Leon felt it was a disservice to all of the men and women that he served with whose lives had been lost in those actions.

This herald looked just as unscrupulous as the rest that he had encountered. He rolled up his scroll, took a few donations, and then went to tack his horse. It looked like the herald was done for the day, so Leon hurried up to him with the hope of persuading him to do one more reading. He held a silver coin out saying, "You don't have to shout if you don't want to."

The others, including the orc family, crowded around as the herald took the silver coin and nodded in appreciation. In a voice that warbled from overuse he said, "I'm dog tired I am, but for a sparrow, I could do one more." Clearing his throat and drinking from the skin at his side, he unfurled the scroll once more and began.

"In attempting to protect the last great city of Agaprya, his royal majesty King Garinth has asked all travelers to undergo simple screening before entering the city. Individuals are to be asked a series of questions relating to their general health, in order to keep the dying away from the general populace. Any refugees from the Lost Lands are welcome in Xaelon, but any who are aware of having disease or illness within them are asked to reside elsewhere– outside of the city."

The herald retook a drink from his belt before he continued. "The Kingdom of Xaelon asks that every able-bodied individual willing to fight for the survival of kin and

Kingdom, inquire at the gates of Agaprya. Of course, as aforementioned, individuals would have to not be sick, or dying."

"King Garinth is still grieving for his son, the Crown Prince Gelan, who fell victim to a fatal crash of the flagship *Dawnfire* due to a dragon attack, five weeks past. There were no survivors, and–"

The blatant lie that escaped the herald's mouth caused Leon's mind to reel.

Was this the story told around the Kingdom?
No survivors?

He recalled how Lord Lucien told him he had bought practically all of the heralds in Xaelon. Apparently, that meant he had also fabricated a lie stating that Leon was dead. No wonder they had been surprised to see him at home! One piece of his personal puzzle fell into place. Leon could only assume that was why his 'former' father had also offered him a job as a Levigem mine foreman. By asking him to leave the next day, he would remain out of sight and dead in their eyes. Or perhaps it was more nefarious than that even, and he would have been soon been dead in truth– considering the dangers of the job that came with mining the precious gems.

Anger for his father resurfaced and seethed through him. He had gone home expecting a civil family reunion only to be cast out and disowned by a man who, unbeknownst to him, had declared him dead to the public. With no mail, no word of his mother's condition, and no warm welcome, Leon might as well have been declared dead five years ago when he had initially left home. To use the heralds to do so was scandalous, but at this point Leon expected nothing less from Lucien.

He shook himself from his memories to listen further, but only caught the last bit of the particular news blurb the herald was reciting. "–and Princess Schalae is nearing the completion of her time of mourning and will be returning soon to the Elvenwood forest."

The herald scanned through the rest of the document, then rolled it up while stating. "The rest is standard rubbish, it is. End of the world, but we will ultimately persevere. Good guys win, bad guys lose, you know how it is." He then asked, "Any news from your neck of the world?"

Lorog began to retell what he had shared earlier about the state of the Lost Lands where he came from. The herald nodded along in obviously feigned interest, but the orc said his piece without care. After a pause, Duamé surprised everyone when he piped in, "Oi, did ya hear about that guy goin' around callin' hisself a new 'Judge'?"

Lorog and his wife turned to Duamé clearly interested, as they had received no information about what transpired in Everbright. Miala's brows knit together as her eyes grew wide, while Kelleren whined and used a paw to cover his own. Leon patiently waited for the punchline, while the Herald looked on with tight-lipped skepticism. Duamé looked around, gauging everyone's reactions before he pushed further, "I'm serious! He's sayin' he's a Judge, ya know, like them old stories!"

The herald, deciding to give the dwarf the benefit of the doubt, quickly produced a quill and ink, and turned his scroll over to write on it. "Please, elaborate. Now, this is good gossip!"

Leon had to give the dwarf credit. Without mentioning anyone's name, Duamé summarized how the Judge routed an undead attack, then found and subsequently defeated an Alukah. He told of how the Judge wasn't even affected by the hypnotic voice of the undead blight, and how he rescued the captured villagers and brought them back safe and sound to Everbright. Thankfully, Duamé omitted the repeated attacks on the town. Overall, Leon thought he had been a bit heavy-handed on the heroics, but also that he wouldn't mind being the Judge that Duamé had described.

"We jus' came from Everbright," Duamé concluded, "They're probably still celebratin'."

The herald became more and more engrossed in the tale as he filled the other side of the scroll with details. Clearly excited, he asked rapidly, "You– you just came from there? Can the rest of you corroborate this?"

"Um, we weren't there." Lorog admitted. The herald looked to Miala and Leon.

"Yeeeees. That did happen." Miala's drawn-out acknowledgment caused the herald to look to Leon, who only nodded.

The herald sighed in relief, "Well, this is exciting! The public could always use a good hero figure. Please, good dwarf, what did this Judge look like?"

Leon pinched the bridge of his nose as the dwarf leaned in conspiratorially, "Well, it's hard ta say. Ya see," he started snickering, "ya humans all look alike!" And with that, Duamé laughed uproariously and walked off towards the waystation lodging.

Fuming, the herald threw the scroll he was writing onto the ground and stomped over to take care of his horse, refusing to turn around and look at anybody. The small crowd that had gathered quickly dispersed, the perceived joke now over.

Miala, Kelleren, Leon, and the orc family followed Duamé over to the lodgings desk, where the dwarf argued with the clerk at the counter. The clerk didn't say a word. Rather the bored-looking heavyset man simply pointed at the sign that said 'all prices final'.

"That's highway robbery that is! An' this IS a highway!" Duamé yelled.

Leon looked at the price listed on the sign, and saw it wasn't that bad. He wondered how many people opted to sleep outside. Looking at the clerk, Leon asked, "Good sir, how many rooms are available?"

His gaze shifted from the dwarf, and he looked at Leon and held up the finger he was pointing with. One room. Leon looked at the dwarf and then Miala. With a sigh, he withdrew the two gold needed for the room from his pack, and slapped it on the table before saying, "I'd like to purchase a room for the family behind me."

Duamé was (for once) rendered speechless, and Miala hid a smirk behind her hand. The clerk snatched the gold, and Lorog looked at the key Leon handed him in wonder. The orc shook his hand and profusely thanked him before they left for their lodging. Leon shrugged under the weight of the others' stares, as the clerk quickly produced a sign saying 'All Sold Out'.

Duamé slapped Leon's arm lightly. "Why'd ya go an' do that?"

"You tell me. Why did you do that to me? To us? And to that herald?" Leon retorted.

"Ha-ha. That was good. Tha best jokes are tha ones with a little truth in em, boyo."

"What we did wasn't a joke, Duamé." Miala objected.

"Nope. He's tha joke." Duamé retaliated, hooking his thumb in Leon's direction.

"That's not a reason." Leon pointed out.

"Well, that's all yer gettin' fer now!" Duamé shouted.

Kelleren woofed loudly, as if he intended to stop them from fighting, and soon they had rented and set up a few tents along the side of the road. The group got a campfire going shortly before the sun set for the night. The spear light suddenly winked on, which resulted in more than a few people casting curious glances their way. After taking

195

note of all the onlookers Duamé shouted, "It's his nightlight! He's very insecure! Don't make fun o' him about it!"

As they settled down around the fire, Duamé stopped chuckling to himself when he noticed everyone staring at him. "Wot?" He shrugged.

Miala looked at Kelleren then back at Duamé, "Kelleren wants to know why you joke around so much to hide your pain."

Duamé's eyes went wide as saucers, and he looked at the dog as if he had spoken the words himself. His mouth wordlessly opened and closed a few times, before he stuttered a bit and emitted a heavy sigh. He reached into his pack and pulled out something that he handed to Miala. Kelleren sniffed at it and whined, before padding over to Duamé and laying his head on Duamé's leg. The dwarf scratched behind Kelleren's ears as he began to talk.

"I grew up in Masterwork Halls. I was happy, I knew me trade, an' I was one o' tha best dolomite'n smiths there. We didn't jus' make things there– we created art. We strived fer perfection. I was good at wot I did, but I didn't need ta make somethin' perfect. Cause I already had it."

"Her name was Rozella. I knew her since we were wee little kids, an' even then, we knew we were made fer each other. Course it helped our pa's were best pals too. Two o' tha three heads o' tha Craftin' Guild, they are. We were happy, an' got married. Married fer forty years. When I was sixty, she surprised me. Told me we were gonna have a wee little girl. We already had a name picked out in advance. Me little Esperella. Our little Hope-Star."

"An' then when tha time came fer her ta join our family…," Duamé teared up, "Me Rozella didn't survive childbirth."

Miala gasped and covered her mouth, "I'm so sorry Duamé!"

"We have a rule with dwarves. If yer spouse dies, ya gotta... ya gotta... be tha one ta make sure they don't come back." Duamé rocked back and forth, struggling to face his past, trying to get through retelling his personal nightmare. Leon honestly didn't know much about the dwarven culture. His father hadn't talked about them much, except to deride them. Of course, his public persona was that he was a man of all the people, but in private he vilified the dwarves. These thoughts brought Leon to a realization. He had never shared with Miala or Duamé that he used to be part of the Rhise family. He would have to do that soon.

"I... I couldn't do it. I couldn't kill her. Me pa had ta." Duamé hung his head in shame. For a long time nobody spoke, they allowed Duamé the quiet as he kept scratching behind Kelleren's ears. Eventually, he continued. "Our families kinda grew apart after that. I still had me work though, an' I had me Esperella. We did wot we could, till when me girl was five, an' she got... sick."

"I prayed ta every mineral we had– cause that's wot we dwarves worship boyo," Duamé seethed, eyeing Leon. "Wot we can see, wot we can touch. I went through all o' them, an' it didn't do a flintin' thing! Me little girl was gone. Luckily, young uns don't turn undead no matter wot race ya are. Nobody knows why. Didn't stop me from goin' mad fer a bit. Lost me wife. Lost me girl. Lost me smithy. Lost me friends an' family, an' respect." Duamé's voice was a rough hollow whisper at this point. A hollow man who had everything he loved ripped from him. "So I wandered fer a bit an' settled in Everbright, content ta just exist till I didn't anymore."

He stabbed an accusing finger at Leon as he stood, "I don't want any part of yer 'Adonai' nonsense. Cause no

'God o' Love' would do that ta a man. Instead, I'm just gonna crack me jokes, an' follow where ya go, cause fer now I found that cavin' in undead heads helps me feel better. At least fer a little bit." With that, Duamé left the campfire and stormed into his tent, whipping the flap shut behind him.

Miala and Leon looked at each other as Miala sniffed and wiped tears from her eyes. She seemed to be looking for Leon to say something, anything, that could help her make sense of the story their companion had just shared. Searching for any sort of rebuttal to Duamé's grievances.

In truth, Leon was every bit as confused and heartbroken as she was and didn't know what to make of it himself. *What kind of answer could there be to something like this?* When she received no response from him, she quietly got up, handed Leon the object Duamé had given her, and headed to bed with Kelleren in tow.

As Leon looked down a lump rose in his throat– in his hands was the most beautifully crafted little doll he had ever seen.

After he deposited the doll in Duamé's tent, his concern and confusion about the dwarf's past led him to go to bed himself. Once in his own tent he stewed on the confusion he felt about Duamé's past, about the false reports of the herald, and why Adonai allowed it all to happen. Somewhere in the midst of all that confusion Leon drifted off to sleep– where he dreamt that he was immersed in a deep fog.

Nothing could be seen, not even the usual pinprick of light in the distance. There were no waves of light to wash over him, no voices in the etherealness– just a thick grey fog that swirled all around. He walked and then ran through it, in every different direction, as he looked for guidance. Clearly lost, Leon looked for any sort of marker, but everything looked the same. His patience already tried and worn, he came to a stop. Leon cried out, his voice echoing in the nothingness all around him.

"What do I say to them? What am I supposed to do? What do you want from me?" He screamed.

When his voice stopped echoing, another answered.

"Trust in Adonai with all your heart and lean not on your own understanding. In all your ways submit to him, and he will make your paths straight."

The voice of Lochemetel had answered in the fog, but Leon could not see her. He knew that running around and screaming did not seem to work, so instead he closed his eyes in the dream and breathed deeply. His thoughts kept going back to Duamé, his tragic tale, and why Adonai would allow such things to happen. As if hearing his thoughts, Lochemetel answered, *"His ways are not our ways. His thoughts are not our thoughts."*

Leon was baffled by the cryptic answers. "What? What does that even mean?"

"You must have faith, Leon."

Faith? There was that word again. *What did 'faith' have to do with anything?*

"You can walk by faith even when you cannot see."

Walk by faith? Leon listened to the voice and breathed deeply again as he attempted to ease his anxiety. He knew that he couldn't see in the fog, so instead he chose to calmly walk forward, trusting that may be the correct direction to go. When that led nowhere after a while, he stopped and wished he had the light of the spear to help cut through this fog.

In an instant, Leon felt the familiar weight of the spear in his right hand. He looked and saw the light emanating from the blade in front of him, heavy fog still surrounding it. Leon raised it and pointed it in front of him, trusting it to help guide him. He slowly turned in a circle until he felt a gentle pull– much like when he needed to address the people of Everbright. Leon stepped, moving forward, and the spearlight flashed briefly.

A moment later, a wave of light from the distant unseen glowing orb washed over Leon and dissolved the fog in its wake. It was a good thing too, for had he taken a few more steps forward, he would have fallen into the first land detail that he had ever seen in the grey expanse– a crevasse that divided the land. It stretched in front of him from horizon to horizon, and was about five feet across to the other side. He peeked over the edge and saw that the fog had been burnt away a good distance down into the depths of the deep gap. Still, this was a crevasse that Leon felt he could easily leap over with some momentum. Retracing his steps, he turned around and sprinted towards it, before leaping over the deep opening. When he landed, he immediately heard Lochemetel again.

"You must learn."

Her voice came from behind him causing him to turn. Leon saw the armored angel on the other side where he had just been. She held out her hand, and the golden spear that she was all too proficient with, coalesced in it. Leon prepared to jump back over to spar with her, but before he moved forward the crevasse began to change.

With another wave of light that came from the point in the distance, the far side of the crevasse of the shifted away. Lochemetel was no longer five feet away but twenty. The fog continued to churn in what was now a canyon between them, and the angel lifted her other hand and beckoned Leon forward.

"It's… impossible!" Leon exclaimed.

"With man this is impossible. With God, all things are possible."

Leon couldn't fathom it. He had never seen anyone capable of jumping that far. *Even ogres couldn't jump that far! Maybe a giant could?*

With God, I could too?

"Our God gives you everything that you need, makes you everything you're meant to be."

Everything I need? Trust in God? Trust in Adonai?

Leon knew he couldn't jump that far by himself, but he could do anything with God? It made sense logically to Leon because if Adonai was the God of everything, he could certainly help Leon make the jump. After all, if he fell in the crevasse, he would wake up, right?

That's what happens in dreams. He reassured himself.

He jogged back several feet, and turned to run and make the jump, but stopped short. Hovering before him was his necklace– the silver chain with the small Levigem pendant at the bottom. Grasping it, Leon tried to comprehend what was occurring.

Levigems helped keep the airships afloat. *Could a tiny Levigem do that for a person?* He didn't know how they worked when installed in an airship, that particular part of the process had never been explained to him. Leon didn't understand it, but he was apparently not supposed to rely on his own understanding. He was just supposed to have faith that Adonai would make it happen.

Grasping the red ten-sided gem, Leon closed his eyes and mentally prepared himself. *Trust in God. His ways are not our ways, lean not on my own understanding, he has given me everything I need.*

Leon opened his eyes, and with one hand on the spear and the other on the Levigem, he ran at a full sprint towards the gap. At the last moment, he planted his last step and slammed the Levigem into the spear. He felt a small jolt as the gem connected to the elvenwood and channeled the energy stored within.

Leon jumped with the full expectation that Adonai would help him get to the other side. Gravity felt as though it was not quite as strict with him as it normally was, and time seemed to slow to a crawl as he hung above the foggy, expansive, void below him. While jumping, Leon heard Lochemetel's musical voice as if she had whispered into his ear.

"Now faith is the assurance of things hoped for, the conviction of things not seen."

As he reached the apex of his jump an image of walking in the forest with Duamé and Miala flashed in front of him, along with the sound of his own words being repeated back to him, "It has been my experience, good friend Duamé, that the absence of knowing about something doesn't mean it's not there."

Something mentally shifted for Leon as he suddenly understood what the angel was trying to teach him. He landed on the other side with his leg muscles flexed, allowing him to absorb the impact and roll to his feet, facing the angel. He was sure that the face of Lochemetel was smiling behind the blur of her helm.

"You are learning."

"I have a good teacher." Leon replied.

"We shall see."

With that, Lochemetel launched herself at him, spear extended, and they began to spar again. Leon knew she was fast, knew she had thousands of years' worth of experience in fighting battles. She wasn't just a warrior, but was a weapon of war herself. As if battling was her very purpose, her art. The spear was a paintbrush, and the battle was her canvas. The difference in their sparring this time was the mere fact that Leon had faith. He had faith that he could hold his own against her.

This was evidenced by him lasting just a few more seconds before Lochemetel disarmed and tripped him, slamming him to the ground.

"Many are the plans in the mind of a man, but it is the purpose of Adonai that will stand."

On the ground, hearing the angel's words and understanding their meaning, Leon started to laugh. Somehow, knowing that angels possessed a sense of humor made him feel a lot better than he had when the dream began. He may not have the answer to the dwarf's tragic tale yet, but he did have faith that Adonai was not done.

Leon got up, grabbed the spear, and continued his lesson.

Chapter 14: The Gates

The group awakened the next morning, and was slow to break camp. Miala and Leon kept casting furtive glances in Duamé's direction, unable to stay focused on the task at hand. It was evident that they both were on edge from the prior evening– still thinking to themselves about the dwarf's self-professed past.

Duamé was the first to break the silence that lingered between them all, "Alright now, don't ya go makin' all this awkward just cause I spilled me guts out yesterday. Who's up fer some bacon, eh?" Kelleren immediately became excited, which brought smiles to everyone's faces, and helped to lighten the mood somewhat.

After they finished eating breakfast, they continued their trek towards Agaprya. They encountered occasional groups of people also travelling along the rode, who walked (or rode) at different speeds, and even saw a passing airship or two high overhead. As they progressed farther along more farmland became visible, and a greater number of creatures from all walks of life began heading in the same direction. Everyone was excited, knowing that they would see civilization soon.

After having walked for days, Miala finally broke down and paid for a small carriage to carry them the rest of the way. "My feet are tired, and my legs are tired, and you all should be grateful that I'm tired!" She reasoned. She sat back and relaxed in her seat– allowing the enterprising young gnome with two painted horses she hired to pull them along at a brisk pace.

The rolling hills and farmland culminated in the city of Agaprya coming into view in the distance. They bounced along the cobblestone path at a slightly faster pace than a small caravan of refugees, whom Leon surmised had hired a guide to show them the way and escort them to the city.

The guide, a small, portly man, rode an equally portly mare. Feeling the need to be heard, he bellowed what sounded to be a prepared speech to both the refugees and anyone else who was close enough to hear his booming voice. "The great city of Agaprya, capital of Xaelon, sits at the edge of lake Xael, with the river flowing through it. Its walls and bridges are centuries old and reinforced every few years to withstand whatever horde may eventually come. Agaprya is then further divided into several quarters and districts, which means newcomers such as yourselves, can easily be lost in the grand city. I can assure you for a modest sum, I can direct you inside the city exactly where you desire to go." The small guide then smiled at the prospective customers that flocked towards him, ready to be bilked out of their last remaining coinage.

A shantytown of ramshackle buildings exploded out from the city, showing them that it was indeed true that some were denied entry. Upon closer inspection, these buildings were made almost entirely out of scraps of wood or cloth. Broken down carts with tarps or wagon trains that did not make it all the way provided whatever shelter it could from the elements, as people of all races and ages occupied the tight quarters when they were not out looking for work or waiting to get better.

Some could not even work for a living at the nearby sprawling farmland. Old and infirm, some missing limbs or fingers, others with wracking coughs or sniffles. They lined the road asking for coins or food. Travelers on the road seemed to shy away from them, not wanting to catch whatever they had.

Seeing their plight and remembering dark times once more, Leon showered some copper crows outside the carriage in some groups. Duamé scoffed at the action and shook his head until one point where a small group of beggar children was huddled together. The clink of coins falling out of the carriage again caught Leon's attention. Since he and Miala were on the other side of the vehicle, Leon and Miala shared a smile as Duamé clumsily put away his gold bag. "Shut it! I got me a new plan instead o' me 'travellin' smithy'. I'll make it back easily."

They moved ever closer to the gates, becoming more keenly aware that there was a line outside the city. While the portcullis was open to the interior, a decent-sized military presence and checkpoint seemed to have been built just before the entrance to Agaprya. Thanking the carriage driver, they exited and approached. Families and caravans were waiting in the long but moderately moving line, and as they took their place in it, a small, fast-moving mail carrier flew overhead. The tiny airship craft maneuvered quickly over the high stone walls and out of sight, as Miala commented. "If only we could move as fast as that."

"Think I'd get sick flyin' in tha air." Duamé replied.

"Some people do, but they get used to it fairly quickly." Leon added instead.

Duamé rolled his eyes and walked past a sign advising to 'Secure all belongings including all weapons.' and to, 'Please

be prepared to declare any magical items before entering.'
While he strapped the spear to his back, Leon wondered
how he was going to explain a weapon that turned undead
to salt and shined in the dark.

They patiently waited for their turns, and as they got
closer, Leon agreed with the guide that got stuck in line
behind them: The walls were indeed getting more layers
built onto them since the last time he was here. Construction
crews were busily working on top of the wall around the
portcullis and turrets. Above the gates flew the emblem of
Xaelon: The black tower of Last Bastion on a light blue
background waved in the gentle wind on the giant flag set
above the entrance.

The line moved further up as an official asked if all three
of them were in a group, and when acknowledged, waved
them to an open queue. A young, pimply, thin soldier was
dressed in the standard chainmail with a sword belted at the
waist. Manning a small podium, he tried to look as officious
as possible. At his side stood two other older soldiers, both
more menacing looking with tabards showing the Xaelon
emblem.

Duamé strode forward first to the young soldier who,
instead of guarding the gates with his sword, pulled out a
sheaf of parchment and quill as the two other guards
stepped in front of Duamé to block his way. The high nasal
voice of the soldier was already enough to crack a smile on
Duamé's face. "Please answer the following questions as
truthfully as you can. What is your name?"

"Nosp Ichor." Duamé said immediately.

The soldier started writing as Duamé winked at the two
other soldiers, who smiled at each other. The young man
continued his questions. "What is your chosen profession?"

"I'm a hairdresser."

The soldier asking the questions scribbled over the answers, and started over again. Pulling out a small milky white cube from his podium, he continued, "Let's try this again, please. What is your real name?"

As soon as the cube was visible, Miala turned to grab Leon's arm. Surprised at the physical contact, Leon looked and saw her eyes wide as she whispered, "They can't know who I am."

"Why? What's wrong?" Leon asked, concerned.

She hesitated for a moment before leaning as close as she dared to Leon and whispered again. "I didn't know they would have a Discerner here! If I am questioned I will be arrested, Leon!"

Discerner cubes were rare, ancient, and couldn't even be replicated. A forgotten form of magic-powered the artifacts, which clarified truth from lies as the name suggested.

Leon racked his brain as to their options and answers he got from Miala.

What would Miala be arrested for?

She was a hermitess.

She did not want to be known.

She was a powerful enough mancer to have a companion.

She was indeed pretty when she stepped out of the cabin…

Stop! She said don't get interested! Focus!

Hints about her knowledge and background fit together in his head as Leon glanced at the guards who were intently watching Duamé spin humorous lie after lie, turning the cube red again and again.

Leon dared to lean closer to her, as one might with a betrothed or spouse, and near her ear asked in a low voice, "Are… are you a deserter?"

Returning to a comfortable distance from her, Leon clearly saw her eyes misting up as she nodded imperceptibly. Leon shifted into a crisis mentality as he was trying to figure a way out of this. Remembering Prince Gelan's lessons in tactics, Leon had three basic options: Run, Fight or Hide. *We can't run or fight...*

The questioner at the gate got frustrated enough at Duamé's antics that he yelled, "Sir, any more infractions, and you can just go to the back of the line!" Getting a new parchment after balling up what appeared to be a completely scribbled out form, he said testily, "Now what is your real full name?"

"Duamé Onyxwill o' Masterwork Halls."

The cube, after a moment, turned a bright green color. Satisfied, the soldier continued. "What is your chosen profession?"

"Mastersmith o' tha eighth degree."

Apparently, Duamé had trouble with the next question as well because the soldier nasally asked, "And are there any magical ITEMS that you have to declare?"

"Nope."

Nodding and satisfied, he asked one last question, "And are you to your knowledge, carrying any sickness, illness, and or disease into Agaprya?"

After thinking about it, Duamé said, "I'm sick o' yer questions, but no."

After a tense moment, the cube turned green again, and the soldier sighed as he waved Duamé through. Duamé smiled as the two other guards chuckled as they stepped aside for him. Near the portcullis gate, Duamé turned and waited for the others.

"Alright, next! You there miss, step forward please."
What can we do?
What can we say?

Leon was racking his brain as Miala looked back at him worriedly, with Kelleren close behind. To make matters worse, a higher-ranking soldier wandered closer after hearing the shouting match between Duamé and the gate questioner. Seeing the insignia and dress on the ranking officer, the grizzled man looked to be a captain and was probably in command of the gate crew itself.

Wait... rank?

"Miss, please state your legal full name." the questioner said.

Holding her arm insecurely, Miala spoke in a soft tone and mumbled.

"What was that miss? I couldn't hear you."

"Miala." she said simply.

The cube on the podium turned a bright yellow as the gate captain stepped closer and next to the questioner. Looking on, Duamé frowned at the development. Leon calculated and weighed the risks of his sudden, desperate idea.

"Miss Miala, you were asked a direct and simple question. Evasiveness will not be tolerated here. What is your legal full name?" The gate captain said sternly. This was a man who was used to being obeyed. A man who exercised his authority over others and more than likely enjoyed that power.

Leon grew up with people like that. Hoping that this would work and asking Adonai in a silent prayer to please let this work, Leon took a few breaths to channel his inner snob and strode forward next to Miala just as she was about to answer.

Taking on a superior air, "What seems to be the problem here commander?" Leon asked.

"Sir, you can wait your turn!" The captain said sternly.

"I will not have you harassing me, or the people in my employ. We will be on our way inside now." Leon hooked his arm around a shocked Miala and walked forward towards Duamé. They were quickly stopped by the two older guards holding their swords at their hips but not drawing them yet. The gate captain huffed and placed a firm hand on Leon's shoulder. "Boy, I'm not going to tell you again. Stay back and wait your turn, or I will place you all under arrest!"

That was the phrase that Leon was hoping someone would say. Leon could tell that Miala was trembling as he shrugged off the gate captain's hand, turned, and said as loudly as he could, "How DARE you! Do you know who I am?"

With that, Leon let go of Miala to pull out the silver chain and the small Levigem pendant, the symbol of being a member of the Rhise family, and shook it vigorously in front of the captain.

The gate captain's eyes seemed to want to pop out of his head as he looked around, frantically trying to give orders to reestablish the authority he had that was suddenly questioned.

"You two, let go of your swords." Turning to the gate questioner, "Carl, start taking the next people." He then turned to Leon, looking at him like he was a live snake. "Um, come with me please, sir."

Leon glanced at Miala, who also stared back, and nodded for her to come along. She and Kelleren followed meekly, which Leon thought was the wrong attitude to portray. Thinking quickly, he turned to her more noticeably and said sternly, "Come along, you are supposed to be a bodyguard right? Guard the body!" Gesturing at himself.

They followed the gate captain up to where Duamé stood, who stared at Leon in what looked to be open hatred.

Leon chided himself on not thinking of this repercussion and reminded himself that he would have to apologize to the dwarf should this work. Meanwhile, Duamé's teeth ground together in a snarl, and his fists clenched and unclenched. Leon certainly understood his reaction: His father Lucien had pretty much-ostracized dwarves from the kingdom courts and stopped the flow of work and income long ago. Dwarves live longer than humans and have long memories, though.

Leon was trying to convey to the dwarf to act casual without saying anything behind the commander's back until the gate captain whirled around and placed his hands on his hips. Expelling a breath, "Alright, what is the meaning of this?"

Leon tried to stay in character, "Do you know who I am?"

The commander averted his eyes and stated. "You're Laric Rhise, son of Lucien Rhise. What are you doing walking through the gates with these… individuals?"

Leon waited silently, not saying anything, just staring at the captain.

The captain, after a few seconds, returned to his eye-popping panic as he suddenly remembered, "My lord."

Leon gave as fake of a smile as he could as he patiently explained, "I was traveling to Agaprya to secure a legitimate business deal, one that must be done in secret! These are my bodyguards." Leon gestured to Duamé and Miala. "You, Sargent, almost announced my presence to the world, and every nearby merchant looking to capitalize on my business venture!"

"I am a Captain, my lord." The captain clarified with gritted teeth.

Leon scoffed, "Not for long if I have my way! What is your name, soldier? Hmm?"

"Gravaisé Orelos of Agaprya, my lord. If I may ask, my lord, why are you dressed in a naval uniform? Why are you walking instead of flying or riding here?" The captain asked shrewdly.

Leon spoke slowly, enunciating every word, "Because the uniform is a disguise. A carriage or airship would be noticed. They would be watched for by my competitors. The idea, soon-to-be-Sargent Orelos, is SECRECY. Now do I need to talk to your superior, or are you going to let us obviously perfectly healthy people through?"

The captain's face registered defeat, knowing that he was outranked, outflanked, and tactically outmaneuvered. With a heavy, stress-laced, sigh, he bowed shortly to Leon. "My apologies, my lord. I hope your business deal is a success."

Leon smirked, "Thank you, captain, now by all means, please secure our city." Then dismissed the captain with a wave. Without looking back, Leon walked through the gate into Agaprya, with his nose held in the air, until the captain was well out of sight.

Heart pounding with adrenaline, Leon took the opportunity to duck into one of the first alleys he came across– he was having trouble catching his breath from the level of stress and anxiety he felt over what he had just done. He leaned against the stone wall, amazed that his ruse had even worked, and glanced at the alley entrance where he saw Miala, Kelleren, and Duamé just standing there, watching him.

"Hey guys, I'm glad that worked. Anyway Duamé, I'm sor–"

The dwarf ran up to Leon and punched him in the gut, causing him to double over, with the wind knocked out of him. Leon knew Duamé was strong, but the pain he felt was like being kicked in the stomach by a horse– a horse that made its living kicking people in the stomach. Coughing and trying to suck in air, Leon squirmed on the alley floor while Duamé stood over him.

"Yer a flintin' Rhise. I knew sumthin' was off about ya."

"Duamé!" Miala chided as Kelleren dashed over to get in between him and the writhing Leon.

"Ya don't know wot his family has done lass! Dwarves fell on hard times before, but never like this. Not from these racist–"

"It wasn't… It wasn't me!" Leon gasped. He was finally able to take a breath.

Duamé was beyond talking to, stuttering and shaking with fury. "I was… I thought we were… I… I shared BACON with ya!" He finally shouted.

Miala strode over to stand between them both as Leon recovered. The truth was, Leon felt like he deserved it. He felt guilty about not telling them his past when Duamé had been so open with his. The pain roiled his stomach as he scrambled up the dirty alley wall. Trying to keep his breakfast (and bile) down, Leon croaked, "I need to explain. Please let me explain."

Looking at them and seeing all of their various states of disbelief and skepticism, Leon's physical pain began to feel paltry compared to the disappointment from those he shared his recent journey with.

"Please." He pled.

Sneering, Duamé said, "Tch. Ya get one response. Make it count, rich boy."

"I'm not rich. I was disowned by my father Lucien." Leon began.

Duamé started to shout again, "THAT'S yer respon… wait wot?"

Miala held up a hand, "Maybe you should explain, Leon."

214

There, in a dirty alley near the entrance of Agaprya, Leon told Miala, Duamé, and Kelleren about growing up in the abusive Rhise household. Leon talked about his sister Liara and his mother, Lady Rhise. He shared about how they were both good people, and how the household was marred by the presence of Lucien and the creepy Seneschal Silas.

"I came to Everbright the day after I was thrown out of my father's manor. I was disowned at my sister's engagement party for objecting to an arranged marriage. To a man twice as old as her, that she doesn't even know or love, and for a simple business merger no less!" Leon continued.

"Ugh. That's disgusting!" Miala looked revolted.

Duamé just stared, arms crossed, frown on his face.

"When I left, I grabbed this rusty old spear that had been hanging on the wall. I was denied a horse by my older brother Laric, and walked to Everbright. You know the rest." Looking at them both, he made his case, "I am truly sorry I did not tell you both earlier. I had to think of something quick to help Miala at the gate, and that was the only option I could think of that had any chance of working."

"Duamé, I swear to you that I have no ill feelings, and bear no ill will, towards you or any dwarf. My 'former' father is the one who bears his grievances– and I want nothing further to do with him." Leon finished.

Duamé's eyes squinted at him, as he tried to see if Leon was being deceptive or not. After a tense moment, he pointed at Leon and said, "Ya wait right there lad. An' don't move!" With that, he gestured for Miala and Kelleren to join him close to the entrance of the alley. They huddled with their backs to Leon, and seemed to be conversing in order to decide his fate.

215

For the first time since the *Dawnfire*, Leon had felt like he was part of a group, part of a crew again. He didn't want it to end, and didn't want to be alone. Silently, he asked Adonai to please let him stay with them. Then, he chided himself for always seeming to come to Adonai in a crisis, but not during other times.

A spark of hope ignited when Miala put a telltale hand in front of her mouth, to cover any indication of her smile. Duamé soon turned back around and strode towards Leon, waving a small hammer in his hand threateningly. "Alright, boyo, listen up."

The nausea that Leon had felt, was suddenly replaced by the feeling of his heart leaping up his throat.

Duamé continued, "That father o' yers is a right Pyrite!"

"Uh, a pirate?"

"No, PYRITE! It's a mineral, boyo. Fool's gold, now pay attention."

Duamé waved the hammer around, gesticulating. "I can understand ye not bein' a racist. Ya ain't Lucien Rhise, an' if I learned one thing on tha surface outside Masterwork, all humans ain't tha same. Ya had our backs up until this point, an' I haven't seen that change yet. So if ya can admit ta me that ya really are a 'meat shield'," Duamé paused for what Leon guessed was theatrics. "Then I guess ya can stick with us."

Leon smiled, relieved as he said questioningly, "I'm a meat shield?"

Duamé narrowed his eyes, "Are ya askin' me, or tellin' me?"

"I'm a meat shield." Leon restated.

"An' don't ya ferget it!" Duamé slung the hammer back on his belt and clapped Leon on the shoulder. Miala laughed a soft peal of musical laughter then said, "Kelleren is hungry. Shall we look for a place to eat lunch?"

"An' yer buying, meat shield!"
Leon grinned from ear to ear as he agreed.

Map of Agaprya

Capital of Xaelon

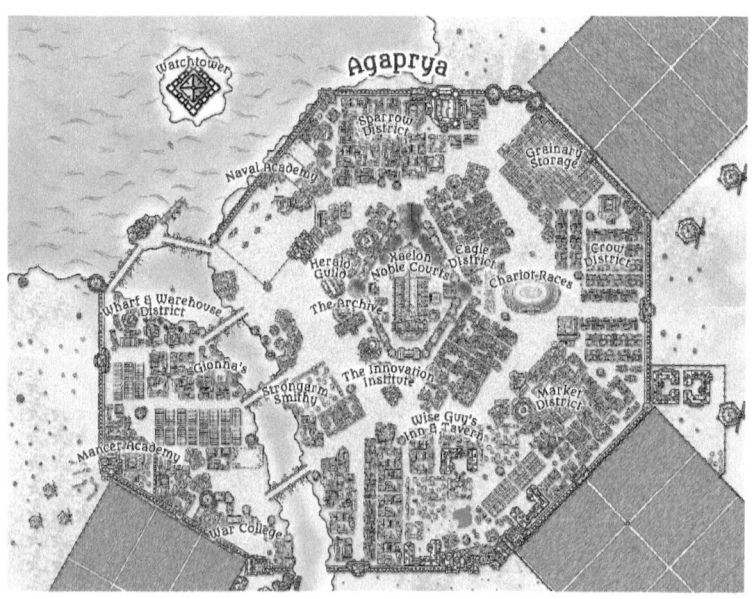

Chapter 15: The Genius

Leon had always thought the city of Agaprya was a tad oversized but simple to navigate if you follow the signs. Entering the city from the southern entrance, they were closest to the market district. There was a clear distinction of class between the established stone buildings which catered to the wealthy, and the market and general grocery stalls where farmers and their families sold produce. Asking around, the group found that the general consensus was that the best food and lodging in the city was a place called Wise Guy's Inn and Tavern, on the northern border of the market district.

Kelleren ran around excitedly, he seemed to want to investigate every square inch of the city they walked through. Miala smiled and let him have his fun, only needing to mentally admonish him a few times for running off too far. It was hard for Leon to not be excited as well. Something about being in the big city with its bustle of activity and the feeling of civilization invigorated him. About the only thing that disinterested him was the politics of the highborn in the city center. That was where the lords and ladies governed the kingdom and held their parties, while the world around them died– one person at a time.

The other place Leon had no inclination to visit was the Wharf area. Dark memories (and even darker actions) from a time spent there, pierced through his misery induced haze to haunt him. While he couldn't recall most of what had occurred before returning to the manor, what he did remember drove shameful spikes through his conscience. Shivers raced down Leon's spine as he danced around the edges of the thoughts that had plagued him many times before. Shaking his head, he looked to his traveling companions and pulled himself out of his reverie.

The cobbled streets had few people on them at this time, as it was just after lunch, and most citizens were already back at work to finish the latter half of their day. That being said, the group did pass several soldiers on patrol, the occasional young man or woman who had tried to skip school (only to be caught by those soldiers), and the random alley cat or dog.

As they reached the first major intersection in the enormous city, they were amazed at the view of the city that opened up before them. There were many small to medium-sized homes crammed closely together to save space, most boasting beautiful tile roofs, crafted from the red clay that was taken from the lake the city sat on. Leon recalled how breathtaking they appeared when the sunlight hit them at just the right angle.

To their left was a gently sloping road that led down to the city's southernmost bridge that crossed the river. Miala warned that they should stay well away from the Mancer Academy, located on the other side of that bridge. The Academy stood out from all of the other buildings that surrounded it. It had multiple spires of different heights, which formed tight circles around the compound–

effectively blocking it off from the public. Since mancers rarely went out of the compound, unless serving in the military, she said it was unlikely that they would run into any unless by a fluke happenstance.

Walking a little further towards the center of the city, Leon pointed out the Naval Academy in the distance. The airborne military trained as many soldiers, as fast as they could– in order to fill their flying ships. It looked as if they had a few new ships in the landing yards, waiting for fresh crew members. Leon counted two frigates, but no destroyer class vessels or replacement flagship.

Supplies must be getting scarce… Or Lord Rhise must be waiting for another payout.

Duamé pointed out several different smithies scattered throughout the city, evidenced by their telltale smoke. He rubbed his hands together and cackled at the inferior human forges, "We are gonna make a fortune I tell ya! A fortune!"

"How?" Miala asked, her interest still piqued at the idea of helping the dwarf create things with her magic.

"By findin' tha right one."

Kelleren didn't have anything to point out to them in the city. Instead, Miala promptly informed them on Kelleren's behalf, "He is so incredibly hungry, he thinks he could die!"

"Isn't that a bit of an exaggeration? He ate not too long ago right?" Looking at Kelleren, Leon couldn't help but be a bit concerned– the dog seemed to be moaning and whining a bit more than usual.

"Oh, don't let him fool you. Dogs can, in fact, lie and exaggerate. He's fine, I assure you. We can wait till lunch, right?" She asked her dog. After a few seconds, she laughed at him and scratched under his chin.

"Wot? Dogs can lie?" Duamé stared at Kelleren, astonished.

"Of course! Usually when they want something from you. Like food."

Duamé started to chuckle, and patted Kelleren's head, "Good boy! Ya lie like a dog on a rug, don't ya Kelleren?"

After groaning at his antics, they continued to look for the tavern.

Once they finally decided to ask for directions, they came across a fairly large and ornate building on their left, near the center of the city. As they were passing it and Miala was commenting on its beauty, an unexpected ruckus occurred. The double front doors banged open with enough force to actually snap one of the top brass hinges! An oversized, muscular, ogre held a small, squirming, figure tightly in its grip. The ogre quickly opened its hand and down plopped a gnome! Then, with a sense of urgency, the ogre ducked back in the building and shut the heavy, but now broken, doors.

The gnome turned out to be an older woman with thick glasses that had several lenses sticking out all around it– making her look as though she had many eyes, if viewed from the right angle. She had bright purple and grey hair tied back into two ponytails, and looked to be a head and a half smaller than Duamé. The gnome sprang up from the ground with a litheness that belied her apparent age, and quickly walked up to the closed doors with her metallic cane. Then, using her cane, she began to rap on them repeatedly– shouting in an elderly, high pitched voice.

"You can't fire me! I'm smarter than the whole lot of you! Blogo, you let me back in this instant!"

A deep baritone rumbled from behind the door, "Sorry miss Gionna. Boss say 'final straw'. Blogo miss you."

She stopped rapping her cane and screamed, "He wouldn't even be there if it weren't for me! None of you would be there!" When there was no response from inside,

222

she yelled again, "Well, you can't fire me because I QUIT! Just TRY to live without me!"

She brandished her cane like a club, and whacked the door one final time before turning away. She saw them watching and gave an imperious grunt, before she walked down the street, and away from their speechless group.

"Um, okay. That was weird." Miala said.

Leon was awestruck. Not just from the shock of seeing an unfortunate lady lose her job, but he could swear that she was someone he had heard of before. Before he could say anything, Duamé spoke in a low voice, "I think that's Gionna Gærheart!"

Leon's head jerked to look at Duamé in shock, "I thought so too! You know who she is?"

"Are ya kiddin' lad? She's a legend at Masterwork Halls!"

Leon smiled at the dwarf– the same one who had knocked the wind out of him earlier in that very day, "Why don't we find out for sure?"

Duamé returned his grin, "Ya, why don't we?"

"EXCUSE ME!" Miala said, perturbed at being left out. "Who is Gionna Gearheart?"

"It's pronounced Gærheart!" Leon and Duamé chorused. They chuckled together as Miala glared at them and stamped her foot in irritation.

"Okay guys. You've had your fun. Seriously, who is she?" She asked again.

Duamé looked to see if she was still visibly walking down the street, while Leon explained, "To put it simply? She invented airships."

Which was only the most notable of her achievements. Over a century old and not slowing down, Gionna had solved the problem of crumbling naval ships that kept getting ripped apart by sea monsters– both alive and undead. Combining mined Levigems with those ships, she created and designed a brand new and highly effective way to deal with the undead.

When paired with the advances in projectile and cannon warfare (which she also had a hand in), the hordes could be dealt with from a distance. Of course, there were some drawbacks and new dangers as a result, but Xaelon would have fallen long ago if it hadn't been for the inventor currently walking away from them.

"I'm gonna see if she wants ta join us fer lunch!" Duamé grinned, before he hurried down the road after her.

Leon shrugged at Miala, then walked around her and Kelleren and suddenly took off after Duamé.

"SERIOUSLY?" Miala yelled, before she huffed and stomped off after them.

It actually required Miala explaining to the elderly gnome that the men were just excited to meet her, before she took her celebrity status in stride and accepted their offer to take her to lunch– on the condition that the boys wouldn't ask for her autograph anymore.

Kelleren smelled the Wise Guy's Tavern and Inn first, and he suddenly raced off down the road. Soon Leon and the others caught a whiff of the same sweet scent mixed with burning wood that had triggered the dog. Everyone's mouths watered and their stomachs grumbled. Their pace subconsciously quickened to follow Kelleren and arrive at the source of the scent.

The Tavern and Inn was a three-story building that, even though the lunchtime hour was over, still boasted a fairly busy dining room. They passed signs outside the establishment that advertised 'package deals' and indoor plumbing in their rooms. When Miala saw that particular sign she exclaimed, "Ha! I'll thank your Adonai for that!"

224

The group entered the building and was met in the lobby by a slightly older man, dressed in a gentlemen's outfit, with short dark hair, and an impressively bushy, perfectly shaped, mustache. In a baritone voice, which rivaled that of the ogre who had thrown Gionna from her building, he recited, "Welcome to the Wise Guy's Tavern. A party of four, and a pet?"

"Yes, please!" Miala exclaimed.

"Well then, right this way miss!" The man beamed, as he pulled a parchment menu from behind his podium, and escorted them into the tavern. They were quickly seated at a round table in a corner. All around the room various signs decorated the walls, each of which told a different pun. Some were good, some were obscure, while others were quite groan-inducing. A quick-footed and also very well-dressed goblin scampered over. A badly pinned black toupee flapped on his head as he ran. He delivered a basket filled with different loaves of bread to the table, then ran back into the kitchen again.

"Is this your first time here?" The mustached man asked.

Everyone in the group nodded, except for Gionna. Seeing this the man immediately began to recommend different options and specials. Gionna interrupted him with a terse, "They're gonna want 'The Farm', Shadric."

"We are also goin' ta want two rooms, his an' hers, fer at least two weeks." Duamé requested.

"Of course, good sir. And welcome back Miss Gærheart." The man crooned.

Leon paid for everyone, as promised, and the man left to put in their food order and arrange their rooms.

"I already love this place." Duamé opined, as he reached for the bread and looked around at the various jokes on the walls.

Leon looked curiously at Gionna, who was silently observing each of them. This lady was supposedly a genius. And while they hadn't met under the best of circumstances, there were very few people that he knew with absolute certainty Lucien respected. One of those people was the elderly gnome who sat at their table, tapping the side of her glasses. Doing so seemed to rotate different lenses in front of the main set that were encased in the frames that rested on her face. Gionna smiled at Leon and remained silent, opting to watch them all take in the atmosphere of the Inn and Tavern.

Soon the well-groomed, mustached, man returned with two keys to third-floor rooms, and Leon handed one to Miala. Then the running goblin brought four glasses of water and a water bowl for Kelleren, without spilling a drop. It promptly dashed away again, as if it never stood still for a moment.

Lastly, two men in aprons, one with a well-trimmed goatee and the other with a full, oiled, beard, brought out a large platter and deposited it in the center of the table after moving the bread. Heaped on it were several cuts of beef, chicken, and pork, all covered in different sauces, which they discovered to be the source of the aroma that had pulled them here. Another few bowls of grains and mixed vegetables were placed around the table, before the servers bowed and departed– leaving them to eat their meal in peace.

The food was indescribably delicious. Everyone had their fill, with even Kelleren mentally saying so. While everyone ate Gionna gave the bone from her steak to Kelleren. "Alright, I think I'm ready to give it a go." She said, wiping her hands on a cloth napkin.

The group looked at her in confusion as she stood on the chair she had previously been seated on. She then pointed at

226

Duamé with her cane. Leon noted, upon closer inspection, the metal cane was definitely not a normal metal. It looked like it was made of silver.

"You, dwarf, are easy enough. You are muscular for your build, but the tools on your belt put you as part of the Crafting Guild. They are smithing tools rightly enough, and not only are they well worn, but they are of exceptional quality and make. You've been doing your profession for quite some time, and based on your apparent age I would put you at a seventh or eighth degree rank. It took me a little bit to try to figure out why you actually have your tools with you. Seeing how you all rented rooms, you are new here to Agaprya. Which means you are not employed at one of the local smithies. I would guess your origin to be Masterwork Halls, and your left hand has a bare spot on your ring finger with no hair on it, which means you were married. But no ring, means not anymore. Don't worry about it dearie, I've had four husbands, and it stinks, but life happens."

Duamé, who seemed to enjoy the food as much as Kelleren, dropped the chicken leg he had been about to bite into on his plate, and stared at the gnome with his mouth hanging open. The old woman then pointed her cane to Miala.

"You dearie took a little bit longer. You're obviously a mancer based on," Gionna tapped the bridge of her glasses, causing tiny gears to move some of the small lenses which surrounded her glasses, "The wand in your robe, and the four-dimensional pockets inside of it. The trouble was figuring out what type of mancer. Not aero, otherwise your companion would be a bird. Not aqua either. I was thinking Geomancer or even a more rare Empamancer. Then I saw," she tapped her glasses again, and a different lens swiveled into place, "Your body heat is higher than everyone else's

227

around you. That means Pyromancer. You are not in the field, and you don't look injured, so that means you are on a special assignment, or on the run. I sincerely hope it's the former. Your companion by the way dearie, is adorable."

Miala's expression grew panicked as Gionna swiveled her cane over to point at Leon. Seeing the cane end up close, Leon noticed the cane's tip was hinged to open somehow.

"You were very odd, my dear. Your demeanor and table mannerisms scream noble, and that spear on your back is radiating a serious aura. That artifact was either expensive to buy, or inherited. Which again, if inherited, means most likely a noble. A smaller magic aura is coming from that ring in your pocket. Then, of course, there is the Levigem around your neck, under your shirt. May I see it?"

Not speaking a word, and allowing Gionna to have her moment, Leon lifted the necklace off of himself and handed it to her. She kept tapping the bridge of her glasses until she found what looked to be a magnifying lens. "Control gem in the standard pentagonal trapezohedron shape, on a silver chain." She handed it back to the impressed Leon, who put it back under his shirt.

"Well, it's obvious you are a Rhise dearie, but which one? Not Lucien, you're too young, and I wouldn't have accepted your invitation to lunch. I would have leaned towards Laric, but the last piece of the puzzle was your armor. Standard Airship Naval. That means the other son. The one who five years ago left to join the military and is the supposed black sheep of the family. Leon Rhise."

Everyone at the table burst into applause as she nodded in acknowledgment and sat back down.

Once everyone stopped clapping she finished speaking, "You were also the hardest because you are supposed to be dead."

"Wait what?" Miala asked, aghast.

"Mm?" Duamé mumbled, food in his mouth.

Leon had heard Gionna described as 'observant' and 'detail-oriented', but this was incredible. No wonder Lord Rhise respected her! Stunned, he asked, "How did you know?"

Gionna smiled and patted Leon's hand, "Oh dearie, you can't believe everything you hear from the Heralds. Plus, the Innovation Institute has regular rosters of all the airships."

"The Innovation Institute?"

Gionna's eyes were magnified by her glasses as she narrowed them, looking in the direction of the building she was thrown from. "The blasted place that wouldn't recognize knowledge even if the Archive itself fell on it."

"Wait, why are ya supposed ta be dead?" Duamé asked, after he finished chewing.

Leon sighed as he looked at Duamé. Knowing that the dwarf shared his past earlier made Leon feel like he owed it to him to reciprocate– even if the whole series of events was incredibly painful to remember. Turning to Miala, he could tell she was interested– her green eyes were locked onto him, marked with a worried expression. Lastly, Leon glanced at Gionna, who gestured with her hand indicating for him to get on with the tale.

After a deep breath, Leon said, "Okay. Well, we are going to need some dessert for this."

As if on cue, the fancy-dressed goblin waiter rushed out of the kitchens to their table. A dessert menu flapped wildly in the air, along with his toupee.

Chapter 16: The Burden

The recent past…

The *Dawnfire* was in flames.

Leon had to slay one after another of his undead crew, his former friends. As he brought their bodies into the blaze of the wrecked ship one by one, he wished that the fire would also burn away the memory of what he had been forced to do to each of his fallen comrades. It would be easier if they could just burn away his memory of them altogether. Memories of camaraderie, friendship, the crash, and cutting his friends down with his own sword when they rose as undead, stubbornly remained with him. The stink of burning bodies combined with the thick smoke that billowed from the wreckage, filled his nostrils. It caused him to shed tears that he never thought would end– part of him didn't want them to.

Leon had insisted Prince Gelan sit and rest. Based on how bloody his impaled arm was, he knew that his friend shouldn't help move any bodies. Eventually, the final corpse had been placed inside the funeral pyre made from the *Dawnfire*. He stumbled over and collapsed on the ground next to the prince. Gelan held a long strip of cloth, a crew member's lost sleeve, and looked at Leon with an unspoken question.

"We need to take it out, or it'll fester." Leon surmised.

Prince Gelan, never one to lack authority, said, "I'll remove it. You will need to bandage it quickly."

Leon replied with, "Yes, Captain," almost as a reflex. Hauling himself up, he came over and looked at the wound. A foot-long splinter of jagged wood pierced straight through Prince Gelan's bicep. Dried blood had caked around it, but it oozed fresh if moved too much. Leon took both ends of the cloth wrapping, "I'm ready, sir." Prince Gelan grit his teeth together and looked straight into Leon's eyes as he grasped the shard with his good hand. He nodded three times, and on the third time ripped the wood out, screaming in agony.

Leon quickly covered the wound, which was bleeding profusely. He wrapped it tightly several times, before placing the knot directly over the wound opening itself. Gelan screamed again as the wrapping was pulled taught, and it seemed as though all of the pain, the loss that they had just experienced, was held in that cry.

When Leon was done he sat back down next to the prince, wiping his bloody hands on the grass. They stayed silent and just sat together for several minutes, then Leon mumbled, "What do we do now, sir?"

Gelan breathed deeply, and thought for a few moments before he said, "We head northeast back to Agaprya. Hopefully, we make it to a well-traveled road first. From there, maybe we will be lucky enough to come across another airship, or even a foot patrol." He grimaced as he tried to move his arm.

"Isn't Bulwark to the northwest, sir? It's a little farther, mind you, but it's more likely we could find a healer there, or medicine– for your arm. Perhaps we would even run into refugees on the way. Shouldn't we head there instead?"

After thinking about it for a few moments Prince Gelan shook his head, "No, no, that wouldn't be prudent. If we can get to Agaprya we can alert my father to what happened. Besides, the longer we're out and exposed, the more likely that we come across roving undead. Between the two of us, we are both good fighters, but my sword arm is useless now. We cannot fight off a horde by ourselves should we come across one."

"Speaking of hordes, we should probably leave here soon, sir," Leon suggested. "We don't know how many undead this fire will attract in the night. Or other creatures for that matter." He added, eyeing the dead dragon.

"Agreed. On your feet sailor." Price Gelan said, as he used his uninjured arm to pull Leon up from where he sat.

They took a minute to scrounge the wreckage for anything that might prove useful. Leon also took the opportunity to scramble up sections of the broken bow of the *Dawnfire*, and dislodge a fang from the dead dragon's open maw with his sword. Resuming the search, Leon and the Prince could only find a few supplies– Leon's tower shield, which was slightly bent, but still usable; both of their swords; a skin of water, luckily undamaged; and a single loaf of bread was all they could find for food. Staring at it and feeling the hopelessness of the situation, Leon handed the bread and the skin to Prince Gelan, "You must keep up your strength, sire."

Gelan's solemn reply was immediate, "We'll ration and share it as we should, Master Leon. Plus, we will hopefully be able to forage."

"Should we maybe cut meat from the dragon, sir? Even though…," Leon started.

Prince Gelan cut him off with a shake of his head and stern chide, "Toxic meat remember? Unless you want to die of dysentery, we should just leave it alone."

Neither of them moved as they watched the flagship, and their friends, burn. With a heavy sigh, Prince Gelan turned and walked away, "Come Master Leon, I feel that if I don't leave now I never will."

Tearing his eyes from the wreckage, Leon faced northeast and instead stared off into the distance, towards Agaprya. Whether they headed to Bulwark Fortress or Agaprya, they both knew they didn't have enough food or water for the journey– but neither said anything about it to the other.

That night they huddled together in a sparse grove of trees. The prince was unable to climb up a tree with his injured arm– not that it would have mattered, as there were no low hanging branches available for them. They shivered in the dark and kept close in order to share body heat. Their outlines were barely visible in the dim starlight. That didn't stop Leon from seeing the faces of his crewmates, and found himself unable to move past the guilt he felt for what he had been forced to do.

"Master Leon." Gelan said, attempting to pass the loaf of bread to him after taking a single small bite. Leon continued to just stare off into the distance, unresponsive. Shaking him a bit, Prince Gelan placed the loaf of bread in his lap and used his good hand to aim and flick.

"Ah!" Leon cried, as he rubbed at his earlobe. "What did you do that for, sir?"

Gelan chuckled a little and offered the loaf to Leon again– who took it, and also ate only one small bite before handing it back.

"Want to talk about it?" Gelan asked.

"I just can't get over seeing them, sir. I see them over and over again." Leon moaned.

Gelan rested his head against the elm tree they had propped themselves against. "No one should have to go through what you did. No one should have to go through any of this at all!" The older man sighed as he closed his eyes and breathed deeply, "We lived for a reason, Master Leon. I intend for both of us to make it back and continue to find that reason."

"I wish they had lived too, sir."

"They can." Prince Gelan said, tapping his head. "In here." Then he tapped his chest, "Here too. Do not ruminate on how they died. Or how you had to make sure they rested. Honor their memories with your thoughts and think about how they lived. Learn from them, and they will never really be gone."

Leon thought it was easy for the prince to say that, but then remembered Queen Dionne died of sickness soon after Gelan's sister was born. The prince had been nine and it was a year before Leon had even been born. "Do you miss her, sir? Your mother?" Leon asked.

"Every day Master Leon. I am sure that you'll miss our crew every day too. It hurts now. It'll hurt less later, I assure you. Get some sleep. We have a long walk ahead of us."

The morning brought rain, and they both tried to refill the waterskin as best they could. Between the two of them, every single muscle seemed to ache. It seemed their bodies were protesting– either from the cold, or the crash's impact the other day, or perhaps a combination of the two. They continued to walk all day, only consuming two bites each of the loaf. Luckily they saw no undead, but neither did they see any living beings who could help them.

The two talked about many things in an effort to keep each other focused and engaged. Leon talked about sneaking into his father's library to find and read stories with his sister, and in turn, Prince Gelan spoke about his younger sister Princess Giselle. Apparently, the prince's younger sister and Leon's older sister got along famously when they were together at court functions. Wondering aloud when he would see her again, Prince Gelan piped in, "When we get back to Agaprya, I'll personally and publicly invite you to my wedding Master Leon. I doubt very highly anyone would argue. You can see them then."

Leon was reminded of the prince's good heart, and the thought energized his steps as they walked onward with renewed purpose. When Leon started to tire later, Prince Gelan walked farther ahead– which motivated Leon to catch up in order to hear him. When the Prince's steps began to slow, Leon reciprocated the gesture by reminding Gelan of their need to get home to the ones they loved. To keep their minds from focusing on their ever increasing hunger, they told every joke they could remember, and shared almost every piece of advice they had ever been given.

At one point, Gelan stopped and looked as if he was about to reach down, before he hissed in discomfort. "Leon, it's time for your next lesson."

Was this really the right time? "Sir?"

The Prince pointed out patches of clover and dandelion on the ground. As he launched into an explanation, he talked about how certain plants and weeds were edible when need absolutely necessitated it. Leon's hunger drove him, and he started to gather everything he could find. The rain from earlier had already washed the plants, so the two had no qualms about immediately chewing on them as they walked.

As they continued forward they gathered wood for a fire to dry themselves, sharing more about their lives the whole time. The random trees they passed reminded the prince about his engagement to Princess Schalae of the Northern Elvenwood. He explained to Leon how she was the one who had taught him what he knew about plants– which ones were edible, toxic, or even medicinal. Gelan recounted how he met and fell in love with the princess– describing her sunny disposition, and its almost infectious quality. Based on her description, Leon couldn't wait to meet her.

When they settled in for the second night of their journey, this time around a fire, Leon noticed Gelan beginning to cough a little. "It's due to the rain from earlier, that's all, Leon." They had dropped their titles and surnames fairly early on in their trek across the wilderness. Leon fell asleep after the prince's reassurances, thinking little of it.

In the morning, a slight fever began to set in for the prince. After using Gelan's sword for an eventful lancing of the infection that had taken root, a fresh makeshift bandage was put on his arm using Leon's shirt sleeve. Leon knew they had to reach Agaprya, or a scouting party, soon. The loaf of bread was stale and more than halfway gone. The skin of water was half empty, and there were no more edible plants to be found anywhere. They both knew time was running out.

Halfway through the day they stumbled across a stray shambler. It immediately went after the prince, but Leon tackled it with his tower shield, and cut its leg off before he completely incapacitated it. Due to the excitement, Gelan's occasional coughing grew to a true fit, which left him struggling to catch his breath. That night he began to wheeze.

"Leon," he whispered.

"Gelan," Leon replied, discarding the formalities.

"I... I think maybe you were right. We should probably have gone the other way."

"I'm sorry sir, I should have…," Leon began.

"It's all your FAULT, Leon!" The Prince shouted with sudden vitriol, as he succumbed to another coughing fit. "You should have had a different idea for the dragon attack! It was pointless to teach you! It's all your fault!" Gelan's eyes rolled around, almost to the back of his head, as Leon reeled from the hurt of accusation. He had failed his crew, and now he was also failing his captain, his Prince. The guilt was already there for Leon– it had taken root when he'd been required to slay his fallen comrades. It had planted itself like a parasite, feeding off of the rest of him. Now with the prince's feverish denunciation, the parasite that was his guilt and remorse burrowed into Leon's very heart.

Gelan recovered soon and shook his head, whispering, "I– I didn't mean it. I don't know what I am saying, Leon."

The words of dismissal did nothing for Leon. The damage had already been done. Feeling the need to bury the moment, his shame, even further he tried to move on and avoid any further outbursts.

"Conserve your strength Gelan. We must be only a day or two from a road, or Agaprya. You have to hold on! For Princess Schalae. For Princess Giselle."

Gelan looked blankly into Leon's eyes, then he blinked and nodded.

The next day they reached a dirt road and both of their spirits lifted significantly. Leon even got Gelan to take the last of the water and bread– convincing him that every time they crested a hill there would be a patrol, or a traveler, ahead. It was when Gelan started to point at birds in the sky, asking if they were airships sent to rescue them, that Leon's worry grew. Especially when Gelan would ask him again only minutes later. After the fifth time the prince asked Leon looked up in a hunger and dehydration induced haze,

237

and realized that the birds were circling them. Vultures, waiting for their demise.

At sunset, Gelan could only speak in a whisper to avoid a wracking, wet, coughing attack. He sat with his back propped against an oak tree by the road and beckoned Leon to come close. He mustered the strength to slowly lift his unmangled arm and clasp his hand behind Leon's neck. Their foreheads touched and Leon noticed the feverish, clammy, oily feeling of the Prince's sweat against his head.

In some deep dark corner of his mind, Leon knew that the prince couldn't make it through another night. That did not stop him from closing his eyes and wishing with every fiber of his being that it could be him dying instead of Gelan– that the prince would be spared to go on, and that he could exist no more.

In the setting sun and his rising grief, Leon heard Gelan start to slowly whisper, "It's okay Leon. It's okay. I've accepted this. You need to as well."

"I– I can't! You must survive!"

"I'll not, and you… need to listen to me." He wheezed.

Leon felt a lump form in his throat as he listened to his friend.

Gelan began, "Just before the crash, you asked me– You asked me how I was so…"

"Fearless in it all, sir?" Leon supplied.

"Yes." Gelan breathed out explosively. He seemed to have a hard time getting it back, but when he finally did, he continued, "When my father gave me command of the *Dawnfire*, he told me something… that had become my code, my mantra. He told me that one day… one day I would pass it on."

Leon felt unworthy. This was a tradition. A message from father to son, from king to prince. Leon thought that he could not, should not know. It was wrong, yet it was the last act from a dying friend, so Leon couldn't help but nod.

"Lead with love, because love conquers all." Gelan stated.

Leon pulled back and sat before the prince, listening intently and waiting for the rest. Gelan leaned back and put his head against the tree trunk, looking at Leon with glassy eyes.

"That's it. That's all he said, and he asked me to think about it. To think hard about it. That it meant more than simple words. And you know what? He was right." Gelan gently cleared his throat, and gave him a weak smile. His voice gained the barest timbre as he continued, "Think about it. Love for your family. For your friends. For your kingdom. If the whole world loved, then fear and hatred would not survive."

"Love can create life. Create a kingdom, a family, and friendship. Love can help you defend others, and prompt you to risk everything to keep them safe. It's out of that love that I stay fearless. For them, and not myself." A cough escaped his lips, which caused another fit. By the time it was done, the prince looked like he had aged years in mere moments. His wheezing returned and he reached out for Leon's hand, which Leon eagerly took.

"Promise me...," he whispered, "Promise me you will remember."

Leon kept nodding until he knew that Prince Gelan could see it.

"Good... It... It's time Leon." Gelan closed his eyes, and his head drooped slightly.

Leon's nodding changed to shaking his head in disbelief, as he grasped his prince's hand more firmly. "No... no... please don't... please don't leave me alone!"

"Don't fear anymore Leon… I'll still be with you…," Gelan moved his hand up to Leon's forehead, then down to his heart, without opening his eyes. That was the moment it lost all of its strength.

It took everything Leon had to unsheathe his sword.

Using the tower shield, and both his and the prince's belts, Leon dragged the prince's wrapped-up remains behind him along the road. He came across no other travelers, the vultures overhead were all that kept him company. The dehydration he suffered made it impossible for Leon to shed any tears for his prince, however, he refused to allow the starvation or dehydration to overtake him until he reached Agaprya. It was due to the love he held for his friend Gelan that Leon managed to arrive at the western gates a day later– promptly collapsing into unconsciousness.

Act Three: The Light

He reveals deep and hidden things; he knows what is in the darkness, and the light dwells with him. - Daniel 2:22 ESV

Chapter 17: The Choice

Present Day

"So yeah, those were pretty much the worst few days of my life. I couldn't believe it when I heard the news at the waystation, about no one having survived the *Dawnfire* crash. That was, as you just heard, a complete lie." Leon finished telling his tale, and looked at the faces of everyone who sat around him. They were all leaning in, listening to his story with rapt attention.

They were still at Wise Guy's Inn and Tavern. Their dessert had been finished long ago, and the dinner crowd was soon approaching. Each time the magnificently mustached man came to check on them, a magnified glare from behind Gionna Gærheart's glasses was the only indicator needed for him to quickly find a different task to do.

"What I don't understand is why lie about that? Why not say that you survived?" Miala asked.

"Because then the Rhise family name would be forever tied to killing the crown prince. It would be known that the Rhise family couldn't protect him. Lord Lucien had to protect HIS good image." Leon snarled. "So it turns out I was written off before I even got home. He said he bought all the heralds or something, and they said whatever he told them to."

Various levels of revulsion painted the faces around the table, but Gionna's elderly voice had a steel edge to it, "I told those fools! I kept telling them over and over they were going about it all wrong!"

"Wot do ya mean?" Duamé asked.

"The *Dawnfire*, like all other airships, had a fatal flaw in it." Gionna looked at everyone's blank faces before she suddenly whacked the edge of the table with her metal cane, causing a small dent to appear. "It was made of wood! They all are! Light, yes, but burnable! Dragons are attracted to Levigems like moths to a flame– only they are the ones who hold the flame! Plus, they have the mass to land on an airship, and weigh it down to crash it. I've been saying for years now that the airship fleet needs an upgrade! Not bigger ships, but better ones!" She shook her cane vigorously at Leon, "The prince was right. That should never have happened!"

Ever since Leon's first dream with the spear, the burden of guilt and responsibility for the *Dawnfire's* outcome had eased slightly. Now after having retold the story, it felt as though the boulder of shame was trying to press him down in the very earth again. This time, however, the weight was mixed with anger towards his father. In Lucien's desperation to keep his public persona as untarnished as possible, Leon had been viewed as an easy sacrifice.

I well and truly hate that man.

Leon shook his head with a sigh, "Well Miss Gærheart, with the pending marriage of my sister to Baron Halomir in a little less than a month, I firmly believe that airships will always be made of wood. Soon enough, thanks to the Baron's lumber empire and whatever arrangement they

243

made, Lucien himself will probably have sole oversight of production. He said as much to me before I was forced out."

Gionna wouldn't have looked more surprised if Leon had bent her cane in half. She began to cackle, as if unable to control herself, until the few people seated at the other ends of the tavern looked over out of curiosity. "Ha! Well, if Lord Rhise pulls that off– and I was ALREADY fired– then everyone else from the airship department at the Institute will soon find themselves thrown out the door too!"

"Ya, why were ya fired exactly?" Duamé asked.

"Pure stubbornness, and not my own for once. I had repeatedly made the case that we needed to sheathe airships in a non-flammable material. I gathered signatures, gave meetings, and even went so far as to speak both publicly and privately to the director. The young whippersnapper was too scared, you see! Too intimidated by a genius that wasn't his own. Plus, why fix the problem when it is more profitable to do the same thing over and over again? So finally, I did what I had to– to get the message across."

"Wot exactly did ya do?" Duamé leaned in.

There was a manic gleam in Gionna's eyes as she exclaimed, "I walked right into the director's office while he was on lunch, and I set his wooden desk on fire to make my point!"

The entire table erupted into howling laughter, causing Miala to wipe tears of mirth from her eyes, and Duamé to pound the table. Gionna's own laughter also led to her needing to dry her eyes, and she sputtered, "Apparently he had all his personal ideas and blueprints inside the desk, and didn't have the presence of mind to make copies. Hence why I got the boot." Still laughing, she slowly got up from her chair, and they all rose out of respect.

She went over to Miala and handed her a folded napkin before she hobbled away. After walking across the tavern, as she was about to exit, she turned suddenly and yelled across the room, "I haven't had fun like this in years– and I even got canned today! See you folks later!" Gionna waved, and cackled in response to the confused looks from the other people around the tavern as she walked out the door.

"She's a barrel o' laughs, make no mistake 'bout that." Duamé commented.

"Completely different from what I expected." Leon stated.

Miala opened the napkin Gionna left and smiled as she read it, "She told us to drop by after we go shopping tomorrow, and gave us her address."

Duamé tried to grab the note to read it, but Miala held it above her head, too far for the dwarf to reach. "She gave it to me! Nope!" She smiled.

They all headed to their rooms, still full from the large lunch. Finding them spacious and comfortable, what really stood out was the large bronze tub and indoor plumbing that came with the small spaces that adjoined them. Unanimous agreement abounded that the next monster which needed to be slain was their own fragrance. Miala emphatically stated that they each had to bathe. Repeatedly.

Each of them took their time, allowing the dirt and grime of the past days to be thoroughly washed away. Leon sat in the tub reflecting on the past few days, using the soap as if it were a weapon that he could scrub his frustrations away with. His thoughts kept circling back to the discussion from earlier. It did not matter how many times the others tried to tell him that the accident was not his fault, there was a part of him that just could not let go of the blame. The flames of the *Dawnfire* always burned brightly in his mind. While he did try to follow the advice Prince Gelan had

245

given to him, Leon's good memories of his crew, and their lives, were overshadowed by their demise.

Gionna's words had raised a valid concern for Leon though. If she was the inventor of the airships, and she had championed changing her invention to improve it, why wouldn't others listen? After thinking about it, Leon could answer his own question. Gionna touched on it earlier: Convenience. It would be easier to keep building the same airships, the same way– and probably more cost-effective too. Why fix a problem when it was more profitable to prolong it? Scoffing to himself, he realized he was thinking along the lines that his 'former' father might. Disowned by him, yet still, it seemed that he could not escape Lord Lucien Rhise.

Leon brooded in the bathtub. He had gotten into Agaprya under the guise of being his stuck-up brother– who tried desperately to mirror their father. Lucien's machinations had caused Duamé and the other dwarves to lose their livelihoods. He bought the Herald Guild for no other reason than to protect himself, and his reputation, with lies. He was also maneuvering to build his own airships– ones that were tragically flawed according to the person who had invented them. Trying to shake himself from his thoughts, Leon got out of the tub and finished getting dressed.

Later, once Leon was clean and dressed, he found he couldn't stop being angry towards Lord Lucien. He stewed in his frustration practically the entire time Duamé had been in the tub. When the dwarf exited the bathroom in his change of clothes, rubbing his dreadlocks with a towel, he pointed, "Oi, wot happened ta yer saltshaker?"

Leon glanced at the spear that rested in the corner of the room. It looked normal, with its metallic blade and strange symbol embedded in it. "What about it?"

Duamé pointed out the window to the cityscape crowned with the night sky. "It's dark outside. Wot happened ta yer nightlight?"

Leon's eyes went wide as he stepped over and picked up the spear. The blade immediately flicked on and glowed, but there was a marked difference to it. What had once been a shining light that illuminated the mine they delved, and had rivaled their campfires with its brilliance on the journey to Agaprya, now barely lit Leon's face as he stared at it. A wave of concern crashed through him.

"Maybe ya broke it?" Duamé suggested. "Did ya refill it with salt?"

"I– I hope it's not broken."

Miala knocked on the door and entered with a sigh of contentment at finally being clean. She was dressed in her brown robe that somehow looked completely spotless from their travels. As she stepped inside, she pursed her lips for a moment and glared back at the door. Kelleren moped in, tail tucked between his legs. His fur was puffed out, and he looked positively miserable.

"Hi guys, do we know where we are going tomorrow?" She sat at a chair and produced a brush from a hidden pocket. When Kelleren padded over, subjugating himself to the torturous grooming, Miala noticed the change in the spear. Concern etched her voice, "What happened?"

"I have no idea!" Leon exclaimed.

Miala frowned and thought, "Maybe you should talk to your Rohiel."

Duamé suggested, "Or wot's her name that keeps kickin' yer behind."

"Now I know I talked to YOU about the dreams." Leon looked at Miala, confused. "But I never mentioned anything to you about them." He stated to Duamé.

The smith and the mancer exchanged glances before Miala explained, "When you're asleep, you talk sometimes. But when you do talk, it's like you are saying both sides of the conversation."

"Ya say stuff like yer you, an' then ya say stuff like yer trying ta be all mysterious."

Leon staggered backward, reeling from the sudden revelation. "Why… why haven't you said anything?"

"I didn't want to listen at first, but then you said what you said to the people of Everbright…," Miala explained, as if trying to convince herself as much as Leon. She kept brushing Kelleren and admitted, "When we camped and made those ingots, Kelleren woke me up to listen to you while you were asleep. He said he liked it when you talked about love. Something about dogs knowing all about 'loving unconditionally'? It's hard to describe."

"I jus' tune it out at this point. Except when ya get thrashed in yer dreams. That I enjoy." Duamé admitted.

Still struggling with the fact that his dreams were more complicated than he thought, Leon wondered if maybe they were right. "So I guess I'll try to find out when I go to sleep tonight."

After a few minutes of silence, where nobody moved, Leon grew even more concerned and confused, "What's up?"

"Think she wants ta stay an' figure out wot's goin' on." Duamé guessed, chortling.

They both looked to Miala and she blushed slightly in the dim light, "I'm kind of interested to see if they tell you anything."

"You want to watch me SLEEP?" Leon asked, dumbfounded. Miala didn't respond, only blushed a little more.

"I can knock ya out if you'd like?" Duamé suggested, as he reached towards the tool belt on his bed.

"Uh, no that's ok."

"Ya sure? It'll only take a second." Duamé said, pulling out a decent-sized mallet and giving it a practice swing.

"I'm going to bed!" Leon scrambled to the cot against the wall, holding the spear against him.

The dwarf chuckled as he blew out a candle on the table before going back to the other cot. Miala remained in her seat and watched in silence. Leon tried to push through the discomfort he felt. Somewhere between wondering if Duamé would take the opportunity to hit him with the mallet anyway, and thinking about Miala's green eyes, he finally fell asleep.

Much like the last time, Leon's dream started with him knowing that he was in a deep fog. The grey expanse with the light in the distance was there all around him, but it was shrouded in a fog so thick that he couldn't see anything. Thoughts from his last lesson in faith came, and Leon started walking while he said aloud, "I can walk by faith, even when I cannot see."

Something large appeared in front of him, through the fog. Leon began to run towards it, until he came to a small clearing. What Leon saw made his heart drop.

There in the clearing was his mother, Lady Erika Rhise. She was just as Leon remembered. Short and thin; with long, straight, blond hair; and kind, warm eyes. Currently, her eyes were red-ringed and wet, and she was running her hand through a younger Leon's hair. This was a Leon from five years ago, and his head was resting in his mother's lap.

Leon couldn't believe how different he had looked back then. No scraggly beard, just a light peach fuzz that he could remember hoping would grow out. Almost as thin as his mother, Leon hadn't filled out and built his natural

249

muscle until joining the navy. The younger version of himself was also crying– but they were tears of pain as much as anger. The anger boiled right through the pain of his prominent black eye, as well as the other better hidden bruises that resided under his tunic.

Leon remembered this day well, because this was the day that he had left Rhise manor for the first time.

Cradling Leon's crying face, Lady Erika whispered gentle, soothing words to him, "My dear sweet boy. I am so sorry."

Teenage Leon eventually stopped crying. After being silently comforted by his mother a bit longer, he spoke the words that had been on his mind for a while, "Mother, I do not think I can stand being here much longer. I do not think I can take being around him anymore."

Lady Rhise's soothing embrace encompassed him. "Leon, I know that it is hard. Your father went through the same thing. His father before him too, I believe. I do not thi–"

Leon stood, and pulled away from her, upset. "That does not give him the right, or excuse! I am serious, mother! I am leaving. Today."

Trying to mask her dismay with concern, Lady Rhise attempted to reason with him, "But where would you go, Leon? What would you do? Live on the street?"

"I have worked it all out. I would go to Agaprya and join the airship navy." Leon lifted his chin and posed grandly.

The Lady reasoned through her son's idea, "You always did love being in the air. Believe it or not, he used to toss you in the air when you were little. You always smiled and laughed… and would squeal in delight."

"I do not remember. Or care. The past is the past and this," the teenager pointed at his black eye, "THIS is the present."

Seeing that he was serious, Leon's mother took a deep breath and closed her eyes. There had certainly been occasions where Leon suffered the wrath of his father, and recently those instances had become more frequent. Even his mother had missed family meals and outings due to feelings of 'unhealth'– per Lord Lucien.

His heart wrenched as he watched his mother's face while she processed through what his younger self had just told her. How many of those days had she truly been unhealthy? How many of them had been days where she had suffered the same wrath from his father as him? Leon had no idea, but he was sure that he had not been the only one in the family to suffer abuse.

Lady Erika rushed over and held her child's shoulders. Fear clouded her eyes, but the same resolve younger Leon had shown now burst from her as well. Asking if he was sure, she told him she would pack him a bundle of clothes and supplies. Further, she told him a mail carrier ship was due at the manor that afternoon, and he would need to spirit away on it to successfully escape.

Watching all of this replay in the dream, Leon couldn't help but be reminded afresh of the hatred he felt for his father. As his thoughts focused on his father, and how much he loathed him, the memory suddenly stopped. Both younger Leon and his mother, Lady Erika, turned and stared straight at him.

Their faces were impassive, as if they had been carved from stone. They began to walk towards him, and the fog became even thicker as it encroached around them. When they opened their mouths to speak, the voices that came out were no longer that of his younger self, or his mother– though they were still familiar.

"There is a difference between righteous anger and outright hatred."

"Rohiel? Lochemetel? What do you mean?"

Leon watched his past self and his mother walk backward into the fog and disappear. He tried to jog after them, but felt as though he was running uphill. When he reached the top of the hill, he found another small clearing in the fog. This opening was somewhat larger than the last, and contained yet another memory from a time long ago.

Almost the entire Rhise family was in the ballroom at the manor. Lady Erika and a young Liara were having a small tea party in the corner, with some of his sister's dolls. Laric looked to be reading a children's book in a nearby chair. Leon gazed upon his family from fifteen years ago—everything seemed so quiet, so idyllic.

A scream came from behind him. He watched his siblings and mother turn at the sound, and saw Lucien– with no grey hairs or worry lines. He was younger, smiling, and… laughing? The scream had come from a wide open mouth that was missing its two front teeth, and belonged to a child with dark hair that was a similar shade to his father's. Leon had his arms out wide as Lucien held him up above his head. His father ran into the ballroom with zest and vigor, while the child pretended to be an airship.

Laric rolled his eyes, an attitude already manifesting in him though he had not yet reached double digits, and looked back at his book while exclaiming, "Does he have to be so LOUD?" Lady Erika shushed him as she smiled, gazing at the father playing with the youngest son. Lucien twirled the child off his head onto the floor, and when the young boy landed on his feet he collapsed into a fit of giggles and laughter as his father tickled him into submission.

Leon stared in amazement, as the memory of a time long forgotten resurfaced from deep within his mind.

Child Leon escaped and ran away from his father. Laughing and looking back, he expected to be chased, and halfway slowed down, so that he could in fact, be caught. Lucien, however, saw Laric reading and walked over to inspect the book. "An advanced book for you Laric, I'm impressed." He praised.

"It has some big words, father, but I can read them!"

After looking, Lucien pointed to a word and had Laric sound it out. Doing so correctly, Lucien praised his firstborn son. Child Leon, seeing he wasn't being chased, decided he was not done playing with his father, and ran over to gently pull on his trouser legs.

"Not now Leon." Lucien mumbled, still pointing at different words for Laric to sound out. Pulling with more demand, child Leon asked to be an airship again.

"No, Leon." Lucien stated, and went back to helping Laric– who stuck his tongue out at his younger brother. A younger, but still emotionless, Silas entered the ballroom to announce the evening's meal was ready.

Seeing that the book was the focus of his father and brother's attention, child Leon pouted, and on an impulse, slapped the book out of his brother's hands.

The sound of another slap resounded in the room, this time that of one on a child. The memory then dissolved into a grey fogbank that rolled towards Leon.

"It is reprehensible. Be angry at the actions, but not the person."

Both angels' voices echoed in the fog that surrounded Leon. He was trying to understand, trying to calm the storm inside his heart, trying to process the injustice of it all. No child should have to go through that abuse. No child should have to wonder if their parents would snap and harm them. The rage that festered inside Leon boiled to the surface.

"HOW?" Leon yelled into the void. "HOW CAN I NOT HATE HIM FOR WHAT HE DID?"

The encroaching fog filled the clearing and touched Leon's skin. It felt different than before, with its ice cold moisture. The red hot anger towards both his father and the physical abuse over the years mixed with the freezing cold of the fog that touched him, causing a numbness to overtake him. He collapsed, tears unashamedly rolling down his face– with the faint whispers of Rohiel and Lochemetel sounding in his ears.

"There is a difference between righteous anger and outright hatred."

"Be angry at the actions, but not the person."

"Forgive, as you have been forgiven."

"All have fallen short of God's glory. Does he deserve unforgiveness, or your prayers that he may see Adonai and repent?"

Leon, numb almost to the core, hated the fact that he had been abused while growing up. How was it possible to forgive the one who abused him, his own father– the one who was supposed to protect him?

"Adonai loves all. He does not want any to suffer, but wants all to follow him."

The hardest internal struggle and debate of his life began to wage war inside of himself. He felt as if he held on to a significant facet of his existence– one that shaped his very being into the person he was today. It was like being asked to cut off a leg that he had been walking on for as long as he could remember. How could he voluntarily let it go?

Leon tried to focus on the abuse and shift his anger towards it. Towards the many nights he spent wondering what he had done to deserve his father's wrath.

Could it be possible for me to separate the man from the actions?

"Lead with love, because love conquers all."

With the angels resounding Gelan's imparted words of wisdom, he was forced to think on them again. For all this time, Leon thought that Gelan meant he would lead his kingdom and his crew with love. That as a leader, love would champion his duty to all who surrounded him. Those words fell to Leon, who had been alone when Gelan died, and felt he couldn't lead anyone.

But the word 'lead' could also mean something else– to start. To have the foundation of every choice and decision made, be love. One could choose to love just like they could choose to hate. If Leon started with love, and led with love– then the next logical step towards his father would be to forgive him for his actions. If Leon continued to choose hatred towards his father, it would eventually burn hot enough to consume him. His every thought would be permeated with it, and he would be left blind to all else.

In the end, there was only one wise choice.

Leon focused on his thoughts and memories of Lucian as the fog numbed him. Mentally viewing Lord Rhise as if he were in front of him, the words escaped Leon's lips, "I forgive him."

The fog exploded outward from Leon and the numbness disappeared in an instant. The grey expanse returned, displaying the far-off light in the distance as it flashed. The wave from it expanded and rolled the remaining bits of fog away. It passed through Leon, leaving him with warmth, a weightlessness, and feeling slightly more at peace with himself.

Another voice pierced the grey expanse that belonged to neither angel nor Leon. In this state of peace, resolved to no longer be a victim, and with a newfound claim of victory over his feelings, Leon heard Miala's voice speak as if from far away.

"I… I forgive them."

Leon jerked awake with a start. He sat up and saw Duamé fast asleep in the cot next to him. He clearly saw Miala bolt from the room, but the door shut rapidly behind her before his mind had processed the image. The ability to see in the darkness of the night caused Leon to gaze at the weapon that was cradled in his hands.

The light of the spear had returned, and was brighter than ever before.

Chapter 18: The Reveal

In the morning Leon intentionally avoided the topic of Miala running out of the room. He had decided it was better to not bring it up. Apparently she decided the same thing, as it went unmentioned during their small breakfast at the Inn. Instead, they focused on that day's activities. Duamé brought up his need for clothes and a few other things– to replace everything that had burned up in his home. As Leon heard this he realized that he was in need of a wardrobe as well. When he mentioned it, Duamé gave him a sidelong glance and asked, "Ya figure out wot kinda armor ya want lad?"

Remembering the dwarf's offer from a few days ago, Leon stumbled to clarify, "Um… good armor?"

"O' course genius! Plate? Scale? Studded? Leather?"

Leon started to feel anxious– and it had nothing to do with fighting undead or dreams with angels.

Miala leaned forward after a moment, appearing quite amused. "What kind of clothes do you want?"

Leon's chest tightened, and he couldn't seem to think about what it was he wanted. *What type of clothes do I want? What armor would be best?* Thinking quickly, he removed the pouches of copper, silver, and gold and handed them to Duamé and Miala.

"I– I don't know." He said. "Just, whatever you guys think is best."

"I don't believe it," Miala remarked. "This is incredible!"

"What?" Leon and Duamé both asked.

Miala pulled out the napkin that Gionna had given her and covered her mouth with a hand– her telltale attempt to hide a smile. She tossed it to the center of their breakfast table and Leon reached for it, flattening it out, as he and Duamé began to read.

You should all come to my house when you are done with your shopping tomorrow. It is in the warehouse and wharf district, on Voelin Lane. Look for the steam.

P.S. Leon is a young noble who spent his recent years in the navy. He probably has no concept of how to shop for things. Be ready for that.

-G. G.

Duamé pointed and laughed uproariously at Leon, who acknowledged with a sheepish, "I've never really shopped for anything before."

Still grinning, Miala asked, "How?"

"The navy gave us everything we needed, and before that, I was just a kid. It's not complicated, right? You just get what looks okay and pay what they ask for, right?"

Miala didn't even attempt to hide her laughter after that.

After spending some of the morning being jokingly harassed by Duamé and Miala, while also being forced to try on several outfits, Leon concluded that he had missed out on some significant life experiences growing up. Getting poked and prodded by puffed-up pompadours was not his idea of a good time, but he bore it patiently because it was better than owning just one, single, ratty outfit. When the whole process was all said and done, Leon had more clothes for travel, as well as a proper backpack. Though, based on the laughter that came from Miala and Duamé, he figured he had still paid too much for it all.

They then visited a jeweler's shop, which was managed by a mismatched trio of women: a middle-aged dwarven woman, a large half-orc woman (who served mostly as the security detail for the store), and a hyperactive gobliness. They argued more with each other than with the group that was trying to sell the assorted jewels. Eventually, with much haggling taking place all around, they exited the jeweler's shop– having almost doubled their gold. Dividing it amongst themselves, they continued their expedition for the day.

Duamé, who had also gotten an assortment of travel wear earlier, announced it was his turn to take charge of the outing. It felt as though he dragged them to every smithy in the city– until Duamé finally found a suitable one, run by a husband and wife team. It looked as though they were endowed with more muscles between the two of them, than all the other smiths the group had encountered that day possessed in total. It also seemed that they were aware of this fact, as their operation was named the Strongarm Smithy.

The couple who owned it, Girard and Josephine, looked skeptical as Duamé patiently explained how they could become the best smiths in the city– if they applied his dwarven techniques. He would upgrade their forge and show them how to be more efficient. In turn, while he would be their private benefactor, they would allow him to use the forge to make what he needed.

"I'm telling ya, ya both got tha best forge setup here in tha city, an' plenty o' space fer an upgrade! Yer even right by tha river, an' have a flintin' water wheel at yer disposal! Ya just need a few tricks an' changes an' ya can ramp up yer production!"

"You haven't even seen us work." Josephine stated, clearly unmoved.

"I know enough about human smithin' around tha city, ta know that none o' ya use molds." Duamé countered.

"Don't use what?" She asked, even more skeptical.

Her husband Girard interjected, his voice like the sound of granite slabs rubbing together, "What does fungus have to do with forging?"

"Me point exactly! Dwarves have efficiency in forgin' down, an' ya two have an opportunity ta get one over on tha rest o' yer competition here."

Appearing quite imposing, Josephine huffed, "What do you want, dwarf?"

"Look at this lump." Duamé pointed at Leon, who was silently watching the exchange. Miala and Kelleren shuffled away from him slightly. "He's thinkin' hisself a hero, but he ain't got no respectable armor ta speak of! Jus' that ratty studded junk they give ya airship navy. Now, I'm gonna make him some scale mail, an' I'll show ya how ta do it too. In a fraction o' tha time, with almost no waste."

Feeling the eyes of everyone on him, Leon walked up and joined the arguing smiths. Girard stepped close to Leon and eyed the spear strapped to his back. Looking him up and down. He turned back to the dwarf before saying, "Why him?"

Duamé was about to open his mouth, but Miala interjected, "He's a Judge."

If Leon had been nervous due to their eyes being on him before, he felt downright uncomfortable after Miala revealed his new title. She shrugged and looked on, amused as people from around the shop peered at him with renewed interest. Josephine then walked up to Leon and cracked her knuckles in front of him. Leon looked up into her eyes, met her penetrating stare, and tried to not wince every time it sounded like bones were breaking as her knuckles popped.

"Is what she said true? Are you a Judge?" Josephine asked.

"I have been called that recently." Leon admitted.

"By who?"

Before Leon could answer, Miala replied for him again. "By the Alukah he killed single-handedly."

Josephine looked to him for confirmation, and he gave her a slight nod in acknowledgement of the statement's truth. She then looked to Duamé, who also affirmed it. The dwarven smith then gave a more abbreviated and accurate account of what happened in the mine to all who listened. The tension that permeated the forge was almost a living thing as everyone watched the dwarf retell the tale.

When he finished, he recapped the deal with the married smiths. Without a word, Josephine stepped behind her husband and placed a hand on his shoulder.

Girard stuck his hand out with a grin, "Deal."

Duamé's confident smile played over his face as he also said, "Deal." He shook Girard's hand, and then Josephine's.

What happened next was a whirlwind of activity, as a leather jacket with multitudes of straps and buckles was brought over to Leon, and put onto him. Adjusting the straps to his frame, the coat soon became the correct basis for how the armor was to fit him. Duamé made a list of materials that would be needed and handed it to Girard, who laughed and rumbled, "What do you need clay and sand in a smithy for?"

"Fer showin' ya how ta shape metal properly, an' if it's small enough pieces, hundreds at a time." Duamé said.

The husband and wife were slightly more interested after that, and sent a few assistants out to get the items the dwarf had requested.

Duamé told Miala and Leon that they could go on to Gionna's without him, "I'm gonna be here a while ta show Mr. an' Mrs. Muscles dwarven smithin'. Tell 'er I'll take a rain check... Alright ya two," Duamé said, as he turned to his new business partners, "Let me tell ya about sumthin' called an 'assembly line'!"

Leon, Miala, and Kelleren left their dwarven friend with his fellow tradespeople and followed the note's directions towards Gionna's house. Navigating the city's twists and turns, they walked along busy midday streets, enjoying the sights and sounds of Agaprya. Making small conversation, Leon knew that they were still avoiding talking about the night before. Even the occasional translating that Miala performed for Kelleren seemed forced– as if it was needed in order to break the silence. Kelleren's input, however, generally revolved around which meat market stalls smelled the best.

Buying a lunch they could eat as they walked, they continued on their way to the gnome's home– until Miala grabbed a hold of Leon's sleeve and uncharacteristically jerked him into a side alley of the street. Eyes wide with panic, she held a finger to her lips as she faced away from the main thoroughfare, and waited. After a few minutes, she nodded and left the alley without explanation, once again joining Kelleren on the street. Leon caught up to her and asked, "What was that all about?"

"Thought I saw a mancer I recognized." She murmured.

"Oh, should we hurry then? Just in case?"

She didn't reply, only quickened her pace– which Leon took as assent.

When Gionna mentioned in her note to look for the steam, it seemed she meant that they should follow the perpetual cloud of steam which emanated from her house like smoke from a chimney. When they reached the outside of the inventor's home, Leon stared in open-mouthed awe at the two story structure– it was a stunning combination of trees and cottage. Bordered by a wooden fence tall enough to be considered private, and each corner of the house had a tree growing from it. Stonework and mortar had then been combined with nature to create traditional walls between them. There were no apparent windows, and nothing which resembled a gate in the fence either.

There were many signs next to a small metal hole in the fence. They warned things such as, 'Go away!', 'Mind the explosions, they are former trespassers!', or 'Antisocial, keep your distance!'. This close to the structure, Leon noticed there was another sign written onto the large flagstone, embedded into the street, in front of the fence's hole. This sign, written in the same handwriting, said, 'Stand here, this is definitely not a trap door.' After some examination, the most relevant sign read, 'No unwelcome visitors! If welcome, please speak into the pipe.' Deciding to take the risk, Leon stepped on the flagstone, leaned down to the pipe, and said, "Miss Gærheart? It's Leon and Miala."

"Woof."

"And Kelleren." He added.

Sounding slightly metallic, Gionna's voice returned through the hole in the wall, and said, "Stand back!"

There was a distinct clanking sound, as a section of the fence seemed to simply drop into the ground– much like the secret wall in the Alukah's lair had done. Inside, they saw that the hole was in fact a pipe that traveled along the ground and into the house. Next to where it entered the building stood a simple door that was large enough for a human to enter, and emitted steam from the cracks around the top. When they were halfway across the yard, the door seemed to open of its own accord. Another pipe end extended from next to the door, and broadcast Gionna's voice as she said, "Come inside quickly, before the door shuts!"

They stepped into the home and saw that it was one huge open area, rather than a traditional house, designed to be made of many rooms. The temperature inside was slightly hotter and definitively more humid than outside, but what drew Leon's attention were the many contraptions spread around the entire area.

Half-built machines of all sizes littered the home. Some could fit in the palm of your hand. Some were meant to be worn. Some were so large you needed to ride them. These were mostly lined along with workbenches and tables that bordered the wall. Other contraptions were suspended in the air– held aloft by wires attached to the vaulted beams of the roof. There were wheeled contraptions, boxes, gears, and cogs. Stacks of metal bars in varying sizes lay on shelving. Some of the contraptions look like they were functional– such as the two airship cannons with piles of cannonballs which Leon clearly recognized. Most of the items looked to be the half-completed, or even the almost skeletal, versions of whatever ideas came to the inventor's head. It looked like a disorganized and completely chaotic mess.

Hobbling up from a small metal spiral staircase in the corner of the room, Gionna's multi-lens glasses magnified her imperious gaze. "Glad you all made it, I– Where is that good looking dwarf?"

Miala hid her smile and Leon stammered awkwardly, "Uh, he's um… smithing."

"Hmph, he reminds me of my second husband! Chiseled from rock that man was. Did you enjoy your shopping trip? Learn anything, dearie?" Gionna asked, as she looked at Leon's new clothes and backpack. "You can just set those over there." She gestured next to the door. They deposited their packs next to a row of canes that gradually became more and more intricate. None compared to the one she had with her, though.

"Yes ma'am, it was… educational." Leon admitted.

"Ha! You can just call me Gionna, dearie. And never forget, you are never too old to learn something. Alright, over here, and let me take a look!" She made her way over to a considerable machine that was set into the back wall, which looked like a bulkier version of her glasses. Various arms on the device had what appeared to be lenses of different colors and crystals. A seat set to her height was there, and in front of her was a small workbench. All of the lenses for the machine were suspended above the workbench.

Leon and Miala stood there, confused. "What are you talking about?" Leon asked.

"Let me take a look at that spear dearie, while you tell me everything you know about it. It's why you are here isn't it?"

Truthfully, Leon hadn't come to the inventor's home to learn about the artifact, but seeing as how the brilliant gnome was just as curious as him, why not? Seizing the opportunity, Leon heartily agreed. Finding a way to position the spear's shaft and the spearhead on the bench in front of her, Miala cautioned that the last being to touch it other than Leon was the Alukah– whose hands had turned to ash.

Turning to Kelleren, Gionna directed the dog to go down the stairwell and fetch her leather gloves. He promptly returned with gloves in mouth, and was rewarded by Gionna scratching him behind the ears before donning them.

"If I lose my finger, I've got nine others." She reasoned, as she opted to use her gloved pinky to touch the spear first.

Nothing happened, allowing everyone to exhale a sigh of relief. Leon recounted how the spear had sat on the wall of his family's home for years, and that it was incredibly rusty at first. He shared how it changed into a polished metallic spearhead over just a couple of hours during the Alukah encounter, and how it now emitted a light at night. However, it was his description of what occurred when it cut into an undead that drove the inventor crazy.

"Salt? SALT?!?" Gionna yelled, outraged at this point.

"Uh, yeah."

The gnome grumbled, irritation masking her face.

"And it also made that sound when the Alukah touched it." Miala commented.

"What sound?" Gionna asked.

When nobody said anything, Leon hummed what he remembered as the long continuous tone he heard. "Hm, sounds like a C five note... anything ELSE?" She asked with exasperation.

"You might as well tell her about the dreams." Miala told Leon.

"Oh, yes... sure. Dreams too, huh?" Gionna scoffed.

So Leon recalled everything he could about his dreams since the first night that he had held the spear: the angels, Adonai, the messages, and how he was told by Rohiel and Rhoxmas that he was a Judge. Miala seemed to listen more intently as Leon repeated the lessons he learned about faith, hatred towards actions but not individuals, and forgiveness.

"Dearie, are you sure you didn't addle your brains in that airship crash?" Gionna asked, as she looked at him with her glasses lens whirling. When he nodded, she threw her hands up in frustration.

"I normally love solving puzzles dear, but this?"

"Puzzles?" Leon asked.

"It doesn't make any sense! It's such a random assortment of magical powers and properties that I have no idea where to start! I mean look at this!" She pointed at the slightly darker symbol in the center of the blade. "I know four languages, have a passing familiarity with six more, and know enough about enchantment runes to teach a basic class at Mancer Academy! That was compliments of my third husband– a Runemancer. Dear was deaf as a post, but he had the most beautiful writing." She brought herself back from her distracted thoughts.

She shook her cane at the spear, much like she had at the Institute doors. "I have no idea what that symbol means, much less how it incorporates everything you told me. Either everything you said is true and you really are a Judge, or you're crazy because you believe it's true."

She stared at the ℵ in the blade like it was taunting her. "The other problem is I could swear I have seen this symbol before."

"What? Where?" Leon exclaimed.

"IF I KNEW I WOULD SAY SO, WOULDN'T I?" She screamed in frustration, as she banged her cane against the wall of her house. Leon looked at the wall and noticed it had multiple deep gouges and scratches. "Alright let's see here…" She reached over and grabbed a few knobs on her device, and with a few clicks and clanks inside the machine, the lenses started to rotate above and closer to the spear.

She then took a file out from a pocket and suddenly ran it across the blade, peering at the results. She looked into the spyglass-looking device on the machine for a few minutes, grumbling and muttering the entire time, and took meticulous notes with her free hand.

Leon's hopes that he might get a few more answers about the weapon were dashed as the elderly genius sat back into her seat and shook her head. "I don't know what this metal is. I can't tell if it's natural, or an alloy of different metals. It's harder than steel but lighter than aluminum. AND in all my years, I have never heard of a metal that could UN-rust– ever! The only conjecture I have is that whatever enchantment it had was reactivated, probably after that tone you heard. Again, it's a theory– but you cannot have an effect without a cause. That also doesn't explain the powers it had before the tone."

"But why was it on the wall in the entrance of Rhise manor in the first place?"

"That is another mystery, dearie. I knew your grandfather, and worked with him on the first generation of airships. Liam Rhise was a great general for the king at that time and knew his weapons, but I never saw him with this."

Dejected by the unsolved mysteries, Leon took the spear off the workbench and re-latched it to his back strap. On an impulse, he pulled out the ring he and Miala had found. "Care to take a look at this and tell us what it can do?"

Gionna snatched the triple-braided ring from his hand and repeated the process of looking at it through her workbench lenses. Sighing, she handed it back after a few minutes. "Part of it is rusted clean through. The iron band, however, isn't rusted for whatever reason, and it looks to be elvenwood on the third braid. The elvenwood on it has densely packed tree rings, which means it came from a very old tree. Likely an elder tree at that. Probably should ask an elf about it."

Gionna handed the ring back, as they thought over what limited information the inventor had been able to provide. As they sat in thought, Kelleren sniffed at a few half-finished inventions, until the gnome suddenly jumped off her stool and shouted, "Don't touch that!"

The dog's nose was up against a metal contraption which looked like a seat that was attached to a large crossbow. The crossbow, however, had a substantial and bulky midsection. With Kelleren's nose pressed against it, the crossbow shifted slightly, and a clank sounded from inside before it twanged. A heavy crossbow bolt shot from it and launched into a wall before it rebounded and hit the workbench– mere inches from where Kelleren was. With his tail between his legs he shamefully crawled over to Gionna. He plopped down in front of her with his head hung low, and Miala translated, "He is sorry for touching your machine."

Gionna placated him, "It's okay, I shouldn't have kept it loaded dearie, I'm just glad no one got hurt."

Leon walked over to the device, "It's too large for a hand crossbow."

Gionna hobbled over from the machine and explained, "That there is a repeating heavy crossbow. Supposed to fire bolts one after another. A good alternative for horde control beyond just cannonballs. It jams up too much though, and I haven't been able to get it to work right. Hmm…" Gionna cocked her head and stared at Miala.

"What else is in here?" Leon interrupted whatever internal dialogue the gnome was having with herself.

The gnome's eyes lit up as she started boasting about all of her half-completed inventions and ideas. War chariots to plow over shamblers. Earmuffs that could make you not hear an Alukah's voice, but also canceled out every other noise. Armor that was nigh impossible to puncture, but too heavy to move in. There were some great ideas here– but as she went further down the line of devices, their drawbacks became greater and greater.

The lab downstairs was for her secret projects, which she wouldn't give any further details about. Mostly though, the inventions were all designed to either explode, or make other things explode. Leon couldn't deny her observational skills or creativity, but the more in-depth she went, the more he wanted to apply the word 'mad' before her title of 'inventor'.

Gionna then ushered everyone outside with a grin. Shuffling out, they were all led around the back of her house, and found that she had an extremely unique backyard. The privacy fence was triple the height of the on in the front, and curved inward. Initially, Leon theorized it was meant to keep prying eyes away. Multiple groups of straw dummies were assembled in different formations. Leon looked around and noticed the lawn was quite uneven– boasting several divots and blackened craters, both large and small. A sense of dread filled him as he realized what he was standing in the middle of. He had seen these patterns many times after a horde bombardment.

"What is this place?" Miala asked, curiosity written on her face.

Leon started to become more concerned about the mental state of the 'genius' he had so admired. "A test range." He answered, his face devoid of all emotion.

"Correct!" shouted Gionna. She went to a small wooden shack that was located in the far corner of the other side of the yard, and brought out a tiny barrel. She set it right into the middle of a small group of straw dummies before hobbling quickly back to the group. Leon immediately raised his concern.

"You built a test range in the middle of a residential district?"

"Of course! I took every precaution for safety. What, you didn't see the signs dearie? Now," Gionna turned to Miala, "Are you well versed in that wand?"

Miala's eyes widened as she pulled the wand from her robe and stared at it. "I um… I know the basic concepts. But I haven't exa–"

Gionna interrupted her, "Okay, a 'No' would do just fine. Do me a favor, and hit the barrel." She rubbed her hands together and waited with baited breath.

Looking quite nervous, and thinking of the houses outside the fence, Miala stammered, "I– I don't think that it would be um… prudent, Miss Gionna."

"Hogwash dearie! You need to practice sometime. Might as well be here, rather than when you are being charged at by wretches! Come on now!"

Concerned, Leon stepped in, "Is there black powder in that barrel?"

"Just a little bit. Enough to do the job."

"How much?" Leon demanded.

With a belligerent sigh, Gionna pointed her walking cane at the barrel and squeezed her index finger on the handle. The entire cane whirred and clicked as two sections of its length sprang out from the middle of it. The transformation created arms with a tensile string between them near the curved handle. Simultaneously, the hinged bottom of the cane also flipped up– the pattern on its end reminding Leon of an archery target. In a matter of moments the mad genius known as Gionna Gærheart, had converted her cane into a crossbow. She lined the cane up, while a crystal lens dropped in front of her glasses. As soon

271

as she was positioned accordingly, she squeezed her pointer finger, releasing a bolt from a hollow chamber in the tube. It streaked toward the small barrel, thunked solidly into it, and ignited.

A small, yet very loud, explosion blew straw dummies apart all over the yard. They lay scattered across the ground. Small remnants of them were still on fire, and the pieces quickly rolled to a stop.

"That much! Ready to try that wand now dearie? I'll get us another barrel!"

Chapter 19: The Consequences

Over the next few days Leon saw some semblance of a routine develop. Waking early, Duamé would grab his breakfast, grumble, and head out to the Strongarm Smithy. On occasion, the dwarf would ask Miala to drop by the forge to do something, and soon the evidence of their actions began to appear. Sleeves of bright chainmail showed up on his arms one day– the beautiful and small rings were some of the finest that Leon had ever seen. After a few questions, and with the passing of a few more days, Miala received some chainmail sleeves of her own. They covered the upper half of her robe sleeves, ending just above her elbows. After another visit to Gionna, her chainmail was altered– boasting a reddish tint and runic inscriptions along the edges.

Leon hated to admit that the entire situation had become slightly frustrating. Duamé and Miala had become very quiet and secretive whenever he was about– but deep down he knew they would tell him anything he needed to know, when they were ready. Instead of focusing on his frustration, Leon worked on the spear techniques Lochemetel had shown him in his dreams. He reflected on the precepts and attributes that Rohiel taught, and how he could best apply them to himself. If his companions wanted to keep secrets, so be it, but Leon was determined to believe that they had a good reason.

Miala took every opportunity that presented itself to head over to Gionna's– always with Kelleren in tow. She was thrilled to be able to practice her magic away from prying eyes. Gionna was more than happy to allow Miala the practice time, fascinated by her use of the wand. She would consistently ask her to try new things with it. "Make a continuous stream of fire dearie, for as long as you can." Or, "That's two projectiles per second. Can you do it faster?" Miala enjoyed the freedom that had been presented to her, and it seemed Gionna had no shortage of straw dummies– or black powder for that matter.

On occasion Gionna would take out a scrap piece of parchment and write fervently on it, before quickly stuffing it away. In the military Leon had met a few people whose minds had continuously seemed to be occupied by one thought or another. However, the genius that he and Duamé had known of by reputation, seemed to take multitasking to the extreme. There was absolutely no doubting her brilliance– but every so often, in the middle of a conversation, she would pause, mumble about something completely off-topic, then return to the original discussion as if nothing had interrupted it.

They all would congregate at the Wise Guy's Inn and Tavern for dinner, and laugh over the stories and events of that day. Gionna regaled the group with tales of her inventions that had gone horribly wrong, and Duamé would talk about hilarious accidents at the forge. As daylight faded they would walk Gionna home, before once again heading back to the Inn, to retire for the evening. Leon's shining spear drew the occasional odd glance, but no passerby ever approached the group to satisfy their curiosity.

One morning in the city, as they sat at breakfast, Miala, Duamé, and Leon overheard the discussion of a group of shabbily dressed workers that sat near their table. They were a rowdy, overly loud group, and garnered more than a few eye rolls from other patrons in the establishment.

Duamé muttered, "Dwarves are loud, but we know better than ta be that loud, this early."

"Wait, listen!" Miala hissed.

"I'm tellin' ya, it's true!" One of the loud men exclaimed. "The guy who saved Everbright, they say he's a Judge!"

"You're still tipsy from last night Gron!" Another chortled, while the others at their table laughed uproariously.

"No, I'm serious! I heard it from my friend who works the fields outside, and he heard it from a herald near here. He killed an Alukah! And he defeated a horde all by himself!"

Varying levels of skepticism played on the faces of the loud man's friends as he described a more fantastical version of what Leon and the others had done. By the end of the man's story, those who had actually been there did not try to hide their laughter at Leon– whose face was crimson with embarrassment.

The loudmouth at the other table concluded, "The Judge then said that the village's safety was thanks enough, and he rode off towards Agaprya on a white horse!"

Soon, the loudmouth and his (now slightly less skeptical) friends left. When they did, Leon turned to face Duamé. The dwarf's dreadlocks shook with his silent laughter.

"Do you see what you did?"

"Ooo, I better be careful. Might get... How'd he say it? Right... 'Smited inta an explosion o' glorious light'!" The dwarf pounded the table, now unable to control his laughter.

They finished their breakfast, and instead of leaving to go by himself to the Smithy, Duamé invited everyone over to see the results of what he had been working on. Hoping the secrecy would finally be done with, Leon followed along– listening as Duamé and Miala quoted parts of the tale they had heard that morning.

When they arrived at Josephine and Girard's smithy, it was hardly recognizable. In the past eight days, the place had expanded and changed drastically. A furnace had been added, and the surrounding area had been converted into individual workstations. Ingots of heated metal, such as the ones they had made at their campsite one night, were shaped, pounded down, and shaped again. Then they were brought to different areas of the smithy, to be improved or refined. What once had been a haphazard; disorganized; free-for-all, was now an organized workshop– optimally designed to assemble various items in specific places.

The husband and wife duo greeted Duamé warmly, almost like one of the family, as they gathered in one corner of the smithy. Miala walked up to Leon, who stood transfixed by the transformation, and said, "Since he couldn't figure out how to lug around an anvil for his mobile smithy idea, he found new business partners instead."

"It's not bad if I say so meself!" Duamé cackled, walking back over with Girard. The owner of the smithy held the result of the shop's work out to Leon, his face beaming with pride.

The armor was primarily scale mail, laid over small interconnected rings. It boasted plate pauldrons and vambraces, held together by its scale mail arms. The chest was designed in such a way that the scale mail seamlessly surrounded a central piece of plate armor– which was engraved with the same symbol that was etched into the spear. Even the rear of the armor had been mindfully designed. It had a couple of loops that could be tightened, to securely hold his spear. Every metallic surface gleamed with a shine so pristine, it was almost as if he looked at a reflective mirror.

It was beautiful.

It was exquisite.

It was the finest piece of armor Leon had ever seen– and it was his.

"That'll be five hundred an' fifty gold!" Duamé stated.

Startled out of his admiration of the armor, Leon recoiled at the price. "What? How much?"

Girard rumbled, as he shook the armor slightly, "Five hundred and fifty eagles."

Wordlessly, Leon counted out the small remainder of money he would have left, and handed the rest to Girard. The smith handed the armor to Leon and smiled as he took the gold. He immediately turned to Duamé and said, "You're right. He doesn't know how to negotiate."

Leon didn't feel embarrassed at all from the laughter that ensued. Instead, he cradled what was now one of his most prized possessions. "Thank you. Really. Thank you for making this."

"I told ya I would make yer armor if ya wanted. An' that's dwarven alloys in there, so it'll be better than yer normal steel."

"I still want to know what you mixed in the steel." Girard rumbled.

"Trade secret, boyo. I gotta keep some stuff ta meself." Duamé countered.

Leon took the next few minutes to put the armor on, over the new padded cloth that had also been provided to him. It was all very snug, but not overly tight or restrictive. He marveled at the freedom of movement around his joints and at the marked improvement it was over his old, worn, naval armor.

Duamé looked down at the leather studded naval pants Leon still wore and commented off-hand, "I'd make ya a matchin' set if ya like, but I doubt ya have tha gold at this point."

"Still, thank you, Duamé."

"Don't mention it."

After settling accounts between Josephine and Girard, as the couple tried to hand Duamé his share, he handed it right back to them. "Save it fer tha buyout account. Ya know wot ta do with it." The married smiths smiled mischievously, and went back to work. Duamé took a few other small things from the shop that belonged to him, and they all left to go to Gionna's.

As they went on their way they passed the markets. Open for early business, the market already had a large crowd– and right in the middle of it all was the very noticeable presence of a herald, who shouted loudly so that anyone near enough to him could hear his words. With the hustle of the stalls that sold meats or produce near them, they couldn't hear the reports of the herald– but they did notice people closer to him shouting in delight. Reaching the gnome's gate, Miala began to talk through the pipe at the entrance, only to be sharply interrupted by the inventor's voice, "Is Leon with you, dearie?"

They looked at Leon who merely shrugged. Miala responded, "Um, yes?"

"All of you get inside– right NOW!" Gionna screeched, as the gate creaked open. They quickly shuffled into the yard and then the house, before both the gate and door slammed shut. Once they were inside the inventor's home, they found her anxiously waiting for them. Gionna walked right up to Leon and thrust a parchment sheaf at him.

"What's all this then?" She demanded.

Leon looked at the parchment and saw a rough sketch of himself with his patchy beard and long hair. Everyone crowded around as he read:

WANTED

'LEON'

THEFT OF PROPERTY

ASSUMING IDENTITY OF NOBLE

CONSPIRACY AGAINST THE KING'S COURT

CAPTURE ALIVE IF POSSIBLE, DEAD IF NECESSARY

REWARD

ONE THOUSAND GOLD ALIVE

FIVE HUNDRED GOLD DEAD

"This is ridiculous!" Leon exclaimed.

"This is going to start popping up all over the city. I ripped down every one that I could!" Gionna replied, poking Leon with her cane. "What did you do?"

Leon's strength left him, and he collapsed to the floor in utter disbelief. All he could do was stare at his likeness and wonder how things had gotten to this point. He was now a wanted criminal– dead or alive!

Some Judge I am!

"I only took the spear!" Leon fretted.

"And you impersonated your brother." Miala added. "It got us into the city, and saved me, but… it happened."

Dejected, Leon reeled from the consequences of his actions. He had known that he had needed to do something to gain entry to Agaprya– he just hadn't thought that this would be a ramification. With a sudden realization, he pulled out the necklace from his undershirt and stared at it with revulsion. The symbol of being a member of the Rhise family was just a reminder that he was, in the eyes of the kingdom, a criminal. Leon wanted nothing to do with it now. He tossed the necklace across the workshop floor, far away from him, and tried to wrap his head around this new development. Distantly, he heard the others as they talked amongst themselves.

Miala must have explained to Kelleren what the notice said, because she replied to the dog's unspoken question, "No, Kelleren. Of course we are not going to turn him in!"

"Then wot are we gonna do with him?" Duamé asked.

"He is depicted with long hair and a beard in the notice," Gionna said, peeking at the parchment on the floor. "It would make sense to cut his hair and give him a shave for a start."

"WOT? Ya can't shave a man's beard! That's barbaric!" Duamé exploded.

"What other option is there?" Gionna poked Duamé in the stomach with her cane.

"Maybe I should just turn myself in." Leon stated.

The others expressed various levels of outrage and dismissal at the idea.

"What else is there to do? I did take the spear, and for that matter I guess, the necklace. I also did pretend to be my brother to get us in the city. I don't know what this whole 'Conspiracy against the King's Court' nonsense is, unless…"

Unless Lord Lucien Rhise had changed his narrative, and had acknowledged that not everyone on the *Dawnfire* had died on impact. Recognized that Leon had tried to bring Prince Gelan back alive, but failed. However, that would go against Lord Rhise's desire to keep the family name disassociated with the deed of killing Gelan– even if it had been out of mercy. But wanted *dead* or alive? Is the Rhise name so valuable that it warranted his life?

Leon continued, "But the only way to prove my innocence is to confront the problem head-on, right?" Leon asked, looking for agreement.

Nobody said anything, they just looked at him as he sat on the floor with his head held in his hands.

Miala sighed and spoke up first, "Maybe… maybe we can give you a new identity."

"What do you mean?" Leon asked.

Miala bent down to pick up the necklace and held it out to Leon. "Well, nobody but us, the people of Everbright, and the Strongarm Smithy know you're the Judge. Does anyone know you are… you? Other than us?"

Leon racked his brain over the events of the past few weeks– ever since he had left the manor. Outside of this group, he realized that, for whatever reason, he hadn't shared his name with anyone. Not Elder Fanem, not anyone in Everbright, nor along the road, or in Agaprya! Amazed at the realization, Leon looked at Miala– who seemed to already know and sported a small smile.

"Maybe you could just hide Leon behind the Judge, and be that for a while." She explained.

Leon looked between her and the necklace, and nodded. He took the Levigem back, once again feeling numb inside.

Gionna piped in, "He would need to get rid of those naval pants, and possibly have a helm to hide his face. I would still recommend a shave, though. We need to find out if there is anything else about Judges that we should know, to mask his identity. We should head to the Arch–" she went wide-eyed and abruptly slammed her cane into the ground, before thrusting it at Leon's new armor. "THAT'S where I have seen that symbol before! The Archive!"

Leon jumped to his feet and pointed at the symbols on his chest and spearhead. "You saw these at the Archive?"

"Wot's tha Archive?" Duamé asked.

Gionna paced back and forth at this point, muttering to herself in an almost manic fervor. "It was almost a century ago when I was researching something for an idea. What was it? Something to do with weight. AH! Weight of naval ships. We had all those beached ships because it was too dangerous to sail anymore. I was figuring out how much weight Levigems could support in the air. I kept staring at this symbol on the wall because I couldn't figure out what it meant! THAT SYMBOL!" she screamed at the end, poking Leon's chest plate.

"We– We have to go there!" Leon exclaimed.

"Go where? Wot's tha Archive?" Duamé asked again, with less patience this time.

"You can't! You'll be recognized!" Miala reminded him.

"She's right dearie, you had better stay here until he," Gionna then waved her cane at Duamé, "can finish your armor and fashion you a helm for a disguise. Then we can go to the Archive."

"OI! WOT IS THA RUSTIN' ARCHIVE?"

Chapter 20: The Archive

Being cooped up in Gionna Gærheart's house was harrowing. For one thing, Leon really didn't know when she slept. Every night that he would be asleep, a loud bang or an explosion under the house would wake him without fail. This would usually be followed by smoke pouring from the tight spiral staircase, and strange noises. When Leon would creep over and yell down to see if she needed help, Gionna would emphatically restate that he was not allowed downstairs, and that she just needed to adjust her ratios.

To say that Leon was frustrated by his inability to leave the giant room was an understatement. Trying to figure out Gionna's contraptions, and how they worked, could only do so much to pass the time. Occasionally, Miala would bring food for both him and Gionna, or Duamé would come by to take measurements. Those encounters reminded Leon of his earlier shopping trip for clothes, as the dwarf seemed to be bent on torturing 'the new Judge'.

After he had basically handed the rest of his coins over to Duamé, the dwarven smith had agreed to finish the set of armor for Leon. This first step of this process resulted in a pair of leather pants, outfitted with a bunch of straps, being brought for measurement. The same was then done for Leon's head. This provided much amusement to Duamé, as he tried to make the straps as tight as he could over Leon's forehead. Leon had trouble believing the dwarf when he said, "So it won't wobble, er fall off yer big Rhise head!"

After several days, a set of scaled leggings to match his chest armor had been produced. They were every bit as exquisite as the chest piece– with interlocking plates above the knees and completed with a pair of new steel-toed, black, leather boots. When the helm appeared, Leon thought it was part protective, and part mask. It covered everything on his face except his mouth and chin. Once his long hair had been sacrificed, he found it did, in fact, fit comfortably.

Miala had surprised them all, and volunteered to cut Leon's hair. Gionna and Leon were wise enough not to make any remarks about the offer, but it took threatening Duamé with the singeing off of his nose hairs to finally silence his joking comments. She produced a brush, razor, and scissors from somewhere in her robe, then set about the task of cutting Leon's hair with a practiced precision that amazed them all.

After Leon sat still for what seemed to be an eternity, Miala turned his head this way and that, and deemed his short hair and lack of beard presentable. Leon looked at himself in the mirror and had to begrudgingly agree. He then went to wash up. A pang of sadness hit him, as he used the last of the soap his sister had given him. He remembered her engagement, and realized with regret that her marriage would happen in only a few days' time. Unfortunately, there was nothing he could do to help her.

"Jus' watch, yer gonna get sick now. Ya ain't got no beard protectin' yer face." Duamé warned.

"Thank you Miala. I truly appreciate it." Leon said, ignoring the dwarf.

"You're welcome." She replied before she stuck her tongue out at Duamé.

Clean and clean-shaven, Leon donned his new armor outfit and helm, then turned to face his companions. "Alright, what do we think?"

"Vaguely like my second husband," Gionna snickered.

"I like starin' at me work, meat shield."

"You look like a Judge to me." Miala praised.

"Why THANK you, Miala!" Leon exaggerated. "AND Kelleren!" He continued, as the dog woofed and wagged his tail.

"Can we go now?" Gionna asked, as she opened her door. "We really should get to the Archive to solve this mystery!"

They walked down the streets of Agaprya towards the Archive– which were a welcome sight to Leon after the several days spent cooped up in the Gærheart house. Leon noticed the occasional wanted poster which displayed his previously hairier visage, but refused to let it bother him, as he trusted that Adonai would protect him. There seemed to be much more joy among the populace– a general happiness and celebration that Leon wanted to ask about, until he heard a herald's words as they passed by.

"No attack from undead at Bulwark Fortress for over a week! Naval ships see no hordes! Could the Dead Wars be over?"

"Is he serious?" Leon questioned.

"Been saying that for a couple of days now." Gionna responded, as they followed her. "Of course, since you told me about Lucien buying the Herald Guild, I tend to take their information very lightly."

They continued to follow the gnome until they got closer to the center of the city. Passing over one of the bridges that crossed the river, they reached the central district in short order. Here the architecture reflected a much older, and more majestic, aesthetic. Tall spires and large ornate buildings peppered the area, all of which were interspersed with the expansive lawns and fancy statues that were proudly displayed along the streets. These buildings surrounded the thick fortress walls of the castle that stood in the center of the capital. It was where the royal courts made their governing decisions, crafted trade agreements, and agreed on military strategies– all while dining and dancing without a care.

Leon was prompted to attempt to pull his helm even further down over his head due to the notably increased presence of guards in this area. Of course, the airship navy was not the only military branch in existence– he had known several people who had not joined the Naval Academy, but joined the War College instead. These patrolling soldiers were graduates of the War College, and fought boredom more than anything else. The most excitement they typically faced was when the occasional panicked citizen asked for help with ensuring a friend or relative who was about to die stayed dead.

In a quick, smooth, motion Miala pulled up the hood of her robe. She moved closer, in an attempt to hide her body behind Leon's frame, as there was no alley to duck into and hide from the pair of middle-aged, ornately robed, mancers that walked by, headed in the other direction. One of them had a large, brown bear lumbering alongside, while the other had no companion, but sported a very unique hairstyle. Each of her auburn hairs stuck straight out from her head. Luckily for Miala, the two were engaged in deep conversation while they walked, and were completely unobservant of the wayward Pyromancer.

After they passed, Miala let out an explosive breath of relief but did not lower her hood again. Curious, Leon asked, "Know them?"

"Of them. You just saw the headmaster of Mancer Academy. That was Geomancer Clyborne. His demeanor and his companion usually settle most arguments."

"One would probably lose most disagreements with a bear sitting across from them." Leon agreed. "And the other one?"

Miala's soft voice grew even quieter, "That was the king's bodyguard. I thought you were a Rhise... You never met her?"

That was Galvamancer Exiosa?

It had been several years since Leon had last been to a court function, he had barely reached into his double digits in years. Even back then, Galvamancer Emirah Exiosa had already become a force to be reckoned with. The past, surrounding her origins, was shrouded in mystery; but there were a few definitive areas of general consensus. At some point in her early years, during a particularly violent storm, she had been struck by lightning. Several times. Rather than most people who would have died, or lost some of their basic functionality, she had become a rare Galvamancer.

In her later years she defended King Garinth from several assassination attempts. The smoking husks of dissatisfied nobles and hired murderers were never afforded the opportunity to turn to undead after she had finished with them. It was rumored that even her mere touch could paralyze someone into submission. The royal family was very well protected whenever she was in the room with them.

This line of thought brought a question to Leon's lips, "I only met her a few times when I was a small boy. But

287

Miala, I have a question. How does a mancer come by their powers anyway? Is it true what they say about her?"

"Usually when you are young they appear. Times of extreme stress make them manifest. Please don't ask me about it." Miala replied. She then stepped out from behind Leon, and moved to the other side of the group– which effectively ended any further probing from Leon.

Eventually, they walked up to a tall stone building with large columns and stained glass windows. It was easily twice the size of Rhise manor, and looked to be older than most of the city.

"The repository of all written knowledge in Agaprya– The Archive." Gionna announced, as she walked up the small steps, cane tapping on the stone.

It was all incredibly impressive to Leon, who entered a grand door and saw quite the bustle of activity inside. A large main room had a front desk that was heaped with every type of book imaginable. Columns that rose three stories high lined the enormous interior, and different sections of book covered shelving lined the walls all the way to the back of the vast building. On either end of the Archive grand staircases led up and down to different levels. They were interspersed with study rooms and specific topic halls, which branched off from the main area.

Several people of all ages and races rushed about, trying to pack books upon books up into different containers. An elvish maiden in a simple green robe with green sash over it seemed to be in charge of trying to keep the great building organized. She directed the other similarly dressed individuals around her as if she were a battlefield commander. She waved around a clipboard with a stack of parchments on it, signifying some semblance of authority. Appearing exasperated over the whole ordeal, she glanced at the approaching group, and decided to ignore them until she finished ranting at the other robed individuals.

"Don't stack the tall books over the small ones you idiot! Start a new pile. And keep the sections together!" She emphasized.

"Excuse me, dearie," Gionna began.

"Trofo, if you put that barrel any closer to the torch, I will stick you inside of it and watch you burn along with the agricultural reports!" The woman continued.

"Lass, wot is going on here?" Duamé tried.

"Dewey, I swear!" She screamed at a robed goblin who rushed about, putting books on other stacks, trying to consolidate space. "If you mess up my system, I will DECIMATE you!"

"Excuse me! Librarian!" Gionna whacked her cane on the floor in front of the yelling elf, which finally caught the woman's attention. Her slightly brown-tinged face, green eyes, and even greener hair swiveled towards the gnome.

"I am a senior archivist miss…"

"Gionna Gærheart."

The twig-like eyebrows of the elf arched slightly, recognizing the name. It did nothing to change her abrasiveness. "What do you, and these… people, want Miss Gærheart? As you can see, we are quite busy."

"Why is that exactly, dearie?" Gionna asked, genuinely curious.

The archivist yelled as she looked over Gionna's small frame. "If the barrel is full Trofo, then 'close' the barrel! Close! I trust you know a five letter word since you are surrounded by so many bigger words!" With that momentary distraction over, she looked to the group and explained, "The Archive is moving to our new facility in Last Bastion. Hence the preparation. Any other inane questions?"

Gionna pushed up her intricate glasses before sighing, "It must be so tedious dealing with vapid idiots all day, dearie. Trust me when I say I know the feeling. Especially at this moment."

The elven maiden's eyes narrowed. Gionna continued, "Since you are obviously busy directing, but not actually doing anything, if you could simply direct us to the historical section of the archive that specifically deals with Judges, we will be on our way." She then slapped the end of her cane on Leon's breastplate, creating a muffled gong sound.

The archivist's attention shifted towards Leon, and she evaluated him with a look of distaste. Voice laced with skepticism, she asked, "This is what those rumors are about? Him?"

Miala, who had silently observed until this point, jumped into the conversation, "He is the new Judge, yes. Where is the section for past Judges?"

The elf tsk'ed, and consulted the clipboard she carried with her. She looked through several sheaves until she got to the last one and the color drained from her face. "No. They are already packed up. So please leave and find your information elsewhere."

Gionna, who had tapped her glasses until a lens that held a tiny cube was in front of her eyes, saw as it emitted a small flash of red. She cleared her throat, "Ok, dearie. I'm sure you, as a seeker of knowledge, appreciate those who also seek knowledge. And not a bunch of horse manure. Why don't you just get Magnus, so we can sort this out."

As soon as Gionna uttered the unfamiliar name, Leon watched the elf's eyes go from narrow at being addressed so rudely, to wide and panicked. "He's– He's not available." She said.

The tiny cube in Gionna's glasses flashed yellow. "He may be unavailable to you dearie, but not to me. Just tell him Gionna is here, we will wait."

After a moment of contemplation the Senior Archivist hurried off. Gionna waited with a smile glued on her face, patiently scratching behind Kelleren's ears.

"So who's Magnus?" Leon asked.

Gionna continued to pet Kelleren, who seemed to enjoy it. "A poor, unfortunate, misguided, brilliant, man. I am truly sorry for what you are about to witness, but I didn't see any other option for getting past that elven windbag."

"Gionna!" Piped a small voice coming down a side stairwell. The voice belonged to an older gnomish man, with a wispy white beard that was tucked into a white sash. His brown robe was fur-trimmed, and he briskly walked over to her, arms outstretched. They hugged, Gionna more fiercely than him, before he resumed a respectable distance and continued, "Gia, what are you doing here?"

"We need access to a specific section of research, Mags." Gionna, whose voice usually held a stern matter-of-fact tone, was noticeably softer when she addressed the other gnome. Leon started to make some assumptions.

"You are welcome to anything we have remaining. As you can see, we are packing up and moving to a newly constructed tower in Last Bastion."

"Why move?" Leon asked. "Isn't the undead threat waning? Aren't there reports of no new assaults for some time at Bulwark?"

Magnus looked at Leon and the rest of the group before shrugging, "Do not believe everything you hear. The reports from the front, before there were no new sightings, were that hordes were traveling away from Bulwark— all in a westerly direction. It's something they have never done before, and that makes certain minds nervous."

This revelation unsettled Leon, as he remembered the recent bone jarring steps of a giant who also moved westward. *Were the two somehow related?* He thought about it and surmised, "You're evacuating?"

Magnus paid a little more attention to Leon as he nodded, "Just a precaution, mind you. We do not want to cause a panic, but we feel that this retreat from the undead is merely temporary. Retreats involve planning, foresight, and strategy. Something not seen in mindless hordes, only with the more dangerous undead. It is better to be safe than sorry."

"Regardless, you asked to see something?" Magnus continued, turning back to Gionna.

"The section on Judges. In the historical portion of the Archive." Gionna stated.

The gnome sighed heavily and then repeated the elven woman's words. "No. No, that section is no longer available."

Practically everyone except Kelleren asked why in unison. Magnus was unyielding, "Because. It. Is. Not. Available."

"Mags…" Gionna started to say, but Magnus interrupted her with a wave of his hand. "I understand your frustration, but there is no way to enter that portion of the Archive anymore. It is gone, sealed, it might as well not exist anymore."

Kelleren turned to Miala, who in turn stated, "He's hiding something."

"Ya think?" Duamé commented.

Before the situation devolved further, Leon stepped forward. "Master Magnus, I understand the section was sealed for a reason. Trust me when I say that it also needs to be unsealed for a reason. It is vitally important."

Magnus was about to dismiss them altogether until his head jerked up to the א symbol in Leon's spear. "Blast it all, you have got the Mark!"

"The mark?"

"The Judge Mark! You are the real thing, aren't you?" Magnus asked in awe.

"It means I'm a Judge?" Leon asked, excited to finally start getting some answers.

"No real Judge is without it!" Magnus looked at them all, thinking before coming to a decision. "A Judge has not been seen in over two centuries. This is amazing! Even bringing one to me though, I... I cannot let you throw away your lives going in there!"

Leon knelt down to eye level with the gnome, and tried a different tactic. "If there is danger, if that is why it was sealed, then I am honor-bound as a Judge to confront it. Please, Master Magnus, I need to know what is in that section of the Archive."

A haunted look washed over the head archivist's face, as he shook his head sadly. "Death is in there. Death for anyone who enters."

Chapter 21: The Sealed

Magnus wrote a quick note and handed it to one of the archivists with a whisper. The small goblin, named Dewey, ran out of the front doors as the elderly gnome turned back to their group. "Come with me, please."

They followed him down a set of marble stairs. Their feet, paws, and cane echoed and tapped a discordant beat, as they journeyed towards the 'death' Magnus had mentioned. The Head Archivist looked back at the group, then around to make sure no other archivists were nearby, before he finally began to speak in a low voice.

"It was about two hundred and forty years ago when an Aeromancer came to the Archive. She said she was hoping to discover the secret of how to actually create a Judge– in order to deal with the Dead Wars during that time. She entered the section, and never came back out."

Dread began to prickle up Leon's spine as Magnus continued. "Two weeks after she failed to come back out, a Gravimancer and Kinetomancer were sent in after her. They also never came back after entering that section."

"Shale." Breathed Duamé.

"Oh no." Miala murmured.

"Indeed," Magnus agreed. "Another week went by, and nothing came out. No noises, no bodies, nothing. Out of fear the archivists refused to come down here, and rightly so. Finally, the king at the time, King Graith I believe, decided in his infinite wisdom, to send an entire platoon in there– to investigate whatever was going on."

"Forty soldiers?" Leon blurted.

"Being a King does not automatically make you the sharpest sword in the stronghold." Magnus quipped, before continuing, "In any case, they too did not return, and it was ordered that the entrance be sealed. None go in, none come out– and so it has been until now."

They reached the bottom of the stairwell, two floors below the main entrance. Ahead, sconces were interspersed down a vast corridor– casting torch-lit shadows along row upon row of floor to ceiling, empty, wooden bookshelves. The musty smell of books was muted down here, but the air was still and dry. The wide corridor echoed their footsteps as they walked along the shelves, heading towards the center of the immense space.

Once they reached the midpoint of the hallway, a branch split off of it, where Magnus turned. More rows of empty shelves lined this corridor, it appeared that there was no written word to be found anywhere on this level of the building. At the end of the branch a decent-sized space had been created, complete with long wooden tables and benches– likely once used for reading and research.

Leon was struck by the unique stonework which made up the far end of the congregational space. More precisely, he was taken by surprise at its similarity to that of the 'temple' which had held Rhoxmas. The walls were angled slightly inward, the bases being wider than the tops, and were constructed with the precisely fitted stonework that needed no mortar to hold the massive blocks.

Duamé noticed it as well and asked, "How old is this here Archive?"

"What you are standing before is probably one of the oldest structures in Agaprya." Magnus explained. "The Archive was built on top of the old library, which was built on top of the Judge's section. What it was originally designed to be was lost to time I suppose."

A stone doorframe was set into the wall, but had no doors. Instead, the entryway had been walled entirely over, using the more recent and known stone and mortar technique. Above the doorframe, carved into the old stone wall, was what Leon now knew to be the Judge's mark. The large symbol א was prominently displayed– clearly marking the entrance to the sealed section in the depths of the Archive.

Magnus gestured at the walled-off doorway, "You see? Now you know why no one can get in. None of them ever came out to wreak their destruction. We do not know why. We only know that the very worst-case scenario would be that you have forty undead soldiers and three former mancers in there waiting. Most of you have the look of experience in dealing with violence. I do not need to tell you what happens when a mancer dies and turns."

Leon knew all too well what happened when a capable magic user died and rose as undead. He recalled airships crashing during significant battles, all due to the lances of magic that struck from the ground, and he remembered the abject terror of veterans and academy soldiers alike at the stories of fallen mancers.

This sealed room held three of them, plus whatever the soldiers had turned into after death. A simple assault would be tantamount to suicide. All of the he had roads taken and decisions he had made brought Leon here though. *This can't be just another dead end.*

Magnus smoothed his long, wispy, white beard, and turned to look at Leon, brows knitted with concern. "I know little of the legends of Judges, but even with all of their power, I do not think you could honestly go in there and come back alive."

Leon wanted more information. He tried to think as a tactician would, like when Prince Gelan made him consider all of the variables before a battle– instead of immediately rushing to a solution. "Do you know the layout of the section beyond that wall?"

"You cannot be serious!" Squeaked the head archivist. "You still want to go in there?"

"It is not a question of 'want to' Master Magnus. I think... I need to go in there." Leon clarified.

Magnus threw his hands up in frustration, and walked over to a long wooden table. He produced a small dagger from his belt and carved a rectangle and a long corridor into the table. "Looks like that. Also, like those more recent sections on either side of it. They were fashioned after it. Go ahead and look at them as much as you want! It will be your grave too!"

Leon took a few minutes to walk around and examine the other specified sections. They were all bare of books– apparently moving the Archive to Bulwark had been going on for some time. The areas that Magnus mentioned had corridors about thirty feet long and six feet wide. They also ended in rooms that were lined with more floor to ceiling bookshelves. The rooms were square and admittedly wide, approximately thirty feet to a side. It would be a tight squeeze to fit more than forty people in there, much less any additional assault force geared to combat the trapped undead.

As he walked back to the main area, Leon thought over any possible options available to him, and saw Magnus trying to talk sense into everyone else.

"Surely you see this is folly, my dear." He said to Miala, who stood with her arms crossed, thinking. "By your robe, and companion, I can see you are a mancer. Do you really think it wise to follow this Judge into the jaws of death itself? Knowing what you will become should you fall?"

Miala glanced up and saw Leon approaching. She must have reached a decision internally, because she smiled slightly at Leon. She focused back on Magnus and echoed words she had heard once before, "We did not come all this way to be defeated by fear."

Magnus, probably thinking her hopeless, turned to Duamé. "Dwarves are sensible, yes? Practical! You all are throwing your lives away! Tell them to leave it well enough alone!"

"I already lost everyone I care about, boyo. If this is how I go, then so be it."

Magnus slumped his shoulders, and shook his head at the responses of those who accompanied Leon.

"I may have an idea, but we will need to come back in a bit." Leon said.

Gionna, who was uncharacteristically silent, watching Magnus the whole time, looked up to Leon from her spot at a table. "What is your idea?"

"Well, first we will need a wagon, if the Archive has one available... Or even a wheelbarrow if necessary."

Several hours later, everything seemed to be ready and in its appointed position. Leon scanned the room once again. The tables and benches had been moved away, creating a clearing for the tools they would need. They had done as much preparation as they could.

News of the Judge, and his assault of the section, seemed to have spread around the Archive like wildfire. The evacuation of books had apparently halted altogether, despite the elvish woman's best efforts to browbeat her fellows into doing their jobs. Instead, Leon and the others had trekked through rows and groups of archivists who simply stared and whispered. Much like the villagers at Everbright, they all craned their necks– trying to get a good look at the armored Judge.

With nothing left to prepare for now, the group waited for someone to magically unseal the blocked-off doorway. Magnus had been incredibly vague about who was coming to perform the task. Still, based on Miala trying to inconspicuously raise her hood to cover her features, Leon surmised they were waiting for another mancer.

In the meantime, Magnus argued with Gionna, who vigorously rapped the ground with her cane to emphasize her points, "I AM helping Mags, and you couldn't stop me if you tried!"

"You are not the same person you were seventy years ago, Gia! I forbid it!" Magnus protested.

Duamé, listening nearby, grimaced and mumbled, "Ooo, shouldn'ta said tha' word."

Gionna waved her cane wildly in Duamé's direction, "At least he has some good sense. You have no right to tell me that I can or can't do anything. You lost the right to have any say in what I do!"

"Ya were married, I take it?" Duamé asked.

"Which time?" Gionna spat.

Everyone in the room winced at the implications.

"Not that it is any of your business, young man." Magnus added, irritated.

"Don't attack him for your failures, Mags." Gionna needled.

"I loved you, Gia. You're the one who ended it!"

"You loved my ideas. My intellect. You never loved me for ME!"

Leon thought this was spiraling out of hand. The two high-pitched gnomes continued to bicker and argue with each other until he and Duamé stepped in, and broke up what would have probably devolved into physical violence. Separating the two gnomes, Leon and Miala led Gionna down to one end of the building, while Duamé stayed with Magnus– giving him unsolicited advice on words and phrases a man should not say to a lady.

Gionna teared up while she whacked her cane against an empty bookshelf. "Ugh! Again, sorry you had to see that dearies. That man is infuriating! Wouldn't know how to make a marriage work if he had an instruction manual written inside his eyelids." Turning to them both, she added, "You know, on the off chance that we do survive and your crazy plan actually does work, you had better enjoy this time of infatuation with each other." Sighing, she finished. "It just goes downhill from there."

Leon started to sputter awkwardly, "Oh, um, we're not…"

Miala pulled her hood back nervously. She was red-faced, and couldn't form a complete sentence, "I don't, um, he's not…"

Leon suddenly couldn't figure out what to do with his hands and fidgeted as he gestured. "Not that I wouldn't…"

Miala held up both hands in front of her, "I like you, just not…"

Leon decided to use his hands to point to the Judge's section. "We just need to focus on…"

"I mean, I'm just focusing on myself right now." Miala finished.

"…staying alive." Leon trailed off.

Gionna looked back and forth at both of them as the tiny Discerner cube in her glasses lens flared red over and over and over again. She patted both of them on the arm, trying to keep a straight face, "Well, I suddenly feel a lot better. I'll leave you two to figure all this out while I'll go… check on Kelleren." Gionna walked back down the rows of shelves in an attempt to sell her flimsy excuse to leave them alone.

The awkward silence that stretched between Leon and Miala could have filled all of the bookshelves around them. Leon started to talk but was interrupted by Miala.

"I've come to a decision." She said.

"Oh? What's that?"

"Um, how do I say this?" She said more to herself than Leon, before huffing and looking at him. "What you said in Everbright, the things you say while you are dreaming, what those beings tell you… I wouldn't mind following a God of Love like that."

Shocked to his core, Leon scrambled to think of something to say, "That's wonderful!"

"The fact is, I don't want to die and become… well, you know." Miala explained further.

"That's certainly understandable."

"So?" She said.

Confused, Leon echoed, "So?"

Rolling her eyes, Miala huffed again and asked, "So, what do I have to do to follow Adonai?"

Leon, who always felt like a fool when it came to Miala, walked her through the basics. He told her about speaking to Adonai, asking forgiveness for past transgressions, and resolving to do no more wrong again.

"How is that even possible?" Miala asked.

Rubbing the back of his neck, and still feeling awkward, Leon tried to explain further, "Well, um, with Adonai, all things are possible. I understand now that the spear," he thumbed at the weapon strapped to his back, "Glowed fainter recently because I had to separate the anger I held against my father from what he did. That anger had gotten in the way of my ability to extend forgiveness. I was still forgiven, but my heart was not in line with Adonai, so the light of the spear wasn't as bright. I have come to realize the two are somehow related."

Miala, patiently listening, nodded slightly, "I– I think I understand."

She proceeded to close her eyes, and say the words that came to her– speaking as if Adonai was in the room. *If he is the true God of the universe, maybe he is.* Leon thought. As Miala spoke the words that were in her heart, Leon couldn't help but feel overjoyed by her decision. It was one thing to speak to villagers that he didn't know, it was another to have someone he knew, someone he might even consider a friend, come to this decision.

Once she was finished, Miala breathed in deeply and exhaled a long breath, before smiling at Leon. Her eyes had teared up slightly, and as she wiped them away she nodded to him, before saying, "We had better get back to the group before they start to get the wrong idea."

Leon's heart fluttered slightly as Miala smiled at him once again, and he agreed.

"We don't want that at all."

"Leon?"

"Yes?"

"Thank you."

"You're welcome, Miala."

They walked back between the shelves, entering into the main room, and saw Gionna had been true to her word. She was petting Kelleren, and the dog appeared to be very appreciative of the inventor's attention. Miala joined the two of them, scratching the dog behind his ears.

In the middle of being petted, Kelleren's head craned up and he sniffed at the air. Padding away from where they had been scratching him, he continued to sniff the air until his ears laid back flat, and his teeth bared in a vicious, low growl. Miala's face shifted from smiling, while silently paying attention to her companion, to wide eyed panic. She flipped her hood back up with a repeated whisper of, "No. No. No. No. No."

Leon, worried about Kelleren's behavior and Miala's reaction, looked to where the dog was growling.

Another hooded figure had stopped at the threshold of the research area, in front of the walled-off section. Her robe was midnight blue, and tight enough for Leon to clearly observe that a woman occupied it. Her companion was wrapped around her– a snake with a triangular head, and alternating brown and yellow bands along its body. It circled the woman's waist, just above her belt, and its head poked up from behind her shoulder. It hissed at Kelleren, displaying the same vehemence that the dog had shown towards it.

The woman proceeded to enter the room, and strode right past Kelleren– not seeming to care about his attitude or proximity. She surveyed their constructed set-up, as well as each of the people in attendance. Her eyes finally locked on Miala and she suddenly pulled her hood back.

Long, lustrous, straight black hair ran down behind the woman's face, which appeared to place her in her mid-twenties. Frown lines creased her pursed lips, and her eyes narrowed dangerously at Miala. She cocked her head slightly as she listened to the hissing that came from her snake. Then, while managing to smile and sneer at the same time, she crooned, "Miala Mytheriyn. Wherever have you been hiding all this time?"

Chapter 22: The Rival

The woman who confronted Miala sauntered around the room, taking in her surroundings. Her movements were a vain, blatant, attempt to be alluring. They almost appeared fluidic, which Leon thought made sense, since the snake that was draped around her was a water moccasin. Venomous and deadly, her snake never took its eyes off of Kelleren– watching the dog unwaveringly, as the woman continued to make her circuit around the room. She stopped at the wall and ran her hand along its surface– inspecting it, before she spoke aloud, "The terms of our agreement have changed, Magnus."

"You are getting paid well enough," the gnome piped.

"I don't care about the money." The woman responded, as she strutted over to stand in front of Miala. "I can unseal the door for you after I come back. Right now, I am taking her with me."

"Now hold on jus' a rustin' minute!" Duamé objected.

"Quiet dwarf! Or I will rip the water from your very body and drown you in it." The woman snapped.

Suspicions confirmed, Leon took the opportunity to step partially in front of Miala and confront the hostile Aquamancer, "Nobody is going anywhere." He said.

Arching a shapely brow, the woman looked at Leon with vague interest. "So, it seems that Miss Mytheriyn has more than one companion."

"Anissa, what are you doing here?" Miala asked, embarrassed but angry.

"I was summoned. The Mancer Academy received a request for someone skilled at unsealing. Naturally, they sent the best." She gestured at herself, staring at Miala. "I guess I have the chore of taking out the Archive's trash as well."

"Anissa, I left because…" Miala began, but the Aquamancer interrupted and pointed an accusing finger at her.

"You deserted, and left the Academy– after you burned our teacher to ashes."

The room was silent as everyone took in the accusation Miala had just been confronted with. Head held high with haughtiness, Anissa laughed, "You never told them, did you? Of course not. Now your days of running are over, and who better to bring you in than your dear, sweet, classmate."

Miala's soft demeanor caved as she stepped around Leon to face her accuser. "You don't understand. You never did. You don't know–"

Anissa interrupted again, sneering at her rival, "Know what?"

Breathing fast, Miala eyes were wide and darted about. She looked like a trapped animal who knew they couldn't escape. She struggled to form the words that she needed to say. Kelleren slowly padded over, eyes never leaving the snake that curled around Anissa. Placing himself next to

Miala, he leaned his medium-sized bulk into her leg. Trying to join the dog's efforts at bolstering her, Leon encouraged, "It's okay Miala. Whatever it is. It won't change the way any of us feel about you."

Miala tried to steady herself by closing her eyes and breathing deep. She was mouthing the words to something, but it took a few tries to put her voice behind it.

"Mancer Psiente, he, he tried to…"

Anissa frowned at her, and prompted, "What? Sleep with you?"

"He was a RAPIST, Anissa!" Miala shrieked, before quickly covering her mouth as tears filled her eyes.

The room had already been tense, but it was as if someone had suddenly thrown heavy boulders on top of the already weighted down atmosphere. Leon remembered the moment when she had slapped him in the darkness of Rhoxmas' throne room. *Were the tears she had cried, and the volatile reaction she had displayed, due to this teacher that she had killed? A man who would stoop so low as to take advantage of his underage students?*

Anissa scoffed at Miala, showing her no sympathy, "Likely story."

"Okay dearie, that is quite enough from you." Declared Gionna, as she walked over brandishing her cane at the Aquamancer. "It's obvious you detest her, and probably because she has talent along with grace and humility. You know, instead of being an overbearing, arrogant, stuck-up…"

The look of murder Anissa's eyes directed towards Gionna was enough to make Magnus slap his hand onto a table– causing everyone to jump and look at him. "Pardon me, but animosity and tragic tales aside, there is a doorway to be unsealed. Mancer Academy's formal agreements, which grant access to the Archive, will be called into

307

question should there be any deviation from the agreed-upon contracts and requests. You will be opening this seal. You will be paid upon completion. Then you may come back and detain whomever you like. Assuming any of them survive."

Anissa walked to Magnus and loomed over him, looking to Leon as if she was trying to intimidate her way into controlling the situation. Stopping well within his personal space, she tilted her head and listened to her hissing snake. Then she asked, "What do you mean, 'assuming any of them survive'?"

While Magnus outlined the history of the Judge's section to her, Leon and the others walked around the room to Miala– who was trying to not break down in front of her school rival. The effort to maintain her composure didn't stop her from also trying to explain the situation to Gionna. The gnome held her hands and listened intently. "I, I was only fifteen. He, he tried to…"

"It's okay, dearie. You're okay." Gionna soothed, patting Miala's hand.

Several minutes later, Miala had regained most of her composure, and the head archivist had finished explaining the situation to Anissa. She had begun to analyze the situation from a slightly different perspective, "Well, you'll die. Then I'll reseal the doors, and then I'll get paid. Never mind, I don't need to take you back to the Academy. You seem perfectly willing to kill yourselves here– while I just stand and watch!"

"Give it a rest, will you?" Miala asked.

Magnus prodded once again, and asked Anissa to get on with it. She shrugged, which caused her snake to drop to the floor. It positioned itself between her and the others while Anissa approached the blocked-off doorway.

Tilting her head once again, she reached inside her dark blue robe and pulled out two wands. Leon heard Miala's sharp intake of breath as they watched the Aquamancer point them to where the walled-over doorway met the floor. With a weapon in each hand and her arms outstretched, Anissa drew the outline of a doorway– leaving behind some sort of watery, gel-like material. When the wands met at the top, she scraped them sharply down the middle and backed away.

The outline of the door crackled and smoked, and the smell of something corrosive entered the air. Gionna mumbled something about acids, and quickly wrote some notes as the gel-like material ate further and further into the stone. Within a few minutes, the stone wall collapsed towards them with a thunderous crash. A large opening stood where the stone facade had been just a moment before. The group could now see the original dry-rotted, wooden, double doors that the stones had previously hidden.

"By all means, head to your oblivion." Anissa gestured towards the doors.

Leon stepped in front of the closed doors, and looked back. "Everyone clear on the plan?"

"Ya know, ya probably shoulda asked that before tha wall came down." Duamé commented.

Miala nodded as she pulled out her wand, "We did this before with an Alukah. We can do it again."

Kelleren woofed, with his eyes still trained on Anissa's snake.

"Just say the word, dearie." Gionna replied.

Magnus, who hid behind a bookshelf, squeaked, "I am ready to run screaming at the first opportunity!"

Leon nodded and turned back to the doorway that provided entrance into the Judge's section of the Archive.

He unstrapped the spear from his back and then pulled on the door's handle. A loud squeal erupted from it as the door proceeded to fall backwards. As it fell from the door frame, it caught on the other door causing it to also break free of its rusted hinges. They hit the floor inside the door frame with a resounding bang, allowing stale musty air to waft out from the dark corridor beyond.

Leon took a deep breath and stepped into the doorway, crossing over the chamber's threshold. As the spear blade passed under the archway's matching Judge's mark, it lit up– brightly illuminating the hallway within. This hallway was also lined on either side with bookshelves, and while they were not empty like their fellows, the books and scrolls that were present all appeared to be molded and defaced. Disheartened, Leon started to worry that this mission was folly.

Air began to move around him slightly. It gently built in strength until a strong breeze pushed against him. *The Aeromancer.* Time did not seem to affect the inhabitants of the Archive. Knowing they were aware of his presence, Leon addressed the dead mancer.

"In the name of Adonai, I have come to reclaim what is His! I have come for your judgement!"

"Rust, here we flintin' go." Leon heard Duamé's faint comment.

The wind that came from the hidden section carried the sound of many people's voices, all whispering at once. Their words were incomprehensible. They overlapped in such a way that it was maddening, almost compounding onto each other.

When they reached a fevered pitch, the whispers blended into one voice, and screamed into the ears of Leon and everyone else present.

"What power does a forgotten God have to pass judgement?" It raged.

Leon did not expect a question like that from the dead. Thinking fast, he tried to stick to the plan they had created. "Adonai is far from forgotten."

A rougher, deeper, whisper echoed in response, *"We have failed."*

"It is only a failure if the Judge remains alive." The original whispering mancer replied.

"Xhormas."

"Agreed."

"Kill them!" A falsetto whisper joined the conversation. *"I can feel others out there as well. Let the adversary's name die with them all."*

"Oh, no!" Magnus squeaked, cowering further into the shelves.

Anissa, listening intently, held up her hands, and spoke into the air. "I am NOT with them!"

"I don't think they care." Miala stated, raising her wand towards the corridor. "You have a better chance of survival if you are with us Anissa. Still good in a fight?"

Anissa tilted her head and momentarily listened to the hissing of her snake. The Aquamancer then stepped next to Miala, with her two wands held at the ready. "Still better than you."

Scraping, clacking, and snapping could be heard from down the corridor and Leon saw dim movement just outside the light of the spear. It quickly proved to be many skeletons, with short swords and round shields at the ready– and they all walked up the corridor towards him. Flesh stripped bare, their dry bones popped with the dark magic that held them upright. Leon saw too many pairs of red glowing eyes advancing towards where he stood in the doorway.

He tried to look as imposing as possible. His muscles were as tense as coiled springs, and it wasn't until the first couple of skeletons were within the spear's reach that he moved. The entire hallway was filled with the clacking bones of undead soldiers as Leon threw himself backward and to the side– just outside the corridor's entrance. He flattened himself against the broken wall and screamed, "NOW!"

From her position, Gionna cackled as she brought the two torches that she held down across short fuses. The fuses sprouted from the two cannons they had transported to the Archive from her home. The wagon that had been used to carry them over served its purpose well, as did some of the more robust, able-bodied, archivists who had been commissioned to carry them down to this level. Once they were on the Archive's bottom level, Gionna had aimed them both very carefully, and then made sure to load them with round shot.

In the airship navy, Leon had seen the destruction round shot caused when fired at undead hordes. Solid metal cannonballs would fly through the air, their weight and velocity knocking through anything that stood in their path. Even upon hitting the ground, they would sometimes bounce and continue on– becoming no less dangerous. Any undead in their path would either be crushed or knocked over and then finished by hand. The undead housed in the Judge's section predated the invention of cannons. Leon wanted to give them an object lesson in their use.

The cannons' cacophonous double boom was even louder than the two sections of wall that had thundered to the floor earlier. The iron projectiles launched into the first row of skeletons, shattering them before continuing into the darkness beyond. Gionna shouted in exaltation as she ran from the cannons towards a cowering Magnus.

Leon's ears, though used to the sound of cannon fire, still rang a bit. He was however, able to hear more destruction coming from the corridor. Stepping around and back in the fray, he saw the chunks of splintered bone and skeletal limbs that lay scattered everywhere in front of him. He shone the spear light forward, but the cannonballs were nowhere to be seen– just the carnage that remained in their wake.

The wind increased in strength once again, and the whispering from earlier returned. It buzzed like a swarm of hornets, sounding even angrier than before. Leon saw the shards of bone and limbs that were all over the floor begin to spin and roll around. They defied all logic as they moved in completely random directions. When they stopped traveling across the floor and congregated in one area, they began to spin in place. They whirled faster and faster as the wind gusted harder and harder.

"Uh, guys?" Leon called behind him.

The jagged bone pieces started to rise and hover off of the ground, at all different heights. The whispering turned into a sharp growl as the multitude of spinning shards suddenly stopped– with the jagged points all directed towards Leon.

Heart racing, he turned and dove out of the corridor again, somehow ending up next to Duamé. "Everyone, take cover!" He shouted, as sharp shards of all sizes flew from the passage in every direction. He covered the back of his neck and cringed further away as the hot sting of a razor-sharp bone blade flew underneath the protection of his helm, and drew a line of blood across his chin.

He felt as shards peppered against his new armor, which thankfully held up against the onslaught. Leon knew that his old naval armor would have been torn apart by these fragments. Duamé shrugged off a bony arm that slapped

313

against him as he reached back and grabbed a wooden table they had propped against the wall earlier. With Leon's help, they dragged it in front of the entrance and felt as bone shards pummeled against the other side. The growling wind carried a guttural, angry whisper that was punctuated by the bone shards continuing to shoot around the room.

"We. Are. Not. Amused."

"It's the Gravimancer!" Miala shouted over the din of the wind and clattering of the bone.

"We need to get down that corridor!" Gionna yelled from a bookshelf.

"You need to kill those mancers already!" Anissa screamed.

"We need ta rethink our line o' work!" Duamé bellowed.

The flying shards of bone eventually died down, and Leon peeked over the small lip of space that was left open from the table blocking the doorway. The hallway was dark, but he could see more movement approaching. Before, many skeletal warriors had crowded towards him, now there was only one lone figure that walked in their direction.

This skeleton's bleached white bones were covered by a black robe, and its hollow eye sockets shone red like lanterns. As Leon watched, it reached out a bony hand that it held curled into a claw, and the table he and Duamé hid behind began to vibrate and shake. They hunched down and looked at each other just as the table started to sound like it was cracking.

"You go high, I'll go low." Leon whispered.

"Yer flintin' insane, boyo!"

"What, just cause you're a dwarf you think you should go low?" Leon jested, trying to temper the insanity of the situation.

Duamé rolled his eyes and tightened the grip he had on his maul.

The table emitted a loud crack as it suddenly splintered in two. Leon turned and leapt toward the Gravimancer as soon as it did. As he pushed through the splinters, a feeling of weightlessness began to come over him. He swept the spear out towards the skeletal mancer's legs and discovered he was still too far away– the spear just barely missed it.

Leon felt himself lifted off the ground, and he now hovered in the air next to Duamé. Both were spinning slightly as the Gravimancer's clawed hands started to close. Indescribable pain and unbelievable pressure began to crush both of them. He saw the rest of his companions at the entrance to the corridor, their wands and cane were held at the ready, but not fired– for fear of hitting Leon or Duamé. They were rotated back around towards the Gravimancer– where they were then stopped and forced to look into its red eyes, without irises, that glowed brightly. Pain wracked Leon's body as its growling whisper grated against his ears.

"Only fools face a Lich."

Chapter 23: The Discovery

Leon refused to cry out in pain as he felt his body being supernaturally crushed by the lich Gravimancer. He had been turned upside down, and blood rushed to his head– along with the thoughts of how he was about to die and fail the mission that he had barely even begun. He had led these people to their deaths. People who had just begun to trust and believe in him; people that he finally thought he could rely on.

Leon was about to blackout from the pain when his Levigem necklace slid out from underneath his armor and cloth shirt. The jewel waved slightly in front of his eyes and a crazy idea suddenly hit him– one that came directly from his dreams. His muscles ached as he strained to grab the gem with his free hand, but he finally managed to catch hold of it as he turned in midair. A shocking stab of pain pierced through him as he felt one of his ribs break under the Gravimancer's pressure, and he knew his time was rapidly running out. He thought the pendant was the key to stopping the torture. So, as he floated and turned, struggling to breathe while still held by the lich's magic, Leon slammed the gem into the elvenwood shaft of the spear. He immediately collapsed to the ground.

"What?" The Gravimancer lich hissed.

Leon held the gem in one hand and spear in the other, as he stepped closer to the creature. He brought the spear up at an angle. It caught the lich's black robe, before continuing onward into the ribcage of the skeleton. The light from the spearhead was faintly muted when it flashed through the robe's fabric, but that didn't stop Leon from seeing what he needed. Finally with a scream of righteous anger, Leon slammed his spear, with the lich stuck to it, into a wall of desiccated books.

The Gravimancer's whispered screech still managed to overpower his own screams, as its bones flew apart. Its skull had remained attached to its neck and rib cage, eyes glowing red, as Leon slammed the spear into the wall full of shelving. That was what it had finally taken for the head to bounce free, and its eye sockets to go dark.

He and Duamé collapsed on the floor. They were both exhausted and in pain.

Clattering bones caused Leon to look up and see even more skeletal soldiers headed into the light of the spear. Tired, and trying to gather himself, he struggled to get off the floor as a ball of fire arched overhead. Miala ran into the corridor with Anissa right next to her, jockeying to get a better shot. Duamé began to pull himself up by the wooden bookshelf that lined the side of the hall, and immediately recoiled from the hiss of watery acid that came from Anissa's wands. It splashed over the approaching skeletons, quickly dissolving through both bone and sinew, to make the horde of undead collapse. Between the Pyromancer and Aquamancer, the undead were held at bay.

317

When no more undead appeared at the edge of the spearlight, the darkness produced a whispering wind that whipped forward as screams of rage overtook the whispers. The screaming escalated until everyone had to clap their hands over their ears in an attempt to muffle the Aeromancer lich's wind carried outcry.

"All that is living DIES! What is the point of your futile flailing endeavors to prolong the inevitable?"

Duamé had already recovered and huffed, "Quit yer whining!" Then he rushed forward into the darkness with his hammer hefted high.

Leon was still recovering when he saw Miala and Anissa wordlessly look at each other, then follow in Duamé's footsteps. Miala's wand tip became incandescent as she lit their way, and their animal companions followed after them– keeping as far away from each other as was possible.

The exhaustion weighed on him, but when he heard steps and small taps approaching he debated on whether he should turn his head to acknowledge the new presence. In the end, he did not. Leon felt a small hand rest on his shoulder. "Are you ok, dearie?" Gionna asked.

Leon nodded slightly, felt a small sense of accomplishment at the movement, and determined to pull himself up to another shelf rung. The extra rung gave him enough space to shift his footing, and with some help from the older gnome, Leon lifted himself upright– leaning heavily on the spear to steady himself.

"How… how did you destroy the Gravimancer?" She asked, nudging the black robe of the former lich with her foot.

"With this." He held up the Levigem necklace, and tapped it against the elvenwood of the spear. He felt slightly lighter again as he did so.

Gionna's eyes widened as she seemed to do mental backflips and somersaults. "How did you know that was going to work?"

"I didn't," Leon said, breathing heavily. "But I had faith that it would."

"That dwarf is right. You have a few pieces of your brain missing, dearie."

Duamé shouted from ahead, which prompted Leon and Gionna to head in that direction, leaning on both spear and cane.

The Judge section of the Archive was a large room that had several shelves which lined the walls. Every shelf was filled with books and scrolls. It was a veritable trove of knowledge for Leon and the past Judges. All of it– every scrap that could be seen, was in some way, shape, or form, defaced.

Books were crumbled to confetti, dry rotted, and cut. Piles of ruined books and destroyed knowledge filled a corner. Paintings interspersed along the wall were ripped and torn to tatters. Glass display cases were shattered, and the contents inside were missing or broken. The only unblemished thing in the room looked to be a perfectly circular stone table that stood in the center of it.

While there were no more skeletal warriors to contend with, the two mancers currently searched the wrong side of the room for the remaining liches. They did not have the same ability to see in the dark as the dwarf, nor did they have Leon's spear– which had placed them at a significant disadvantage. With the spear now providing light to the room, Leon saw Duamé on the opposite side as the mancers, facing the second lich. Gionna was headed in his direction.

Duamé fought against intense winds that were being directed towards him, causing his dreadlocks to undulate against his dark skin. The lich was backed against a corner, with one boney hand outstretched to direct its wind attack. The dwarf was moving inexorably toward the lich– one concentrated step at a time, and was almost within striking distance.

Nearer to Leon, Gionna lifted her cane and pressed a few buttons in its handle, which unfolded the small crossbow. In one moment she lined up her shot, fired, and watched as her trajectory allowed the storm force winds to pick the bolt out of the air. The lich, distracted by the sudden movement, turned its skull her way.

That was all the distraction Duamé needed. He took one last step, and swung his maul high. The hammer's head connected with the side undead skull, before it also collided with the stone wall, breaking it into a shower of bone fragments.

"Ha! Two down!" Duamé exalted.

"Where is the last one?" Leon asked. He looked around and noticed that there was something on the table in the center of the room. While everyone else searched for the lich, Leon approached the small, stone, circular table. There were no chairs around it. The surface was smooth but dusty. What had drawn Leon's attention to it was the oddly-shaped, fist-sized lump that sat on top of it.

"Is that…" Gionna started to ask behind him.

"Looks like it." Leon replied.

It reminded Leon of the blob-like shape that adorned the fountain in front of Rhise manor. There were no blemishes or impurities. But it looked as though it was made of the same blue-tinged metal as the spearhead– when it wasn't iridescent. He decided it was best to deal with this discovery later, as there was still one last lich to handle.

When nobody could find the final lich, Duamé was the first to pose a theory, "Maybe it got hit in tha cannon blast."

"Why would it be among the warriors though?" Leon countered.

"I don' know, boyo! Wot tha hematite is a Kinetomancer anyway?"

Miala answered, "They are really rare. They manip– HEY!"

She was interrupted by a bubble of acidic water splashing next to her. Anissa pointed one of her wands at Miala. Her hand shook violently, while her face appeared strained, and held a look of consternation. She stuttered in an effort to get words out, "It's– It's not me! Get–".

Anissa struggled as she brought her other wand up and shot an acidic stream of water straight at Duamé. He was barely able to block it with the massive head of his maul– which caused it to spit, hiss, and smoke, and made Duamé drop it. "Oi! Tha' was me favorite hammer!"

"GET OUT OF MY HEAD!" Anissa screeched, as she brought both wands to point at Miala, and fired continuous bubbles of water. Miala brought up her hand, and a circle of flame emanated from it, blocking the streams and creating steam to form all around her.

Kelleren bounded over and rushed at Anissa to stop her, but was intercepted by the water moccasin. It launched itself and tackled the dog, causing both animals to roll into the rapidly growing steam cloud. Both the companions and mancers were effectively obscured from the others' sight.

Miala's voice rose from within the fog, "Anissa! Fight it! The Kinetomancer is controlling you!"

"I can't! I can't stop it!" Anissa cried.

The cloud enveloped the entire room as neither mancer would give up. Leon knew, however, that neither of their endurances would last very long. "Find the lich! It has to be here!" He shouted.

321

It was impossible to see anything in the room anymore. With minimal vision, and the only audible sounds being the hiss of water and fire colliding, growls from Kelleren fighting the snake, and those of everyone bumping into things– they were not successful at finding anything.

After a few moments, Leon called out, "Anything?"

"Can't see anything in this fog! Where is that thing?" Cried Gionna.

Anissa's voice was mixed with a more guttural tone that laughed and echoed throughout the room. Almost as if she and the Kinetomancer were speaking together. *"Worry not, you will all join us one by one."*

A sharp yip came from Kelleren, and Leon knew that Anissa was lost. Somehow the lich was controlling her, and now thanks to the fog they couldn't even find the thing! Miala heard Kelleren's hurt cry and screamed. A large yellow glow, which came from her general direction, pulsed in the fog. She rapidly began to change color, transitioning to hotter and hotter hues. The temperature in the room rose, keeping pace with her changing color, and it began to feel like a bathhouse.

"Miala, you… you need to stop me!" Anissa yelled amidst the screaming.

Leon clearly heard both women shout the same thing simultaneously, as he saw their shapes take form through the steam cloud. "I'm sorry!"

The glow moved across the room to where Anissa was, and braving the blistering heat, Leon staggered over to try and help. As he approached he saw the flame that enveloped Miala change to a bright white; then watched as a beam of that white fire shot towards Anissa. The Aquamancer was somehow able to deflect the blast a little, directing it to the shelves behind her. The wood was extremely dry, and she shelving easily caught and burst into flame.

Groaning under the sudden energy and strain, the shelves fell onto Anissa. The mingled voices of her and the Kinetomancer were laughing maniacally– until they were suddenly cut off. Miala ran over. She had cooled down and her skin was back to normal. Miala's unblemished robe and chainmail sleeves, with their red glowing runes across the seams and hems, had also faded back to normal. She had tears in her eyes as she saw the bookshelves collapsed over Anissa in the corner. Leon found the physical strength to catch her, before she collapsed on the floor sobbing.

Leon tried to get her to refocus, "Kelleren! You need to find Kelleren!"

His attempt seemed to work, because she stumbled off to try to find her dog. Leon looked over the rubble until he found a part that wasn't burning, so he could grab it and pull the fallen bookshelf off of Anissa. As he was about to put the effort in to move it something dark slithered out from underneath, causing him to step back.

At first glance he thought that it was the Aquamancer's snake. Instead, what he saw was a dark shadow that moved independently of an owner. It glided slowly across the smooth stone floor, oozing towards him. Acting on pure instinct, he brought the shining spear blade down onto it, the light flashed, and caused a falsetto whispering scream to fade quickly. A small pile of salt, in the outline of the shadow, confirmed Leon's suspicions. *Not a lich after all.* He thought. *Some sort of shadowy thing.*

"Was that the Kinetomancer? Did you find it?" Gionna yelled.

"Yeah!" Leon called over his shoulder.

One hand on the spear, and another grasping a shelf, Leon slightly lifted and maneuvered the burning wood off of Anissa's broken body. A third of her body was burned, and the rest was bloody and swollen. Her breathing was

323

shallow. One of her eyes was swollen shut but the other looked at Leon. He crouched down next to her, knowing she would soon be gone. Miala returned and crouched next to him. With tears still in her eyes, she reported, "Kelleren is hurt, but alive."

"I'm... sorry, Mi... Miala." Anissa breathed.

"I'm sorry too." Miala replied.

Anissa reached out a trembling hand and grabbed Miala's arm, "It's... ok. Don't... don't let me turn..."

Feeling a gentle tug on his soul, Leon thought that with all of the animosity she had harbored towards Miala, perhaps Anissa could use some peace in her last moments. "Do you want to not turn undead, without us killing you?"

Her breathing ragged, Anissa's one good eye looked to Leon as she stuttered, "Is this a... a Judge thing? You... you could do that?"

"I can't, but let me tell you who can..."

After a while, Duamé carried a whining Kelleren in his arms and walked over with Gionna. Leon and Miala were still crouched over Anissa, with Leon's spear blade ready to strike her unmoving body. It took Gionna a few seconds before she pushed Leon aside, and raised her cane high to bring it down on the body.

"Wait!" Miala commanded.

"Are you insane, dearie? We have to make sure she doesn't come back as another lich!"

"I think we already did." Leon said, still staring at her.

"Wot do ya mean?" Duamé asked.

"She's been dead for ten minutes." Leon stated.

Everyone looked at the slain Aquamancer– unable to believe what was occurring, or not occurring.

"That's not funny." Duamé said.

"It's not a joke." Miala said in a hollow voice.

"Did ya whack her in tha back o' tha head? An' we jus' can't see it?" Duamé hedged.

"No! We just," Miala began, "We just made sure she accepted Adonai before she died."

Another ten minutes passed, making it twenty in all, well after anyone would turn into undead, when the emotion overtook Leon. Tears of vindication just kept flowing as the faith that he had held since his first dream with Rohiel was proven true. Faith that believed he was on the right path– which had carried him here. The truth of Adonai, and his having the power to ensure that those who knew and accepted him would not turn undead, was altogether real.

Eventually, Magnus worked up enough courage to come inside. Gionna regaled him with the story of what happened, and he too could not stop staring at Anissa. Gionna walked away and went to inspect the fallen skeletons and liches, picking up the robes of the two long undead mancers. When the smoke from the flaming bookcases became too much, well over an hour after Anissa had died, and with her still not rising, they filed from the room one by one. Leon waited for Miala, as she was the last to walk away from the body. She whispered something before she stood, but Leon couldn't hear her words. He did, however, see that Anissa's two wands had found a new owner.

Chapter 24: The Aftermath

Everyone was exhausted from the endeavor they had just undertaken. That did not stop Magnus as he frantically shooed everyone up the stairs– as if their leaving the Archive would be enough to wipe away everything that had happened. On their way back to the main level every step they climbed felt like ten. The group passed by archivists who stared at them in wonder. Defeating one lich on the Bulwark Fortress cliffs was no easy task; defeating two and the shadowy whatever-it-was, was unheard of.

That was not to say that the group hadn't taken a beating. Anissa was dead. A mancer had been sent to do a simple job, and she would not return to the Academy. Leon knew that would raise serious questions and repercussions. The small cuts he had received from the flying bone shards, and the broken rib that was felt with every breath, plagued him. Miala had both revealed old trauma and experienced new trauma that she would have to deal with. Gionna seemed quieter than usual after observing Anissa, but she had encountered her own issues with her ex-husband today.

Even Duamé griped about his maul– Anissa's acid having destroyed the metal head beyond repair. He didn't seem to suffer from the same physical pain as Leon though. The Gravimancer must have focused more of its energy on the Judge.

Just as Leon brought his assessing thoughts to Kelleren, Miala looked sharply at the dog in Duamé's arms with a cry. She cradled her companion's head with one hand and yelled, "You think you're WHAT?"

"Oi! That was right in me ear!" Duamé complained. "Wot did he say?"

"He thinks he's been poisoned! He thinks he's dying!" Miala cried.

They all crowded around Kelleren as the dog's wide eyes gazed around slowly. Miala carefully unwrapped the makeshift bandage that covered one of Kelleren's forepaws. The short yellow fur did not hide the inflammation of the leg around a purple snake bite wound.

Leon didn't want to waste a moment, his exhaustion no longer a priority. "What do we do?"

"Ya, is there a healin' mancer 'er somethin'?" Duamé asked– concern lacing his voice.

"No. nothing like that!" Miala said, still looking over the bite.

Gionna took control with a breath, "We need to go to an apothecary. The nearest one is almost halfway across the city in the far end of the market district."

"Then let's move!" Miala said, climbing the stairs as she waved for Duamé to follow.

"I don't know if we can make it in time before the poison spreads too much." Gionna scowled. Internally, Leon had to agree.

They all rushed up the last of the stairs, desperation fueling their adrenaline. Reaching the main hall, they rushed to the front doors when the snooty elven senior archivist saw Magnus with them and tried to grab his attention, "Uh, excuse me, sir?"

Magnus, head pivoting between his ex-wife who was urging him to go with them, and the elven archivist, asked impatiently, "What is it, Xieth? We are a little busy as you can see!"

She looked at the battle-weary group, likely smelling the smoke and sweat of the battle. The archivist, Xieth, shook her head to clear it of the distraction and pressed on. "Well, sir, the Princess Schalae is here to take a selection with her on her return to the Northern Elvenwood tomorrow."

Leon looked behind Archivist Xieth to where a figure stood on the other side of the room. She was dressed in a slim black gown and had a black lace veil that covered her braided green hair. Her light brown face was pensive, and her eyes kept darting towards Magnus and the others in their group. Other archivists, knowing who she was, walked warily around her, as they went about their jobs.

Princess Schalae.

The princess was here.

Is this fate?

"Hey, wait! I think she can help Kelleren!" Leon said to Duamé and Miala, who were both almost out the door. They turned and instead followed Leon as he rushed over to the princess, who watched their approach with apprehension.

Leon bowed slightly as his words tumbled out. "Excuse me, your highness, I was hoping you could help us."

A look of confusion crossed the princess' face, but was soon followed by one of intrigue. She spoke with a lilt that was typical of the northern elves, "Do I know you? Are you in the habit of asking favors of strangers?"

"Only ones who are reputed to be masters of medicine. Our dog– he was bitten by a snake." Leon gestured to Kelleren, who was still held in Duamé's arms.

"Oh, my fir trees!" Princess Schalae exclaimed, as she approached the dog. A bare, unblemished, arm reached out of the black gown and toward the dog as she examined his wound with expertise. "Here, place him on the floor."

Duamé gently laid Kelleren down as Schalae gathered her gown and sat next to him. Reaching back, she grabbed a light, leather, rolled-up bundle that she carried, and laid it on the ground next to her. She unstrapped it, helped it roll out, and row after row of secured, stoppered, vials clinked. Miala hovered over them and asked, "Can you save him, your highness?"

"A snakebite, you say? What type of snake?" Schalae asked, while pulling a few of the vials out.

"Water Moccasin." Miala and Leon stated.

Princess Schalae reached and took out yet another vial after the type of snake was mentioned. "How long ago was the bite?"

"A little over an hour." Miala said, sitting down next to Kelleren.

"Hm... Alright, let us save your companion." The princess said, as she started to unstopper some of the ingredients.

Miala's eyes darted to Leon, caught off guard by how Schalae seemed to know what the dog was. They then watched as the princess mixed a couple of vials and shook the concoction– all the while constantly checking on the wound. After that process was finished, the liquid was still clear. Then the princess leaned over, and one amber tear fell from her eye. The drop plopped into the vial, and the princess shook the vial some more.

With quick reflexes, she poured the contents of the vial directly over the bite mark. The wound began to bubble and hiss as more liquid than what the vial had originally contained began to ooze out. The swelling in Kelleren's forepaw seemed to reduce immediately, and he moved his head slightly, looking at the princess. She stroked the dog underneath his chin and spoke to him with a smile, "You are welcome."

While Schalae was cleaning up her vials and kit, Miala asked, "Will he be okay?"

Rolling up her bundle, the princess exclaimed, "Gopher wood, yes! You should be proud of your companion. Keep the wound covered for a few days with a clean, dry cloth, and he will be just fine."

Breaths that had been held in suspense were suddenly expelled with relief, as their group watched Miala gently hug Kelleren.

"We owe you a debt of thanks, your highness." Leon said with gratitude.

"Hmph! You all owe me a lot more than that!" Princess Schalae exclaimed. After a tense moment where everyone silently questioned what she meant, the elf laughed and said, "I want an explanation! How did a snake get into the Archive? Why do you all look as if you just fought a war? Why is the blade of that spear shining? Why, as I keep asking questions, does Magnus look as though he might explode?"

Magnus was quick to nervously jump in as soon as the princess finished speaking, "Ah, yes, well, we have all got quite the ah, story for you your highness. But unfortunately they were just, uh, leaving! Yes. Leaving." He finished, with a knowing stare at Gionna.

"Well, that IS unfortunate." Princess Schalae agreed. After a moment, she continued, smiling sweetly at Magnus.

"Especially considering how I had thought that your hospitality towards me, Magnus, was due to your general respect towards everyone. I see now that you only respect my title, is that correct?"

The head archivist looked as if he had just swallowed a vial of cottonmouth poison himself. "Why no, of– of course not your highness. Why…" Leon thought he could almost see the wheels turning in the gnome's head– trying to extricate himself from the situation. "Why, they were just going to, um, find lodging for the evening. Before returning in the morning! Yes!" He smiled at the princess, thinking he had succeeded.

Schalae's smile turned slightly vicious, she knew she had trapped her quarry. "Surely you have lodgings here that you could provide to be more hospitable! I would hate to have my patient brave the cool evening air. In fact, I must insist. Then, perhaps we could meet in the morning to hear what happened. I am quite intrigued."

Magnus opened and closed his mouth a few times, like a gasping fish, before he bowed and acquiesced, "Of course, your highness. I will see to it."

Princess Schalae picked up her black gown as she stood– everyone else also rose, as necessitated by proper etiquette. "Then I shall see you all at breakfast when I return tomorrow. I will bring it, do not worry! I fully expect a most exciting tale!" She brought her black veil in front of her face once again and departed with a nod and curtsey. Two other elves, dressed more for battle than mourning, waited at either side of the door that led outside. They followed behind her as she exited the Archive.

"How'd ya know? About her medicine an' all that?" Duamé asked.

"Prince Gelan told me almost everything about her, remember?" Leon replied.

331

"Thank you, thank you so much!" Miala exclaimed, still holding onto Kelleren.

Embarrassed, Leon muttered, "Don't thank me, thank Princess Schalae when we see her tomorrow."

Magnus, having calmed down slightly, announced with a resigned tone, "Well, if you would follow me, I will show you to your rooms."

The rooms given to them at the archive were simple, almost monastic. A bed, a chair, and a table were all that adorned the cramped quarters. Miala went to her room first, carrying Kelleren there with her. Her eyes met Leon's, and an unspoken thanks passed from her to him.

Duamé left for his room next, still shaking his head– probably in disbelief. He had been griping about his lost hammer, too corroded from the acid to be useful again. Leon figured the hammer wasn't all that the dwarf was upset about.

Leon overheard Gionna ask Magnus if she could stay with him for the night. He assumed she was trying to mend a bridge after their harrowing experience that day. The offer that he overheard was declined by Magnus, who gave a lame excuse, before he then bid her goodnight. Gionna closed her eyes, shook her head ever so slightly, then left for her own room with a sigh.

Leon entered his room and laid his pack down before unbuckling his armor. Taking it off, he removed the cloth undershirt next, and saw the bruising that was already around his ribs. He used his fingers to probe around the most tender rib and see how bad the break was. Surmising that it would probably heal on its own, he pulled another shirt from his pack, put it on, and collapsed in bed. Soon, Leon was asleep– but in his dream, he was not alone.

The flat, grey expanse was featureless save the light in the distance. It was noticeably larger, compared to when

Leon had first dreamt of it, and the rainbow glow that emanated from it felt warm. It was like a sun, made just for him– all he needed to relax now was a beach and the sound of ocean waves.

Instead, a wave pulsed from the distant light. It bathed Leon in a glow that helped him feel at peace. A peace that overpowered his feelings of loss or pain, a peace that surpassed all understanding. It was a peace that was broken by the voice of Rohiel, who stepped next to Leon.

"I have not seen the light so bright in a long time."

Leon thought that the angel's conversational tone was different from his past dreams. Rohiel, having heard Leon's inner monologue, laid a gauntleted hand on his shoulder.

"A great victory has been won today."

Leon thought of the battle in the Judge's section.

"You have seen but a part of the battle. Witness it all."

Rohiel waved his other hand and the grey expanse shifted, causing Leon to feel unbalanced. His vision swam, but as his head cleared a moment later, the Judge's room of the Archive appeared. It looked very different in this vision. Colors were infinitely brighter than they had been and shadows were darker than he remembered. It occurred to Leon that he saw this room the same way that he had seen Rhise manor in his earlier dream.

The room interior was dark– the only light source was the glow of the multitude of skeleton and lich eyes. They all circled the stone table in the center of the room. From the dim light, Leon was able to see a shadowy cloud undulating above the heads of all the undead. Dim red light from the undead eyes fell upon the lump of metal in the center of the table. While the metal did not shine, or do anything overt, it was clearly important as it was the only thing that captured the attention of the entire horde.

Leon watched as within the darkness of the sealed room, hidden for decades, the undead showed that they had not been dormant. While their bodies were unmoving, they were, in fact, chanting. In low, hollow, whispering voices, Leon heard one word repeated over and over.

"Xhormas. Xhormas. Xhormas."

The idea of the undead chanting baffled Leon, and curiosity overcame him.

"Rohiel, what is Xho–"

"Observe."

Leon continued to watch as the undead chanted. He still burned with curiosity, but hoped that answers would come. Then sounds came from down the hall. It was the sound of hissing acid, followed by the slam of the unsealed section of wall which echoed into the room. The undead stopped chanting, and wordlessly the eyes nearest to the table looked down the corridor at where Leon and his companions were about to enter. Whispers from the three dead mancers conversed.

"More are coming."
"More will die."
"Xhormas."
"They are too late."
"Their knowledge is lost."
"The horde will not be stopped."
"The Aeonyte remains."
"Xhormas."
"Defend it we must."
"Charged with the task."
"Xhormas."
"Kill them all."

The echo of the wooden doors falling inward down the hall signaled the start of the short siege. Rohiel waved a hand, and the scene proceeded forward as Leon watched the battle again– this time with the vision Rohiel granted. What it showed was a new facet of the battle.

Every time a skeletal warrior or a lich was defeated, every time the red lights in their eyes winked out, a shadow fell straight from the bones, seeped into the earth, and disappeared. It reminded Leon of when he saw Lochemetel fight the large Nephilim creature. When defeated, an inky black smudge had seeped down and disappeared.

The light that flashed from the strikes he made with the spear was reminiscent of the light in the expanse, and the glow that suffused him. Seeing the Gravimancer crush him and Duamé for half a minute made Leon instinctively rub at his chest where his rib had cracked. He felt no pain in his dream, and Leon was about to ask Rohiel about that, when his attention was caught by something else.

There had been no actual black clouds churning over the table, instead it was a countless number of other creatures. He recalled from another of his visions that Rohiel had called them 'Mazzikin.' They made tight loops near the ceiling, much like the vultures that had circled overhead when he had been dragging Gelan's body. When the shadow lich of the Kinetomancer was slain, the dark cloud of Mazzikin screeched in a chorus and flew in masse down the hallway, towards the Archive. Leon moved to follow them down the hall with Rohiel, and saw that the section's doorway was guarded against their escape.

There, at the entrance, stood Lochemetel.

There was not one moment as Leon watched her, that she stood unmoving. She whirled in a dance of death with her golden spear. Mazzikin rapidly puffed out of existence– not a single one escaped her reach. When her dance was done, she knelt down on one knee as a clarion bell sounded all around. It was a tone reminiscent of when Rhoxmas grasped the spear with Leon, and it emanated from the interior of the Judge's chamber. They moved again, and now stood behind the crouched forms of himself and Miala with Anissa. He saw the frozen figures of everyone else around the room.

"Animosity, hatred, jealousy. Love conquers all, Leon."

Leon looked closer at Anissa's still form, and saw the unmistakable light of the expanse surrounding her, infusing her. Interestingly, he saw the same glow around himself and Miala.

Seeing Anissa at rest, Leon stated his thoughts aloud– knowing the angel could hear them anyway. "Nobody could believe that she didn't turn. Even I couldn't believe it to some extent."

"Seeing is believing. You see the power of Adonai. You will all need to believe in the times ahead."

"Why? What is ahead?" Leon asked.

With another wave of Rohiel's hand the vision began to dissolve around them, until the grey void had returned.

Questions swirled around Leon's mind as Rohiel started to walk forward, towards the light in the distance. A few steps behind, Leon hurried to catch up, and then kept pace with the angel. As he was about to start asking his questions, Rohiel responded before even one could pass from his lips.

"You must learn."

Baffled, and feeling slightly impudent, Leon had become frustrated by all of the questions that were piling up in his life. When one question received an answer, it seemed that two more would take its place. Throwing up his hands, he demanded, "Well, what else can I learn?"

The laugh that came from the angel was infectious. It was deep, rich, and Leon could not help but chuckle with him. "What?" Leon halfway pled with him.

"You must all learn."

As he listened to Rohiel's instructions for what to do when he awakened, a smile crept up Leon's face. For the first time in what felt like ages, he knew for certain this was his path. Now he was sure that the flood of undead hordes could be eradicated– that Adonai, the God of the universe, could stop the curse of undeath from continuing. Adonai was a far greater weapon in the Dead Wars than a hundred *Dawnfires*. As a Judge, Leon now knew his true purpose too. He knew that following the angel's instructions would be the next step to save the kingdom's people. To save the entire world.

He couldn't wait to awaken from his slumber so he could share what he had learned with his new friends. That was just one more certainty he now had– these were, in fact, his friends.

Epilogue: The Machination

Irritated, he dipped his quill into the inkwell once more. Another signature for a shipping order. He sealed it and added it to the pile for the next mail carrier. It was a commitment of more iron ore to an enterprising smithy couple in Agaprya. A distraction, one he did not need, but part of the tedium he dealt with on a daily basis.

Lucien was tired. He sat at the desk in his study, dealing with the issues of that day. He ran a hand through his mane of still mostly dark hair, and sighed. Everything needed to be on schedule– even with the higher demand for resources. The next few days were crucial. The dreadnought airships needed to be ready, with the guards and mercenaries from the mining crews ready to fly them. Halomir had proven to be quite resourceful, and had practically all of the lumber for the dreadnoughts ready to use as soon as their agreement had been reached. It was yet another one of Silas' suggestions that had proven quite fruitful. Now, the Baron's part was done.

After so many years of careful planning, everything was finally coming to a head. They were almost ready. He was so very close. It had been a long road, with more than a few compromises made along the way. Reflecting back on it, Lucien was proud of the work he had accomplished.

Moreover, he was proud of the workers and refugees under his employ that kept the production and supply steady. Lucien had always admired those who came from nothing, but were able to make something of themselves due to their hard work. This business was his kingdom, his empire– and it's success continued due to the dedication of Lucien and those in his employ.

That is not to say he had no regrets. Lucien knew that his work had taken its toll on his family. In the interest of securing more stability and comfort for his family, and also in securing his legacy, he had distanced himself from everyone. Even talking to his wife, Lady Erika, about his accomplishments seemed to fall on deaf ears. Only her eyes responded– and those were usually undecipherable.

Nobody understood, no one realized, just how much he had sacrificed. Hard work was something he had learned to respect from his father, Lord Liam, and he knew that a day not filled with merit was a day wasted. However, one simple fact remained– he was far too busy securing their future. Once this campaign was complete, Lucien was sure there would be more time to spend with his family.

Long ago he had wished for the impossible. He wished for there to be more hours in a day– perhaps then he would be able to spend more time with those that mattered to him. Such wishes were proven to be foolish though, as whenever he made the effort, those same family members would invariably just let him down. The only one who had not yet disappointed him, sat in one of the chairs across the desk from him, reading over foreman reports from the mines.

Lucien had very high hopes for his son, Laric, who had proven to be just as ambitious and dedicated as himself. Laric must have felt his gaze, as he looked up from his report and smiled at him. An act which Lucien wordlessly reciprocated before he returned to his own reading.

His ruminations were interrupted before tackling the next supply request, as the study door opened to admit the unnervingly silent Seneschal Silas. He quietly shut the door behind himself, and turned to look at Lucien. Irritation and tension flared once again, as it always did whenever Silas was around. Lucien glared at his long time butler and advisor as he asked, "Well?"

Face devoid of all expression, Silas stepped over to the remaining unoccupied chair in front of the desk, and sat with his back rigidly straight. "Disappeared."

"We should have moved sooner." Lucien replied, rubbing his temples.

"You should not have thrown him out." Silas shot back brazenly. "But mistakes once made, cannot be undone."

Lucien hated when Silas tried to sound as if he were wiser than him. Simple directness was his preferred mode of communication, with no sugar coating of words that wasted time.

"Where was he last seen?" Laric asked, eager to assert his authority in the room. The Seneschal glanced impassively at him before looking back to Lord Lucien.

With a gesture from Lucien indicating he should answer, Silas responded, "He was seen in Agaprya, but disappeared before we sent out notices. Presumably, he is in hiding."

Impulsively, Lucien slammed a fist on the hard wooden desk. It hurt his hand, but he refused to let the pain show. "Double the reward Silas. I want him found!"

A wide smile spread across the Seneschal's face which looked out of place when paired with his monotonous voice,

"Of course. Perhaps if I were to hire a few from the dreadnought crews, or our shipbuilders, to start searching..."

Rubbing his hand below the desktop, to hide it from Silas, Lucien fought through his building headache as he nodded, "Brilliant. Do it, and then prepare our bags. Laric and I will be making a trip with the mail carrier to Agaprya. We have a lot of moving pieces on the board Silas. The endgame is almost here."

"Indeed it is, sir. As you wish." Silas bowed, and the grin he wore returned to his expressionless mask. He exited the room as quietly as he had come.

Laric waited until the door closed before asking, "Surely we are not looking for him ourselves?"

"Do not be ridiculous." Lucien snapped, still rubbing his injured hand. "I need to talk to the Herald Guild about how to proceed from here, as well as attend the monthly council meeting. There are people that I need to talk to. Those who have roles to play and those who need a firm hand to stay in line." Lucien's ire rose as he was reminded of the dwarf who had not followed instructions, and thus made his situation much more complicated. *That idiot should be grateful that all he lost was his position, but still,* "Ugh! Incompetent fools! Never trust a dwarf, Laric. Do you hear me?"

"Yes, father." Laric replied. His eyes widened, and he grew excited and exclaimed, "Maybe we can try to find that new Judge everyone is talking about! Have you heard anything more about him?"

Lucien rolled his eyes. He had heard more than enough of the commoners' gossip. Long ago, he had been fascinated by those tales himself, but now that he had a business empire to rule, he had more important things to focus on. "Stop chasing legends and dreams and focus on the here and now, son! You need to focus your attention on more royal prey."

"The Princess Giselle, you mean?" Laric ran a hand through his hair, smoothing it. "She never attended Liara's engagement party."

Lord Lucien steepled his fingers on the desk, inhaling deeply, "Still mourning her brother. Just like her father."

"I could be a comforting shoulder for her to cry on." Laric reasoned.

Lord Lucien smiled as his son finally caught on, "And I will speak with King Garinth about another… arrangement."

Bible Verses

Used for Rhise of Light

The Nephilim were on the earth in those days, and also afterward, when the sons of God came in to the daughters of man and they bore children to them. These were the mighty men who were of old, the men of renown.
- Genesis 6:4 (ESV)

"You shall have no other gods before me.
- Exodus 20:3 (ESV)

For where your treasure is, there your heart will be also.
- Matthew 6:24 (ESV)

Many are the plans in the mind of a man, but it is the purpose of the LORD that will stand.
- Proverbs 19:21 (ESV)

And Jesus said, "Father, forgive them, for they know not what they do."
- Luke 23:34a (ESV)

But Jesus looked at them and said, "With man this is impossible, but with God all things are possible."
- Matthew 19:26 (ESV)

Whenever the LORD raised up judges for them, the LORD was with the judge, and they saved them from the hand of their enemies all the days of the judge. For the LORD was moved to pity by their groaning because of those who afflicted and oppressed them.

- Judges 2:18 (ESV)

For we do not wrestle against flesh and blood, but against the rulers, against the authorities, against the cosmic powers over this present darkness, against the spiritual forces of evil in the heavenly places.
- Ephesians 6:12 (ESV)

"Son of man, you dwell in the midst of a rebellious house, who have eyes to see, but see not, who have ears to hear, but hear not, for they are a rebellious house.
- Ezekiel 12:2 (ESV)

They have neither knowledge nor understanding, they walk about in darkness; all the foundations of the earth are shaken.
- Psalm 82:5 (ESV)

He reveals deep and hidden things; he knows what is in the darkness, and the light dwells with him.
- Daniel 2:22 (ESV)

Everyone who is called by my name, whom I created for my glory, whom I formed and made.
- Isaiah 43:7 (ESV)

It is the glory of God to conceal things, but the glory of kings is to search things out.
- Proverbs 25:2 (ESV)

Blessed is the one who finds wisdom, and the one who gets understanding.
- Proverbs 3:13 (ESV)

Our God gives you everything you need, makes you everything you're to be.
- 2 Thessalonians 1:2-4 (MSG)

Trust in the LORD with all your heart, and do not lean on your own understanding. In all your ways acknowledge him, and he will make straight your paths.
- Proverbs 3:5-6 (ESV)

Now faith is the assurance of things hoped for, the conviction of things not seen.
- Hebrews 11:1 (ESV)

For we walk by faith, not by sight.
- 2 Corinthians 5:7 (ESV)

If we confess our sins, he is faithful and just to forgive us our sins and to cleanse us from all unrighteousness.
- 1 John 1:9 (ESV)

Again Jesus spoke to them, saying, "I am the light of the world. Whoever follows me will not walk in darkness, but will have the light of life."
- John 8:12 (ESV)

But the fruit of the Spirit is love, joy, peace, patience, kindness, goodness, faithfulness, gentleness, self-control; against such things there is no law.
- Galatians 5:22-23 (ESV)

Be kind to one another, tenderhearted, forgiving one another, as God in Christ forgave you.
- Ephesians 4:32 (ESV)

Surely goodness and mercy shall follow me all the days of my life, and I shall dwell in the house of the LORD forever.
- Psalms 23:6 (ESV)

Acknowledgements

This story has hovered on the edges of being written for years, but it took family and faith to see it through to completion. Therefore I would first like to thank my wife Crystal, and sons Cameron and Aiden, for providing the motivation to get it done.

I would next like to thank my Alpha and Beta Readers: Debbie, Travis, Autumn, Tim, and my mother and father, Kate and Bob Sternberg, who also created the cover art. Pastor Derrick Rawlings (Freedom Worship Center, VA), thank you for helping me to find resources when I needed them, and for the teachings that continually sparked my desire to learn more. Derek P. and Sharon Gilbert, your ministry and teachings are profound. Nathan Dezago http://njdezago.com/ (My first 5-star review!), C. S. Wachter (Didn't kill the dog), and Pastor Tony Suarez, I thank God for the work I have seen Him do through you, and others, to help usher in a revival of the Holy Spirit. https://www.tonysuarez.com/.

I would also like to thank Inkarnate - Create Fantasy Maps Online for the tools that allowed me to create the Map of Xaelon and the city of Agaprya. I highly recommend them for fictional map creation.

Finally, I would like to thank you for laughing, crying, and learning along with Leon and company. If, like me, this work has challenged you, convicted you, or changed how you view life, then I consider it well worth the hours of writing.

My request to the readers of this series is twofold. First, ***please share it!!!*** If you enjoyed reading this story as much as I have enjoyed writing it, then it is a story that needs to be shared. Family, places of worship, friends, enemies, pets large and small, etc. Please like, share, and review!

Secondly, wherever you find yourself on your spiritual walk, my personal advice is to do your research. Look into the origins of what you believe. If a deeper understanding can be reached through finding the original translations, look for it. If there is archeological evidence that can support your belief, be your own Indiana Jones and dig for it. Repeating verbatim what you hear from someone else, without sourcing and researching all sides, is quite frankly *dangerous.* That is just a little food for thought.

Rest assured, I am diligently working on books two and three. If you thought The Rhise of Light was full of action and intrigue, you haven't seen anything yet! Until the next book's release, remember to lead with love, because love conquers all!

Author Bio

Max B. Sternberg lives in Virginia with his wonderful wife and two incredible boys. When he is not working, or filling his time with the activities of a husband and dad, he enjoys delving deeper into biblical scripture and telling dad jokes. He strives to live his life as best he can – in all areas – for Jesus. Max believes that humor, mixed with truth, and tied together in a relatable way, can be an amazing way to reach people for the Lord. It is his sincere hope that readers will find his imaginings, paired together with biblical truth, inspirational for a deeper relationship with Christ.

The Rhise of Light is his first literary work, and he is currently working on two additional novels for the *Darkness Overcome* series.